RELIQUARY

DOUGLAS PRESTON and LINCOLN CHILD are the number one bestselling co-authors of the celebrated Pendergast novels, as well as the Gideon Crew books. Preston and Child's *Relic* and *The Cabinet of Curiosities* were chosen by readers in a National Public Radio poll as being among the one hundred greatest thrillers ever written, and *Relic* was made into a number one box-office hit movie. Readers can sign up for their monthly newsletter, The Pendergast File, at www.PrestonChild.com and follow them on Facebook.

Also by Douglas Preston and Lincoln Child

PRESTON & CHILD

RELIQUARY

HEAD
ZEUS

First published in the US in 1997 by Tom Doherty Associates, LLC
This paperback edition first published in the UK in 2018 by Head of Zeus Ltd

9 7 5 3 1 2 4 6 8

A catalogue record for this book is available from
the British Library.

ISBN (PB): 9781788547031
ISBN (E): 9781784970499

Typeset by Divaddict Publishing Solutions Ltd

Printed and bound in Great Britain by
CPI Group (UK) Ltd, Croydon CR0 4YY

Head of Zeus Ltd
5–8 Hardwick Street
London EC1R 4RG

WWW.HEADOFZEUS.COM

*Lincoln Child dedicates this book to
his daughter, Veronica*

*Douglas Preston dedicates this book to
James Mortimer Gibbons, Jr., M.D.*

RELIQUARY

We listen to the unspoken, we gaze upon the unseen.

—Kakuzo Okakura, *The Book of Tea*

PART 1

OLD BONES

REL-I-QUARY *relic-wary* (n): a shrine or coffer for displaying an object, bone, or body part from a saint or deity

I

Snow tested his regulator, checked both air valves, ran his hands along the slick neoprene of the suit. Everything was in order, just as it had been when he last checked it, sixty seconds before.

"Another five minutes," the Dive Sergeant said, cutting the launch to half speed.

"Great," came the sarcastic voice of Fernandez over the sound of the big diesel. "Just great."

Nobody else spoke. Already, Snow had noticed that small talk seemed to die away when the team neared a site.

He looked back over the stern, watching the froth of the Harlem River spread out behind the propeller in a brown wedge. The river was wide here, rolling sluggishly under the hot gray haze of the August morning. He turned his gaze toward the shore, grimacing slightly as the rubber cowl pulled at the skin of his neck. Towering apartment buildings with broken windows. Ghostly shells of warehouses and factories. An abandoned playground. No, not quite abandoned: one child, swinging from a rusty frame.

"Hey, Divemaster," Fernandez's voice called to him. "Be sure you got your training diapers on."

Snow tugged at the ends of his gloves and continued looking toward the shore.

"Last time we let a virgin out on a dive like this," Fernandez continued, "he shat his suit. Christ, what a mess. We made him sit on the transom all the way back to base. And that was off Liberty Island, too. A frigging Cakewalk compared to the Cloaca."

"Fernandez, shut up," the Sergeant said mildly.

Snow continued to gaze over the stern. When he'd come to Scuba from regular NYPD, he had made one big mistake: mentioning that he'd once worked a Sea of Cortez dive boat. Too late, he'd learned that several of the Scuba team had at one time been commercial divers laying cable, maintaining pipelines, working oil platforms. To them, divemasters like him were pampered, underskilled wimps who liked clear water and clean sand. Fernandez, in particular, wouldn't let him forget.

The boat leaned heavily to starboard as the Sergeant angled in closer to shore. He cut the power even further as they approached a thick cluster of riverfront projects. Suddenly, a small, brick-lined tunnel came into view, breaking the monotony of the gray concrete facades. The Sergeant nosed the boat through the tunnel and out into the half-light beyond. Snow became aware of an indescribable smell wafting up from the disturbed waters. Tears sprang involuntarily to his eyes, and he stifled a cough. In the bow, Fernandez looked back, sniggering. Beneath Fernandez's open suit, Snow could see a T-shirt with the Police Scuba team's unofficial motto: We dive in shit and look for dead things. Only this time it wasn't a dead thing, but a massive wrapped brick of heroin, thrown off the Humboldt Rail Bridge during a shootout with police the previous night.

The narrow canal was lined on both sides by concrete embankments. Ahead, a police launch was waiting beneath the railroad bridge, engine off, bobbing slightly in the striped shadows. Snow could see two people on board: the pilot and a heavyset man in a badly fitted polyester suit. He was balding and a wet cigar projected from his lips. He hiked up his pants, spat into the creek, and raised one hand toward them in greeting.

The Sergeant nodded toward the launch. "Look who's here."

"Lieutenant D'Agosta," one of the divers in the bow replied. "Must be bad."

"Anytime a cop is shot, it's bad," said the Sergeant.

The Sergeant killed the engine, swinging the stern around so the two launches drifted together. D'Agosta stepped back to speak with the dive team. As he moved, the police launch heeled over slightly under his shifting weight, and Snow could see that the water left an oily, greenish residue on the hull as it slid away.

"Morning," D'Agosta said. Normally ruddy-faced, in the darkness beneath the bridge the Lieutenant blinked back at them like a pale cave creature that shunned the light.

"Talk to me, sir," the Dive Sergeant replied, strapping a depth gauge to his wrist. "What's the deal?"

"The bust went bad," D'Agosta said. "Turns out it was just a messenger boy. He tossed the stuff off that bridge." He nodded upward toward the overhanging structure. "Then he shot up a cop and got his own ass aired out good. If we can find the brick, we can close this piece-of-shit case."

The Dive Sergeant sighed. "If the guy was killed, why call us out?"

D'Agosta shook his head. "What, you just gonna leave a six-hundred-grand brick of heroin down there?"

Snow looked up. Between the blackened girders of the bridge, he could see the burnt facades of buildings. A thousand dirty windows stared down at the dead river. Too bad, he thought, the messenger had to throw it into the Humboldt Kill, aka Cloaca Maxima, named after the great central sewer of ancient Rome. The Cloaca was so called because of its centuries-old accumulation of shit, toxic sludge, dead animals, and PCBs. A subway lumbered by above, shuddering and screeching. Beneath his feet the boat quivered, and the surface of the glistening thick water seemed to jiggle slightly, like gelatin that had begun to set.

"Okay, men," he heard the Sergeant say. "Let's get wet."

Snow busied himself with his suit. He knew he was a first-rate diver. Growing up in Portsmouth, practically living in the

Piscataqua River, he'd saved a couple of lives over the years. Later, in the Sea of Cortez, he'd hunted shark, done technical diving below two hundred feet. Even so, he wasn't looking forward to this particular dip.

Though Snow had never been near it before, the team talked about the Cloaca often enough back at the base. Of all the foul places to dive in New York City, the Cloaca was the worst: worse than the Arthur Kill, Hell Gate, even the Gowanus Canal. Once, he'd heard, it had been a sizeable tributary of the Hudson, cutting through Manhattan just south of Harlem's Sugar Hill. But centuries of sewage, commercial construction, and neglect had turned it into a stagnant, unmoving ribbon of filth: a liquid trash can for everything imaginable.

Snow waited his turn to retrieve his oxygen tanks from the stainless-steel rack, then stepped toward the stern, shrugging them over his shoulders. He still was not used to the heavy, constricting feel of the drysuit. Out of the corner of his eye, he could see the Sergeant approaching.

"All set?" came the quiet baritone.

"I think so, sir," Snow said. "What about the headlamps?"

The Sergeant stared at him blankly.

"These buildings cut out all the sunlight. We'll need lamps if we're going to see anything, right?"

The Sergeant grinned. "It wouldn't make any difference. The Cloaca's about twenty feet deep. Below that, there's ten, maybe fifteen feet of suspended silt. As soon as your flippers touch that silt, it balloons out like a dustbomb. You won't be able to see beyond your visor. Below the silt is thirty feet of mud. The brick'll be buried somewhere in that mud. Down there, you see with your hands."

He looked at Snow appraisingly, hesitating a moment. "Listen," he said in a low voice. "This won't be like those practice dives in the Hudson. I only brought you along because Cooney and Schultz are still in the hospital."

Snow nodded. The two divers each had gotten a case of the "blastos"—blastomycosis, a fungal infection that attacked the solid organs—while searching for a bullet-ridden body in a limo at the bottom of the North River the week before. Even with mandatory weekly blood work to screen for parasites, bizarre diseases ruined the health of divers every year.

"If you'd rather sit this one out, it's okay," the Sergeant continued. "You can stay here on deck, help with the guide ropes."

Snow looked over at the other divers as they strapped on their weight belts, snugged the zippers of their drysuits tight, let the lines over the sides. He remembered the first rule of the Scuba team: Every man dives. Fernandez, making a line fast to a cleat, looked back toward them and smirked knowingly.

"I'm diving, sir," Snow said.

The Sergeant stared at him for another long moment. "Remember basic training. Pace yourself. First time down in that muck, divers have a tendency to hold their breath. Don't do it; that's the fastest way to an embolism. Don't overinflate your suit. And, for Christ's sake, don't let go of the rope. In the mud, you forget which way is up. Lose the rope, and the next body we come looking for will be yours."

He pointed to the sternmost guide rope. "That'll be you."

Snow waited, slowing his breathing, while the mask was slipped over his head and the lines attached. Then, after a final check, he went over the side.

Even through the stifling, constrictive drysuit, the water felt strange. Viscous and syrupy, it didn't rush past his ears or eddy between his fingers. Pushing against it was an effort, like swimming in crankcase oil.

Tightening his grip on the guide rope, he allowed himself to sink a few feet below the surface. Already the keel of the launch was invisible overhead, swallowed by a miasma of tiny particles that filled the fluid around him. He looked around through the feeble, greenish light. Immediately in front of his face, he could see his gloved hand gripping the rope. At a greater distance, he could make out his other hand, outstretched, probing the water. An infinity of motes hung in the space between. He could not see below his feet: there was only blackness. Twenty feet down into that blackness, he knew, lay the ceiling of a different world: a world of thick, encasing mud.

For the first time in his life, Snow realized just how much he had depended on sunlight and clean water for his sense of security. Even at fifty meters down, the waters in the Sea of Cortez had been clear; light from his torch had given a sense of openness and space. He let himself drop another several feet, eyes straining into the blackness below.

Suddenly, at the outermost reaches of his vision, he saw or thought he saw through the dim currents a solid haze beneath him, an undulating, veined surface. It was the layer of silt. He sank toward it slowly, feeling a knot of apprehension grow in his stomach. The Sergeant had said that divers often imagined they saw odd things in the thick waters. It was sometimes hard to tell what was real and what was not.

His foot touched the strange floating surface—passed through it—and instantaneously a cloud roiled out, folding around him, shutting out all sight. Snow panicked for an instant, scrabbling at the guide rope. Steadying himself with the thought of sniggering Fernandez, he descended. Each movement sent a new storm of black liquid eddying against his visor. He found himself instinctively holding his breath against it, and he forced himself to breathe long, regular breaths. *This is bullshit,* he thought. *My first real dive on the force, and I'm practically a basket case.* He stopped for a moment, controlling his breathing, forcing it back into a steady rhythm.

He let himself down the rope a few feet at a time, moving sparingly, trying to relax. With some surprise, he realized that it no longer mattered whether his eyes were open or shut. His mind kept returning to the thick mantle of mud that waited beneath him. *Things* were in that mud, encased, like insects in amber...

Suddenly, his boots seemed to touch bottom. But it was unlike any seabed Snow had felt before. This bottom seemed to be decomposing; it yielded beneath his weight with a disgusting kind of rubbery resistance, sneaking up his ankles, then his knees, then his chest, like sinking into clammy quicksand. In a moment it was over his head, and he was beneath it and still descending, slower now, encased wholly in an ooze that could not be seen but only felt, pushing close against the neoprene of his drysuit. He could hear the bubbles of his own exhalations working their way upwards around him; not with the quick abandon he was used to, but instead with a slow flatulent rolling. The mud seemed to offer more resistance as he descended. How far down was he supposed to go in this shit?

He swung his free hand about as he had been taught, sweeping it through the muck. It bumped into things. In the blackness with his thick gloves it was hard to tell what they were: limbs of trees, crankshafts, nasty snarls of wire, the collected waste of centuries trapped in this graveyard of mud.

Another ten feet, and he'd go back up. Even that bastard Fernandez couldn't snigger after this.

Abruptly, his swinging arm bumped against something. When Snow pulled at it, the thing drifted toward him with the kind of slow resistance that implied weight. Snow tucked the guide rope around the crook of his right arm and felt the thing. Whatever it was, it was not a brick of heroin. He let it go, pushing himself away.

The thing swung around in the treacly eddy of his flippers and bumped up against him in the blackness, knocking his visor back and momentarily loosening his regulator. Regaining his balance, Snow began moving his hand over the object, looking for a hold with which to push it away.

It was like reaching into a tangle of something. A large tree branch, maybe. But it was inexplicably soft in places. He felt along it, feeling the smooth surfaces, the rounded knobs, the pliable lumps. Then, in a flash of understanding, Snow realized he was feeling along a bone. Not just one bone, but several, connected by leathery strips of sinew. It was the half-skeletonized remains of something, a horse maybe; but as he felt farther along its length he realized that it could only be human.

A human skeleton. He tried again to slow his breathing, get his mind working properly. Common sense and training told him he couldn't just leave it there. He'd have to bring it up.

He began threading the guide rope through the hip joint and down around the long bones as best he could in the thick muck. He figured there was still enough gristle on the bones to hold the thing together on its trip to the surface. Snow had never tried to tie a knot with gloved fingers in pitch-black mud before. This was something the Sergeant hadn't gone into during Basic.

He hadn't found the heroin. But it was still a stroke of luck: Snow had stumbled onto something important. An unsolved murder, perhaps. Muscle-bound Fernandez would shit a brick when he found out.

Yet, somehow, Snow felt no exhilaration. All he wanted was to get the hell up and out of this mud.

His breath was coming in quick, short pants, and he no longer made any effort to control it. His suit was cold, but he couldn't stop to inflate it now. The rope slipped and he tried again, holding the skeleton close to him in the ooze to make sure it didn't slip away. Again and again he thought of the yards of mud above his head, the whirlpool of silt above that, the viscous water through which sunlight never penetrated...

The rope pulled tight at last and he gave a mental whimper of thanks. He'd just make sure it was secure, then give three tugs on the line, signaling he'd found something. And then he'd climb up the line and out of this black horror, onto the boat and onto dry land, and maybe then he'd shower for ninety minutes, get drunk, and think about getting his old job back. Dive boat season was just a month away. He checked the rope, feeling it tight around the corpse's long bones. His hands moved up, probing for the ribs, the sternum, threading more rope through the bones, ensuring the fit was snug and that the rope would not slip off when they hauled it topside. His fingers continued to travel upward, only to find that the spinal column tapered off into nothing but black muck.

No head. Instinctively Snow jerked his hand away, then realized in a surge of panic that he had let go of the guide rope. He windmilled his arms and bumped against something: the skeleton again. He grabbed at it desperately, almost hugging it with relief. He quickly felt downward for the rope, grasping and feeling along the long bones, trying to remember just where he'd tied it.

The rope wasn't there. Had it come loose? No, that was impossible. He tried to shove it, to turn it, looking for the rope, and suddenly felt his air hose catch on something. He jerked back, disoriented again, and felt the seal on his mask loosening. Something warm and thick began trickling underneath. He tried to shake loose and felt his mask pulled aside, a surge of mud flooding his eyes, oozing into his nose, sucking across his left ear. With escalating horror he realized that he was tangled in a macabre embrace with a *second* skeleton. And then came blind, mindless, screaming panic.

On the deck of the police launch, Lieutenant D'Agosta watched with detached interest as the novice diver was hauled to the surface. He was a remarkable sight: thrashing around, bubbling yells partly muffled by mud, streams of the ochre-colored stuff bleeding away from his drysuit and staining the water chocolate. The diver must've lost his hold on the rope at some point; he was lucky, very lucky, to have found his way back to the surface. D'Agosta waited patiently while the hysterical diver was brought on board, unsuited, rinsed off, and calmed down. He watched the man vomit over the side—not on deck, D'Agosta noted approvingly. He'd found a skeleton. Two of them, apparently. Not what he'd been sent down for, of course, but not bad, for a virgin dive. He would write the poor guy a commendation. The kid would probably be okay if he hadn't breathed in any of that shit that clung to his nose and mouth. If he had... well, it was miraculous what they could do with antibiotics these days.

The first skeleton, when it appeared at the churning surface, was still coated with sludge. A sidestroking diver dragged it to the side of D'Agosta's launch, eased a net around it, and clambered onto the deck. It was hoisted up the side, scraping and dribbling, sliding onto a tarp at D'Agosta's feet like some grisly catch.

"Jesus, you could have rinsed it off a bit," D'Agosta said, wincing at the smell of ammonia. Above the surface the skeleton became his jurisdiction, and he fervently wished it could simply go back from whence it came. He could see that where the skull should have been there was nothing.

"Shall I hose it down, sir?" the diver asked, reaching for the pump.

"Hose yourself down first." The diver looked ridiculous, an unraveled condom plastered to the side of his head, filth dribbling from his legs. Two divers climbed aboard and began gingerly hauling in another rope while a third diver brought up the other skeleton, buoying it with a free hand. When it landed on the deck and those aboard saw that it, too, had no head, an awful silence fell. D'Agosta glanced over at the huge brick of heroin, also recovered and safely sealed in a rubber evidence bag. Suddenly, the brick had grown a lot less interesting.

He drew thoughtfully on his cigar and looked away, scanning the Cloaca. His eyes came to rest on the ancient mouth of the West Side Lateral Drain. A few stalactites dripped from the ceiling, like small teeth. The West Side Lateral was one of the biggest in the city, draining practically the entire Upper West Side. Every time Manhattan got a hard rain, the Lower Hudson Sewage Treatment Plant hit capacity and shunted thousands of gallons of raw sewage out the West Side Lateral. Right into the Cloaca.

He tossed the remains of his cigar over the side. "You guys are gonna have to get wet again," he said, exhaling loudly. "I want those skulls."

2

Louis Padelsky, Assistant Medical Examiner for the City of New York, glanced at the clock, feeling his gut rumble. He was, quite literally, starving. He'd had nothing but SlimCurve shakes for three days, and today was his day for a real lunch. Popeye's fried chicken. He ran his hand over his ample gut, probing and pinching, thinking that there might be less there. Yup, definitely less there.

He took a gulp from his fifth cup of black coffee and glanced at the ref sheet. Ah—at last, something interesting. Not just another shooting, stabbing, or OD.

The stainless steel doors at the end of the autopsy suite banged open, and the ME nurse, Sheila Rocco, rolled in a brown corpse and laid it out on a gurney. Padelsky glanced at it, looked away, glanced back again. Corpse was the wrong word, he decided. The thing on the gurney was little more than a skeleton, covered with shreds of flesh. Padelsky wrinkled his nose.

Rocco positioned the gurney under the lights and began hooking up the drainage tube.

"Don't bother," Padelsky said. The only thing that needed draining around here was his coffee cup. He took a large swallow, tossed it into the wastebasket, checked the corpse's tag against the ref sheet and initialed it, then pulled on a pair of green latex gloves.

"What have you brought for me now, Sheila?" he asked. "Piltdown Man?"

Rocco frowned and adjusted the lights above the gurney.

"This one must've been buried for a couple of centuries, at least. Buried in shit, too, from the smell of it. Perhaps it's King Shitankhamen himself."

Rocco pursed her lips and waited while Pàdelsky roared with laughter. When he was finished, she silently handed him a clipboard.

Padelsky scanned the sheet, lips moving as he read the typed sentences. Suddenly, he straightened up. "Dredged out of Humboldt Kill," he muttered. "Christ almighty." He eyed the nearby glove dispenser, considered putting on an extra pair of gloves, decided against it. "Hmm. Decapitated, head still missing... no clothing, but found with a metal belt around its waist." He glanced over at the cadaver and spied the ID bag hanging from the gurney.

"Let's have a look," he said, taking up the bag. Inside was a thin gold belt with an Uffizi buckle, set with a topaz. It had already been run through the lab, he knew, but he still wasn't allowed to touch it. He noticed the belt had a number on its back plate.

"Expensive," Padelsky said, nodding toward the belt. "Maybe it's Piltdown Woman. Or a transvestite." And he roared again.

Rocco frowned. "May we show the dead a little more respect, Dr. Padelsky?"

"Of course, of course." He hung the clipboard on a hook and adjusted the microphone that hung above the gurney. "Switch on the tape recorder, will you, Sheila darling?"

As the machine snapped on, his voice suddenly became clipped and professional. "This is Dr. Louis Padelsky. It's August 2, 12:05 P.M. I am assisted by Sheila Rocco, and we're commencing examination of"—he glanced at the tag—"Number A-1430. We have here a headless corpse, virtually skeletonized—Sheila, will you straighten it out?—perhaps four feet eight inches in length. Add the missing skull and you probably got someone five foot six, seven. Let's sex the skeleton. Pelvic rim's a little wide. Yup, it's gynecoid; we've got a woman here. No lipping of the lumbar vertebrae, so she's under forty. Hard to say how long she's been submerged. There is a distinct smell of, er, sewage. The bones are a brownish orange color and look like they've been in mud for a long time. On the other hand, there is sufficient connective tissue to hold the corpse together, and there are ragged ends of muscle tissue around the medial and lateral condyles of the femur and more clinging to the sacrum and ischium. Plenty of material for blood typing and DNA analysis. Scissors, please."

He snipped off a piece of tissue and slipped it into a bag. "Sheila, could you turn the pelvis over on its side? Now, let's see... the skeleton is still mostly articulated, except of course for the missing skull. Looks like the axis is also missing... six cervical vertebrae remaining... missing the two floating ribs and the entire left foot."

He continued describing the skeleton. Finally he moved away from the microphone. "Sheila, the rongeur, please."

Rocco handed him a small instrument, which Padelsky used to separate the humerus from the ulna.

"Periosteum elevator." He dug into the vertebrae, removing a few samples of connective tissue, cutting away at the bone. Then he pulled a pair of disposable plastic goggles over his head.

"Saw, please."

She handed him a small nitrogen-driven saw and he switched it on, waiting a moment while the tachometer reached the correct rpm. When the diamond blade touched the bone, a high-pitched whine, like an enraged mosquito, filled the small room. Along with it came the sudden smell of bone dust, sewage, rotten marrow, and death.

Padelsky took sections at various points, which Rocco sealed in bags.

"I want SEM and stereozoom pictures of each microsection," Padelsky said, stepping away from the gurney and turning off the recorder. Rocco wrote the requests on the Ziploc bags with a large black marker.

A knock sounded at the door. Sheila went to answer, stepped outside for a moment, then poked her head back in.

"They have a tentative ID from the belt, Doctor," she said. "It's Pamela Wisher."

"Pamela Wisher, the society girl?" asked Padelsky, taking off the goggles and backing off a little. "Jeez."

"And there's a second skeleton," she continued. "From the same place."

Padelsky had moved to a deep metal sink, preparing to remove his gloves and wash up. "A second one?" he asked irritably. "Why the hell didn't they bring it in with the first? I should have been looking at them side by side." He glanced at the clock: one-fifteen already. Goddammit, that meant no lunch until at least three. He felt faint with hunger.

The doors banged open and the second skeleton was wheeled under the bright light. Padelsky turned the tape recorder back on and went to pour himself yet another cup of coffee while the nurse did the prep work.

"This one's headless, too," Rocco said.

"You're kidding, right?" Padelsky replied. He walked forward, glanced at the skeleton, then froze, coffee cup to his lips.

"What the—?" He lowered the cup and stared, open-mouthed. Laying the cup aside, he stepped up quickly to the gurney and bent over the skeleton, running the tips of his gloved fingers lightly over one of the ribs.

"Dr. Padelsky?" Rocco asked.

He straightened, went back to the tape recorder, and brusquely switched it off. "Cover it up and get Dr. Brambell. And don't breathe a word about this"—he nodded at the skeleton—"to anyone."

She hesitated, looking at the skeleton with a puzzled expression, her eyes gradually widening.

"I mean *now*, Sheila darling."

3

The phone rang abruptly, shattering the stillness of the small museum office. Margo Green, face mere inches from her computer terminal, sat back guiltily in her chair, a shock of short brown hair falling across her eyes.

The phone rang again, and she moved to answer it, then hesitated. No doubt it was one of the computer jocks in data processing, calling to complain about the enormous amount of CPU time her cladistic regression program was soaking up. She settled back and waited for the phone to stop ringing, the muscles of her back and legs pleasantly sore from the previous night's workout. Picking up the hand trainer from her desk, she began squeezing it in a routine so familiar it had grown almost instinctive. Another five minutes and her program would be finished. Then they could complain all they wanted.

She knew about the new cost-cutting policy requiring that large batch jobs be submitted for approval. But that would have meant a flurry of e-mail before she could run the program. And she needed the results right away.

At least Columbia, where she'd been an instructor until accepting the assistant curatorship at the New York Museum of Natural History, wasn't always in the midst of some new round of budget cutting. And the more the Museum got into financial trouble these days, the more it seemed to rely on show instead of substance. Already, Margo had noticed the early buildup for next year's blockbuster exhibition, *21st-Century Plagues*.

She glanced up at the screen to check the progress of her regression program, then put down the hand trainer, reached into her bag and drew out the *New York Post*. The *Post* and a cup of black Kilimanjaro coffee had become her weekday morning ritual. There was something refreshing about the *Post*'s truculent attitude, like that of the Fat Boy in *The Pickwick Papers*. Besides, she knew she'd catch hell from her old friend Bill Smithback if he ever found out she'd missed a single homicide article carrying his byline.

She smoothed the tabloid on her knees, grinning at the headline despite herself. It was vintage *Post*ean, a screaming 96-point banner that covered three-quarters of the front page:

SEWAGE CORPSE
IDENTIFIED AS MISSING DEB

She glanced down at the opening paragraph. Sure enough, it was Smithback's work. *Second front-page article this month*, she thought; on the strength of this, Smithback would be strutting and primping, even more impossible to be around than usual.

She quickly skimmed the article. It was quintessential Smithback: sensationalist and macabre, full of loving attention to the gruesome details. In the opening paragraphs, he quickly summarized the facts that were by now well known to all New Yorkers. The "beautiful trust-funder" Pamela Wisher, known for her marathon late-night carousings, had disappeared two months earlier from a basement club on Central Park South. Ever since, her "smiling face with its dazzling teeth, vacant blue eyes, and expensive blond hair" had been plastered at every street corner from 57th to 96th. Margo had often seen the color photocopies of Wisher as she jogged to the Museum from her apartment on West End Avenue.

Now, the article breathlessly announced, the remains found the previous day—"buried in raw sewage" in Humboldt Kill and "locked in a bony embrace" with another skeleton—had been identified as Pamela Wisher's. The second skeleton remained unidentified. An accompanying photo showed Wisher's boyfriend, the young Viscount Adair, sitting on the curb in front of the Platypus Lounge with his head in his hands, minutes after learning of her grisly death. The police were, of course, "taking vigorous action." Smithback closed with several man-on-the-street quotations of the "I-hope-they-fry-the-bastard-who-did-this" variety.

She lowered the paper, thinking of the grainy face of Pamela Wisher staring out at her from the numerous posters. She deserved a better fate than becoming New York's big story of the summer.

The shrill sound of the phone again interrupted Margo's thoughts. She glanced over at her terminal, pleased to see that the program had finished at last. *Might as well answer it,* she thought; she'd have to get this lecture over with sooner or later.

"This is Margo Green," she said.

"Dr. Green?" came the voice. "About time."

The thick Queens accent was distantly familiar, like a half-forgotten dream. Gruff, authoritarian. Margo searched her memory for the face belonging to the voice on the other end of the phone.

...All we can say is that a body has been found on the premises, under circumstances we are currently investigating...

She sat back in surprise.

"Lieutenant D'Agosta?" she asked.

"We need you in the Forensic Anthropology lab," D'Agosta said. "Right away, please."

"Can I ask—?"

"You may not. Sorry. Whatever you're doing, forget it and come downstairs." The line went dead with a sharp click.

Margo held the phone away from her face, looking at the mouthpiece as if waiting for further explanation. Then she opened her carryall and replaced the *Post*—carefully covering a small semiautomatic pistol in the process—pushed the chair away from the computer, and stepped quickly out of her office.

4

Bill Smithback strolled nonchalantly past the grand facade of Nine Central Park South, a stately McKim, Mead, and White building of brick and carved limestone. A brace of doormen stood beneath the gold-trimmed awning that stretched to the curb. He could see a variety of other service people standing at attention inside the opulent lobby. As he'd feared, it was one of those ridiculously overstaffed parkfront apartment buildings. This was going to be tough. Very tough.

He turned the corner of Sixth Avenue and paused, considering how best to proceed. He felt in the outside pocket of his sports jacket, locating the record button of his microcassette recorder. He could turn it on unobtrusively when the time came. He glanced at his image, reflected among countless Italian shoes in a nearby shop window: he was the very model of preppiedom, or as near as his wardrobe would permit. He took a deep breath and returned around the corner, walking with confident step toward the cream-colored awning. The closer of the two uniformed doormen gazed at him imperturbably, one gloved hand on the great brass handle of the door.

"I'm here to see Mrs. Wisher," Smithback said.

"Name, please?" the man asked in a monotone.

"A friend of Pamela's."

"I'm sorry," the man said, unmoving, "but Mrs. Wisher is not receiving any visitors."

Smithback thought quickly. The doorman had asked who was calling before telling him this. That meant Mrs. Wisher was expecting someone.

"If you must know, it's about this morning's appointment," Smithback said. "I'm afraid there's been a change. Could you ring her for me?"

The doorman hesitated a moment, then opened the door, leading Smithback across the gleaming marble floor. The journalist looked around. The concierge, a very old and very gaunt-looking man, was standing behind a bronze construction that looked more fortress than front desk. At the back of the lobby, a security guard sat behind a Louis XVI table. An elevator operator stood beside him, legs slightly apart, hands folded across his belt.

"This gentleman is calling on Mrs. Wisher," the doorman said to the concierge.

The concierge gazed down at him from his marble pillbox. "Yes?"

Smithback took a deep breath. At least, he'd broached the lobby. "It's about the appointment she's expecting. There's been a change."

The concierge paused a moment, his hooded eyes checking out Smithback's shoes, running up his sport coat, examining his haircut. Smithback waited, silently chafing under the examination, hoping he'd captured the look of an earnest young man from a well-to-do family.

"Who may I say is calling?" the concierge rasped.

"A friend of the family will do."

The concierge waited, staring at him.

"Bill Smithback," he added quickly. Mrs. Wisher, he was certain, did not read the *New York Post*.

The concierge looked down at something that was spread in front of him. "What about the eleven o'clock appointment?" he asked.

"They sent me instead," Smithback replied, suddenly glad that it was 10:32 A.M.

The concierge turned around and disappeared into a small office. He came out again sixty seconds later. "Please pick up the house telephone on the table beside you," he said.

Smithback held the receiver to his ear.

"What? Did George cancel?" said a small, crisp, expensive voice.

"Mrs. Wisher, may I come up and speak with you about Pamela?"

There was a silence. "Who is this?" the voice asked.

"Bill Smithback."

There was another silence, longer this time. Smithback continued. "I have something very important, some information about your daughter's death, that I am sure the police haven't told you. I feel sure you would want to know—"

The voice broke in. "Yes, yes, I'm sure you do."

"Wait—" Smithback said, his mind racing again.

There was a silence.

"Mrs. Wisher?"

He heard a click. The woman had hung up.

Well, Smithback thought, he had given it his best shot. Maybe he could wait outside, on a park bench across the street, on the chance she'd emerge later in the day. But even as he considered this, Smithback knew that Mrs. Wisher would not be leaving her elegant fastness for the foreseeable future.

A phone rang at the concierge's elbow. Mrs. Wisher, no doubt. Eager to avoid a bum's rush, Smithback turned and started walking quickly out of the lobby.

"Mr. Smithback!" the concierge called loudly.

Smithback turned. This was the part he hated.

The concierge gazed at him expressionlessly, telephone at his ear. "The elevator is over there."

"Elevator?" Smithback asked.

The concierge nodded. "Eighteenth floor."

The elevator operator slid open first the brass cage, then the heavy oak doors, depositing Smithback directly into a peach-colored foyer crammed top to bottom with flower arrangements. A side table was overflowing with sympathy cards, including a fresh stack that had not been opened. At the far end of the silent room, a set of French doors stood ajar. Smithback walked toward them slowly.

Beyond the doors lay a large drawing room. Empire sofas and chaise longues were placed at neat symmetric angles on the dense carpet. Along the far wall stood a series of tall windows. Smithback knew that, when open, they would afford a spectacular view of Central Park. But now they were tightly closed and shuttered, throwing the tastefully appointed space into heavy gloom.

There was a brief movement to one side. Turning, Smithback saw a small, neat woman with well-coiffed brown hair seated at one end of a sofa. She was wearing a dark, simple dress. Without speaking, she motioned him to sit down. Smithback selected a wing chair opposite Mrs. Wisher. A tea service had been laid out on a low table between them, and the journalist's eye roved over the array of scones, marmalades, dishes of honey and clotted cream. The woman made no move to offer any, and Smithback realized the setting had been for the intended appointment. A brief uneasiness came across him at the thought that George—no doubt the real eleven o'clock arrival—might appear at any moment.

Smithback cleared his throat. "Mrs. Wisher, I'm very, very sorry about your daughter," he said.

As he spoke, he realized he might actually mean it. Seeing this elegant room, seeing how little all this wealth mattered in the face of ultimate tragedy, somehow brought the woman's loss forcefully home to him.

Mrs. Wisher continued to gaze back, hands folded in her lap. She may have made a barely perceptible nod, but Smithback couldn't be sure in the dim light. *Time to get the show on the road,* he thought, reaching casually into his jacket pocket and slowly pressing the record button.

"Turn off that tape recorder," said Mrs. Wisher quietly. Her voice was thin and a little strained, but remarkably commanding.

Smithback jerked his hand out of the pocket. "I'm sorry?"

"Please remove the recorder from your pocket and place it here, where I can see that it's turned off."

"Yes, yes, of course," Smithback said, fumbling with the machine.

"Have you no sense of decency?" the woman whispered.

Smithback, placing the recorder on the low table, felt his ears begin to burn.

"You say you're sorry about my daughter's death," the quiet voice continued, "while at the same time turning on that filthy thing. After I invited you into my home."

Smithback shifted uncomfortably in his chair, reluctant to meet the woman's eyes. "Yes, well," he babbled. "I'm sorry, I'm just... well, it's my job." The words sounded lame even as he spoke them.

"Yes. I've just lost my only child, the only family I had left. Whose sensitivities do you think should take precedence, Mr. Smithback?"

Smithback fell silent, forcing himself to look at the woman. She sat unmoving, staring steadily back at him across the gloom, hands still folded on her lap. A strange thing was happening to him, a very strange thing, so foreign to his nature that he almost didn't recognize the emotion. He was feeling embarrassed. No, that wasn't it: he was feeling ashamed. If he'd fought for the scoop, unearthed it himself, perhaps it would be different. But to be brought up here, to see the woman's grief... All the excitement of getting assigned a big story drained away beneath this novel sensation.

Mrs. Wisher raised one of her hands and made the briefest of movements, indicating something on a reading table beside her.

"I assume you are the Smithback who writes for this paper?"

Smithback followed her gesture and noticed, with a sinking feeling, a copy of the *Post*. "Yes," he said.

She folded her hands again. "I just wanted to be sure. Now, what about that important information regarding my daughter's death? No, don't say it—no doubt that was a ruse, as well."

There was another silence. Now, Smithback found himself almost wishing that the real eleven o'clock appointment would show up. Anything to get out of here.

"How do you do it?" she asked at last.

"Do what?"

"Invent this garbage? It isn't enough for my daughter to be brutally murdered. People like you have to sully her memory."

Smithback swallowed. "Mrs. Wisher, I'm just—"

"Reading this filth," she continued, "one would think that Pamela was just some selfish society girl who got what she deserved. You make your readers glad my daughter was murdered. So, what I wonder is simple. *How do you do it?*"

"Mrs. Wisher, people in this town don't pay attention to something unless you slap them in the face with it," Smithback began, then stopped. Mrs. Wisher wasn't buying his self-justification any more than he was.

The woman sat forward very slowly on the sofa. "You know absolutely nothing about her, Mr. Smithback. You only see what's on the surface. That's all you're interested in."

"Not true!" Smithback burst out, surprising himself. "I mean, that's not all I'm interested in. I want to know the real Pamela Wisher."

The woman regarded him for a long moment. Then she stood up and left the room, returning with a framed photograph. She handed it to Smithback. A girl of about six was pictured, swinging on a rope tied to a massive oak branch. The girl was hollering at the camera, her two front teeth missing, pinafore and pigtails flying.

"That's the Pamela I'll always remember, Mr. Smithback," Mrs. Wisher said evenly. "If you really are interested, then print this picture. Not that one you keep running that makes her look like a brainless debutante." She sat down again, smoothing her dress across her knees. "She was just beginning to smile again, after the death of her father six months ago. And she wanted to have some fun before starting work this fall. What's criminal about that?"

"Work?" Smithback asked.

There was a short silence. Smithback felt Mrs. Wisher's eyes on him in the funereal gloom. "That's correct. She was starting a job in a hospice for AIDS patients. You would have known that if you'd done your research."

Smithback swallowed.

"That's the *real* Pamela," the woman said, her voice suddenly breaking. "Kind, generous, full of life. I want you to write about the real Pamela."

"I'll do my best," Smithback mumbled.

Then the moment was over, and Mrs. Wisher was again composed and distant. She inclined her head, made a brief movement of her hand, and Smithback realized he had been released. He mumbled his thanks, retrieved his tape recorder, and headed for the elevator as quickly as he dared.

"One other thing," Mrs. Wisher said, her voice suddenly hard. Smithback stopped at the French doors. "They can't tell me when she died, why she died, or even how she died. But Pamela will not have died in vain, I promise you that."

She spoke with a new intensity, and Smithback turned to face her. "You said something just now," she went on. "You said that people in this town don't pay attention to something unless you slap them in the face with it. That's what I intend to do."

"How?" Smithback asked.

But Mrs. Wisher withdrew onto the sofa, and her face fell into deep shadow. Smithback walked through the foyer and rang for the elevator, feeling drained. It wasn't until he was back on the street, blinking in the strong summer light, that he looked down again at the childhood picture of Pamela Wisher, still clutched in his right hand. It was beginning to dawn on him exactly how formidable a woman Mrs. Wisher was.

5

The metal door at the end of the gray hallway was discreetly marked FORENSIC ANTHROPOLOGY in stenciled capitals. It was the Museum's state-of-the-art facility for analyzing human remains. Margo tried the knob and to her surprise found it locked. This was odd. She'd been here countless times, assisting in examinations of everything from Peruvian mummies to Anasazi cliff dwellers, and the door had never been locked before. She lifted her hand to knock. But the door was already being opened from the inside, and she found her rap falling onto thin air.

She stepped in, then stopped abruptly. The lab, normally brightly lit and bustling with grad students and curatorial assistants, looked dim and strange. The bulky electron microscopes, X-ray viewers, and electrophoresis apparatus sat against the walls, silent and unused. The window that normally boasted a panoramic view of Central Park was covered by a heavy curtain. A single pool of brilliant light illuminated the center of the room; at its edge, a semicircle of figures stood among the shadows.

In the center of the light lay a large specimen table. Something brown and knobby lay on it, along with a blue plastic sheet covering some other long, low object. As she stared curiously,

Margo realized that the knobby object was a human skeleton, decorated with desiccated strips of sinew and flesh. There was a faint but unmistakable odor of corpse-reek.

The door closed and locked behind her. Lieutenant Vincent D'Agosta, wearing what looked like the same suit she remembered from the Museum Beast murders of eighteen months before, walked back to join the group, nodding briefly at her as he passed. He seemed to have shed a few pounds since she'd last seen him. Margo noticed that his suit matched the dirty brown color of the skeleton.

Margo scanned the row of figures as her eyes adjusted to the dim light. To D'Agosta's left was a nervous man in a lab coat, a cup of coffee gripped in his pudgy hand. Next came the tall, thin form of the Museum's new director, Olivia Merriam. Another figure stood farther back in the shadows, too dim for Margo to make out anything but a vague outline.

The Director gave Margo a wan smile. "Thank you for coming, Dr. Green. These gentlemen"—she waved vaguely in D'Agosta's direction—"have asked for our help."

There was a silence. Finally, D'Agosta sighed irritably. "We can't wait for him any longer. He lives way the hell out in Mendham, and didn't seem too thrilled about coming in when I telephoned last night." He looked at each person in turn. "You saw the *Post* this morning, right?"

The Director looked at him with distaste. "No."

"Let me backtrack a bit, then." D'Agosta gestured toward the skeleton on the stainless steel table. "Meet Pamela Wisher. Daughter of Anette and the late Horace Wisher. No doubt you've seen her picture all over town. She disappeared around 3:00 A.M. on the morning of May 23. She spent the evening at the Whine Cellar, one of those basement clubs off Central Park South. Went to make a phone call and never came back. At least, not until yesterday, when we found her skeleton—minus the skull—in the Humboldt Kill. Apparently it was flushed out of a West Side storm drain, probably during a recent heavy rain."

Margo looked again at the remains on the table. She had seen countless skeletons before, but none belonging to anyone she'd known, or even heard of. It was difficult to believe that this grisly assemblage of bones had once been the pretty blond woman she had been reading about barely fifteen minutes before.

"And with the remains of Pamela Wisher we also found *this*." D'Agosta nodded at the thing lying beneath the blue plastic sheet. "So far, the press knows only that a second skeleton was found—thank God." He glanced at the figure standing apart in the shadows. "I'll let Dr. Simon Brambell; Chief Medical Examiner, do the talking."

As the figure stepped into the light, Margo saw a slender man of about sixty-five. The skin lay tight and smooth across a devious old skull, and a pair of beady black eyes glittered at the assembled company behind ancient horn-rims. His long lean face was as devoid of expression as his head was devoid of hair.

He laid a finger across his upper lip. "If you would all take a few steps forward," he said in a soft Dublin accent, "you might have a better view."

There was a sound of reluctant shuffling. Dr. Brambell grasped the end of the blue sheet, paused a moment to look impassively around again, then flipped it off with a deft motion.

Beneath, Margo saw the remains of another headless corpse, as brown and decayed as the first. But as her eyes scanned the remains, she sensed there was something odd. Her breath drew in sharply as she realized what it was: the bizarre thickening of the leg bones, the odd curvatures of several of the major joint structures, was all wrong.

What the hell? she thought.

There came a sudden thump on the door.

"Christ." D'Agosta moved toward it quickly. "At last."

The door swung wide to reveal Whitney Cadwalader Frock, the famous evolutionary biologist, now a reluctant guest of Lieutenant D'Agosta. His wheelchair creaked as it approached the specimen table. Without looking at the assembled company, he examined the bony corpses, his eyes coming to rest on the second skeleton. After a few moments, he leaned back, a shock of white hair falling away from his wide pink forehead. He nodded at D'Agosta and the Museum Director. Then he saw Margo, and a look of surprise came over his face, changing quickly to a delighted smile.

Margo smiled and nodded in return. Although Frock had been her primary adviser during her graduate work at the Museum, she had not seen him since his retirement party. He had left the Museum to concentrate on his writing, yet there was still no sign of the promised follow-up volume to his influential work, *Fractal Evolution*.

The Medical Examiner, who had paid Frock's entrance only the briefest of glances, now continued. "I invite you," he said pleasantly, "to examine the ridging of the long bones, the bony spicules and osteophytes along the spine and at the joints. Also the twenty-degree outward rotation of the trochanters. Note that the ribs have a trapezoidal, instead of the normal prismatic, cross section. Finally, I would direct your attention to the thickening of the femurs. On the whole, a rather unbecoming fellow. Of course, these are only some of the more outstanding features. You can no doubt see the rest for yourselves."

D'Agosta breathed out through his nose. "No doubt."

Frock cleared his throat. "Naturally, I haven't had a chance for a thorough examination. But I wonder if you've considered the possibility of DISH."

The ME looked at Frock again, more carefully this time. "A very intelligent guess," he said. "But quite wrong. Dr. Frock is referring to diffuse idiopathic skeletal hyperostosis, a type of severe degenerative arthritis." He shook his head dismissively. "Nor is it osteomalacia, though if this wasn't the twentieth century I'd say it was the most nightmarish case of scurvy ever recorded. We've searched the medical databases, and can find nothing that would account for this condition."

Brambell ran his fingers lightly, almost affectionately, along the spinal column. "There is another curious anomaly shared by both skeletons, which we only noticed last night. Dr. Padelsky, would you please bring the stereozoom?"

The overweight man in the lab coat disappeared into the gloom, then returned, rolling before him a large microscope with an open stage. He positioned it over the neck bones of the deformed skeleton, peered through the eyepieces, made a few adjustments, then stepped back.

Brambell gestured with the palm of his hand. "Dr. Frock?"

Frock rolled forward and, with some difficulty, fit his face to the visor. He remained motionless for what seemed several minutes, leaning over the skeletonized cadaver. At last he rolled his wheelchair back, saying nothing.

"Dr. Green?" the ME said, turning to her. Margo stepped up to the microscope and peered in, aware of being the focus of attention.

At first, she could make nothing of the image. Then she realized that the stereozoom was focused on what appeared to be a cervical vertebra. There were several shallow, regular scores along one edge. Some foreign brownish matter clung to the bone, along with bits of cartilage, strings of muscle tissue, and a greasy bulb of adipocere.

Slowly she straightened up, feeling the old familiar fear return, unwilling to consider what those scores along the bone reminded her of.

The ME raised his eyebrows. "Your opinion, Dr. Green?"

Margo drew in her breath. "If I were to guess, I'd say they look like teeth marks."

She and Frock exchanged glances.

She knew now—they *both* knew—exactly why Frock had been called to this meeting.

Brambell waited while the others took turns staring through the microscope. Then, wordlessly, he wheeled the stereozoom over to Pamela Wisher's skeleton, focusing this time on the pelvis.

Again, Frock took up a position at the microscope, followed by Margo. No denying it this time; Margo noticed that some of the marks had punctured the bone and penetrated into the marrow spaces.

Frock blinked in the cold white light. "Lieutenant D'Agosta told me these skeletons came out of the West Side Lateral Drain."

"That's right," said D'Agosta.

"Flushed out by the recent storm."

"That's the theory."

"Perhaps feral dogs worried our couple while their dead bodies lay in the drain system."

"That's one possibility," said Brambell. "I would estimate the pressure required to make the deepest of those pressure marks at around 1200 psi. A bit high for a dog, don't you think?"

"Not for, say, a Rhodesian Ridgeback," said Frock.

Brambell inclined his head. "Or the Hound of the Baskervilles, Professor?"

Frock frowned at the sarcasm. "I'm not convinced those marks are as powerful as you believe."

"Alligator," said D'Agosta.

All heads turned toward him.

"Alligator," he repeated, almost defensively. "You know. They get flushed down the toilets as babies, then grow big in the sewers." He looked around. "I read it somewhere."

Brambell issued a chuckle as dry as dust. "Alligators, like all reptiles, have cone-shaped teeth. These marks were made by small triangular mammalian teeth, probably canines."

"Canine, but not dog?" Frock said. "Let's not forget the principle of Occam's razor. The simplest explanation is usually the correct one."

Brambell tilted his head in Frock's direction. "I know that Occam's razor is held in great esteem in *your* profession, Dr. Frock. In *mine*, we find the Holmesian philosophy more apt: 'When you have eliminated the impossible, whatever remains, *however improbable*, must be the truth.'"

"So what answer remains, Dr. Brambell?" Frock snapped.

"As of this moment, I have no explanation."

Frock settled back in the wheelchair. "This second skeleton is interesting. Perhaps even worth the trip in from Mendham. But you forget that I am now retired."

Margo watched him, frowning. Normally, the professor would have been more entranced by a puzzle such as this. She wondered if—perhaps in the same way as herself—Frock was reminded of the events of eighteen months before. If so, perhaps he was resisting. It was not the kind of reminiscence likely to ensure tranquil retirement.

Olivia Merriam spoke up. "Dr. Frock," she said, "we were hoping that you would be willing to assist in the analysis of the skeleton. Because of the unusual circumstances, the Museum has agreed to put its laboratory at the disposal of the police. We'll be happy to provide you an office on the fifth floor, with secretary, for as long as necessary."

Frock raised his eyebrows. "Surely the City Morgue has all the latest equipment. Not to mention the luminous medical talents of Dr. Brambell here."

"You are correct about the luminous talent, Dr. Frock," Brambell replied. "But as for having the latest equipment, you are sadly in error. The budget shortfalls of recent years have left us rather behind the times. Besides, the Morgue is a bit public for this sort of thing. Right now, we are infested with reporters and television crews." He paused. "And, of course, we don't have your particular expertise at the City Morgue."

"Thank you," Frock said. He gestured at the second skeleton. "But how hard could it be to identify someone who in life must have looked like, ahem, the Missing Link?"

"Believe me, we've tried," said D'Agosta. "Over the last twenty-four hours, we've checked every missing Tom, Dick, and Harry in the Instate area. Nothing. And as far as we can tell, no freak like this ever existed, let alone one who got himself lost and chewed up in the New York City sewers."

Frock seemed not to hear the answer to his question. His head sunk slowly to his chest and he remained motionless for several minutes. Except for an impatient cluck from Dr. Brambell, the laboratory was still. At last, Frock roused himself, sighed deeply, and nodded with what to Margo seemed like weary resignation. "Very well. I can give you a week. I have other business in the city to attend to. I assume you wish Dr. Green here to assist me?"

Too late, Margo realized she hadn't given any thought to why she had been invited to this secret gathering. But now it was clear. She knew that Frock trusted her completely. Together, they had solved the mystery of the Museum Beast killings. *They must have figured,* she thought, *that Frock would work with me and nobody else.*

"Wait a minute," she blurted. "I can't do that."

All eyes turned toward her, and Margo realized she had spoken more sharply than she'd meant to. "What I mean is, I don't think I can spare the time right now," she stammered.

Frock looked at her, comprehension in his eyes. More than anyone else, he understood this assignment was guaranteed to stir up fearsome memories.

Director Merriam's narrow features creased into a frown. "I'll speak to Dr. Hawthorne," she said. "You'll be given whatever time necessary to assist the police."

Margo opened her mouth to protest, then decided against it. Too bad, she thought, that her curatorial appointment at the Museum was too recent for her to refuse.

"Very good," said Brambell, a tight smile briefly cracking his face. "I will be working alongside the two of you, of course. Before we disperse, I might just emphasize that the utmost discretion will be required. It was bad enough having to release the news that Pamela Wisher had been found dead and decapitated. If word ever gets out that our socialite was nibbled on after death... or perhaps before..." His voice trailed off, and he smoothed a hand over his baldpate.

Frock glanced up sharply. "The teeth marks are not postmortem?"

"That, Dr. Frock, is the question of the hour. Or one of them, at least. The Mayor and the Chief of Police are waiting rather impatiently for results."

Frock made no reply, and it was clear to everybody that the meeting was at an end. The group turned to go, most of them eager to distance themselves from the gaunt brownish things that lay on the specimen tables.

As she walked past, the Museum Director turned briefly toward Margo. "Let me know if I can help in any way," she said.

Dr. Brambell took in Frock and Margo with one last sweep of his eyes, then followed the Director out the door.

Last to leave was Lieutenant D'Agosta. In the doorway, he paused for a moment. "If you have to talk to anyone, talk to me." He opened his mouth as if to say more, then stopped, nodded, and turned away abruptly. The door closed behind him and Margo was alone with Frock, Pamela Wisher, and the bizarrely malformed skeleton.

Frock sat up in his wheelchair. "Lock the door please, Margo," he said, "and get the rest of the lights up." He wheeled himself toward the specimen table. "I guess you'd better wash and put on scrubs."

Margo glanced at the two skeletons. Then she looked toward her old professor.

"Dr. Frock?" she began. "You don't think this could be the work of a—"

He turned suddenly, an odd expression on his ruddy face. Their eyes locked, and he shook his head.

"Don't," he whispered fiercely. "Not until we're certain."

Margo held his gaze for a moment. Finally she nodded and turned toward the bank of light switches. What had not been said between them was much more unsettling than the two grisly skeletons.

6

In the smoky recesses of the Cat's Paw bar, Smithback wedged himself into a narrow telephone booth. Balancing his drink in one hand and squinting at the buttons in the dim light, he dialed the number of his office, wondering how many messages would be waiting for him this time.

Smithback never doubted that he was one of the greatest journalists in New York. Probably *the* greatest. A year and a half ago, he'd brought the story of the Museum Beast to the world. And not in the usual dickless, detached way: he'd been there with D'Agosta and the others, struggling in the dark on that April night. On the strength of the book which quickly followed, he'd secured this position as *Post* crime correspondent. Now the Wisher thing had come along, and none too soon, either. Big stories were rarer than he could have guessed, and there were always others—like that stain-on-the-wall Bryce Harriman, crime reporter for the *Times*—out to scoop him. But if he played it right, this could be as big as the Mbwun story had been. Maybe bigger.

A great journalist, he mused as he listened to the phone ring, *adapts himself to the options offered him.* Take the Wisher story. He had been totally unprepared for the mother. She'd been impressive. Smithback found himself embarrassed and deeply moved. Fired by those unfamiliar emotions, he'd written a new article for that morning's edition, labeling Pamela Wisher the Angel of Central Park South and painting her death in tragic colors. But the real stroke of genius had been the $100,000 reward for information leading to the murderer. The idea had come to him in the middle of writing the story; he had carried the half-written piece and his reward idea straight into the office of the *Post*'s new editor, Arnold Murray. The man had loved it, authorizing it on the spot without even bothering to check with the publisher.

Ginny, the pool secretary, came on the line excitedly. Twenty phone calls about the reward, all of them bogus.

"That's it?" Smithback asked, crestfallen.

"Well, there was, like, this really *weird* visitor for you," the secretary gushed. She was short and skinny, lived in Ronkonkoma, and had a crush on Smithback.

"Yeah?"

"He was dressed in rags and he smelled. God, I could hardly *breathe*. And he was, like, high or something."

Maybe it's a hot tip, Smithback thought excitedly. "What did he want?"

"He said he had information about the Wisher murder. He asked you to meet him in the Penn Station men's room—"

Smithback almost dropped his drink. "The men's room? You've got to be kidding."

"That's what he said. You think he's a pervert?" She spoke with undisguised relish.

"Which men's room?"

He heard papers shuffling. "I've got it right here. North end, lower level, just to the left of the track 12 escalator. At eight o'clock tonight."

"What information, exactly?"

"That was all he said."

"Thanks." He hung up and checked his watch: seven forty-five. The men's room in Penn Station? *I'd have to be crazy or desperate,* he thought, *to follow up a lead like that.*

Smithback had never been inside a men's room at Penn Station before. Nobody he knew would ever go in one, either. As he opened the door into a vast, hot room, suffocating with the stench of urine and old diarrhea, he thought that, in fact, he'd rather piss his pants than use a Penn Station men's room.

He was five minutes late. *Probably the guy's gone already,* Smithback thought gratefully. *Assuming he'd ever been here in the first place.* He was just about to duck back outside when he heard a gravelly voice.

"William Smithback?"

"What?" Smithback looked around quickly, scanning the deserted men's room. Then he saw two legs descend in the farthest stall. The door opened. A small, skinny man stepped out and walked up to him unsteadily, his long face grimy, his clothes dark with grease and dirt, his hair matted and knotted into alarming shapes. A beard of indescribable color descended to twin points near his belly button, which was exposed through a long ragged tear in his shirt.

"William Smithback?" the man repeated, peering at him through filmy eyes.

"Who else?"

Without another word, the man turned and moved back toward the rear of the men's room. He stopped at the open last stall, then turned, waiting.

"You have some information for me?" Smithback asked.

"Come with me." He gestured back toward the stall.

"No way," said Smithback. "If you want to talk, we can talk out here, but I'm not going in there with you, pal."

The man gestured again. "But this is the way to go."

"Go where?"

"Down."

Cautiously, Smithback approached the stall. The man had stepped inside and was standing behind the toilet, prying back a large piece of painted sheet metal that, Smithback now saw, covered a ragged hole in the dirty tile wall.

"In there?" Smithback asked.

The man nodded.

"Where does it go?"

"Down," the man repeated.

"Forget it," said Smithback. He started to back away.

The man held his gaze. "I'm supposed to bring you to Mephisto," he said. "He has to talk to you about the murder of that girl. He knows important things."

"Give me a break."

The man continued to stare at him. "You can trust me," he said simply.

Somehow, despite the filth and the drugged eyes, Smithback found himself believing the man. "What things?"

"You have to talk to Mephisto."

"Who's this Mephisto?"

"He's our leader." The man shrugged as if no other information was necessary.

"Our?"

The man nodded. "The Route 666 community."

Despite his uncertainty, Smithback felt a tingle of excitement. An organized community underground? That would make good copy all by itself. And if this Mephisto really knew something about the Wisher murder... "Where exactly is this Route 666 community?" he asked.

"Can't tell you. But I'll show you the way."

"And your name?" he asked.

"They call me Tail Gunner," the man said, a small gleam of pride flaring in his eyes.

"Look," said Smithback. "I'd follow you, but you can't expect me to just crawl into a hole like this. I could get ambushed, mugged, anything."

The man shook his head vehemently. "I'll protect you. Everyone knows I'm Mephisto's chief runner. You'll be safe."

45

Smithback stared at the man: rheumy eyes, running nose, dirty wizard's beard. He had come all the way to the offices of the *Post*. That was a lot of trouble for a guy who looked both broke and homeless.

Then the image of Bryce Harriman's smug face filled his mind. He imagined Bryce's editor at the *Times,* asking him again how come that hack Smithback had gotten the story first.

He liked that image.

The man known as Tail Gunner held back the large piece of tin while Smithback clambered through. Once they were both inside he carefully maneuvered it back into place, propping it closed with some loose bricks.

Looking around, Smithback found himself in a long, narrow tunnel. Water and steam pipes ran overhead like thick gray veins. The ceiling was low, but not so low that a man as tall as Smithback couldn't stand upright. Evening light filtered in through ceiling grates spaced at hundred yard intervals.

The reporter followed the stooped, low figure, moving ahead of him in the dim light. Once in a while the rumble of a nearby train would fill the dank space; Smithback could feel the sound more in his bones than his ears.

They began walking northward along what seemed to be an endless tunnel. After ten or fifteen minutes, Smithback began to feel a nagging worry. "Excuse me," he said, "but why the long walk?"

"Mephisto keeps the nearest entrances to our community secret."

Smithback nodded, making a wide detour around the swollen body of a dead dog. It wasn't surprising these tunnel dwellers were a little paranoid, but this was getting ridiculous. They'd walked far enough north to be under Central Park.

Soon, the tunnel began to curve gently to the right. Smithback could make out a series of steel doors set into the thick concrete wall. Overhead a large pipe ran, water dripping from its padded covering. A sign on the padding read DANGER: CONTAINS ASBESTOS

FIBERS. AVOID CREATING DUST. CANCER AND LUNG DISEASE HAZARD. Stopping and digging one hand into his rags, Tail Gunner extracted a key and placed it in the lock of the closest door.

"How'd you get that key?" Smithback asked.

"We have many skills in our community," the man replied, pulling open the door and ushering the journalist through.

As the door shut behind Smithback, the blackness of night rushed forward to meet him. Realizing how much he'd instinctively relied on the dim light that had filtered down from the grates, Smithback had a sudden feeling of panic.

"Don't you have a flashlight?" he stammered.

There was a scratching sound, then the flaring of a wooden match. In the flickering illumination, Smithback saw a series of cement steps leading downward as far as the matchlight penetrated.

Tail Gunner snapped his wrist and the match went out.

"Satisfied?" came the dull, monotonic voice.

"No," Smithback replied quickly. "Light another."

"When it is necessary."

Smithback felt his way down the staircase, his hands spread on the cool slick walls for balance. They descended for what seemed an eternity. Suddenly, another match flared, and Smithback saw that the stairs ended in an enormous railroad tunnel, its silver tracks gleaming dully in the orange light.

"Where are we now?" Smithback asked.

"Track 100," the man said. "Two levels down."

"Are we there yet?"

The match flickered out, and darkness descended again.

"Follow me," came the voice. "When I say stop, you stop. Immediately."

They ventured onto the tracks. Smithback found himself fighting down panic once again as he stumbled over the iron rails.

"Stop," came the voice. Smithback halted as another match flared. "See that?" Tail Gunner said, pointing to a gleaming bar

47

of metal with a bright yellow line painted next to it. "That's a third rail. It's electrified. Don't step on it."

The match died out. Smithback heard the man take a few steps in the close, humid darkness.

"Light another!" he cried.

A match flared. Smithback took a broad step over the third rail.

"Are there any more of those?" he asked, pointing to the rail.

"Yes," the little man said. "I'll show you."

"Jesus," said Smithback as the match died. "What happens if you step on one?"

"The current explodes your body, blows off your arms, legs, and head," the disembodied voice said. There was a pause. "It's always better not to step on it."

A match flared again, illuminating another yellow-painted rail. Smithback stepped gingerly over it, then watched as Tail Gunner pointed to a small hole in the far wall about two feet high and four across, chiseled out of the bottom of an old archway that had been bricked up with cinder block.

"We go down here," Tail Gunner said.

Smithback could feel a hot draft coming up from below, tinged with a foul odor that made his gorge rise. Interwoven with the stench Smithback thought he caught, for a moment, the smell of wood smoke.

"Down?" he asked in disbelief, turning his face away. "Again? What, you mean slide in there on my belly?"

But his companion was already wriggling his way through.

"No way," Smithback called out, squatting down near the hole. "Listen, I'm not going down there. If this Mephisto wants to talk, he has to come up here."

There was a silence, and then Tail Gunner's voice echoed out of the gloom on the far side of the cinder block. "Mephisto never comes higher than level three."

"He's gonna have to make an exception, then." Smithback tried to sound more confident than he felt. He realized that he had put himself into an impossible situation, relying totally on this bizarre, unstable man. It was pitch black again, and he had no way of finding his way back.

There was a long silence.

"You still with me?" Smithback asked.

"Wait there," the voice demanded suddenly.

"You're leaving? Give me some matches," Smithback pleaded. Something poked him in the knee and he cried out in surprise. It was Tail Gunner's grimy hand, holding something out to him through the hole.

"Is that all?" Smithback asked, counting the three matches by touch.

"All I can spare," came the voice, faint now and moving away. There were some more words, but Smithback could not make them out.

Silence descended. Smithback leaned back against the wall, afraid to sit down, clutching the matches tightly in one hand. He cursed himself for being foolish enough to follow the man down here. *No story is worth this,* he thought. Could he get back with only three matches? He shut his eyes and concentrated, trying to remember every twist and turn that had brought him here. Eventually, he gave up: the three matches would barely get him across those electrified rails.

When his knees began to protest he rose from the squatting position. He stared into the lightless tunnel, eyes wide, ears straining. It was so utterly black that he began to imagine things in the dark: movement, shapes. He remained still, trying to breathe calmly, as an infinity of time passed. This was insane. If only he—

"Scriblerian!" a ghostly, incorporeal voice sounded from the hole at his feet.

"What?" Smithback yelped, spinning around.

"I am addressing William Smithback, scriblerian, am I not?" The voice was cracked and low, a sinister sing-song rising from the depths beneath him.

"Yes, yes, I'm Smithback. Bill Smithback. Who are you?" he called, unsettled at speaking to this disembodied voice out of the darkness.

"Mephisto," came the voice, drawing the *s* of the name into a fierce hiss.

"What took you so long?" Smithback replied nervously, stooping down again toward the hole in the cinder block.

"It is a long way up."

Smithback paused a minute, contemplating how this man—now standing somewhere below his feet—had needed to travel several levels *up* to reach this place. "Are you coming up?" he asked.

"No! You should feel honored, scriblerian. This is as close as I have been to the surface in five years."

"Why is that?" Smithback asked, groping in the darkness for the microcassette recorder.

"Because this is my domain. I am lord of all you survey."

"But I don't see anything."

A dry chuckle rose from the hole in the cinder block. "Wrong! You see *blackness*. And blackness is my domain. Above your head the trains rumble past, the surface dwellers scurry on their pointless errands. But the territory below Central Park—Route 666, the Ho Chi Minh trail, the Blockhouse—is mine."

Smithback thought for a moment. The ironic place-name of Route 666 made sense. But the others confused him. "The Ho Chi Minh trail," he echoed. "What's that?"

"A community, like the rest," hissed the voice. "Joined now with mine, for protection. Once upon a time, we knew the trail well. Many of us here fought in that cynical struggle against an innocent backward nation. And were ostracized for it. Now we live our lives down here in self-imposed exile, breathing, mating, dying. Our greatest wish is to be left alone."

Smithback fingered the tape recorder again, hoping it was catching everything. He'd heard of the occasional vagrant

retreating to subway tunnels for shelter, but an entire population...
"So all your citizens are homeless people?" he asked.

There was a pause. "We do not like that word, scriblerian. We *have* a home, and were you not so timid, I could show it to you. We have everything we need. The pipes provide water for cooking and hygiene, the cables provide electricity. What few things we require from the surface, our runners supply. In the Blockhouse, we even have a nurse and a schoolteacher. Other underground spaces, like the West Side railyards, are untamed, dangerous. But here, we live in dignity."

"Schoolteacher? You mean there are children down here?"

"You are naive. Many are here *because* they have children, and the evil state machine is trying to take them away and put them in foster care. They choose my world of warmth and darkness over your world of despair, scriblerian."

"Why do you keep calling me that?"

The dry chuckle rose again from the hole in the cinder block. "That is you, is it not? William Smithback, scriblerian?"

"Yes, but—"

"For a journalist, you are ill read. Study Pope's *The Dunciad* before we speak again."

It began to dawn on Smithback that there was more to this person than he had originally supposed. "Who are you, really?" he asked. "I mean, what's your real name?"

There was another silence. "I left that, along with everything else, upstairs," the disembodied voice hissed. "Now I am Mephisto. Never ask me, or anyone, that question again."

Smithback swallowed. "Sorry," he said.

Mephisto seemed to have grown angry. His tone became sharper, cutting through the darkness. "You were brought here for a reason."

"The Wisher murder?" asked Smithback eagerly.

"Your articles have described her, and the other corpse, as being headless. I am here to tell you that being headless is the least of it." His voice broke into a rasping, mirthless laugh.

"What do you mean?" Smithback asked. "You know who did it?"

"They are the same that have been preying on my people," Mephisto hissed. "The Wrinklers."

"Wrinklers?" Smithback said. "I don't understand—"

"Then be silent and mark me, scriblerian! I have said my community is a safe haven. And so it has always been, until one year ago. Now, we are under attack. Those who venture beyond the safe areas disappear or are murdered. Murdered in the most horrific ways. Our people have grown afraid. My runners have tried time and again to bring this matter to the police. The police!" There was an angry spitting sound, then the voice rose in pitch. "The corrupt watchdogs of a society grown morally bankrupt. To them, we are filth to be beaten and rousted. Our lives mean nothing! How many of our people have died or disappeared? Fat Boy, Hector, Dark Annie, Master Sergeant, others. But one shiny thing in silks gets her head torn off, and the entire city grows enraged!"

Smithback licked his lips. He was beginning to wonder just what information this Mephisto had. "What do you mean exactly, under attack?" he asked.

There was a silence. "From outside," came the whispered answer at last.

"Outside?" Smithback asked. "What do you mean? Outside, meaning out here?" He looked around the blackness wildly.

"No. Outside Route 666. Outside the Blockhouse," came the answer. "There is another place. A shunned place. Twelve months ago, rumors began to emerge, rumors that this place had become occupied. Then the killings began. Our people began disappearing. At first, we sent out search parties. Most of the victims were never found. But those we did find had their flesh eaten, their heads ripped from their bodies."

"Wait a minute," Smithback said. "Their flesh *eaten*? You mean there is a group of cannibals down here, murdering people and stealing their heads?" Perhaps Mephisto was nuts, after all.

Once again, Smithback began to wonder how he would return to the surface.

"I do not appreciate the doubting tone in your voice, scriblerian," Mephisto replied. "That is *exactly* what I mean. Tail Gunner?"

"Yes?" said a voice in Smithback's ear. The journalist jumped to one side, neighing in surprise and fright.

"How did he get back here?" Smithback gasped.

"There are many ways through my kingdom," came the voice of Mephisto. "And living here, in lovely darkness, our night vision becomes acute."

Smithback swallowed. "Look," he said, "it isn't that I don't believe you. I just—"

"Be silent!" Mephisto warned. "We have spoken long enough. Tail Gunner, return him to the surface."

"But what about the reward?" Smithback asked, surprised. "Isn't that why you brought me here?"

"Have you heard nothing I told you?" came the hiss. "Your money is useless to me. It is the safety of my people I care about. Return to your world, write your article. Tell those on the surface what I have told you. Tell them that whatever killed Pamela Wisher is also killing my people. And the killings must stop." The disembodied voice seemed farther away now, echoing through the dark corridors beneath Smithback's feet. "Otherwise," he added with a fearful intensity, "we will find *other* ways to make our voices heard."

"But I need—" Smithback began.

A hand closed around his elbow. "Mephisto has gone," came the voice of Tail Gunner beside him. "I'll take you topside."

7

Lieutenant D'Agosta sat in his cramped, glass-sided office, fingering the cigar in his breast pocket and eyeing a stack of reports about the Humboldt Kill dive. Instead of closing one case, he now had two cases, both wide open. As usual, nobody knew nothing, nobody saw nothing. The boyfriend was prostrate with grief and useless as an eyewitness. The father was long dead. The mother was as uncommunicative and remote as an ice goddess. He frowned; the whole Pamela Wisher business felt like nitroglycerine to him.

His eye traveled from the stack of reports to the NO SMOKING sign outside his door, and the frown deepened. It and a dozen like it had gone up around the precinct station just the week before.

He slid the cigar out of his pocket and removed its plastic wrapping. No law against chewing on the thing, at any rate. He rolled it lovingly between thumb and index finger for a moment, examining the wrapper with a critical eye. Then he placed it in his mouth.

He sat for a moment, motionless. Then, with a curse, he jerked open the top drawer of his desk, hunted around until he located a kitchen match, and lit it on the sole of his shoe. He applied the flame to the end of the cigar and sat back with a sigh, listening to the faint crackle of tobacco as he drew in the smoke and bled it slowly out his nose.

The internal phone rang shrilly.

"Yes?" D'Agosta answered. Couldn't be a complaint already. He'd just lit up.

"Lieutenant?" came the voice of the departmental secretary. "There's a Sergeant Hayward here to see you."

D'Agosta grunted and sat up in his chair. "Who?"

"Sergeant Hayward. Says it's by your request."

"I didn't ask for any Sergeant Hayward—"

A uniformed woman appeared in the open doorway. Almost instinctively, D'Agosta took in the salient features: petite, thin, heavy breasts, jet black hair against pale skin.

"Lieutenant D'Agosta?" she asked.

D'Agosta couldn't believe such a deep contralto could come from such a small frame. "Take a seat," he said, and watched as the Sergeant settled herself in a chair. She seemed to be unconscious of anything irregular, as if it was standard procedure for a sergeant to burst in on a superior anytime he—or she—felt like it.

"I don't recall asking for you, Sergeant," D'Agosta finally said.

"You didn't," Hayward answered. "But I knew you'd want to see me anyway."

D'Agosta sat back, drawing slowly on his cigar. He'd let the Sergeant say her piece, then chew her out. D'Agosta wasn't a stickler for process, but approaching a senior officer like this was way out of line. He wondered if perhaps one of his men had come on to her in some filing room or something. Just what he needed, a sexual harassment suit on his hands.

"Those corpses you found in the Cloaca," Hayward began.

"What about them?" D'Agosta snapped, suddenly suspicious. A security lid was supposed to be clamped down over the details of that business.

"Before the merger, I used to be with the Transit Police." Hayward nodded, as if that explained everything. "I still do the West Side duty, clearing the homeless out of Penn Station, Hell's Kitchen, the railyards, under the—"

"Wait a minute," D'Agosta interrupted. "You? A rouster?"

Immediately, he knew he'd said the wrong thing. Hayward tensed in the chair, her eyebrows contracting at the obvious disbelief in his voice. There was a moment of awkward silence.

"We don't like that term, Lieutenant," she said at last.

D'Agosta decided he had enough to worry about without humoring this uninvited guest. "It's my office," he said, shrugging.

Hayward looked at him a moment, and in those brown eyes D'Agosta could almost see her good opinion of him falling away. "Okay," she said. "If that's how you want to play it." She took a deep breath. "When I heard about these skeletons of yours, they rang a bell. Reminded me of some recent homicides among the moles."

"Moles?"

"Tunnel people, of course," she said with a condescending look D'Agosta found irritating. "Underground homeless. Anyway, then I read that article in today's *Post*. The one about Mephisto."

D'Agosta grimaced. Trust that scandal-hound Bill Smithback to whip readers into a frenzy, make a bad situation worse. The two of them had been friends—after a fashion—but now that Smithback was a homicide reporter, he'd grown almost intolerable. And D'Agosta knew better than to give him the slightest speck of the inside information he was always demanding.

"The life expectancy of a homeless person is very short," Hayward said. "It's even worse for the moles. But that journalist was right. Lately, some of the killings have been unusually nasty. Heads missing, bodies ripped up. I thought I'd better come to you about it." She shifted in her seat and gazed at D'Agosta with her clear brown eyes. "Maybe I should have saved my breath."

D'Agosta let that pass. "So how many recent homicides we talking about, Hayward?" he asked. "Two? Three?"

Hayward paused. "More like half a dozen," she said at last.

D'Agosta looked at her, cigar halfway to mouth. "Half a *dozen*?"

"That's what I said. Before coming up here, I looked through the files. Seven murders among the moles in the last four months match this MO."

D'Agosta lowered the cigar. "Sergeant, let me get this straight. You got some kind of underground Jack the Ripper here, and nobody's on top of it?"

"Look, it was just a hunch on my part, okay?" Hayward said defensively. "Back off me. These aren't my homicides."

"So why didn't you go through channels and report this to your superior? Why are you coming to me?"

"I *did* go to my boss. Captain Waxie. Know him?"

Everyone knew Jack Waxie. The fattest, laziest Precinct Captain in the city. A man who had reached his position by doing nothing and offending nobody. A year earlier, D'Agosta had been up for promotion to captain himself, thanks to a grateful mayor. Then there was the election, Mayor Harper was thrown out of office, and a new mayor rode into City Hall on promises of tax cuts and reduced spending. In the resulting fallout at One Police Plaza, Waxie got a captainship and a precinct, but D'Agosta was passed over. Some world.

Hayward crossed one leg over the other. "Mole homicides aren't like homicides on the surface. Most of the corpses we don't even find. And when we do, the rats and dogs have usually found them long before. Many are John Does, can't be ID'd even in good condition. And the other moles sure as hell won't talk."

"And Jack Waxie just files everything away."

Hayward frowned again. "He doesn't give a shit about those people."

D'Agosta looked at her for a minute, wondering why an old-school chauvinist like Waxie would have taken a five-foot-three female rouster onto his staff. Then his eyes lighted once again on her narrow waist, pale skin, and brown eyes, and he knew the answer. "Okay, Sergeant," he said at last. "I'll bite. You got locations?"

"Locations is about all I've got."

D'Agosta's cigar had gone out, and he fumbled through his drawer for another match. "So where were they found?" he asked.

"Here and there." Hayward dug a computer printout out of a pocket, unfolded it, and slid it across the desk.

D'Agosta glanced at the sheet as he lit up. "First one was found April 30, at 624 West Fifty-eighth Street."

"Boiler room in the basement. There's an old access to a railway turnabout there, which is why it was TA jurisdiction."

D'Agosta nodded and glanced at the sheet. "Next one was found May 7 beneath the Columbus Circle IRT station. The third one was found May 20, RR Stem B4, track 22, milepost 1.2. Where the hell is that?"

"Closed freight tunnel that used to connect to the West Side railyard. The moles break through the walls to get into some of those tunnels."

D'Agosta listened, enjoying his cigar. A year earlier, after hearing about the promised promotion, he'd switched from Garcia y Vegas to Dunhills. Though the promotion had never materialized, D'Agosta hadn't been able to convince himself to switch back. He glanced again at Hayward, still looking back at him impassively. She wasn't very good at respecting superior officers. But despite her small frame, she carried an air of natural self-confidence and authority. It had taken initiative, coming to him like this. Guts, too. For a moment he regretted starting off on the wrong foot with her.

"This isn't exactly departmental procedure, your coming to see me like this," he said. "Still, I appreciate your taking the time."

Hayward nodded almost imperceptibly, as if acknowledging his compliment without accepting it.

"I don't want to bust in on Captain Waxie's jurisdiction," D'Agosta continued. "But I can't pass this up, just in case there's a connection. I guess you figured that out already. So what we're going to do is, we're going to forget you came to see me."

Hayward nodded again.

"And I'm gonna call up Waxie like I got these reports on my own, and then we'll do a little sight-seeing."

"He isn't going to like that. The only sight he likes is the view out the precinct window."

"Oh, he'll come along. It wouldn't look too good if a lieutenant did his job for him while he sat there on his ass. Especially if this turns out to be big. A serial killer among the homeless—that could be politically explosive. So we'll take a little stroll, just the three of us. No use getting the brass stirred up."

Immediately, Hayward frowned. "Not smart," she said. "Lieutenant, it's dangerous down there. It's not our turf; it's theirs. And it's not what you think, either. These aren't just a handful of burnt-out mainliners. There're some pretty radicalized people down there, whole communities, Vietnam vets, ex-cons, hardcore SDS remnants, parole violators. There's nothing they hate more than cops. We'll need at least a squad."

D'Agosta found himself growing irritated at her brusque, disrespectful tone. "Look, Hayward, we're not talking about D day here. We're talking about a quiet peek. I'm going out on a limb as it is. If it looks like something, then we can make it official."

Hayward said nothing.

"And Hayward? If I hear any talk about this little party of ours, I'll know where it came from."

Hayward stood up, smoothed her dark blue trousers, straightened her service belt. "Understood."

"I knew it would be." D'Agosta stood up, exhaling a jet of smoke in the direction of the No SMOKING sign. He watched as Hayward glanced at the cigar with either disdain or disapproval, he wasn't sure which. "Care for one?" he asked sarcastically, sliding another out of his breast pocket.

For the first time, Hayward's lips twitched in what might almost have been a smile. "Thanks, but no thanks. Not after what happened to my uncle."

"What was that?"

"Mouth cancer. They had to cut his lips off." D'Agosta watched as Hayward turned on her heel and walked quickly out of his office. He noticed she hadn't bothered to say good-bye. He also noticed that, suddenly, the cigar didn't taste as good anymore.

8

He sat in the listening darkness, unmoving.

Although the chamber was devoid of light, his eyes flicked from surface to surface, lingering with a loving glance on each object they encountered. It was still a novelty; he could sit motionless for hours, enjoying the marvelous acuteness of his own senses.

Now he closed his eyes and allowed himself to listen to the distant sounds of the city. Slowly, from the background murmur, he sorted out the various strands of conversation, filtering the nearest and loudest from those more distant, many rooms or even floors away. Then those, too, faded into the haze of his concentration, and he could hear the faint scamperings and squeals of the mice as they carried out their own secret cycles of life within the walls. At times he thought he could hear the sound of the earth itself, rolling and churning, swathed in its atmosphere.

Later—he was not sure how much later—the hunger started again. Not a hunger exactly, but the feeling of something *missing*: a deep craving, unlocalized, subtle for the time being. He never allowed the craving time to grow.

Standing quickly, he stepped across the laboratory, surefooted in the blackness. Turning on one of the gas spigots along the far wall, he lit the attached nozzle with a sparker, then positioned a retort of distilled water over the burner. As the water heated, he reached into a secret pocket sewn into the lining of his coat and withdrew a slender metal capsule. Unscrewing its end, he poured a trace of powder onto the surface of the water. Had there been light, the powder would have shone the color of light jade. As the temperature rose, a thin cloud began to spread downward from the surface until the entire retort became a miniature storm of roiling liquid.

He turned off the heat, then emptied the distillate into a Pyrex beaker. This was the point at which the decoction should be placed between the hands, the mind emptied, the ritual movements performed, the caressing vapor allowed to rise and fill the nostrils. But he could never wait; once again, he felt his palate burn as he swallowed the liquid greedily. He laughed to himself, amused at his own inability to follow the precepts he had set so sternly for others.

Even before he was seated again, the hollow feeling was gone, and the long slow rush had started: a flush that began in his extremities, then spread inward until it seemed that the very core of his being was on fire. An indescribable feeling of power and well-being surged through him. His senses, already hyperacute, seemed to expand until he could see infinitesimal dust motes hanging in the pitch black; until he could hear all of Manhattan in conversation with itself, from cocktail chat in the Rainbow Room seventy stories above Rockefeller Center, to the hungry wailing of his own children, far below-ground in secret forgotten spaces.

They were growing hungrier. Soon, not even the Ceremony would control them all.

But by then it would no longer be necessary.

The darkness seemed almost painfully bright, and he closed his eyes, listening to the vigorous rush of blood through the natural gates and alleys of his inner ears. He would keep his eyelids closed until the peak of sensation—and the odd, silvery sheen that temporarily covered his eyes—had gone. *Whoever named it glaze,* he thought with amusement, *named it well.*

Soon—all too soon—the fierce bloom faded. But the power remained, a constant reminder in his joints and sinews of what he had become. If only his former colleagues could see him now. Then they'd understand.

Almost regretfully, he stood again, unwilling to leave the site of so much pleasure. But there was much that needed doing.

It would be a busy night.

9

Margo approached the door, noting with distaste that it was as dirty as ever. Even in a museum known for its high dust tolerance, the door to the Physical Anthropology lab—or Skeleton Room, as the staff universally referred to it—was almost unbelievably grimy. *This can't have been washed since the turn of the century,* she thought. A patina of hand oils coated the knob and the surrounding area like a shiny varnish. She considered getting a tissue out of her carryall, then dismissed the thought, grabbed the knob tightly, and turned.

As usual, the room was dimly lit, and she had to squint to make out the tiers of metal drawers that rose to the ceiling like the stacks of some vast library. Each of the twelve thousand drawers contained, either whole or in part, the remains of a human skeleton. Although most belonged to native peoples of Africa and the Americas, Margo was interested in the subset of skeletons that had been collected for medical, rather than anthropological, purposes. Dr. Frock had suggested that, as a first step, they examine the remains of people with acute bone disorders. Perhaps, he'd hypothesized, the victims of such ailments as acromegaly or Proteus syndrome could help shed some light on the bizarre skeleton that waited for them under the blue plastic sheet in Forensic Anthropology.

As she threaded her way between the giant stacks, Margo sighed. She knew the impending encounter would be unpleasant. Sy Hagedorn, administrator of the Physical Anthropology lab, was almost as old and desiccated as the skeletons he watched over. Along with Curley manning the staff entrance, Emmaline Spragg of Invertebrate Biology, and a few others, Sy Hagedorn was the last remnant of the Museum old guard. Despite the Museum's computerized collection database, and despite the high-tech laboratory that lay just beyond the Skeleton Room, he steadfastly refused to bring his cataloguing methods into the twentieth century. When her erstwhile colleague Greg Kawakita had made his office in the lab, he'd had to endure Hagedorn's withering scorn every time he opened up his laptop. Behind Hagedorn's back, Kawakita had nicknamed the administrator "Stumpy." Only Margo and a few of Frock's other graduate students had known the name referred not to Hagedorn's diminutive size, but to *Stumpiniceps troglodytes,* a particularly mundane kind of bottom-feeder that populated the oceans of the Carboniferous period.

At the thought of Kawakita, Margo frowned guiltily. He'd left a message on her answering machine maybe six months before, apologizing for dropping out of touch, saying he needed to speak to her, that he'd try again the same time the following evening. When her phone had rung again at the appointed time twenty-four hours later, Margo had reached for it automatically, then frozen, her hand inches from the handset. Nobody left a message when the machine picked up, and she had drawn her hand back slowly, wondering exactly what instinct had prevented her from answering Kawakita's call. But even as she'd done so, she'd known the answer. Kawakita had been a part of it all... along with Pendergast, Smithback, Lieutenant D'Agosta, even Dr. Frock. His extrapolation program had been the key that helped them understand Mbwun: the creature that had terrorized the

Museum and that still roamed her uneasy dreams. Selfish as it was, the last thing she'd wanted was to talk to someone who would unnecessarily remind her of those awful days. Silly, in retrospect, now that she was chin-deep in an investigation that—

The sudden fussy clearing of a throat brought Margo back to the present. She looked up to see a short man standing before her, wearing a worn tweed suit, his leathery face lined with innumerable wrinkles.

"I thought I heard somebody wandering around my skeletons," Hagedorn said, frowning, tiny arms crossed in front of his chest. "Well?"

Despite herself, Margo felt annoyance begin to take the place of her daydreams. His skeletons, indeed. Stifling her irritation, she pulled a sheet of paper from her carryall. "Dr. Frock wants these specimens sent up to the Forensic Anthropology lab," she replied, handing the sheet to Hagedorn.

He scanned it, the frown deepening. "*Three* skeletons?" he said. "That's somewhat irregular."

Up yours, Stumpy. "It's important we get these right away," she said. "If there's a problem, I'm sure Dr. Merriam will give whatever authorization you need."

Mentioning the Director's name had the desired effect. "Oh, very well. But it's still irregular. Come with me."

He led her back toward an ancient wooden desk, heavily scarred and pitted from years of neglect. Behind the desk—in rows of tiny drawers—was Hagedorn's filing system. He checked the first number on Frock's list, then ran a thin yellow finger down drawers. Stopping at last, he pulled out a drawer, rifled through the cards within, and plucked one out, harrumphing in displeasure. "1930-262," he read. "Just my luck. On the very top tier. I'm not as young as I used to be, you know. Heights bother me."

Suddenly he stopped. "This is a medical skeleton," he said, pointing to a red dot in the upper right-hand corner of the card.

"All of the requests are," Margo replied. Though it was clear Hagedorn wanted an explanation, she fell into a stubborn silence. At last the administrator cleared his throat again, his eyebrows contracting at the irregularity of the request. "If you insist," he said, sliding the card across the desk toward her. "Sign this, add your extension and department, and don't forget to place Frock's name in the Supervisor column."

Margo looked at the grimy paper, its edges soft with wear and age. *It's a library card,* she thought. *How quaint.* The skeleton's name was printed neatly at the top: Homer Maclean. That was one of Frock's requests, all right: a victim of neurofibromatosis, if she remembered correctly.

She bent forward to scrawl her name in the first blank row, then stopped abruptly. There, three or four names up the list of previous researchers, was the jagged scrawl she remembered so well: G. S. Kawakita, Anthropology. He'd taken this very skeleton out for research five years earlier. Not surprising, she supposed: Greg had always been fascinated by the unusual, the abnormal, the exception to the rule. Perhaps that's why he'd been attracted to Dr. Frock and his theory of fractal evolution.

She remembered how Greg had been notorious for using this very storage room for fly-casting practice, snapping nymphs down the narrow rows during practically every coffee break. When Hagedorn was not around, of course. She suppressed a grin.

That does it, she thought. *I'll look up Greg's number in the phone book this evening. Better late than never.*

There was a high-pitched, rattling wheeze, and she looked up from the card into the small impatient eyes of Hagedorn. "It's just your *name* I want," he said waspishly. "Not a line of lyric poetry. So stop thinking so hard and let's get on with it, shall we?"

10

The broad ornate front of the Polyhymnia Club squatted on West 45th Street, its marble and sandstone bulk heaving outward like the stern of some Spanish galleon. Above its awning, a gilt statue of the club's namesake, the muse of rhetoric, stood on one foot as if poised to take flight. Beneath it, the club's revolving door did a brisk Saturday evening business; although patronage was limited to members of the New York press, that still let in, as Horace Greeley once complained, "half the unemployed young dogs south of Fourteenth Street."

Deep within its oak fastness, Bill Smithback stepped up to the bar and ordered a Caol Ila without ice. Though he was for the most part uninterested in the club's pedigree, he was very interested in its unique collection of specially imported scotch whisky. The single malt filled his mouth with the sensation of peat smoke and Loch nam Ban water. He savored it for a long moment, then glanced around, ready to drink in the congratulating nods and admiring glances of his fellow pressmen.

Getting the Wisher assignment had been one of the biggest breaks of his life. Already, it had netted him three front-page stories in less than a week. He'd even been able to make the ramblings and vague threats of the homeless leader, Mephisto, seem incisive and pertinent. Just that afternoon, as Smithback was leaving the office, Murray had thumped him heartily on the back. Murray, the editor who never had a word of praise for anyone.

His survey of the clientele unsuccessful, Smithback turned toward the bar and took another sip. It was extraordinary, he thought, the power of a journalist. A whole city was now up in arms because of him. Ginny, the pool secretary, was at last growing overwhelmed by the volume of calls about the reward, and they'd had to bring in a dedicated switchboard operator. Even the mayor was taking heat. Mrs. Wisher had to be pleased with what he'd accomplished. It was inspired.

A vague thought that somehow Mrs. Wisher had deliberately manipulated him flitted across his field of consciousness and was quickly pushed aside. He took another sip of scotch, closing his eyes as it trickled down his gullet like a dream of a finer world.

A hand gripped his shoulder, and he turned eagerly. It was Bryce Harriman, the *Times* crime reporter who was also covering the Wisher case.

"Oh," Smithback said, his face falling.

"Way to go, Bill," said Bryce, his hand still on Smithback's shoulder as he elbowed up to the bar and rapped a coin on the zinc. "Killians," he said to the bartender.

Smithback nodded. Christ, he thought, of all the people to run into.

"Yup," said Harriman. "Pretty clever. I bet they loved it over at the *Post*." He paused slightly before uttering the final word.

"They did, as a matter of fact," Smithback said.

"Actually, I ought to thank you." Harriman picked up his mug and sipped daintily. "It gave me a good angle for a story."

"Really?" said Smithback, without interest.

"Really. How the whole investigation's ground to a halt. Paralyzed."

Smithback looked up, and the *Times* reporter nodded smugly. "With this reward posted, too many crazy calls have been flooding in. The police have no choice but to take every last one seriously. Now they're chasing after a thousand bullshit tips, wasting time. A bit of friendly advice, Bill: I wouldn't show your face around One Police Plaza for a while, like maybe ten years."

"Don't give me that," Smithback said irritably. "We've done the police a big favor."

"Not the ones I talked to."

Smithback turned away and took another sip of his drink. He was used to being needled by Harriman. Bryce Harriman, the Columbia J-School grad who thought he was God's gift to journalism. In any case, Smithback still had a good relationship with Lieutenant D'Agosta. That's what really mattered. Harriman was full of shit.

"So tell me, Bryce, how did the *Times* do on the newsstand this morning?" he asked. "We're up forty percent at the *Post* since last week."

"I wouldn't know and I wouldn't care. Sales shouldn't be of concern to a real journalist."

Smithback pressed his advantage. "Face it, Bryce, you got scooped. I got the interview with Mrs. Wisher and you didn't."

Harriman's face darkened: he'd hit a nerve there. The guy had probably been scolded by his editor.

"Yeah," Harriman said. "She got your number, all right. Wrapped you around her little finger. While the real story is taking place somewhere else."

"And what real story might that be?"

"Such as the identity of the second skeleton. Or even, where they took the bodies." Harriman eyed Smithback as he nonchalantly drained his beer. "You mean you didn't know? Too busy talking to nutcases in railroad tunnels, I guess."

Smithback glanced back at the reporter, struggling to conceal his surprise. Was this some kind of false lead? But no; the cool eyes behind the tortoise-shell glasses were scornful, but serious. "Haven't been able to find that out yet," he said guardedly.

"You don't say." Harriman slapped him on the back. "Hundred thousand bucks reward, huh? That might just pay your salary for the next two years. If the *Post* doesn't go belly up again." He laughed, dropped a five-dollar bill on the counter, and turned to go.

Smithback watched Harriman's retreating back with irritation. So the bodies had been moved from the Medical Examiner's office. He should have learned that himself. But where? There had been no funeral arrangements, no burial. They must be in a lab somewhere, a lab with better equipment than the NYME. Someplace secure, not like Columbia or Rockefeller University, with students wandering around everywhere. After all, Lieutenant D'Agosta was in charge of the case. He was a cool customer, Smithback knew. Not the kind of guy to do something rash. Why would D'Agosta move the bodies...

D'Agosta.

Suddenly, Smithback guessed—no, he *knew*—where the bodies must be.

Draining his glass, he slid off the stool and moved across the plush red carpet to a bank of phones in the front foyer. Dropping a quarter in the nearest one, he dialed a number.

"Curley here," said a voice thick with age.

"Curley! It's Bill Smithback. How you doing?"

"Fine, Dr. Smithback. Haven't seen you around for a while." Curley, who checked badges at the staff entrance to the Museum of Natural History, called everyone Doctor. Princes lived and died; dynasties rose and fell; but Curley, Smithback knew, would remain in his ornate bronze pillbox, checking IDs forever.

"Curley, what time on Wednesday night did those ambulances come in? You know, the two that drove in together?" Smithback spoke fast, praying that the ancient guard didn't know he'd become a reporter after leaving his writing assignment at the Museum.

"Well, let's see," Curley said in his unhurried way. "Can't say I remember anything like that, Doctor."

"Really?" Smithback asked, crestfallen. He'd been absolutely sure.

"Not unless you mean that one that came in with the lights and sirens off. But that was early Thursday, not Wednesday." Smithback could hear Curley rustling through his log. "Yup, just after five A.M., it was."

"That's right, Thursday. What was I thinking of?" Smithback thanked Curley and hung up exultantly.

Grinning, he returned to the bar. With one phone call, he'd discovered what Harriman had no doubt been searching for—unsuccessfully—for days.

It made perfect sense. He knew that D'Agosta had used the Museum's laboratory on other cases, not least of all the Museum Beast murders. It was a high-security lab in a high-security museum. No doubt he'd have called in that pompous old curator, Frock. And maybe Frock's ex-assistant, Margo Green, Smithback's own friend from his days at the Museum.

Margo Green, Smithback thought. That merited some looking into.

He called the bartender over. "Paddy, I think I'll stay on Islay, but switch distilleries. Laphroaig, please. The fifteen-year-old."

He took a sip of the marvelous whisky. Ten bucks a shot, but worth every penny. *A hundred thousand might just pay your salary for the next two years,* Harriman had teased. Smithback decided that, after the next front-page story, he'd have to hit Murray up for a raise. Nothing like striking while the iron was hot.

11

Sergeant Hayward descended a long metal staircase, opened a narrow door filmed in brown rust, and stepped out onto an abandoned railroad siding. Behind her, D'Agosta emerged from the doorway, hands in pockets. Murky sunlight filtered down through a series of gratings far above their heads, illuminating dust motes in the still air. D'Agosta looked first left, then right. In both directions, the tracks dissolved into the gloom of the tunnel. He noticed that Hayward had an unusual way of moving belowground, a kind of silent, wary step.

"Where's the Captain?" Hayward asked.

"He's coming," said D'Agosta, scraping the underside of his heel on the metal rail of the siding. "You go ahead." He watched Hayward move catlike down the tunnel, her flashlight throwing a narrow beam into the darkness ahead. Any hesitation he felt at letting this petite woman lead the way had evaporated as he watched the ease with which she handled herself underground.

Waxie, on the other hand, had slowed considerably in the two hours since they'd visited the brownstone basement where the first body had been found more than three months before. It was a damp room, crammed with old boilers. Rotting wires dangled from the ceiling. Hayward had pointed out the mattress tucked behind a blackened furnace, littered with empty plastic water bottles and torn newspapers: the dead man's living space. There was an old bloodstain on the mattress, three feet in diameter, heavily chewed on by rats. Above it, a pair of ragged athletic socks were draped over a pipe, covered in a furry mantle of green mold.

The body found there had been Hank Jasper, Hayward said. No witnesses, no known relatives or friends. The case file had been equally useless: no photographs or scene reports, just some routine paperwork, a brief report referring to "extensive lacerations" and a badly crushed skull, and the notice of a quick burial at Potter's Field on Hart Island.

Nor had they found much of anything in the defunct Columbus Circle station bathroom, where the second body had been discovered: a lot of trash, and a half-hearted attempt to clean up the red blizzard of blood that clung to the ancient tile sinks and cracked mirrors. No ID on that one at all: the head was missing.

There was a stifled curse behind him, and D'Agosta turned to see the round form of Captain Waxie emerging from the rusted door. He looked around distastefully, his pasty visage shining unnaturally in the half-light.

"Jesus, Vinnie," he said, picking his way over the tracks toward D'Agosta. "What the hell are we doing? I told you before, this isn't any job for a police captain. Especially on a Sunday afternoon." He nodded his head in the direction of the dark tunnel. "That cute little thing put you up to this, didn't she? Amazing set of knockers. You know, I offered her a job as my personal assistant. Instead, she chose to stay on rousting detail, dragging bums out of holes. Go figure."

Funny thing about that, D'Agosta thought, imagining what life under Waxie would be like for a woman as attractive as Hayward.

"And now my damn radio's gone on the fritz," Waxie said irritably.

D'Agosta pointed upward. "Hayward tells me they don't work underground. Not reliably, anyway."

"Great. How are we supposed to call for backup?"

"We don't. We're on our own."

"Great," Waxie repeated.

D'Agosta looked at Waxie. Beads of sweat had sprung up along his upper lip, and his dough-colored jowls, usually firm, were starting to sag. "This is your jurisdiction, not mine," D'Agosta said. "Just think how good it will make you look if this turns out to be big: taking charge right away, visiting the scene personally. For a change." He fingered his jacket pocket for a cigar, then decided against it. "And think how bad it will look if these deaths *are* connected somehow, and the press starts talking about how you just looked the other way."

Waxie scowled at him. "I'm not running for mayor, Vinnie."

"I'm not talking about being mayor. All I know is, when the rain of shit begins to fall like it always does, your ass will be covered."

Waxie grunted, looking somewhat mollified.

D'Agosta could see Hayward's light playing down the tracks toward them, and soon the woman appeared again out of the gloom.

"Almost there," she said. "It's one more down."

"Down?" said Waxie. "Sergeant, I thought this *was* the lowest level!"

Hayward said nothing.

"So how are we supposed to go down?" D'Agosta asked her.

Hayward nodded in the direction from which she'd come. "North along the tracks about four hundred yards, there's another staircase along the right wall."

"What if a train comes?" Waxie asked.

"This is a deserted stem," Hayward said. "No trains have come along here in a long time."

"How do you know?"

Hayward silently played her beam along the rails beneath their feet, illuminating the thick orange rust. D'Agosta's eyes traveled up the flashlight beam until they reached Hayward's face. She did not look very happy.

"Is there anything unusual about the next level?" D'Agosta asked quietly.

Hayward was silent for a moment. "Ordinarily, we only sweep the upper levels. But you hear stories. They get crazier the lower you go." She paused. "That's why I suggested backup," she said pointedly.

"People *living* down here?" Waxie asked, sparing D'Agosta the necessity of a reply.

"Of course." Hayward made a face as if Waxie should know better. "Warm in the winter, no rain or wind. Only people they have to worry about down here are the other moles."

"So when was the last time they rousted that level?"

"They don't roust the lower levels, Captain."

"Why not?"

There was a silence. "Well, for one thing, you can't find the deeper moles. They've got night vision, living in the dark. You hear something, and by the time you've turned around, they're gone. They only do a couple random sweeps a year with dogs trained to find bodies. And even they don't go that deep. Besides, it's very dangerous. Not all the moles come down here just for shelter. Some come to hide. Some are running from something, the law, usually. Still others are predatory."

"What about that article in the *Post*?" D'Agosta asked. "It said there was some kind of underground community. Didn't sound all that hostile."

"That was under Central Park, Lieutenant, not the West Side railyards," Hayward said. "Some areas are tamer than others. And don't forget that article mentioned something else. Something about cannibals." She smiled sweetly.

Waxie opened his mouth to respond, then closed it again, swallowing loudly.

They began moving down the tracks in silence. As they walked, D'Agosta realized he was unconsciously fingering his S&W Model 4946 double-action. Back in '93, there'd been some controversy in the department about moving to a 9-millimeter semiautomatic. Now D'Agosta was glad he had it.

The staircase, when they reached it, was fronted by a steel door canted at a crazy angle across the doorframe. Hayward pulled it open, then moved to one side. D'Agosta stepped through and immediately felt his eyes begin to water. A smell like ammonia violated his nostrils.

"I'll go first, Lieutenant," Hayward said.

D'Agosta stepped aside. No argument there.

The lime-coated staircase descended to a landing, then made a turn. D'Agosta felt his watering eyes begin to sting. The smell was searing, indescribable.

"What the hell is that?" he asked.

"Piss," said Hayward matter-of-factly. "Mostly. Plus other things you don't want to hear about."

Behind them, Waxie's wheezing became more pronounced.

They stepped through a ragged opening into a dark, humid space. As Hayward played her light about, D'Agosta saw that they were in what looked like the cavernous end of an old tunnel. But there were no tracks here: just a rough dirt floor, scattered with pools of oil and water and the charred remains of small campfires. Garbage lay strewn everywhere: old newspapers; a torn pair of pants; an old shoe; a plastic diaper, freshly soiled.

D'Agosta could hear Waxie blowing hard behind him. He was beginning to wonder why the Captain had abruptly stopped complaining. *Maybe it's the stench,* he thought.

Hayward was moving toward a passage that led away from the cavern. "Over here," she said. "The body was found in a cubby down this way. We'd better stay close. Watch out you don't get piped."

"Piped?" D'Agosta asked.

"Someone reaches out from the dark and whacks you over the head with a pipe."

"I don't see anyone," D'Agosta said.

"They're here," Hayward replied.

Waxie's breathing became more labored.

They began following the passage, moving slowly. Hayward periodically pointed her light along the sides of the tunnel. Every twenty feet, a large rectangular space had been cut into the rock: work and storage areas, she explained, of railway crews a century before. Filthy bedding lay in many of the cubbyholes. Frequently, large brown rats, disturbed by the light, would stir among the trash, waddling away from the flashlight beams with insolent slowness. But there were no signs of people.

Hayward stopped, removed her police cap, and drew a damp strand of hair back into place behind one ear. "The report said it was the cubby directly across from a collapsed iron catwalk," she said.

D'Agosta tried breathing through his hand, and when that didn't help he loosened his tie and pulled his shirt collar over his mouth, as a kind of mask.

"Here it is." Hayward shone her beam on a rusted heap of iron struts and I-beams. She swept the flashlight across the tunnel, locating the cubby. From the outside, it looked just like the others: five feet across, three feet deep, cut into the rock about two feet above grade.

D'Agosta stepped closer and peered in. Naked bedding lay askew, caked thickly with dried blood. Blood was also spattered about the walls, along with bits of something that D'Agosta didn't want to think about. There was the ubiquitous packing crate, tipped over and partly crushed. The floor of the cubby was lined with newspapers. The stench was beyond description.

"This guy," Hayward whispered, "was also found without his head. They identified him from prints. Shasheen Walker, thirty-two years old. Rap sheet as long as your arm, a serious user."

At any other time, D'Agosta would have found it ludicrous to hear a police officer whispering. Now, he felt somehow glad. There was a long silence while D'Agosta played his own light around. "Did they find the head?" he asked at last.

"Nope," said Hayward.

The foul little den showed zero signs of a police search. Thinking he'd rather be anywhere else, *doing* anything else, D'Agosta reached into the cubby, took hold of a corner of a filthy blanket, and jerked it back.

Something brown tumbled out of the folds and rolled toward the nearest edge. What was left of its mouth was wide open in a frozen scream.

"I guess they didn't look too hard," D'Agosta said. He heard a small moan escape from Waxie. "You okay, Jack?" he asked, glancing back.

Waxie said nothing. His face looked like a pale moon, hovering in the noisome dark.

D'Agosta turned his light back on the head. "We're gonna have to get an SOC team down here for a full series." He reached for his radio, then remembered it wouldn't work.

Hayward edged forward. "Lieutenant?"

D'Agosta paused. "Yes?"

"The moles left this place alone because someone died in it. They're superstitious that way, some of them. But as soon as we leave, they're going to clean this whole mess up, get rid of the head themselves, and you'll *never* find it. More than anything else, they don't want cops down here."

"How the hell will they know we were here?"

"I keep telling you, Lieutenant, they're *around*. Listening."

D'Agosta shone his light about. The corridor was silent and dead. "So what's your point?"

"If you want the head, you're going to have to take it with you."

"Shit," breathed D'Agosta. "Okay, Sergeant, we'll have to improvise. Grab that towel over there."

Stepping in front of the motionless Waxie, Sergeant Hayward picked up a water-logged towel and spread it on the damp concrete next to the head. Then, pulling the sleeve of her uniform over her hand, she nudged the head toward the towel with her wrist.

D'Agosta watched with mixed disgust and admiration as Hayward gathered the ends of the towel into a ball. He blinked his eyes, trying to wipe away the smart of the foul reek. "Let's go. Sergeant, you may do the honors."

"No problem." Hayward lifted the towel, holding it away from her body.

As D'Agosta stepped forward, shining his flashlight back down the corridor toward the staircase, there was a sudden whistling sound and a bottle came winging out of the dark, just missing Waxie's head. It shattered loudly on the wall. Farther down the passageway, D'Agosta could hear a rustling noise.

"Who's there?" he yelled. "Halt! Police officers!"

Another bottle came flying wildly out of the dark. D'Agosta realized, with a strange crawly feeling at the base of his spine, that he could *feel,* but not see, shapes moving toward them.

"There's only three of us, Lieutenant," Hayward said, tension suddenly evident in her dusky voice. "May I suggest we get the hell out of here?"

There was a raspy call from out of the dark, then a shout and the sound of running. He heard a neigh of terror at his shoulder and turned to see Waxie, still transfixed.

"For Chrissakes, Captain, get hold of yourself!" D'Agosta shouted.

Waxie began to whimper. From the other side, D'Agosta heard a hissing noise, and he turned to see Hayward's petite figure standing tense and erect. Her slender hands were at her sides with the knuckles pointed in, the towel and its burden dangling from her fingers. She took another deep, hissing breath, as if in preparation. Then she looked around quickly and turned back toward the staircase, once again holding the head at arm's length.

"Jesus, don't leave me!" Waxie howled.

D'Agosta gave Waxie's shoulder a vicious tug. With a low groan, Waxie began to move, first slowly and then faster, bursting past Hayward.

"Move!" D'Agosta called, pushing Hayward ahead of him with one hand. He felt something whiz past his ear, and he stopped, turned, drew his gun, and fired toward the ceiling. In the muzzle flash he saw a dozen or more people coming up the dark tunnel, dividing, preparing to circle him; they ran low across the ground, moving with horrible speed through the darkness. He turned and fled for the stairway.

One level up, on the far side of the hanging door, he stopped at last to listen, gulping air. Hayward waited beside him, gun in hand. There was no sound except the footsteps of Waxie, far ahead of them now, running down the rail siding toward the pool of light.

After a moment, D'Agosta stepped back. "Sergeant, if you ever suggest backup in the future—or make any other suggestion, for that matter—remind me to pay attention to it."

Hayward holstered her gun. "I was afraid you'd wig out down there, like the Captain did," she said. "But you did well for a virgin, sir."

D'Agosta looked at her, realizing this was the first time she had addressed him as a superior officer. He thought about asking just what the hell that weird breathing of hers had been about, but decided against it. "Still got it?" he said instead.

Hayward raised the towel.

"Then let's get the hell out. We'll see the rest of the sites some other time."

On the way to the surface, the image that kept returning to D'Agosta was not the circling mob, or the endless dank tunnel. It was the freshly soiled baby's diaper.

12

Margo washed her hands in the deep metal sink of the Forensic Anthropology lab, then dried them on a coarse hospital cloth. She glanced over at the gurney on which the sheeted remains of Pamela Wisher lay. The samples and observations had all been taken, and the corpse would be released to the family later that morning. Across the room, Brambell and Frock were at work on the unidentified skeleton, bending over its grotesquely twisted hips and taking elaborate measurements.

"If I may make an observation?" Dr. Brambell said, putting a vibrating Stryker saw to one side.

"Be my guest," Frock replied in his buttery rumble, waving a hand magnanimously.

They detested each other.

Margo slipped two latex gloves onto each hand, turning to hide a smile. It was probably the first time she'd seen Frock face a man with an intellect, or an ego, equal to his own. It was a miracle that any work had been accomplished. Yet over the past few days they had performed antibody testing, osteological analysis, tests for toxic residues and teratogens, as well as numerous other procedures. All that remained was the DNA sequencing and forensic analysis of the teeth marks.

Yet the unknown corpse remained a riddle, refusing ʋ its secrets. Margo knew this only added to the highly cⱼ atmosphere within the lab.

"It should be obvious to the meanest intelligence," Brambell was saying, his high Irish voice trembling with irritation, "that the puncture can*not* have originated on the dorsal side. Otherwise, the transverse process would have been clipped."

"I fail to see what clipping has to do with anything," muttered Frock.

Margo tuned out the argument, most of which was uninteresting to her anyway. Her specialty was ethnopharmacology and genetics, not gross anatomy. She had other problems to solve.

She leaned over the latest gel electrophoresis run on tissue from the unidentified corpse, feeling her trapezius muscles cry out in protest as she reached forward. Five sets of ten reps with the upright rows the night before, instead of her normal three. She'd upped her workout routine dramatically over the last several days; she would have to be more careful not to overdo it.

Ten minutes of close scrutiny confirmed her suspicions: the dark stripes of the various protein elements could tell her little beyond being common human muscle proteins. She straightened up with a sigh. Any more detailed genetic information would have to come from the much more sensitive DNA sequencing machine. Unfortunately, reliable results would not be available for several more days.

As she placed the gel strips to one side, rubbing her shoulder thoughtfully, she noticed a manila envelope lying next to the SPARC-10 workstation. *X rays,* she thought. *They must have arrived first thing this morning.* Obviously, Brambell and Frock had been too busy arguing over the corpse to look at them. It was understandable: with a body that was almost completely skeletonized already, X rays weren't likely to tell them very much.

"Margo?" Frock called.

She walked over to the examining table.

"My dear," Frock said, pushing his wheelchair away and gesturing toward the microscope, "please examine this groove running down the right femur."

The stereozoom was on lowest power, yet it was still like gazing into another world. The brown bone leaped into view, revealing the ridges and valleys of a miniature desert landscape.

"What do *you* make of this?" he asked.

It wasn't the first time Margo had been called to give an opinion in a dispute, and she didn't relish the role. "It looks like a natural fissure in the bone," she said, keeping her voice neutral. "Part of the suite of bone spurs and ridges that seem to have affected the skeleton. I wouldn't necessarily say it was caused by a tooth."

Frock settled back in his wheelchair, not quite able to mask a smile of triumph.

Brambell blinked. "I'm sorry?" he asked in disbelief. "Dr. Green, I don't mean to contradict you, but that's a longitudinal tooth mark if ever I saw one."

"I don't mean to contradict *you*, Dr. Brambell." She switched the stereozoom to higher power, and the small fissure immediately turned into a vast canyon. "But I can see some natural pores along the inside, here."

Brambell bustled over and looked into the eyepieces, holding his old horn-rims to one side. He stared at the image for several moments, then stepped away much more slowly than he had approached.

"Hmm," he said, replacing his glasses. "It pains me to say it, Frock, but you may have a point."

"You mean *Margo* may have a point," said Frock.

"Yes, of course. Very good, Dr. Green."

Margo was spared a reply by the ringing of the lab phone. Frock wheeled over and answered it energetically. Margo watched him, realizing that this was the first time she had really stopped to look at her old adviser since D'Agosta's call had brought them back together the week before. Though still portly, he seemed thinner than she remembered from their days together at the Museum. His wheelchair, too, was different: old and scuffed. She wondered, in sudden sympathy, if her mentor had fallen on hard times. Yet if so, it hadn't seemed to affect him adversely. If anything, he looked more alert, more vigorous, than during his tenure as Anthropology Department chairman.

Frock was listening, clearly upset about something. Margo's gaze drifted away from him and up to the laboratory window and its gorgeous view of Central Park. The trees were rich with the dark green foliage of summer, and the reservoir shimmered in the brilliant light. To the south, several rowboats drifted lazily across the pond. She thought how infinitely preferable it would be in one of those boats—basking in the sun—instead of here in the Museum, pulling apart rotten bodies.

"That was D'Agosta," Frock said, hanging up with a sigh. "He says our friend here is going to have some company. Close the blinds, will you? Artificial light is preferable for microscope work."

"What do you mean, company?" Margo asked sharply.

"That's how he put it. Apparently, they discovered a badly decomposed head during a search of some railroad tunnels yesterday afternoon. They're sending it over for analysis."

Dr. Brambell muttered something in fervent Gaelic.

"Does the head belong..." Margo began, then nodded in the direction of the corpses.

Frock shook his head, a somber expression on his face. "Apparently it's unrelated."

Silence descended on the lab for a moment. Then, as if on cue, the two men slowly returned to the unidentified skeleton. Soon, murmurs of dissent began to rise once again. Margo sighed deeply and turned back toward the electrophoresis equipment. She had at least a morning's worth of cataloging to get through.

Her eye moved toward the X rays. They'd raised a fearful stink with the lab in order to get them that morning. Maybe she ought to take a quick look before starting the cataloging.

She slid out the first series, clipping them to the viewer. Three shots of the unidentified skeleton's upper torso. As she expected, they showed—much less clearly—what they had already observed from direct examination: a skeleton suffering bizarre bone deformities, with a grotesque thickening and ridging of almost every osteological process in the body.

She pulled them down and slid the next series into the clips. Another set of three views, this time of the lumbar region.

She saw it immediately: four small spots, crisp and white. Curious, she swiveled the magnifier over for a closer look. The four spots were sharp triangles, arranged in a precise square at the very bottom of the spine, completely enclosed in a fused mass of bony growth. They had to be metal, Margo knew: only metal would be that opaque to X rays.

She straightened up. The two men were still bending over the cadaver, their mutterings floating toward her across the quiet room.

"There's something over here you should take a look at," she said.

Brambell reached the viewer first and peered closely. He stepped away, adjusted his horn-rims, and peered again.

Frock rumbled over a moment later, curious, brushing against the Medical Examiner's legs in his haste. "If you *don't* mind," he said, using the heavy wheelchair to crowd Brambell off to the side. He leaned forward, face inches from the viewer.

The room fell silent except for the hiss of air from the duct above the gurney. For once, Margo thought, both Brambell and Frock were completely baffled.

13

It was the first time D'Agosta had been in the Chief's office since Horlocker's appointment, and he gazed around in disbelief. It looked to him like a suburban steakhouse trying to go upscale. The heavy fake-mahogany furniture, the low lighting, the thick drapes, the cheap Mediterranean-style ironwork fixtures with the ripply yellow glass. It was so perfect, it made him want to ask a waiter to bring him a Gibson.

Chief Redmond Horlocker sat behind a vast desk absolutely bare of paper. In the nearest wing chair, Waxie had settled his bulk comfortably and was describing their movements of the previous day. He had just gotten to the point where the three of them had been set upon by a mob of enraged homeless, and he, Waxie, was holding them at bay so that D'Agosta and Hayward could escape. Horlocker listened, his face impassive.

D'Agosta's gaze fastened on Waxie, growing ever more animated as he talked. He considered speaking up himself, but long experience told him it wouldn't make any difference. Waxie was a precinct captain; he didn't get many chances to come down to One Police Plaza and impress the head honcho. Maybe the end result would be more manpower allocated to the case. Besides, a little voice in the back of D'Agosta's head said this was going to be one of those cases where the shit-rain would fall especially hard. Even though he was officially in charge, it didn't hurt to let Waxie take some credit. The more visible you were at the beginning, the closer they mowed your ass at the end.

Waxie finished his story, and there was a silence as Horlocker let a bit of *gravitas* build up in the room. Then he cleared his throat.

"Your take, Lieutenant?" he asked, turning to D'Agosta.

D'Agosta straightened up. "Well, sir, it's too early to tell whether there's a connection or not. It bears looking into, though, and I could use some extra manpower to—"

The antique phone jangled, and Horlocker picked up the receiver, listening for a moment. "It can wait," he said curtly, then hung up and turned back to D'Agosta.

"You a *Post* reader?" he asked.

"Sometimes," D'Agosta replied. He knew where this was leading.

"And you know this Smithback who's writing all the garbage?"

"Yes, sir," said D'Agosta.

"He a friend of yours?"

D'Agosta paused. "Not exactly, sir."

"Not exactly," the Chief repeated. "In that book of his about the Museum Beast, Smithback made it seem like you two were bosom buddies. To hear him tell it, the pair of you single-handedly saved the world during that little problem at the Museum of Natural History."

D'Agosta kept quiet. The role he'd played in the disastrous opening-night party for the *Superstition* exhibition was ancient history. And nobody in the new administration wanted to give him any credit for it.

"Well, your not-exactly pal Smithback is running us ragged, chasing down all the crank calls his reward offer has generated. *That's* where your extra manpower has gone. You should know that better than anyone." The Chief shifted irritably in his huge leather throne. "So you're telling me that the homeless murders and the Wisher murder have the same MO."

D'Agosta nodded.

"Okay. Now we don't like homeless being murdered here in New York. It's a problem. It doesn't look good. But when we get socialites being murdered, then we got a *real* problem. You get my drift?"

"Absolutely," said Waxie.

D'Agosta said nothing.

"What I'm saying is, we're concerned about the homeless murders, and we're going to try to take care of it. But look, D'Agosta, we've got homeless dying every day. Between you and me, they're a dime a dozen. We both know it. On the other hand, I got a whole city on my butt about this headless debutante. The mayor wants that case *solved*." He leaned forward and put his elbows on the desk, a magnanimous look settling across his features. "Look, I know you're going to need more help on this. So I'm going to keep Captain Waxie here on the case. I've put someone else on the precinct desk to free him up."

"Yes, sir!" said Waxie, straightening up.

As he listened, something inside D'Agosta crumpled and died. A walking disaster like Waxie was exactly what he didn't need. Now instead of more manpower, he'd have to nursemaid Waxie through every step. He'd better put him on some peripheral assignment, where he couldn't screw up. But that led to a whole new chain-of-command problem: putting a precinct captain on a case being run by a lieutenant in the Homicide Division. Just how the hell was *that* going to fall out?

"D'Agosta!" the Chief snapped.

D'Agosta looked up. "What?"

"I asked you a question. What's going on at the Museum?"

"They've completed tests on the Wisher corpse and have released it to the family," D'Agosta replied.

"And the other skeleton?"

"They're still trying to identify it."

"What about the teeth marks?"

"There seems to be some disagreement about their origin."

Horlocker shook his head. "Jesus, D'Agosta. I thought you said those people knew what they were doing. Don't make me sorry I took your advice and moved those corpses out of the Morgue."

"We've got the Chief ME and some top Museum staff working on it. I know these people personally, and there aren't any better—"

Horlocker sighed loudly and waved his hand. "I don't care about their pedigrees. I want results. Now that you've got Waxie on the case, things should move faster. I want something by the end of the day tomorrow. Got that, D'Agosta?"

D'Agosta nodded. "Yes, sir."

"Good." The Chief waved his hand. "Then get to it, you two."

14

It was, Smithback thought, the most bizarre demonstration he had seen in the ten years he had lived in New York. The signs had been professionally painted. The sound system was first-class. And Smithback felt distinctly underdressed.

The crowd was remarkably diverse: Central Park South and Fifth Avenue ladies, dressed in diamonds and Donna Karan, along with young bankers, bond salesmen, commodity traders, and various young turks eager for civil disobedience. There were also some well-dressed prep school teenagers. But what astonished Smithback was the size of the crowd. There must have been two thousand people milling around him. And whoever organized the rally obviously had political clout: their permit allowed them to close off Grand Army Plaza on a weekday rush hour. Behind a series of well-manned police barricades and ranks of television cameras were endless lines of angry traffic.

Smithback knew that this group represented tremendous wealth and power in New York City. Their demonstration was no joke—not for the mayor, not for the police chief, not for anyone involved in New York City politics. These people simply did not go into the streets and hold demonstrations. And yet, here they were.

Mrs. Horace Wisher stood on a large redwood platform in front of the gilded victory statue at the intersection of Central Park South and Fifth Avenue. She was speaking into a microphone, the powerful PA system amplifying her crisp tones into an unavoidable presence. Behind her was a massive full-color blowup of the now-famous childhood picture of her daughter Pamela.

"How long?" she asked the assembled throng. "How long are we going to let our city die? How long are we going to tolerate the murders of our daughters, our sons, our brothers, our sisters, our parents? How long are we going to live in fear, in our own homes and in our own neighborhoods?"

She gazed over the crowd, listening to the rising murmur of assent.

She began again more softly. "My ancestors came to New Amsterdam three hundred years ago. It has been our home ever since. And it has been a good home. When I was a little girl, my grandmother used to take me for evening walks in Central Park. We used to walk home alone from school after nightfall. We did not even lock the door to our townhouse.

"Why has nothing been done, while crime, drugs, and murder have reared up all around us? How many mothers will have to lose their children before we say, *enough*!"

She stood back from the microphone, collecting herself. A murmur of anger was beginning to ripple through the crowd. This woman had the simplicity and dignity of a born orator. Smithback held his cassette recorder higher, scenting another front-page story.

"The time has come," Mrs. Wisher said, her voice rising once again, "to take back our city. To take it back for our children and grandchildren. If it means executing drug dealers, if it means erecting a billion dollars in new prison space, it must be done. This is war. If you don't believe me, look at the statistics. Every day they are killing us. One thousand nine hundred murders in New York City last year. Five murders a day. We are at war, my friends, and we are losing. Now we must fight back with everything we've got. Street by street, block by block, from Battery Park to the Cloisters, from East End Avenue to Riverside Drive, we must take back our city!"

The angry murmur had grown. Smithback noticed that more younger men were now joining the throng, attracted by the noise and the crowd. Hip flasks and pint bottles of Wild Turkey were being passed around. *Gentlemen bankers, my ass,* he thought.

Suddenly, Mrs. Wisher turned and pointed. Smithback turned to see a flurry of activity beyond the barricade: a sleek black limousine had pulled up, and the mayor, a small balding man in a dark suit, stepped out, accompanied by several aides. Smithback waited, eager to see what would happen. The size of this rally had obviously taken the mayor by surprise, and now he was scrambling to get involved, to show his concern.

"The mayor of New York!" Mrs. Wisher cried as the mayor made his way toward the podium with the help of several policemen. "Here he is, come to speak to us!"

The voice of the crowd rose.

"But he shall *not* speak!" cried Mrs. Wisher. "We want action, Mr. Mayor, not talk!"

The crowd roared.

"Action!" she cried. "Not talk!"

"*Action!*" roared the crowd. The young men began jeering and whistling.

The mayor was stepping up to the podium now, smiling and waving. It appeared to Smithback that the mayor was asking Mrs. Wisher for the microphone. She took a step backward. "We don't want to hear another speech!" she cried. "We don't want to hear any more *bullshit!*" And with that she ripped the microphone out of its plug and stepped down from the platform, leaving the mayor standing alone above the crowd, a plastic smile frozen on his face, deprived of any possibility of being heard over the roar.

More than anything, it was her final expletive that caused the crowd to explode. A great unintelligible roar rose up and the crowd surged toward the podium. Smithback watched, a strange sensation rippling up his spine as the assembled group turned dangerously angry before his eyes. Several empty liquor bottles came sailing toward the stage, one shattering not five feet from the mayor. The groups of younger men had consolidated into a single body, and they began muscling their way toward the stage, cursing and jeering. Smithback caught a few isolated words: *Asshole. Faggot. Liberal scum.* More pieces of trash came flying out of the crowd, and the mayor's aides, realizing all was lost, quickly hustled him off the stage and back into his limousine.

Well, Smithback thought, *interesting to see how mob mentality affects all classes.* He couldn't remember having seen quite so brief or so fine a display of mob oratory as Mrs. Wisher's. As the sense of menace faded and the crowd began dissolving into seething knots, the journalist threaded his way toward a park bench to jot down his impressions while they were fresh. Then he checked his watch: five-thirty. He stood up and began trotting northwest through the Park. Better get in position, just in case.

15

As Margo jogged around the corner onto 65th Street, her portable radio tuned to an all-news channel, she stopped short, surprised to see a familiar lanky form lounging against the front railing of her apartment building, cowlick rearing above the long face like a brunette antler.

"Oh," she panted, snapping off the radio and tugging the speakers from her ears. "It's you."

Smithback reared back, mock incredulity flooding his features. "Can it be? 'How sharper than a serpent's tooth,' indeed, is a thankless friend. All we've been through together—all that vast shared reservoir of memories—and I merit just an 'Oh, it's you'?"

"I keep trying to put that vast reservoir of memories behind me," Margo said, stuffing the radio into her carryall and bending forward to massage her calves. "Besides, whenever you run into me these days, it's to talk about one subject: My Career and How Great It Is."

"'A hit, a palpable hit.'" Smithback shrugged. "Fair enough. So let's pretend I'm here to make amends, Lotus Blossom. Let me buy you a drink." He eyed her appreciatively. "My, my, you're looking good these days. Going for the Miss Universe title?"

Margo straightened up. "I've got things to do."

He caught hold of her arm as she maneuvered past him toward the door. "Café des Artistes," he said teasingly.

Margo stopped and sighed. "Very well," she said with a slight smile, disengaging her arm. "I'm not cheap, but I guess I can be had. Give me a few minutes to shower and change."

They entered the venerable cafe through the lobby of the Hotel des Artistes. Smithback nodded at the maître d'hôtel, and they made their way toward the quiet old bar.

"Looks good," Margo said, nodding toward the quiche tray that was waiting to make its rounds among the tables.

"Hey, I said a drink, not an eight-course dinner." Smithback selected a table, positioning himself beneath the Howard Chandler Christy painting of naked women frolicking tastefully in a garden.

"I think the redhead likes me," he said, winking and pointing his thumb at the painting. An ancient waiter, his face creased by wrinkles and a perpetual smile, came by and took their drink orders.

"I like this place," Smithback said as the waiter shuffled away, a study in white and black. "They're nice to you in here. I hate waiters who make you feel like low-class shit." He caught Margo in an interrogating gaze. "So. Quiz time. Have you read all my articles since last we met?"

"I'll have to plead the fifth on that," Margo replied. "But I did see your pieces on Pamela Wisher. I thought the second article was especially well done. I liked the way you made her out to be a real human being, not just something to exploit. New tack for you, isn't it?"

"That's my Margo," Smithback said. The waiter returned with their drinks and a bowl of filberts, then departed. "I just came from the rally, actually," Smithback continued. "That Mrs. Wisher is a formidable woman."

Margo nodded. "I heard about it on NPR just now. Sounds wild. I wonder if this Mrs. Wisher realizes what she's unleashed."

"It became almost scary toward the end. The rich and influential have suddenly discovered the power of the *vulgus mobile*."

Margo laughed, still careful not to drop her guard. You had to be wary around Smithback. For all she knew, he had a tape recorder running in his pocket as they spoke.

"It's strange," Smithback continued.

"What is?"

He shrugged. "How little it takes—a few drinks, maybe the stimulant of being part of a mob—to strip a group of its upper-class veneer, make it ugly and violent."

"If you knew about anthropology," Margo said, "you wouldn't be so surprised. Besides, from what I heard that crowd wasn't as uniformly upper-crust as some of the press like to think." She took another sip and sat back. "Anyway, I assume this isn't just a friendly drink. I've never known you to spend money without an ulterior motive."

Smithback put down his glass, looking genuinely wounded. "I'm surprised. I really am. That doesn't sound like the Margo I knew. I hardly see you these days. When I do, you talk this kind of trash. And just look at you: all muscled up like some gazelle. Where's the frumpy, slope-shouldered Margo I used to know and love? What's happened to you, anyway?"

Margo started to reply, then paused. God only knew what Smithback would say if he knew she now carried a pistol in her carryall. *What* has *happened to me?* she wondered. But even as she asked the question, she knew the answer. It's true, she hadn't seen much of Smithback. But it was for the same reason she hadn't seen much of her old mentor, Dr. Frock. Or Kawakita, or Pendergast the FBI agent, or anyone she'd known from her earlier days at the Museum. The memories they all shared were still too fresh, too dreadful. The nightmares that still troubled her sleep were bad enough; the last thing she'd wanted was more reminders of that terrible ordeal.

But even as she pondered, Smithback's hurt expression dissolved into a smile. "Oh, God, there's no point in dissembling," he cackled. "You know me too well. There *is* an ulterior motive. I know what you've been doing, working late at the Museum."

Margo froze. *How had it leaked?* But then she checked herself; Smithback was a clever fisherman, and there might be less bait on his line than he was letting on.

"I thought as much," she said. "So exactly what am I doing, and how did you find out about it?"

Smithback shrugged. "I have my sources. You of all people should remember that. I looked up some old Museum friends and learned that Pamela Wisher's body, and the unidentified body, were brought to the Museum last Thursday. You and Frock are assisting in the autopsies."

Margo said nothing.

"Don't worry, this is not for attribution," Smithback said.

"I think I've finished my drink," said Margo. "Time to go." She stood up.

"Wait." Smithback put a restraining hand on her wrist. "There's one thing I don't know. Was the reason you were called in the teeth marks on the bones?"

Margo jerked around. "How did you know that?" she demanded.

Smithback grinned in triumph and Margo realized, with a sinking feeling, how expertly she had been baited. He'd been guessing, after all. But her reaction had confirmed it.

She sat down again. "You're a real bastard, you know that?"

The journalist shrugged. "It wasn't all guesswork. I knew the bodies had been brought to the Museum. And if you read my interview with Mephisto, the underground leader, you know what he said about cannibals living beneath Manhattan."

Margo shook her head. "You can't print it, Bill."

"Why not? They'll never know it came from you."

"That's not what I'm worried about," she snapped. "Think, just for one moment, beyond your next deadline. Can you imagine what a story like that could do to the city? And how about your new friend, Mrs. Wisher? She doesn't know. What do you suppose she'd say if she knew her daughter was not only murdered and decapitated, but partially devoured, as well?"

A look of pain briefly crossed Smithback's face. "I know all that. But it's news, Margo."

"Delay it one day."

"Why?"

Margo hesitated.

"You'd better give me a reason, Lotus Blossom," Smithback urged.

Margo sighed. "Oh, very well. Because the teeth marks may be canine. Apparently, the bodies were lying underground for a long time before they were washed out in a storm. Probably some stray dog took a few bites out of them."

Smithback's face fell. "You mean it wasn't cannibals?"

Margo shook her head. "Sorry to disappoint you. We should know tomorrow, when the lab tests are finished. Then you can have the exclusive, I promise. We have a meeting scheduled at the Museum for tomorrow afternoon. I'll talk to Frock and D'Agosta about it myself afterward."

"But what difference will a day make?"

"I already told you. Break the story now and you'll cause an unholy panic. You saw those Upper Crusters out there today; you said so yourself. What happens if they think some kind of monster is loose—another Mbwun, say—or some weird cannibalistic serial killer? Then the next day we'll announce it was a dog bite and you'll look like an idiot. You've already pissed off the police with that reward business. If you panic the city for no reason, they'll ride you out of town on a rail."

Smithback sat back. "Hmm."

"Wait just one day, Bill," Margo pleaded. "It's not a story yet."

Smithback was silent, thinking. "All right," he said at last, grudgingly. "All my instincts tell me I'm crazy. But you can have one more day. Then I get an exclusive, remember. No leaking the story to anyone."

Margo smiled slightly. "Don't worry."

They sat for a moment in silence. At last, Margo sighed. "Earlier, you asked what's happened to me. I don't know. I guess these killings are just bringing back all the bad memories."

"The Museum Beast, you mean," Smithback said. He was methodically attacking the bowl of filberts. "That was a tough time."

"I guess you could put it that way." Margo shrugged. "After all that happened... well, I just wanted to put everything behind me. I was having bad dreams, waking up in a cold sweat night after night. After I went to Columbia, things got better. I thought it was over. But then I came back to the Museum; all this started happening..." She fell silent for a moment.

"Bill," she said suddenly. "Do you know whatever happened to Gregory Kawakita?"

"Greg?" Smithback asked. He'd finished the bowl of filberts and was turning it over in his hands, as if looking for more underneath. "Haven't seen him since he took that leave of absence from the Museum. Why?" His eyes narrowed craftily. "You and he didn't have a thing going, did you?"

Margo waved her hand dismissively. "No, nothing like that. If anything, we were always in competition for Dr. Frock's attention. It's just that he tried to reach me once, several months ago, and I never followed through. I think maybe he was sick or something. His voice sounded different than I remembered it. Anyway, I was feeling kind of guilty about it, so I finally looked him up in the Manhattan directory. He's not listed. I was curious if he'd moved away, maybe gotten a position elsewhere."

"Beats me," Smithback said. "But Greg's the kind of guy that always lands on his feet. He's probably moonlighting in some think tank, earning three hundred grand a year." He checked his watch. "I've got to file my story on the rally by nine. Which means we have time for another drink."

Margo stared at him in mock amazement. "Bill Smithback, buying a friend a second round? How could I leave now? History is being made here tonight."

16

Nick Bitterman eagerly climbed the stone steps of Belvedere Castle, then waited at the parapet for Tanya to catch up. Below him, the dark bulk of Central Park was spread out beneath a setting sun. Nick could feel the icy coldness of the bottle of Dom Pérignon creeping through the paper bag under his arm. It felt pleasant in the heat of evening. The glasses clinked in his jacket pocket as he moved. Automatically, he felt for the square box that contained the ring. A Tiffany-cut one-carat diamond set in platinum that had cost him four large on 47th Street. He'd done well. Here came Tanya, giggling and gasping. She knew about the champagne but she didn't know about the ring.

He remembered seeing a movie in which two characters drank champagne on the Brooklyn Bridge, then threw the glasses into the river. That was pretty good, but this was going to be better. You couldn't get a more spectacular view of Manhattan than from the ramparts of Belvedere Castle at sunset. You just had to make sure you got your ass out of the Park before dark.

He grabbed Tanya's hand as she climbed the last steps, and they walked together to the edge of the stone parapet. The tower rose above them, black in the gloaming, its Gothic trappings humorously offset by the weather apparatus protruding from the topmost crenelations. He looked back the way they had come. At their feet lay the small castle pond, and beside it the Great Lawn, leading up to the row of trees that shaded the Reservoir. The Reservoir itself was a sheet of beaten gold in the sunset. To his right, the buildings of Fifth Avenue marched stolidly northward, their windows flashing orange; to his left sat the dark outlines of the ramparts of Central Park West, in shadow below a layer of clouds.

He pulled the bottle of champagne from its brown tissue, tore off the foil and the wire netting, took careful aim, then wiggled the cork inexpertly out of the neck. They watched as it burst free with a loud pop, sailing out of sight. In a few seconds there was a splash as it hit the pond far below.

"Bravo!" cried Tanya.

He filled the glasses and handed her one.

"Cheers." They clinked glasses and he drank his down in a gulp, then watched as Tanya sipped gingerly. "Drink up," he urged, and she drained the glass, wrinkling her nose as she did so.

"It tickles," she giggled as he refilled the glasses, drinking his off again in a few quick gulps.

"Attention, citizens of Manhattan!" he yelled from the ramparts, holding up the empty glass, his voice disappearing into space. "This is Nick Bitterman speaking! I proclaim August seventh to be Tanya Schmidt day in perpetuity!"

Tanya laughed, as he filled the glasses a third time, overflowing the rims and draining the bottle. When the glasses were empty, Nick wrapped his arm around the girl. "Custom demands that we throw them off, too," he said sternly.

They winged the glasses into space, leaning over the parapet to watch as they flashed in a downward arc, landing in the pond with a splash. As he watched, Nick noticed that the sun-bathers, roller skaters, and various Park loungers were now gone, and the base of the castle was deserted. He'd better get the show on the road. Plunging his hand into his jacket pocket, he removed the box and handed it to her. He stepped backward, watching proudly as she opened it.

"Nick, my *God*!" she cried. "It must have cost a fortune!"

"You're worth a fortune," Nick smiled as she placed it on her finger, then pulled her to him and gave her a quick, hard kiss. "You know what it means?" he asked.

She turned to him, eyes shining. Over her shoulders, the gloom was starting to gather in the trees.

"Well?" he urged.

She kissed him back and whispered in his ear.

"Until death do us part, baby," he replied, and kissed her again, longer this time, cupping one of her breasts in his hand.

"Nick!" she said, laughing and pulling away.

"There's nobody here," he said, placing his other hand on her rear and pulling her hips hard against his.

"Just the whole city watching," she said.

"Let them. They might learn something." His hand slipped inside her shirt and teased her hard little nipple as he glanced around at the encroaching darkness. "We'd better move this to my apartment," he whispered into her ear.

She smiled, then moved away from him toward the stone stairs. Watching her, admiring the natural grace in her walk, Nick felt the expensive champagne running through his veins. *Nothing like a champagne buzz,* he thought. *Goes straight to the head.*

Straight to the bladder, too. "Hold on," he said aloud. "I've got to drain the main vein."

She turned to wait as he walked to the tower. There were rest rooms hidden on its back side, he remembered, beside the metal maintenance staircase that led up to the weather equipment and down to the pond. Under the shadow of the tower it was still; the sounds of the traffic on the East Drive seemed muffled and distant. He located the men's room door and pushed through, unzipping his fly as he crossed the scuffed tile, past the row of dark stalls toward the bank of urinals. The room was deserted, as he knew it would be. He leaned against the cool porcelain and closed his eyes.

He opened them again quickly as a slight sound broke his champagne reverie. No, he realized; it was nothing. He laughed, shaking his head at the paranoia that was always bubbling just under the skin of even the most jaded New Yorker.

The sound came again, much louder, and he turned in surprise and fear, his dick still in his hand as he saw that someone was in one of the stalls, after all, and was coming out, fast.

Tanya waited, standing at the parapet, the night breeze quickening on her face. She felt the engagement ring, heavy and foreign on her finger. Nick was taking his sweet time. The Park was dark now, the Great Lawn deserted, the bright lights of Fifth Avenue winking off the surface of the pond.

Impatient, she walked toward the tower, then skirted around its dark bulk. The men's room door was shut. She knocked, timidly at first, then louder.

"Nick? Hey, Nick! You in there?"

There was no sound, only the wind sighing through the trees. The wind carried a strange smell: a pungent odor that reminded her, unpleasantly, of feta cheese.

"Nick? Stop playing games."

She pushed open the door and stepped inside.

For a moment, silence settled again over Belvedere Castle. And then the screams began: ululating, rising louder and louder as they rent the soft summer night.

17

Smithback took a seat at the counter of his favorite Greek coffeeshop, nodding at the griddleman for his usual breakfast order: two poached eggs on a double portion of red flannel hash. He sipped the cup of coffee that was placed in front of him, sighed contentedly, and slipped the newspapers out from under his arm. He turned first to the *Post,* frowning slightly as he scanned Hank McCloskey's front-page article on the Belvedere Castle murder. His own piece on the rally at Grand Army Plaza had been demoted to page four. By rights, he should have owned the front page that day, with his story on the Museum's involvement and the teethmark angle. But he'd promised Margo. Tomorrow would be different. Besides, maybe his forbearance would land him more scoops down the road.

The breakfast arrived and he dug into the hash with relish, putting aside the *Post* and cracking open the *New York Times* as he did so. He scanned the top headlines—tastefully understated and tidy—with derision. Then his eye, traveling below the fold, stopped at a one-column headline that read merely "Museum Beast Returns?" It was bylined Bryce Harriman, Special to the *Times*.

Smithback read on, the hash turning to wallpaper paste in his mouth.

August 8—Scientists at the New York Museum of Natural History are continuing their analysis of the headless corpses of Pamela Wisher and an unknown person, trying to determine if teeth marks found on the bones are the postmortem work of feral animals or possibly the cause of death itself.

The brutal murder and decapitation of Nicholas Bitterman at Belvedere Castle in Central Park yesterday evening has increased the pressure on the forensic team to find answers. Several deaths among homeless persons over the past months also may fit the pattern. It is not known if these corpses will also be brought to the Museum for analysis. Pamela Wisher's remains have been returned to her family, and will be interred in a 3:00 P.M. service this afternoon at Holy Cross Cemetery, Bronxville.

The autopsies have been proceeding under a cloak of secrecy at the Museum. "They don't want to have a panic on their hands," said a source. "But the unspoken word on everyone's lips is *Mbwun*."

Mbwun, as the Museum Beast is known to scientists, was an unusual creature that was inadvertently brought back to the Museum by a failed Amazonian expedition. In April of last year, the creature's presence in the Museum's subbasement became known when several museumgoers and some guards were killed. The creature also attacked a large crowd during a Museum opening, causing panic and a mistriggering of the Museum's alarm system. This resulted in 46 deaths and nearly three hundred injuries, one of the worst disasters in New York in recent years.

The name *Mbwun* was given to the creature by the now-extinct Kothoga tribe, who lived in the animal's original habitat along the Upper Xingu River in the Amazon Basin.

For decades, anthropologists and rubber tappers had heard rumors of a large, apparently reptilian animal in the Upper Xingu. Then, in 1987, a Museum anthropologist, Julian Whittlesey, organized an expedition to the Upper Xingu to seek clues about the tribe and the creature. Whittlesey disappeared in the rain forest, and the other members of the ill-fated expedition were tragically killed in a plane crash as they were returning to the United States.

Several crates containing relics from the expedition made their way back to New York. The artifacts were packed in plant fibers which contained a substance that the Mbwun animal craved. Although the manner in which the creature reached the Museum is not known, curators theorize that it was inadvertently locked into a freight container along with the expedition's collections. The creature lived in the Museum's vast subbasement until it ran out of its natural food and began attacking visitors and guards.

The animal was killed during the resulting melee, and its carcass was removed by authorities and destroyed before detailed taxonomic research could be performed. Although there are still many mysteries about the creature, it was determined that it lived on an isolated plateau in the Amazon called a tepui. Recent hydraulic gold mining in the Upper Xingu has severely impacted the area and probably caused the extinction of the species. Professor Whitney Cadwalader Frock of the Museum's anthropology department, author of *Fractal Evolution,* believed the creature to be an evolutionary aberration produced by its isolated rain forest habitat.

It was suggested by the source that the recent killings might be the work of a second Mbwun animal, perhaps the mate of the original. That, it seems, is also the unspoken worry of the New York City Police Department. Apparently, the police have asked the Museum laboratory to determine if the teeth marks on the bones are consistent with a feral dog or something far more powerful—something like Mbwun.

Smithback pushed the uneaten eggs away with a hand that was trembling with rage. He didn't know what was worse: having that prick Harriman scoop him, or the knowledge that he, Smithback, had already *had* the story and had allowed himself to be talked out of running it.

Never again, Smithback vowed. Never again.

On the fifteenth floor of One Police Plaza, D'Agosta put aside the same newspaper with a withering expletive. The NYPD public affairs spin doctors were going to have to work overtime to avert hysteria. Whoever had leaked this, he thought, was going to have his barbecued butt served up on a rôtisserie. At least, he thought, this time it wasn't his pain-in-the-ass friend Smithback.

Then he reached for the telephone and dialed the office of the Chief of Police. While on the subject of asses, he'd better take care of his own while he still had one. With Horlocker, it was always better to call than be called.

All he got was the voice mail of the Chief's secretary.

D'Agosta reached for the newspaper again, then pushed it away, frustration welling up inside him. Waxie would be here in a minute, no doubt bawling about the Belvedere Castle murder and the Chief's deadline. At the thought of seeing Waxie, D'Agosta shut his eyes involuntarily, but the feeling of weariness that surged over him was so great that he immediately opened them again. He'd only had two hours of sleep, and was bone tired after spending much of the night clambering over Belvedere Castle in the aftermath of the Bitterman murder.

He stood up and walked over to the window. Below, amidst the gray urban sprawl, he could make out a small square of black: the playground of PS 362. The tiny shapes of young kids were racing around it, playing tag and hopscotch, no doubt screeching and hollering their way through midmorning recess. God, he thought, what he wouldn't give to be one of them now.

As he turned back to the desk, he noticed that the edge of the newspaper had knocked over the framed photograph of his ten-year-old son, Vinnie Junior. He righted it carefully, smiling involuntarily at the face that smiled back at him. Then, feeling a little better, he dug into his coat pocket and pulled out a cigar. The hell with Horlocker. What was going to happen was going to happen.

He lit up, tossed the match into an ashtray, and walked over to a large map of the west side of Manhattan tacked to a bulletin board. The precinct board was pocked with white and red pins. A legend taped to one corner showed that the white pins indicated disappearances over the last six months, while the red pins indicated deaths that fit the suspect MO. D'Agosta reached into a plastic tray, pulled out a red pin, located Central Park Reservoir on the board, and carefully pressed the pin directly to its south. Then, he stood back, staring at it, trying to see the pattern through the visual noise.

The white pins outnumbered the red pins ten to one. Of course, many of those wouldn't pan out. People disappeared for a lot of reasons in New York. Still, it was an unusually high number, over three times the norm for a six-month period. And a remarkable number seemed to be in the region of Central Park. He kept staring. The dots didn't look random somehow. His brain told him there was a pattern, but he hadn't any idea what it was.

"Daydreaming, Lieutenant?" came the familiar, dusky voice. D'Agosta jumped in surprise, then turned around. It was Hayward, now officially on the case along with Waxie.

"Ever hear of knocking?" D'Agosta snapped.

"Yeah, I've heard of it. But you said you wanted this stuff as soon as possible." Hayward held a thick sheaf of computer printouts in her slender hand. D'Agosta took the papers and began leafing through them: more homeless murders going back six months, most in Waxie's Central Park/West Side jurisdiction. None had been investigated, of course.

"Christ," he muttered, shaking his head. "Well, we'd better get these mapped." He began reading out locations while Hayward pressed red pins into the precinct board. Then he paused for a moment, glancing up at her shock of dark hair, her pale skin. Though he hadn't let her know it, of course, D'Agosta was secretly glad Hayward was assisting him. Her imperturbable self-assurance was like a calm haven at the center of a howling storm. And he had to admit she didn't hurt the eyes either.

From the hall came the sound of running and raised voices. Something heavy fell over with a crash. Frowning, D'Agosta nodded for Hayward to check it out. Soon there was more yelling, and D'Agosta heard his own name being spoken in a whiny, high-pitched voice.

Curious, he poked his head out the door. An almost unbelievably filthy-looking man was standing in the Homicide lobby, struggling with two cops who were trying to subdue him. Hayward was on the sidelines, her small frame tensed as if awaiting an opportunity to wade in. D'Agosta took in the dirt-clotted hair; the sallow, jaundiced skin; the narrow, hungry frame; the ubiquitous black garbage bag holding the man's worldly possessions.

"I want to see the Lieutenant!" the homeless man screeched in a thin, reedy voice. "I have information! I demand—"

"Fella," said one officer, a look of disgust on his face as he restrained the man by his greasy coat, "if you have anything to say, say it to me, okay? The Lieutenant's busy."

"There he is now!" the man pointed a trembling finger at D'Agosta. "See, he's not busy! Get your hands off me, you, or I'll file a complaint, you hear me? I'll call my lawyer!"

D'Agosta retreated into his office, shut the door, and resumed his scrutiny of the map. The barrage of voices continued, the shrill whine of the homeless man particularly grating, punctuated by the increasingly irritated tones of Hayward. This one didn't want to leave.

Suddenly the door banged open and the homeless man half-fell, half-stumbled inside, a furious Hayward on his heels. The man backed into a corner of the office, holding the garbage bag in front of him protectively.

"You have to listen to me, Lieutenant!" he yelped.

"He's a slippery bastard," Hayward panted, wiping her hands on her slender thighs. "Quite literally."

"Stay back!" the homeless man squealed at Hayward.

D'Agosta sighed wearily. "It's okay, Sergeant," he said. Then he turned to the homeless man. "All right. Five minutes. But leave that outside." He gestured toward the bag as its ripe smell reached his nostrils.

"They'll steal it," the man said hoarsely.

"This is a police station," snapped D'Agosta. "Nobody's gonna steal any of your shit."

"It's not shit," the man whined, but he nevertheless handed the greasy bag to Hayward, who hurriedly deposited it outside, returning and closing the door against the stench.

Suddenly the demeanor of the homeless man changed dramatically. He shambled forward and sat down in one of the visitor's chairs, crossing his legs, acting for all the world like he owned the place. The smell was stronger now. It reminded D'Agosta, faintly and unsettlingly, of the smell in the railroad tunnel.

"I hope you're comfortable," said D'Agosta, strategically placing the cigar in front of his nose. "You got four minutes left."

"Actually, Vincent," said the homeless man, "I'm about as comfortable as can be expected, given the condition in which you see me."

D'Agosta slowly dropped the cigar to the desk, stunned.

"I'm sorry to see you still smoking." The homeless man eyed the cigar. "However, I notice that your taste in cigars has improved. Dominican Republic leaf, if I'm not mistaken, with a Connecticut Shade wrapper. If you must smoke, that Churchill is a vast improvement over the packing twine you used to indulge in."

D'Agosta remained speechless. He knew the voice, he knew the melodious southern accent. He just couldn't connect it with the stinking, filthy bum sitting across from him.

"Pendergast?" he breathed.

The homeless man nodded.

"What—?"

"I hope you'll forgive the histrionic entrance," said Pendergast. "I wanted to test the effectiveness of my costume."

"Oh," said D'Agosta.

Hayward stepped forward and glanced at D'Agosta. For the first time she appeared to be at a loss. "Lieutenant—?" she began.

D'Agosta took a deep breath. "Sergeant, this"—he waved a hand at the bedraggled figure who was now sitting, hands folded in his lap, one leg crossed carefully over the other—"is Special Agent Pendergast of the FBI."

Hayward looked at D'Agosta, then at the homeless man. "Bullshit," she said simply.

Pendergast laughed delightedly. He placed his elbows on the arms of the chair, tented his hands, rested his chin on his fingertips, and looked at Hayward. "Delighted to meet you, Sergeant. I would offer to shake hands, but..."

"Don't bother," said Hayward, hastily, a lingering look of suspicion on her face.

Suddenly, D'Agosta stepped over and crushed the visitor's slender, grubby hands in his. "Christ, Pendergast, it's good to see you. I wondered what the hell had happened to your skinny ass. I heard you'd refused the directorship of the New York office, but I haven't seen you since—"

"Since the Museum murders, as they've become known." Pendergast nodded. "I see they are front-page news again."

Sitting down again, D'Agosta scowled and nodded.

Pendergast glanced up at the map. "Quite a problem you have on your hands, Vincent. A string of vicious murders above and belowground, angst plaguing the city's elite, and now rumors that Mbwun has returned."

"Pendergast, you got no idea."

"Pardon my contradicting you, but I have a very good idea. In fact, I came by to see if you would care for some assistance."

D'Agosta's face brightened, then grew guarded. "Officially?" he asked.

Pendergast smiled. "Semiofficial is the best I can do, I'm afraid. These days, I more or less choose my own TDYs. I've spent the past year working on technical projects we can go into some other time. And let's just say I've received sanction to assist the NYPD on this case. Of course, I must maintain what we so delicately call 'deniability.' At this point, there is no evidence that a federal crime has been committed." He waved his hand. "My problem, quite simply, is that I cannot stay away from an interesting case. An annoying habit, but very hard to break."

D'Agosta looked at him curiously. "So why haven't I seen you in almost two years? Seems like New York would offer lots of interesting cases."

Pendergast inclined his head. "Not for me," he replied.

D'Agosta turned toward Hayward. "This is the first good thing that's happened to the case since day one," he said.

Pendergast glanced from D'Agosta to Hayward and back again, his pale blue eyes in stark contrast to his dirty skin. "You flatter me, Vincent. But let's get to work. Since my appearance seems to have convinced both of you, I'm hoping to test it out belowground as soon as possible. If you two will bring me up to date, that is."

"So you agree that the Wisher murder and the homeless murders are connected?" Hayward asked, still a little suspicious.

"I agree completely, Sergeant—Hayward, was it?" Pendergast said. Then he straightened noticeably. "That wouldn't be Laura Hayward, would it?"

"What of it?" Hayward said, suddenly guarded.

Pendergast relaxed in his chair again. "Excellent," he said in a low voice. "Please let me congratulate you on your article in last month's *Journal of Abnormal Sociology*. A most revealing look at the hierarchy among the underground homeless."

For the first time since D'Agosta had met her, Hayward looked distinctly uncomfortable. Her face flushed, and she looked away, unused to the compliment.

"Sergeant?" he asked.

"I'm getting my master's from NYU," she said, still looking away. Then she turned back quickly, glaring at D'Agosta, as if challenging him to taunt her. "My thesis is on caste structure in underground society."

"That's great," D'Agosta said, surprised at her defensiveness, but feeling a little defensive himself. *How come she never told me? She think I'm stupid?*

"But why publish in such an obscure journal?" Pendergast continued. "I'd have thought the *Law Enforcement Bulletin* would be the obvious choice."

Hayward gave a low laugh, her poise fully recovered. "Are you kidding?" she said.

All at once D'Agosta understood. Hard enough to be a pint-sized, pretty female rouster in the TA division, which had more than its share of hulking thugs. But to be working on an advanced academic degree on the very people she had to roust... He shook his head, imagining the kind of relentless derision she would have been subjected to in the ranks.

"Ah yes, I see," Pendergast said, nodding. "Well, it's a pleasure to meet you, in any case. But let's get to business. I'll need to see the analyses of the crime scenes. The more we can learn about the UnSub, the sooner we'll find him. Or them. He's not a rapist, correct?"

"Correct."

"Perhaps he's a fetishist. He—or they—certainly does seem to enjoy his souvenirs. We'll have to check the files on any inactive serial killers or assassin-types. Also, I wonder if you could have Data Processing ran cross-correlations on the known data for all victims. You might want to run a second query for all the missing persons, too. We should check for any points of commonality, no matter how subtle."

"I'll get on it," Hayward said.

"Excellent." Pendergast stood and approached the desk. "Now, if I could just see the case files—"

"Please sit down," D'Agosta said quickly, his nose wrinkling. "Your disguise is all too convincing, if you get my meaning."

"Of course," Pendergast said airily, sitting down again. "Convincing to a fault. Sergeant Hayward, if you'd be so kind as to pass those over?"

18

Margo took a seat in the vast Linnaeus Hall, deep within the original massing of the Museum of Natural History, and looked curiously around. It was an elegant space, originally constructed in 1882. Soaring vaults rose above dark oak paneling. Around the long dome of the hall, an intricate frieze had been carved, displaying Evolution in all its grandeur: from beautifully carved animalcules at one end to the great figure of Man at the other.

She gazed at the image of Man, dressed in frock coat, top hat, and walking stick. It was a marvelous monument to the early Darwinian view of evolution: the steady upward march from simple to complex, with Man the crowning glory. Margo knew that the modern view was very different. Evolution was proving to be a more random, haphazard affair, full of dead ends and bizarre twists. Dr. Frock—sitting in his wheelchair in the aisle next to her—had made major contributions to this understanding with his theory of fractal evolution. Now, evolutionary biologists no longer considered man the apotheosis of evolution, but merely the dead end of a minor side branch of a generalist, less-evolved subgroup of Mammalia. And, she thought with an inward smile, the word *Man* itself had gone out of favor—a definite improvement.

She craned her neck to look back toward the narrow projectionist's booth high up in the rear wall. The grand old facade had become a very modern lecture hall, retrofitted with concealed mechanical blackboards, retractable movie screens, and the latest in computerized multimedia equipment.

For the hundredth time that day, she wondered who had leaked the story of the Museum's involvement. Whoever it was, they obviously didn't know everything—they hadn't mentioned the grotesque deformities on the second skeleton—but they knew enough. Her relief at not having to intervene on Smithback's behalf was tempered by what she now knew about the nature of the teeth marks on the corpses. She was dreading the arrival of the Bitterman corpse, almost afraid of what corroborative evidence it might hold.

A loud humming sound brought Margo's eyes forward again. At the front of the hall, the proscenium and wings were retracting as a massive screen descended toward the floor.

There were exactly seven tense people in the two-thousand-seat hall.

Beside her, Frock was humming a tune from a Wagner opera, his thick fingers tapping on the battered arms of his wheelchair. His face was expressionless, but Margo knew that inside he was fuming. Protocol held that Brambell, as Chief Medical Examiner, should do the presentation, but Frock was obviously rankled by the arrangement. Several rows nearer the front, Margo could see Lieutenant D'Agosta, sitting with an overweight police captain in a rumpled uniform and two bored-looking Homicide detectives.

By now the main lights were fully dimmed, and Margo could see only Brambell's long bony face and baldpate, illuminated from below by the light on the lectern. In one hand he clutched an odd-looking plastic rapier that acted as wireless slide controller and light pointer. He looked positively cadaverous, she thought; Boris Karloff in a lab coat.

"Let's get right to the evidence, hey?" Brambell said, his high-pitched, cheerful voice booming from numerous speakers along both sides of the hall. Beside her, Margo could feel Frock stiffen with irritation.

The huge image of a magnified bone appeared on the screen, bathing the hall and its occupants in a ghostly gray light.

"Here is a photograph of Pamela Wisher's third cervical vertebra. Notice the dentition pattern that's clearly visible."

The next slide came up.

"Here is one of those tooth marks, magnified two hundred times. And here is a cross section reproduction. As you can see, the tooth is clearly mammalian."

The next series of slides displayed results of lab tests done on a variety of bones from the two corpses, recording the pressures per square inch needed to make marks of varying depths.

"We identified twenty-one clear marks, punctures, or scratches made by teeth on the bones of the two victims," Brambell continued. "There are also some marks that seem to come from a dull instrument: too regular for teeth, but too rough for a well-finished knife. Such as you'd see, perhaps, from a primitive ax or stone knife. These are particularly prevalent on the cervical vertebrae, perhaps indicative of the mode of decapitation. In any case, the pressure required to make the teeth marks"—Brambell indicated the results with his electronic pointer—"varied from 500 to about 900 pounds per square inch. This is considerably less than our initial estimate of 1,200 pounds per square inch."

Less than your initial estimate, Margo thought, glancing toward Frock.

Another photograph came on the screen. "Our detailed study of thin bone sections here, around the marks, shows blood leakage through the interstitial areas of the bone and into the marrow itself. That indicates they were made pre-mortem." There was a silence.

"In other words, the marks occurred at the time of death." Brambell cleared his throat. "Due to the highly advanced state of decomposition, it is impossible to determine a *definitive* cause of death. But I think we can say with fair certainty that these victims died of massive trauma and blood loss inflicted at the time these teeth marks were made."

He turned toward his audience dramatically. "There is, I know, a question on all of your minds. *The* question. What made these marks? As we know, there has been speculation in the press that the killer might be another Mbwun."

He's enjoying this, Margo thought. She could feel the tension building in the room. D'Agosta, in particular, was on the edge of his seat.

"We did a thorough analysis of these marks vis-à-vis those made by Mbwun eighteen months ago, which of course this Museum of all places has a great deal of data on. And we have come to two firm conclusions."

He took a deep breath and looked around.

"One, these teeth marks are not consistent with the teeth of Mbwun. They do not match the cross section, the size, or the length."

Margo saw D'Agosta's shoulders relax, almost slump, with relief.

"Two, the force used to make these marks never exceeded 900 pounds per square inch, which definitely puts it squarely in the canine, or even more squarely, in the *human* category. Not in the Mbwun category."

The slides were flashing by more quickly now, showing various micrographs of teeth marks and bite patterns. "A healthy, habitual gum-cracking male can exert 850 to 900 pounds per square inch of pressure with a hard bite," Brambell said. "There is nothing inconsistent between these marks and the bite of human eyeteeth. On the other hand, it could have been, say, a pack of feral dogs roaming the tunnels, attacking, killing, and dismembering. In my opinion, however, the patterns we see here are more suggestive of a human than of a dog, or any other hypothesized feral inhabitant of the underground."

"There are perhaps more types of underground inhabitants, Dr. Brambell, than are dreamt of in your philosophy."

The accent was from the deep south, perhaps Alabama or Louisiana; the laconic voice was soft, with the slightest hint of genteel cynicism. Margo turned to find the familiar lean figure of Special Agent Pendergast reclining in a seat near the top of the hall. She had neither seen nor heard him come in. He caught her glance and nodded, his pale eyes flashing in the dark. "Miss Green," he said. "Pardon me, it's Dr. Green now, isn't it?"

Margo smiled and nodded in return. She hadn't seen the FBI agent since the good-bye party in Frock's Museum office. Then again, that was the last time she had seen a lot of people involved in the Museum Beast murders: Dr. Frock, say, or Greg Kawakita.

Frock turned around in his wheelchair with an effort, nodded his recognition, then turned back toward the screen.

Brambell was looking at the new arrival. "You are—?" he began.

"Special Agent Pendergast of the FBI," replied D'Agosta "He'll be assisting us with this case."

"I see," Brambell said. "Delighted." He turned briskly back toward the screen. "Let's move on to the next question: the identification of the unknown body. I have some rather good news on this front. I'm afraid it may come as a surprise to my colleagues"—he nodded at Frock and Margo—"because it just recently came to my own attention."

Frock sat forward in his wheelchair, an unreadable expression on his face.

Margo looked back and forth between the two scientists. Was it possible that Brambell had kept them in the dark or something, intending to garner the credit himself?

"Please take a close look at this next slide." A new image appeared on the screen: the X ray showing the four white triangles that Margo had first noticed.

"Here we have four small triangles of metal embedded in the lumbar vertebrae of the unknown skeleton. We were all perplexed as to their meaning after Dr. Green here first pointed them out. Then, just last night, I had a stroke of inspiration as to their possible origin. I spent much of today in contact with orthopedic surgeons. If I am correct, we will know the identity of the murdered individual by the end of the week, perhaps sooner."

He grinned and gazed about the hall triumphantly, lingering for an insolent moment on Frock.

"I assume you believe those triangles to be—" Pendergast began.

"For the time being," Brambell interrupted pointedly, "I can say no more on the subject." He waved the remote and a new slide flashed up, showing an extensively decomposed head, eyes missing, teeth exposed in a lipless grin. Margo was as repelled by the sight as she had been when the head was first wheeled into the lab.

"As you all know, this head was also brought to us yesterday for analysis. It was discovered by Lieutenant D'Agosta while investigating recent murders among the homeless population. Although we won't be able to give you a full report for several more days, we know that it belongs to an indigent man who was murdered approximately two months ago. Numerous marks can be seen, some from teeth and some apparently from a crude weapon—again especially noticeable around the remaining cervical vertebrae. We're planning to have his corpse exhumed from Potter's Field for a more thorough investigation."

Oh no, Margo thought.

He flashed several more slides. "We studied the excoriation of the neck and concluded that, again, the force used was most consistent with a human attacker, certainly not Mbwun."

The screen flashed to white, and Brambell placed the pointing remote on a table next to him. As the lights came up, D'Agosta rose from his seat. "That's a bigger relief than you'll ever know," he said. "But let me get this straight. You're saying that a person made those bite marks?"

Brambell nodded.

"Not a dog or some other animal that might be living down in the sewers?"

"Given the nature and condition of the marks, it's hard to rule out a dog completely. But it's my belief that a human, or perhaps several humans, fit the bill better. If we had even one clear dentition pattern we would know, but, alas..." He spread his hands. "And if certain of those marks turn out to be made by a rough weapon of some sort, then a dog would obviously be out of the question."

"And you, Dr. Frock? What do you think?" D'Agosta turned.

"I concur with Dr. Brambell," Frock said curtly, shifting in his chair. "If you will recall," he rumbled, "I was the one who originally suggested that this was *not* the work of some creature like Mbwun. I am pleased to be vindicated. However, I must protest the way Dr. Brambell has proceeded on his own with the identification of Cadaver A."

"Duly noted," Brambell said, with a thin smile.

"A copycat killer," said the fat policeman triumphantly.

There was a silence.

The man stood up and looked around the room. "We've got a weirdo out there who was inspired by the Museum Beast," he said loudly. "Some nut running around, killing people, cutting off their heads, and maybe eating them."

"That," said Brambell, "is consistent with the data, except—"

The fat policeman cut him off. "A serial killer who is also a homeless man."

"Look, Captain Waxie," D'Agosta began, "that doesn't explain—"

"It explains everything!" the man named Waxie said obstinately.

Suddenly a door banged open at the top end of the hall, and a raised voice echoed angrily down over the group.

"Why the hell wasn't I told of this meeting?"

Margo turned, instantly recognizing the pitted face, the immaculate uniform, the heavy encrustation of stars and braids. It was Police Chief Horlocker, coming down the aisle at a brisk walk, followed by two aides.

A weary look flitted across D'Agosta's face before a mask of neutrality descended. "Chief, I sent—"

"What? A memo?" Glowering, Horlocker approached the row of seats where D'Agosta and Waxie were sitting. "Vinnie, the way I hear it, you made the same goddamn mistake at the Museum. You didn't involve the top brass from the beginning. You and that jackass Coffey kept insisting it was a serial killer, that you had it under control. By the time you realized what it really was, you had a museum full of dead people."

"If you'll pardon my saying so, Chief Horlocker, that's a highly inaccurate rendition of what happened." Pendergast's mellifluous voice rang clearly across the hall.

Margo watched Horlocker look toward the voice. "Who is this?" he demanded.

D'Agosta began to speak, but Pendergast raised his hand to stop him. "Allow me, Vincent. Chief Horlocker, I am Special Agent Pendergast of the FBI."

Horlocker frowned. "I've heard of you. You were part of that whole balls-up in the Museum, too."

"Colorful metaphor," Pendergast replied.

"So what is it you want, Pendergast?" Horlocker asked impatiently. "This isn't your jurisdiction."

"I'm assisting Lieutenant D'Agosta in an advisory capacity."

Horlocker frowned. "D'Agosta doesn't need any help."

"Forgive me for contradicting you," Pendergast said, "but I think he—and you—need all the help you can get." His eyes moved from Horlocker to Waxie, and back to Horlocker again. "Don't worry, Chief, I'm not after the collar. I'm here to help in profiling, not to scoop the case."

"Very reassuring," Horlocker snapped. He turned back to D'Agosta. "So?" he demanded. "What have you got?"

"The Medical Examiner believes he can ID the unknown skeleton by Friday," D'Agosta said. "And he thinks the teeth marks probably belong to a human. Or several."

"Several?" Horlocker asked.

"Chief, in my opinion the evidence is beginning to point to more than one perp," D'Agosta said. Brambell nodded his assent.

Horlocker looked pained. "What, you think we've got two cannibalistic psychos running around? For Chrissakes, Vinnie, use your head. What we've got is a homeless serial killer who's preying on his own kind. And once in a while a real person wanders into the wrong place at the wrong time—like Pamela Wisher, or that guy Bitterman—and gets their ass killed."

"A real person?" Pendergast murmured.

"You know what I mean. A productive member of society. Somebody with an address." Horlocker frowned, turning to D'Agosta. "I gave you a deadline, and I expected a lot more than this."

Waxie heaved himself up from his chair. "I'm convinced this is the work of a single perpetrator."

"Exactly," said Horlocker, looking around the room, waiting for a challenge. "Now, we've got a homeless man, out of his gourd, probably living in Central Park somewhere, who thinks he's the Museum Beast. And with this damn *Times* article, half the city's going apeshit." He turned to D'Agosta. "So how are you planning to handle it?"

"*Du calme, du calme,* Chief," Pendergast said soothingly. "I have often found it true that the louder a person speaks, the less they have to say."

Horlocker looked at him in disbelief. "You can't talk to me like that."

"On the contrary, I'm the only one in this room who *can* talk to you like that," Pendergast drawled. "So it is left up to me to point out that you have made a string of quite remarkable and unsupported assumptions. First, that the murderer is a homeless man. Second, that he lives in Central Park. Third, that he is psychotic. And fourth, that there is only one of them." Pendergast gazed at the Chief almost benignly, like a patient parent humoring a fretful child. "You've managed to cram a remarkably large number of guesses into just one sentence, Chief Horlocker."

Horlocker stared at Pendergast, opened his mouth, closed it again. He took a step forward, then stopped. Then, with a single blazing glance at D'Agosta, he turned on his heel and strode out of the hall, his aides scampering to keep up with him.

There was silence in the wake of the slamming door. "What a bloody charade," Margo heard Frock mutter as he moved restlessly in his wheelchair.

D'Agosta sighed and turned to Brambell. "You'd better send a copy of your report to the Chief. Edit it down, okay, so only the really important stuff is there. And put in a lot of pictures; try to make it readable. Like at a fourth-grade level."

Brambell burst into delighted, high-pitched laughter. "Yes, indeed, Lieutenant," he cackled, his bald dome incandescent in the glow of the projector. "I will do my literary best."

Margo watched as Waxie shot both of them a disapproving look, then started for the door himself. "I don't find this humor at the expense of the Chief very professional," he said. "I, for one, have more important things to do than joke around."

D'Agosta stared at him. "On second thought," he said slowly, "make it third-grade level, so that Captain Waxie here can read it, too."

From his aerie in the projectionist's booth high up on the rear wall, Smithback drew back from the observation slit and switched off his tape recorder with satisfaction. He waited, listening, as the last of the attendees left Linnaeus Hall.

The projectionist came in from the control room, his features narrowing as he saw Smithback. "You said—"

The journalist waved his hand. "I know what I said. I didn't want to make you any more nervous than you already were. Here." Smithback pulled a twenty out of his wallet and handed it to him.

"I wouldn't take it, except the Museum's salaries are ridiculous; you can't even begin to live in New York..." The fellow nervously stuffed the bill into his pocket.

"Yeah," Smithback replied, taking a final glance out of the observation slit. "Listen, you don't have to explain it to me. You're contributing to freedom of the press. Go buy yourself a nice dinner, okay? And don't worry. Even if they put me in jail, I wouldn't reveal my sources."

"Jail?" the projectionist whinnied. Smithback soothed him with a pat on the back, then ducked out of the booth into the control room, clutching his notebook and tape recorder and passing into the old, dusty corridors he remembered so well. He was in luck: old Pocahontas—nicknamed for the ferocity with which she slashed rouge across her generous cheeks—was manning the north exit. He passed her in a flurry of smiles and salacious winks, his thumb discreetly covering the expiration date on his aging Museum ID card.

19

Margo pushed through the revolving door of the 27th Precinct House, made a sharp left, and trotted down the long, steep staircase to the basement. The banister had been removed from the ancient yellow wall decades before, and she had to take care not to slip on the concrete steps. Despite the thickness of the stone foundations around her, she could hear muffled popping sounds below long before she reached the bottom of the staircase.

As she yanked open the heavily soundproofed door on the landing, the muffled pops turned suddenly to roars. Wincing against the noise, she stepped forward to the duty desk. The officer recognized her and waved dismissively as she began to pull the letter of privilege and special permit from her carryall. "Take number seventeen," he said over the blasts, passing over a dozen target sheets and a set of battered ear cups.

Margo scribbled her name and entry time in the book, then turned and walked down the gallery, putting on the ear cups as she did so. Immediately, the roaring became bearable once more. To her left, the line of police officers in their open-topped booths ran almost unbroken to the far wall of the range: reloading, clipping targets, assessing results. Early evening was a popular time. And of the dozen twenty-five-yard indoor ranges scattered across the NYPD station houses, the 27th Precinct boasted the largest and best-equipped.

Reaching booth seventeen, she removed her weapon, a box of 120-grain FMJ ammunition, and some spare clips from the carryall. Placing the ammunition on a ledge at her side, she inspected the small autoloader. The movements were as habitual now as they had been foreign a year before, when she'd first purchased the gun. Satisfied, she slapped a full clip home, pinned a standard target to the guide line, and ran it out to ten yards. Then she quickly settled into the Weaver stance, as she'd been taught: right hand on trigger, left hand gripping the right in the classic push-pull dynamic. Focusing on the front sight, she squeezed the trigger, letting her bent elbows absorb the recoil. She stopped a moment to squint at the target, then quickly emptied the rest of the ten-round clip toward it.

She went through several more clips almost mechanically, settling into the standard firing range routine: reload, reset target, fire. When the ammunition box was half empty, she switched to silhouette targets at twenty-five yards. Emptying the final clip at last, she turned away to clean her weapon and was surprised to see Lieutenant D'Agosta behind her, arms folded, watching.

"Hi," she said, removing her ear cups and shouting over the din.

D'Agosta nodded toward her target. "Let's see how you did," he mouthed, and waited for her to pull the silhouette in. "Nice rosette," he said approvingly.

Margo laughed. "Thanks," she said. "I have you to thank for that. Just like I have you to thank for the permit." She dumped the empty clips into her carryall, thinking about how strange it must have seemed to D'Agosta at the time: her bursting into his office three months after the conclusion of the Museum murders, asking him to arrange for a handgun permit. For protection, she'd told him. How could she have brought herself to explain the lingering fear, the sweat-drenched nightmares, the feeling of vulnerability that plagued her?

"Brad told me you were a good student," D'Agosta said. "I figured you'd get on well, that's why I recommended him. But as for the permit, you don't have me to thank. Pendergast took care of it personally. Now, let's see what kind of gun Brad set you up with."

Margo handed it over. "It's a baby Glock. Model 26, with a factory-modified 'New York trigger.'"

D'Agosta hefted it. "Nice and light. Short sight radius, though."

"Your friend Brad was very helpful with that. Taught me Kentucky windage, helped me set up the adjustable sight. I've done all my training with it. I'd probably be useless with anything else."

"I doubt it." D'Agosta handed the subcompact back. "With scores like those, you could probably handle just about anything." He nodded toward the exit. "Come on, let's get away from this noise. I'll walk you out."

Margo stopped at the desk to sign out and return the ear cups, and was surprised when D'Agosta signed the log as well. "You were shooting?" she asked.

"Why not?" D'Agosta turned to her. "Even old farts like me get rusty." They stepped out of the range and began climbing the long, steep staircase. "Actually, cases like this get everybody on edge," he said. "A little practice seemed like a good idea. Especially after that briefing."

Margo didn't bother to reply. At the top of the steps, she stopped and waited for the Lieutenant to catch up. He emerged, puffing slightly, and they passed through the revolving door onto 31st Street. It was a cool evening, and traffic was light. Margo looked at her watch: almost eight. She could jog home, fix herself a light dinner, then try to catch up on her sleep.,

"I'll bet those damn stairs have caused more coronaries than all the pastry in New York," D'Agosta said. "Doesn't seem to have bothered you any, though."

Margo shrugged. "I've been working out."

"So I noticed. You're not the same person I met eighteen months ago. Not on the outside, anyway. What's your routine?"

"Strength workout, mostly. You know, high weight, low reps."

D'Agosta nodded. "Couple times a week?"

"I work the upper and lower muscle groups on alternating days. I try to work in some interval training, as well."

"What are you currently benching? One twenty?"

Margo shook her head. "One thirty-five, actually. It's nice, because for the first time I don't have to change all those little weights on the bar. I can just use the forty-fives."

D'Agosta nodded again. "Not bad." They started toward Sixth Avenue. "And has it worked?"

"Excuse me?"

"I said, has it worked?"

Margo frowned. "I don't know what you mean," she replied, but even as she said the words, she understood.

"No," she said a moment later, in a lower voice. "Not completely, anyway."

"Don't mean to be nosy," D'Agosta replied, patting his pockets, absently searching for a cigar. "I'm a blunt kind of guy, just in case you didn't know." Finding one, he picked off the label with his fingernail and inspected the wrapper. "That shit at the Museum affected all of us, I suppose."

They reached the avenue, and Margo hesitated a moment, looking northward. "Sorry," she said. "I guess it's just hard for me to talk about."

"I know," D'Agosta said. "Especially now." There was a brief silence as he lit up. "Take good care of yourself, Dr. Green."

Margo smiled slightly. "You too. And thanks again for this." She patted her carryall, then eased into a jog, moving northward through the traffic, aiming for the West Side and home.

20

D'Agosta looked at his watch: 10:00 P.M., and they still had jack shit to show for all their work. Details of beat cops had checked the shelters, redemption centers, and soup kitchens, searching fruitlessly for word of anyone who might have an excessive interest in Mbwun. Hayward, whose knowledge of the underground homeless was becoming an ever more valuable resource, had led a number of special rousting details. Unfortunately, the results had also been disappointing: the moles had melted before their sweeps, disappearing into ever darker and more obscure recesses. Besides, as Hayward explained, the sweeps could only scratch the surface of the vast tunnel networks beneath the city's streets. At least the stream of nutcases calling in to claim the *Post* reward was beginning to slow to a trickle. Maybe everyone was too worried about the *Times* report and the Bitterman murder.

He looked down at his desk, still buried under the half-coordinated results of the sweeps. Then he glanced up at the precinct board for the hundredth time that evening, staring fixedly at the map as if the fierceness of his glare would force it to yield up an answer. What was the pattern? There had to be one; it was the first rule of detective work.

He didn't give a shit what Horlocker said: his gut told him that these killings were the work of more than one murderer. And it wasn't only his gut—there were just too many; and the MOs, while similar, weren't similar enough: some decapitated, some with their heads crushed, others simply mutilated. Perhaps it was some kind of truly screwed-up cult. But whatever it turned out to be, Horlocker's threatening deadlines were time-consuming distractions. What was needed here was patient, methodical, intelligent detective work.

D'Agosta laughed to himself. *Christ, I'm sounding more like Pendergast all the time.*

From beyond the closed door of the storage room at one side of his office, he began to make out a series of odd shuffling noises. Hayward had gone in there a few minutes earlier on her coffee break. He stared at the door for a moment while the noises continued. At last, he rose, walked to the door, turned the handle, and stepped in. Hayward stood in the middle of the storage room, crouched in an animal-like stance, her left hand stuck rigidly in front of her like an arrow, her right cocked back to the side of her head. Her hands were tensed and slightly curved, bent thumbs protruding upward. As he watched, she swiveled her small form through ninety degrees of the compass, reversed the position of her arms in a silent punching motion, then turned another ninety degrees. It looked like some kind of dangerous ballet.

The movements were punctuated by sharp exhalations, not unlike the breathing she'd done during the confrontation in the tunnels. As he watched, she swiveled again, facing him this time, and brought her hands together in front of her with a slow, deliberate motion.

"Need something, Lieutenant?" she asked.

"Just an explanation of what the hell you're doing," he replied.

Hayward straightened up slowly to her full height, released a deep breath, then looked up at him. "It's one of the *heian* series of kata."

"What's that again?"

"Formal exercises of *shotokan* karate," she said. Then she caught his look. "It helps keep me relaxed, in shape," she explained. "And it *is my* break, Lieutenant."

"Then get on with it." D'Agosta turned toward the door, then stopped and looked back. "What's your belt?"

She looked up at him for a moment. "White," she replied at last.

"I see."

Hayward smiled slightly. "*Shotokan* is the original Japanese school of karate. They don't usually believe in all sorts of pastel belt colors, Lieutenant. There are six degrees of white belt, three brown, then black."

D'Agosta nodded. "So what degree are you?" he asked curiously.

"I go for my *sankyu* brown belt examination next month."

From his office beyond D'Agosta could hear the rattle of a knob. Stepping out of the supply room and closing the door behind him, he found himself looking at the corpulent form of Captain Waxie. Without a word, Waxie sauntered over to the precinct board. He studied the riot of red and white pins intently, hands clasped behind his back.

"There's a pattern here," he said at last.

"Really?" D'Agosta asked, fighting to keep his voice neutral.

Waxie nodded sagely, keeping his back turned.

D'Agosta said nothing. He knew he was going to regret to his dying day bringing Waxie into the case.

"It originates *here*." Waxie's finger hit a green spot on the map with a soft thump. D'Agosta saw that he had fingered the Ramble, the wildest area of Central Park.

"How do you figure?"

"Simple," said Waxie. "The Chief had a talk with the top actuary in human resources. He looked at the murder locations, did a best-fit linear analysis, and said they were radiating right from this spot. See? The deaths form a semicircle around this point. The Belvedere Castle murder was the key."

He turned. "Out there in the Ramble, there are rocks, caves, dense woods. Lots of homeless, too. It's a perfect hideout. *That's* where we'll find the killer."

This time, D'Agosta was unable to keep the incredulity off his face. "Let me get this straight. Some insurance dweeb in *personnel* gave you this tip? Did he try to sell you on the savings plan, too?"

Waxie frowned, his jowly cheeks turning a rich crimson. "I don't appreciate your tone, Vinnie. It wasn't appropriate in the meeting this afternoon, and it isn't appropriate here."

"Look, Jack," D'Agosta said, struggling to keep his patience. "What the hell would an actuary, even a police actuary, know about a murder pattern? That just isn't enough. You have to take into account ingress, egress, everything. Besides, the Belvedere Castle murder is the one that *least* fits the pattern." Then he gave up. There was no point in telling Waxie anything. Horlocker was one of those chiefs who loved specialists, experts, and consultants. And Waxie was such a yes-man that...

"I'm going to need this map," Waxie said.

D'Agosta stared at the broad back in front of him. As he did, a light suddenly turned on inside his head. Now he knew what this was all about.

He stood up. "Be my guest," he said. "The primary case files are in these cabinets here, and Sergeant Hayward has some valuable—"

"I won't be needing her," said Waxie. "Just the precinct board and the files. Have them sent over to my office by eight tomorrow morning. Suite 2403. They're moving me here to headquarters."

He slowly turned on his heel and eyed D'Agosta. "Sorry, Vinnie. I think it boiled down to a question of chemistry. Me and Horlocker. He needs someone he can relate to. Someone who can keep a lid on the press. Nothing personal, you know. You'll still be on the case, in one capacity or another. And now that we're going to start making progress, you might even feel better about things. We'll be staking out the Ramble, and we're going to catch this guy."

"Sure," said D'Agosta. He reminded himself that this was a no-win case, that he hadn't wanted it in the first place. It didn't help.

Waxie held out his hand. "No hard feelings, Vinnie?"

D'Agosta shook the plump warm hand. "None at all, Jack," he heard himself saying.

Waxie took another look around the office, as if searching for other items worth appropriating. "Well, I gotta go," he said at last. "I wanted to tell you in person."

"Thanks."

They stood for a moment as the uncomfortable silence grew. Then Waxie patted him awkwardly on the shoulder and walked out of the office.

There was a soft rustle as Hayward came up beside him. They stood silently, listening to the footsteps retreat down the linoleum corridor until they were finally lost amidst the low buzz of typing and distant conversations. Then Hayward turned to D'Agosta.

"Lieutenant, how can you let him get away with it?" she asked bitterly. "I mean, when our backs were against the wall down in those tunnels, that mother ran."

D'Agosta sat down again, feeling inside the upper drawer of his desk for a cigar. "Respect for superiors isn't your strong suit, is it, Sergeant?" he asked. "Anyway, what makes you so sure this isn't a reward?" He located the cigar, dug a hole in its crown with a pencil, and lit up.

It was two hours later, as D'Agosta was making final arrangements to move the case files upstairs, that Pendergast strolled into his office. It was Pendergast as D'Agosta remembered him: impeccable black suit severely tailored to his spare frame, blond-white hair combed back from his high forehead, handmade English loafers in polished oxblood. As usual, looking more like a fashionable undertaker than an FBI agent.

Pendergast indicated the visitor's chair with a brief nod of his head. "May I?"

D'Agosta hung up the phone and nodded. Pendergast slipped into the chair with his catlike grace. He looked around, taking in the boxed files and the bare patch on the wall where the map had once hung. He turned back to D'Agosta, eyebrows raised quizzically.

"It's Waxie's headache now." D'Agosta answered the unspoken question. "I've been placed on modified assignment."

"Indeed," Pendergast replied. "Lieutenant, you don't seem dismayed by the turn of events."

"Dismayed?" D'Agosta said. "Look around again. The precinct board's gone, the files are packed, Hayward's in bed, the coffee is hot, the cigar is lit. I feel terrific."

"I doubt it very much. Still, you'll probably sleep better tonight than Squire Waxie will. 'Uneasy lies the head that wears the crown,' and all that." He looked at D'Agosta with an amused expression. "So what's next?"

"Oh, I'm still assigned to the case," D'Agosta replied. "Exactly how, Waxie hasn't bothered to say."

"He probably doesn't know himself. But I think we can ensure that you won't be sitting idle." Pendergast fell silent and D'Agosta leaned back in his chair, enjoying his cigar, content to let the silence spread out to fill the room.

"I was once in Florence," Pendergast said at last.

"Oh, yeah? I was just in Italy. Took my son there last fall to see his great-grandmother."

Pendergast nodded. "Did you visit the Pitti Palace?"

"Pity who?"

"It's an art museum, actually. Quite exquisite. There's an old medieval map painted as a fresco on one of its walls, done the year before Columbus discovered America."

"No kidding."

"In the place where the continent of America would later be found, the map is blank except for the words *Qui ci sono dei mostri.*"

D'Agosta screwed up his face. "Here there are... *mostri.* What's that?"

"It means, 'Here there be monsters.'"

"Monsters. Yeah. Jesus, I've forgotten my Italian. I used to speak it with my grandparents."

Pendergast nodded. "Lieutenant, I want you to hazard a guess at something for me."

"Shoot."

"Guess the largest inhabited region on earth that remains unmapped."

D'Agosta shrugged. "I don't know. Milwaukee?"

Pendergast smiled mirthlessly. "No. And it's not Outer Mongolia. Or the Antipodes. It's underground New York."

"You're shitting me, right?"

"I am not 'shitting you,' as you so charmingly put it." Pendergast shifted in his chair. "Vincent, underground New York reminds me of that map in the Pitti Palace. It is truly unexplored territory. And it is, apparently, unimaginably vast. For example, there are almost a dozen stories' worth of structures below Grand Central—not counting the sewers and storm drains. The levels below Penn Station go even deeper."

"So you've been down," D'Agosta said.

"Yes. After meeting with you and Sergeant Hayward. It was an exploratory journey, really. I wanted to get a sense of the environment, test my ability to move around and learn what I could. I was able to speak with a few of the underground dwellers. They told me much, and they hinted at even more."

D'Agosta sat forward. "Learn anything about the murders?"

Pendergast nodded. "Indirectly. But those who know the most are deeper underground than I dared go on my first descent. It takes a while to gain these people's trust, and I have a long way to go. Especially now. You see, the underground homeless are terrified." Pendergast turned his pale eyes toward D'Agosta. "From piecing together various whispered conversations, I've gathered that a mysterious group of people have colonized the underground. And most of the rumors don't even use the word *people*. Supposedly, they are feral, cannibalistic, subhuman. And it is these beings who are responsible for the killings."

There was a pause. D'Agosta stood and moved to the window, gazing out at the nocturnal cityscape of Manhattan. "You believe this?" he asked at last.

"I don't know," Pendergast replied. "I need to speak to Mephisto, the leader of the community beneath Columbus Circle. Many of the things he told the *Post* in that recent article ring disturbingly true. Unfortunately, he's a difficult man to contact. He is distrustful of all outsiders and hates the authorities with a passion. But I feel he is the one person who can lead me where I have to go."

D'Agosta's lips twitched. "Need a partner?" he asked.

A small smile appeared on Pendergast's face, then disappeared again. "It's an extremely dangerous and lawless place. However, I will consider the offer. Fair enough?"

D'Agosta nodded.

"Good. Now, I suggest you go home and get some sleep." Pendergast rose. "Although he doesn't know it, friend Waxie is going to need all the help he can get."

21

Simon Brambell zippered up his portfolio, humming "Macushla" to himself. He cast a loving glance over the lab: the safety shower in the corner, the rows of chrome and steel instruments lined up neatly behind glass, winking at him in the subdued light. He was feeling enormously pleased with himself. Once again, he replayed in his head the scene of his little coup, in particular the impassive look on Frock's face as he'd been speaking. Impassive, yet no doubt fuming inside. It made up for Frock's little sneer of triumph over the strength of the bites. Though he worked for the city government, Brambell enjoyed the one-upmanship of academia as much as anybody.

He tucked the soft leather portfolio under his shoulder and once again cast his eyes about the laboratory. It was a wonderful laboratory, well designed and well equipped. He longed for something as elegant and comprehensive at the Medical Examiner's office. It would never happen, he knew; the city was chronically short of money. If he didn't find the detective work of forensic pathology so absorbing, he'd move to some well-endowed ivory tower in half a second.

He closed the door behind him softly, surprised as always by the emptiness of the corridor. He'd never seen a bunch so averse to working late as the Museum staff. Still, he didn't mind the quiet. It was refreshing and different, just as the Museum's smell of dust and old wood was so different from the stench of formalin and decay that pervaded the Medical Examiner's office. He decided to take the long way out of the Museum, as he did every evening, through the Hall of Africa. He found the dioramas in that particular hall to be true works of art. And they looked especially good at such an advanced hour, the hall lights turned off, each diorama glowing with internal light like a window into another world.

He walked down the long corridor and, being averse to elevators, skipped down three flights of stairs. Passing beneath a metal archway, he found himself in the Hall of Ocean Life. Only the nocturnal lighting was on, and the hall looked dark and mysterious, quiet except for the ever-present clicks, groans, and creakings of the ancient fabric of the Museum. *Lovely,* he thought. This was the way to see the Museum, with all those horrid shrieking children and their braying teachers absent. He passed under the replica of a giant squid, through a brace of yellowed elephant tusks, and entered the Hall of Africa.

Midnight. He passed slowly through the hall, the herd of elephants at its center barely emerging from the darkness, the habitat groups arranged in a double tier around the walls on both sides of him. The gorilla group was his favorite, and he paused in front of it, pursing his lips, letting himself merge with the scene. It was so very real, and he wanted to enjoy it. Things would be wrapping up here very soon; his work was almost done. If he was right, this poor Bitterman fellow and the remains of Shasheen Walker would fall right into the pattern.

At last, he turned with a sigh under a low doorway, then down a stone corridor toward the Tower. He knew the story of the famous Tower: how in 1870 Endurance S. Flyte, railroad baron and third director of the NYMNH, had commissioned a monstrous, fortresslike addition to the original Museum building. It was to be modeled after the Welsh castle of Caernarvon, which

Flyte had tried—unsuccessfully—to purchase for himself. Saner heads eventually prevailed, and Flyte was removed from office with only the central tower of his fortress completed. Now the cornerstone of the institution's southwest facade, the six-sided Tower was used primarily to store the Museum's endless collections. It was also, Brambell had heard, a favorite trysting place for the more ghoulish-minded of the Museum's staff.

The dim, cathedral-like hall at the base of the Tower was empty, and Brambell's footsteps echoed hollowly as he crossed the marble floor toward the staff exit. Nodding at the guard, he passed into the humid night air of Museum Drive. It was midnight, but the avenue beyond was still bustling with people and taxis.

He took a few steps, then looked back in admiration. No matter how many times he saw it, he'd never get tired of staring at that Tower. Rearing several hundred feet into the air, topped by fanglike crenelations, it threw a dark shadow as far south as 59th Street on cloudless days. Tonight, pale under the light of a waxing moon, it looked troubled, full of ghosts.

At last, with a sigh, he started forward again, turned the corner onto 81st, then walked west toward the Hudson and his modest apartment, once again humming under his breath. As he went, the street gradually took on a seedier character, and the number of pedestrians began to dwindle. But Brambell took no notice, walking briskly, inhaling the night air. There was a lovely breeze blowing in, crisp and sharp, ideal for a midsummer's night. A bite of dinner, a quick washing-up, a toothful of Green Spot, and he'd be between the covers in an hour. As usual, he'd be up at 5:00 A.M., being one of those fortunate people who needed hardly any sleep. It was a great advantage to a medical examiner not to need sleep, especially one who wanted to get to the top of his profession. Brambell couldn't begin to count the number of times he'd been the first on the scene of an important crime, simply by virtue of being awake when everybody else was fast asleep.

The neighborhood looked even seedier now, but it was only a block to Broadway and its bustling bagel shops, bookstores, and delis. Brambell walked along the row of shabby brownstones, now subdivided into Single Room Occupancies and tiny apartments. A few harmless drunks lingered at the far corner.

As he reached the center of the block, he detected movement out of the corner of his eye: something in the dark well of the basement entrance of an abandoned walk-up. He hastened his step. There was an unusually foul odor wafting from the dark entrance, pungent even for New York. Hearing something moving swiftly along the sidewalk behind him now, he instinctually reached into his portfolio for the scalpel he always carried. His mouth tightened as his fingers closed on its cold ergonomic handle. He felt no real alarm; he'd been mugged once at gunpoint and twice at knifepoint, and he now knew exactly how to handle things. He drew the scalpel from the portfolio as he spun around, but there was nothing there. He looked around for a moment in surprise before an arm slid around his neck and dragged him into the darkness. He assumed, in a surprisingly detached sort of way, that it was an arm; it had to be an arm, yet it felt slippery and so very strong. Then, almost immediately, he felt a curious digging sensation just below his Adam's apple. Yes, it was a most curious sensation, indeed.

22

Margo unlocked the door to the Forensic Anthropology laboratory, smugly pleased to find the room dark and empty. This was the first morning she'd managed to beat Dr. Brambell into work. Most mornings, he would be sitting on a lab stool when she arrived, sipping a cup of Museum coffee and arching his narrow eyebrows over the rim at her in greeting. He would then go on to point out that the Museum must percolate its coffee in secondhand formaldehyde borrowed from the Animal Conservation department. Other mornings, she would arrive to find Frock in before her as well, the two scientists bent over a table or a report, carrying on their usual argument in polite undertones.

She slung her carryall into a drawer and shrugged into her scrubs, stepping over to the window as she did so. The sun had broken over the Fifth Avenue buildings, bathing the magisterial frontage in hues of gold and copper. Below the window, the Park was waking up: mothers walking children toward the zoo, joggers trotting the long oval course around the Reservoir. Her eye moved southward, lighting at last on the purple bulk of Belvedere Castle, and she shuddered slightly as she stared into the dark wooded area at its rear where Nicholas Bitterman had met with violent death. His headless corpse, she knew, was due to arrive in their lab later that morning.

The door opened and Dr. Frock wheeled himself inside, a large silhouette against the dimness of the lab. As he came forward into the sunlight, Margo turned to wish him good morning. Seeing the expression on his face, she stopped short.

"Dr. Frock?" she asked. "Are you all right?"

He came toward her slowly, the normally ruddy face drawn and pale.

"There's tragic news," he said in a low voice. "I received a call very early this morning. Simon Brambell was murdered last night on his way home from the Museum."

Margo frowned, drawing in her breath. "Simon Brambell?" she repeated, uncomprehending.

Frock rolled closer and took her hand. "I'm sorry to be the one to tell you, my dear," he said. "This is all so horribly sudden."

"But how?" Margo asked.

"It appears he was attacked on Eighty-first Street," Frock said. "His throat was cut. Beyond that..." Frock spread his hands, which Margo noticed were shaking with emotion.

It seemed unreal, like some kind of dream; she could not believe the man who had been standing in front of that huge screen the previous afternoon, manipulating the remote pointer like a samurai sword, was now dead.

Frock sighed. "Though you may not have known it, Margo, Simon and I didn't always see eye to eye. We had our professional differences. But I always had great respect for the man. It's a huge loss to the Medical Examiner's office. And to our work, coming at this critical moment."

"Our work," echoed Margo automatically. She paused. "But who did it?"

"There were no witnesses."

They remained motionless for a moment, Frock's hand on hers, warm and gently reassuring. Then he slowly rolled away. "I don't know who the ME's office will give us as a replacement, if anyone," he said. "But I think Simon would want us to continue in the spirit in which he began." He rolled over to the far wall and switched on the theater lights, flooding the center of the room. "I've always found work the best antidote for grief." He was silent for a long moment. Then he sighed, as if forcing himself to continue. "Would you mind removing Cadaver A from the refrigerator? I have a theory about a potential genetic anomaly that might have caused this deformity. Unless you would like the day off?" He raised his eyebrows.

"No," Margo said, shaking her head. Frock was right. Brambell would want them to continue. Standing slowly and walking across the room, she knelt, opened a cabinet door, and pulled out the long metal tray inside. The unidentified body which lay on it had been reduced and rearranged to a mere series of irregular lumps under the blue sheet. She slid it onto a stretcher and rolled it under the lights.

Frock carefully pulled off the sheet and began the painstaking process of measuring the carpal bones of the deformed skeleton with a pair of electronic calipers. Feeling an eerie sense of unreality, Margo went back to examining yet another series of MRI scans. The lab fell into a long silence.

"Do you have any idea what lead Simon was referring to yesterday?" Frock asked at last.

"I'm sorry?" Margo said, looking up. "Oh. No, I don't. He never discussed it with me. I was as surprised as you were."

"A shame," said Frock. "As far as I know, he left no notes about it, either." He fell silent again for some time. "This is a real setback, Margo," he said at last in a quiet voice. "We may never learn what it is he discovered."

"Nobody ever makes their plans as if they're going to die the next day."

Frock shook his head. "Simon was like most of the MEs I've known. Exciting, high-profile cases like this are rare, and when one comes along... well, they can't always resist the drama." He looked suddenly at his watch. "Oh, dear. You know, I almost forgot that I have an appointment in Osteology. Margo, I wonder if you would be willing to leave that aside and take over here for a while. Maybe it's this tragic news, or maybe I've just been staring at these bones too long. But I think the work could benefit from a fresh eye."

"Of course," said Margo. "What exactly are you looking for?"

"I wish I knew. I'm quite sure this person had a congenital disease. I want to quantify the morphological changes to see if there's been a genetic shift. Unfortunately, that means measuring almost every bone in the body. I thought I'd start with the wrist and finger bones, since as you know they're the most sensitive to genetic change."

Margo looked down at the examining table. "That could take days," she said.

Frock shrugged in exasperation. "I'm only too aware of that, my dear." He gripped the rails of his wheelchair and gave himself a powerful push toward the door.

Wearily, Margo began measuring each bone with the electronic calipers and entering the measurements on the workstation keyboard. Even the smallest bones required a dozen measurements, and soon a long column of numbers was scrolling up the nearby screen. She tried not to grow impatient with the tedious work and the tomblike silence of the lab. If Frock was right, and the deformation was congenital, this would greatly narrow their search for the identity of the body. And at this point, they could use any lead they could find: the skeletons from the Physical Anthropology lab had provided no clues. As she worked, she found herself wondering what Brambell would have thought. But the memory of Brambell was too awful. To think of the man, set upon and murdered... She shook her head, forcing herself to concentrate on other things.

The sudden ringing of the telephone jarred her from a particularly complicated measurement. It rang again—two short beeps—and she realized it was an outside call. Probably D'Agosta, calling about Dr. Brambell.

She picked it up. "Forensics."

"Is Dr. Brambell there?" asked a clipped, youthful-sounding voice.

"Dr. Brambell?" Margo's thoughts raced. What if it was a relative? What should she say?

"Hello?" came the voice.

"Yes, yes," said Margo. "Dr. Brambell isn't available. Can I help you?"

"I'm not sure. It's a confidential matter. May I ask who I'm speaking to?"

"The name is Dr. Green," said Margo. "I'm assisting him."

"Ah! That's fine, then. This is Dr. Cavalieri from St. Luke's in Baltimore. I've identified that patient he's looking for."

"Patient?"

"Yes, the one with the spondylolisthesis." Margo could hear the shuffling of paper on the other end of the line. "This is one bizarre set of X rays you sent me. At first I thought there was some kind of joke. I almost missed it."

Margo fumbled for a pad of paper and a pencil. "You'd better start from the beginning."

"Fine," came the voice. "I'm an orthopedic surgeon down in Baltimore. There are only three of us here who do corrective surgery to reduce a spondylolisthesis. Dr. Brambell knew that, of course."

"Spondylolisthesis?"

There was a silence. "You're not a physician?" Cavalieri asked, his tone suddenly disapproving.

Margo took a deep breath. "Dr. Cavalieri, I might as well tell you. Dr. Brambell was... well, he died last night. I'm an evolutionary biologist helping him analyze the remains of several homicide victims. Since Dr. Brambell is no longer here, I'll need you to tell me everything."

"Died? Why, I just spoke to him yesterday!"

"It was very sudden," said Margo. She did not want to go into any more detail.

"But that's terrible. Dr. Brambell was well known across the country, not to mention the United Kingdom..."

The voice petered out. Margo, holding the silent phone to her ear, thought again about the last time she'd seen the Medical Examiner: at the front of Linnaeus Hall, smiling deviously, eyes flashing behind the horn-rims.

She was roused by a sigh on the other end of the line. "A spondylolisthesis is a fracture and slippage of one of the lumbar vertebrae. We correct it by fixing a metal plate to the spine with pedicle lag screws. As you tighten the screws to the plate, it draws the fractured vertebrae back into place."

"I'm not sure I see the connection," Margo said.

"Do you remember those four white triangles on the X rays Dr. Brambell sent me? Those are the lags for the plate screws. This fellow had an operation for spondylolisthesis. Very few surgeons do the procedure, which makes it easy to trace."

"I see," said Margo.

"I know that this X ray is from a patient of mine, for one very good reason," Cavalieri continued. "It's clear that these particular lag bolts were manufactured by Steel-Med Products of Minneapolis, which went out of business in 1989. I performed about three dozen operations using Steel-Med lag screws. I used a special technique of my own, a particular placement of the screws behind the transverse process of the second lumbar. A rather brilliant technique, actually. You can read about it in the Fall 1987 issue of the *Journal of American Orthopedics,* if you're interested. It held the bone better, you see, and required less bone fusion. No one else performed it but myself and two residents I instructed. Of course, it was considered obsolete after the Steinmann procedure was developed. So in the end I was the only doctor who used it." Margo could hear the pride in the doctor's voice.

"But here's the mystery: no surgeon that I ever knew would *remove* the corrective plate for this kind of spondylolisthesis.

It simply isn't done. Yet these X rays clearly show that my patient had the metal plate and screws removed, God knows why, leaving only the lags behind. You can't remove the lags, of course; they're set into the bone. But why this fellow had the plate removed..." his voice trailed off.

Margo scribbled notes furiously. "Go on."

"As I said, when I saw the X rays, I knew immediately that this was one of my patients. However, I was astonished at the condition of the skeleton. That *riot* of bone growth. I knew I'd never operated on anyone with a condition like that."

"So the bone growth occurred afterwards?"

"Absolutely. In any case, I went back to my records and, based on the X-ray evidence, I was able to identify the patient. I operated on him the morning of October 2, 1988."

"And who was the patient?" Margo asked, pencil at the ready. Out of the corner of her eye she saw that Frock had reentered the lab and was rolling toward her, listening intently.

"It's right here somewhere." She could hear another rustling of papers. "I'll fax all these records to you, of course, but I'm sure you'll still want... here we are. The patient was named Gregory S. Kawakita."

Margo felt her blood freeze. "Greg Kawakita?" she croaked.

"Yes, Gregory S. Kawakita, Ph.D. No question about it. Funny, it says here that he was an evolutionary biologist, too. Maybe you knew him?"

Margo hung up the telephone, unable to speak. First Dr. Brambell, and now—She glanced at Frock, alarmed to see that his face had gone ashen. He was slumped to one side of the wheelchair, a hand pressed hard to his chest, his breathing labored.

"Gregory *Kawakita*?" Frock breathed. "This is Gregory? Oh, my good lord."

His breathing eased, and he shut his eyes and slowly hung his head. Margo turned quickly and ran to the window, choking back sobs.

Of its own accord, her mind flashed back to that horrible week eighteen months before, when the murders started at the Museum. Then, the opening of the *Superstition* exhibition, the mass slaughter, and the final killing of the Mbwun. Greg Kawakita had been an assistant curator at the Museum, a colleague of hers, a student of Frock's. More than anyone else, Greg had helped identify and stop the monster. It had been his genetic extrapolation program that provided the key, that told them what Mbwun was, and how it could be killed. But the horror that followed had affected everyone, especially Greg. He'd left the Museum soon after, abandoning a brilliant career. No one had heard from him since.

No one except her. He'd tried to reach her, leaving a message on her answering machine several months before. At the time, he said he'd needed something, needed her help. She hadn't even bothered to respond.

And now she could guess why he must have left the Museum: he'd been suffering from some dreadful disease that was deforming his bones, turning him slowly into that twisted skeleton on the gurney. No doubt he was ashamed, probably afraid. Perhaps he had tried to seek treatment. Maybe toward the end he had become homeless. And then, the ultimate insult to a life once so full of promise: murder, decapitation, the frenzied gnawing of bones in the dark.

She stared out the window, shuddering in the warm sun. Whatever end he had suffered, it must have been horrible. Perhaps she could have helped him, had she known. But she'd been too wrapped up in trying to forget it all herself: losing herself in her workouts and her work. And she'd done nothing.

"Dr. Frock?" she called out.

She heard the rumbling of the wheelchair behind her.

"Dr. Frock—" she whispered, unable to continue.

She felt a gentle hand touch her elbow. It was trembling with emotion.

"Let me think for a moment," Frock said. "Just for a moment, please. How could this be? To think this pathetic collection of bones—that we've studied, picked at, disassembled—could be Gregory..." His voice broke. A beam of light shone through the window and highlighted the hand as it slipped from her elbow.

Margo stood motionless, closing her eyes now against the light, feeling the oxygen stream in and out of her lungs. Eventually, she felt able to turn away from the window. But not toward the examining table—she wasn't sure she would ever be able to face the contents of that table again. Instead, she turned toward Frock. He was there behind her, motionless, his eyes dry and far away.

"We'd better call D'Agosta," she said.

For a long time, Frock did not speak then, silently, nodded his assent.

PART 2

QUI CI SONO DEI MOSTRI

For obvious reasons, no reliable census of Manhattan's underground population exists. However, the Rushing-Bunten study of 1994 indicates that 2,750 persons live in just the small area bordered by Penn Station on the southwest and Grand Central Terminal on the northeast, with the population rising to 4,500 during the winter months. In this writer's experience, such a number seems conservative.

Similarly, there is no accurate record of the births and deaths that take place in the communities beneath New York. However, given the disproportionate number of drug abusers, criminals, ex-convicts, mentally handicapped, and mentally unstable people who gravitate to the world below the surface, it is clear that the environment can be an extremely difficult and dangerous one. People have given many reasons for retreating from society into the darkness of the railroad tunnels and other subterranean spaces: privacy, security, a deep alienation from society. It has been estimated that, once a person goes underground, the average life expectancy is approximately twenty-two months.

L. Hayward, *Caste and Society Beneath Manhattan*
(forthcoming)

23

West 63rd Street stretched toward the Hudson, the procession of magnificent co-ops yielding gradually to manicured brownstones. D'Agosta walked resolutely, keeping his eyes down, feeling acutely self-conscious. The shabby, fragrant form of Pendergast shuffled along just in front of him.

"Hell of a way to spend my afternoon off," D'Agosta muttered.

Though he found himself itching in many remote places, he decided not to scratch. Scratching meant touching the ancient, greasy London Fog raincoat he wore, or the filthy Kmart plaid polyester shirt, or the shiny, threadbare trousers. He wondered where Pendergast had gotten all this stuff.

On top of all that, the dirt and grease on his face were real, not something out of a makeup tin. Even his shoes were disgusting. But when he'd balked, Pendergast had said simply, "Vincent, your life depends on it."

He hadn't even been allowed to carry his gun or shield. "You don't want to know," Pendergast had said, "what they'll do to you if they find a badge." In fact, D'Agosta thought morosely, this whole expedition was a direct violation of departmental regulations.

Glancing up briefly, he spotted a woman approaching, spotless in a crisp summer dress and high heels, walking a Chihuahua. She stopped abruptly, stepping to the side and averting her eyes with a distasteful look. As Pendergast passed by, the dog suddenly lunged forward, erupting with a shrill volley of squeaky barks. Pendergast shuffled aside, and the dog redoubled its hysterical efforts, tugging against the leash.

Despite his discomfort, or perhaps because of it, D'Agosta found himself growing annoyed at the look of loathing on the woman's face. *Who the hell is she to judge us?* he thought. As he was passing, he suddenly stopped and turned to face her. "Have a nice day," he growled, thrusting his chin forward.

The woman shrank backwards. "You revolting man," she shrieked at D'Agosta. "Stay away from him, Petit Chou!"

Pendergast grabbed D'Agosta and pulled him around the corner onto Columbus Avenue. "Are you mad?" he said under his breath. As they hurried on, D'Agosta could hear the woman calling, "Help! Those men threatened me!"

Pendergast dashed southward, D'Agosta struggling to keep up. Moving into the shadow of a large driveway halfway down the block, Pendergast knelt quickly above the steel plates set into the sidewalk that marked an emergency subway exit. Using a small hooked tool, he levered up the plates, then ushered D'Agosta down the iron stairs beneath. Closing them behind him, Pendergast followed D'Agosta into the darkness. At the bottom were two sets of train tracks, dimly illuminated. Crossing the tracks, they reached an archway leading to another descending set of stairs, which they took two steps at a time.

On the lowest step, Pendergast stopped. D'Agosta came to a halt beside him in the pitch blackness, fighting for breath. After a few moments, Pendergast switched on a penlight, chuckling. "'Have a nice day'... Vincent, what could you have been thinking?"

"Just trying to be friendly," D'Agosta said truculently.

"You could have sunk our little expedition before it left the dock. Remember, you're here simply to complete my disguise. The only way I'm certain to see Mephisto is if I pose as the leader of another community. And I'd never travel without an aide-de-camp." He gestured with his penlight into a narrow side tunnel. "That way leads east, into his territory."

D'Agosta nodded.

"Remember my instructions. I'll do the talking. It's imperative that you forget you're a police officer. No matter what happens, don't try to interfere." He reached into the pocket of his grimy trenchcoat, bringing out two floppy woolen hats. "Put this on," he said, handing one to D'Agosta.

"Why?"

"Headgear disguises the true contours of a person's head. Besides, if we're forced to make a quick escape, we can 'break our profiles' by discarding them. Remember, we're not used to the darkness. We'll be the ones at a disadvantage." He dug into the pocket again and took out a small, dull object which he fitted into his mouth.

"What the hell is that?" D'Agosta asked, pulling the hat onto his head.

"A false rubber palate for changing tongue position, thus modifying the harmonic resonances of the throat. We will be consorting with criminals, remember? I spent a fair amount of time last year at Riker's Island, profiling murderers for Quantico. It's possible that I'll come in contact with some of them down here. If so, they must not recognize me, either by appearance or voice." He waved his hand. "Of course, makeup alone isn't enough. I must adapt my posture, way of walking, even mannerisms. Your job is easier: keep silent, blend in, follow my lead. We must not in any way stand out. Understood?"

D'Agosta nodded.

"With any luck, this Mephisto will be able to point us in the right direction. Perhaps we'll return with evidence of the killings he described to the *Post*. That could provide additional forensics material we desperately need." He paused. "Any leads on the Brambell murder?" he asked. He took a step forward, shining the penlight ahead.

"No," said D'Agosta. "Waxie and the top brass think it was just another random killing. But I'm wondering if it didn't have something to do with his work."

Pendergast nodded. "An interesting theory."

"Seems to me that these killings—or at least some of them—aren't random at all. I mean, Brambell was on the verge of discovering who the second skeleton belonged to. Maybe somebody didn't want that known."

Pendergast nodded again. "I have to admit, Lieutenant, I was flabbergasted when I heard the second skeleton belonged to Kawakita. It opens up a vista of"—he paused—"complexity and ugliness. And it suggests that Dr. Frock, Dr. Green, and the others working on the case should be protected."

D'Agosta scowled. "I went up to Horlocker's office this morning with that in mind. He dismissed any kind of protection for Green or Frock. Said he suspected Kawakita must've been involved with Pamela Wisher somehow, just got caught in the wrong place and the wrong time. A random killing, like Brambell. All he cared was that we didn't leak anything about it to the press, at least until Kawakita's family is tracked down and alerted—assuming there're any left to alert; I think somebody once said he was an orphan. Waxie was there, too, strutting and preening like an overstuffed rooster. He told me to do a better job of keeping this under wraps than I did with Wisher."

"And?"

"I suggested he go put a poultice on it. Politely, of course. I'd been thinking it was best not to alarm Frock or Green. But after that meeting, I talked to them both, gave them some advice. They promised to be very careful, at least until their work is finished."

"Have they discovered what caused the skeletal deformation in Kawakita?"

"Not yet." D'Agosta nodded absently.

Pendergast turned toward him. "What is it?" he asked.

D'Agosta hesitated. "I suppose I'm a little worried about how Dr. Green is taking all this. I mean, it was my idea to tap her and Frock in the first place, but now I'm not so sure. Frock seems to be his usual ornery self, but Margo..." He paused. "You know how she reacted to the Museum murders. Conditioning herself, running every day, packing a pistol."

Pendergast nodded. "It's not an uncommon type of post-traumatic stress reaction. People who emerge from terrifying situations sometimes look for ways to gain control, to limit their feelings of vulnerability. Actually, it's a relatively healthy response to severe stress." He smiled grimly. "And I can think of few more stressful situations than the one she and I found ourselves in, there in that darkened Museum corridor."

"Yeah, but she's overdoing it. And now, with all this shit happening... Well, I'm not sure I made the right decision, calling her in like I did."

"It was absolutely the right decision. We need her expertise. Especially now that we know Kawakita is dead. You'll be investigating his last known whereabouts, I trust?"

D'Agosta nodded.

"You might consider asking Dr. Green to lend a hand with that." Pendergast resumed his scrutiny of the tunnel, peering into the darkness with his sooty face. "Ah, well. Ready, Vincent?"

"I guess so. What if we meet hostiles?"

Pendergast smiled slightly. "Trading in local commerce tends to keep the natives peaceful."

"Drugs?" D'Agosta asked in disbelief.

Pendergast nodded, opening his coat. In the gleam of the penlight, D'Agosta could make out several tiny pockets stitched into the filthy lining. "It appears that virtually everyone down here is or has been an addict of one kind or another." His finger moved from one pocket to the next. "I have an entire pharmacopoeia here: crack cocaine, methylphenidate, Carbrital, Seconal, military-grade Blue 88s.

They may well save our lives, Vincent. They saved mine on my first descent."

Pendergast dug into one of the small pockets and pulled out a slender black capsule. "Biphetamine," he said. "Known in the underground fraternity as a black beauty."

He stared at the capsule for a moment. Then, with a quick movement, he popped it into his mouth.

"What the—?" D'Agosta began, but the FBI agent held his hand out for silence.

"It's not enough for me to *act* the part," Pendergast whispered. "I have to *be* the part. This Mephisto is undoubtedly a suspicious, paranoid individual. Scenting fraud is his stock in trade. Remember that."

D'Agosta said nothing. They really had stepped outside society, outside the law, outside everything.

They passed into the side tunnel and moved along an abandoned rail line. Every few minutes, Pendergast would stop to consult some notes. Following the FBI agent deeper into darkness, D'Agosta was amazed at how quickly he lost his own orientation, his sense of time.

Suddenly Pendergast pointed toward a wavering reddish light, seemingly suspended in the darkness perhaps a hundred yards ahead of them. "There are people around that fire," he whispered. "It's probably a small 'upstairs' community, squatters living at the edge of Mephisto's domain." He stared speculatively at the glow for a few moments. Then he turned.

"Shall we retire to the drawing room?" he asked, and, without waiting for an answer, began moving toward the distant glow.

As they drew closer, D'Agosta made out a dozen or so figures, lounging on the ground or hunched atop milk crates, staring into the fire. A bubbling black coffeepot sat among the coals. Pendergast ambled into the firelight and squatted down beside the blaze. Nobody paid any attention. He reached into one of the many layers of his outfit and pulled out a pint bottle of

English Lord De Luxe Tokay wine. D'Agosta watched as all eyes swiveled in the direction of the bottle.

Pendergast unscrewed the cap and took a long pull, sighing contentedly. "Anybody want a slug?" he asked, turning the bottle's label toward the firelight so all could see. D'Agosta was momentarily taken aback: the FBI agent's voice had changed utterly. It now sounded thick, drugged, with a distinct Flatbush accent. Pendergast's pale skin, eyes, and hair looked alien and menacing in the flickering glare.

A hand reached out. "Yeah," came a voice. A man on a milk crate took the bottle and placed it to his lips. There was a long sucking noise. When he handed it back to Pendergast, a quarter of the contents were gone. Pendergast passed the bottle to another, and it went around the circle, returning empty. There was a single grunt of thanks.

D'Agosta tried to maneuver into the plume of smoke, hoping to dilute the stench of unwashed human bodies, bad wine, and rancid urine.

"I'm looking for Mephisto," Pendergast said after a moment.

There was a momentary stir around the campfire. The men seemed suddenly wary. "Who wants to know?" the one who'd first taken the bottle asked belligerently.

"*I* want to know," said Pendergast, immediately belligerent himself.

There was a short silence while the man eyed Pendergast, sizing him up. "Up yours, Jack," he said at last, sinking back into his chair.

Pendergast moved so quickly that D'Agosta jumped away, startled. When he looked back, the man was facedown in the rubble, and Pendergast was standing over him, one foot planted on his neck.

"Shit!" the man howled.

Pendergast pressed down. "Nobody disses Whitey," he hissed.

"I didn't mean nothing, man. Jesus!"

Pendergast eased up slightly.

"Mephisto hangs out at Route 666."

"Where's that?"

"Stop it, man, that shit hurts! Look, head down track 100, watch for the old generator. Take the ladder down to the catwalk."

Pendergast released his foot, and the man sat up, rubbing his neck. "Mephisto don't like outsiders."

"Him and I have business to discuss."

"Yeah? About what?"

"About the Wrinklers."

Even in the dark, D'Agosta sensed the group stiffen. "What about them?" a new voice asked sharply.

"I talk to Mephisto only." Pendergast nodded to D'Agosta, and they moved away from the campfire, continuing on into the darkness of the tunnel. When the fire had receded to a dwindling point, Pendergast once again snapped on the penlight.

"You can't let anyone disrespect you down here," Pendergast said quietly. "Even a marginal group like that. If they sense weakness, you're as good as dead."

"Those were some pretty slick moves," D'Agosta said.

"It's not difficult to knock down a drunk. On my last trip down, I learned that alcohol is the drug of choice on these upper levels. Except for that one thin fellow, farthest from the fire. I'd wager, Lieutenant, that he was a skin-popper. Did you notice how he was absently scratching himself during the entire meeting? A side effect of fentanyl, quite unmistakable."

The tunnel branched, and after consulting a railyard map from one of his pockets Pendergast took the narrower, left-hand passage. "This leads to track 100," he said.

D'Agosta shuffled on behind. After what seemed an interminable distance, Pendergast stopped again, pointing out a great rusting machine with several huge belt gears, each at least twelve feet in diameter. The rotted belt lay underneath in a heap on the ground. On the far side was a metal staircase, ending at a catwalk suspended above an ancient tunnel. Ducking under a stalactite-covered pipe stenciled H.P.ST., D'Agosta followed Pendergast down the staircase and along the rickety grating. At the end of the catwalk, a hinged plate in the floor led to a metal ladder, which descended into a large, unfinished tunnel. Rock and rusted metal I-beams lay in untidy piles against the walls. Although D'Agosta could see the remains of several camps, the place appeared deserted.

"We have to climb down this rock, it seems," said Pendergast, shining the penlight beam into a large area at the end of the tunnel. The edges of the rock were slick with the impressions of countless hands and feet. A caustic smell drifted up.

D'Agosta went first, clinging desperately to the sharp, wet basalt. It was the work of five terrifying minutes to reach the bottom. He felt like he was entombed in the very bedrock of the island.

"I'd like to see someone climb that thing messed up on drugs," he said as Pendergast dropped to the ground beside him. The muscles in his arms were shaking from the exertion.

"Below here, nobody leaves," said Pendergast. "Except the runners."

"Runners?"

"As I understand it, they are the only community members who have contact with the surface. They collect and cash AFDC checks, rummage for food, 'bust' recyclables for spare change, pick up medicine and milk, buy drugs."

Pendergast shone his light around, revealing a rough, rocky pit. On the far wall, a five-foot piece of corrugated tin covered an abandoned tunnel. A crude message painted on the wall beside it read FAMILIES ONLY. ALL OTHERS KEEP OUT.

Pendergast grabbed the sheet of metal and it swung open with a loud screech. "Doorbell," he explained.

As they stepped into the tunnel, a ragged-looking figure suddenly appeared in front of them, a large firebrand in one hand. He was tall and terrifyingly gaunt. "Who are you?" he demanded, standing in Pendergast's way.

"Are you Tail Gunner?" Pendergast asked.

"Outside," the man said, pushing them toward the tin door. In a moment they were back out in the rocky pit. "The name's Flint. What do you want?"

"I'm here to see Mephisto," Pendergast replied.

"What for?"

"I'm the leader of Grant's Tomb. A small community beneath Columbia University. I've come to talk about the killings."

There was a long silence. "And him?" Flint said, gesturing at D'Agosta.

"My runner," said Pendergast.

Flint turned back to Pendergast. "Weapons or drugs?" he asked.

"No weapons," said Pendergast. In the lambent glow of the firebrand, he looked suddenly embarrassed. "But I do carry my own little supply—"

"No drugs here," said Flint. "We're a clean community."

Bullshit, D'Agosta thought, looking into the man's burning eyes.

"Sorry," said Pendergast, "I don't give up my stash. If that's a problem—"

"What've you got?" Flint asked.

"None of your business."

"Coke?" he asked, and D'Agosta thought he detected a faint hopeful tone in his voice.

"Good guess," said Pendergast after a moment.

"I'm gonna have to confiscate that."

"Consider it a gift." Pendergast brought out a small folded piece of tinfoil and handed it to Flint, who quickly tucked it into his coat.

"Follow me," he said.

D'Agosta pulled the metal sheet closed behind them and followed Flint as he led them down a metal staircase. The staircase ended in a narrow opening that led onto a cement landing, suspended far above a vast cylindrical room. Flint turned and began moving down a cement ramp that spiraled along the wall. As he walked down the ramp, D'Agosta noticed that several cubbyholes had been cut into the rock. Each cubbyhole was occupied by individuals or families. Candles and kerosene lamps flickered over dirty faces and filthy beddings. Looking across the vast space, D'Agosta could see a broken pipe jutting from the wall. Water spilled from the pipe and fell into a muddy pool that had been excavated out of the cavern floor. Several figures huddled around it, apparently washing clothes. The dirty water ran away in a stream and disappeared into the broken mouth of a tunnel.

Reaching the bottom, they crossed the stream on an ancient board. Groups of underground dwellers dotted the cavern floor, sleeping or playing cards. A man lay in a far corner, his eyes open and milky, and D'Agosta realized he was awaiting burial. He turned away.

Flint led them through a long, low passage from which many tunnels seemed to branch. In the dim light at the end of some of the corridors, D'Agosta could see people at work: storing canned goods, mending clothes, distilling grain alcohol. At last, Flint brought them out into a space filled with the glow of electric light. Looking up, D'Agosta saw a single light bulb dangling from a frayed cord that ran to an old junction box in one corner.

D'Agosta's eyes traveled down from the bulb along the crack-riddled bricks that lined the chamber. Then he froze, a gasp of disbelief on his lips. In the center of the room was a battered and ancient train caboose, tilted at a crazy angle, its rear wheels suspended at least two feet above the floor. How it had ended up in this strange lunatic place he couldn't begin to imagine. Along its side, he barely could make out the letters NEW YO CENTRA in faded black on the rusted red metal.

Motioning them to stay put, Flint entered the caboose. He emerged a few minutes later, beckoning them forward.

Stepping inside, D'Agosta found himself in a small antechamber, the far end of which was covered with a thick dark curtain. Flint had vanished. The caboose was dark and stupefyingly hot.

"Yes?" hissed a strange voice from beyond the curtain.

Pendergast cleared his throat. "I'm known as Whitey, leader of Grant's Tomb. We heard about your call for the underground people to band together, to stop the killings."

There was a silence. D'Agosta wondered what lay beyond the curtain. *Maybe nothing*, he told himself. *Maybe it's like in* The Wizard of Oz. *Maybe Smithback had just made half the article up. You could never tell with journalists...*

"Come in," the voice said.

The curtain was pulled aside. Reluctantly, D'Agosta followed Pendergast into the chamber beyond.

The interior was dark, lit only by the reflected glow of the naked bulb outside and by a small fire that smoldered beneath a vent in one corner. In front of them, a man sat in a massive, thronelike chair that had been placed in the exact center of the room. He was tall, with large limbs and long, thick gray hair. The man was dressed in an ancient bell-bottom suit of tan corduroy and wore a threadbare Borsalino hat. A heavy silver Navajo squash blossom necklace set with turquoise hung around his neck.

Mephisto stared at them with unusually penetrating eyes. "Mayor Whitey. Unoriginal. Not likely to induce reverence. But in your albinoid case, appropriate." The hiss had taken on a slow, formal tone.

D'Agosta felt the gaze turn on him. *Whatever else this guy is,* D'Agosta thought, *he ain't crazy. At least, not completely crazy.* He felt uneasy; Mephisto's eyes glittered with suspicion.

"And this one?" he asked.

"Cigar. My runner."

Mephisto stared at D'Agosta for a long time. Then he turned back to Pendergast. "I've never heard of a Grant's Tomb community," he said, voice laced with doubt.

"There's a large network of service tunnels beneath Columbia and its outbuildings," Pendergast said. "We're small, and we mind our own business. The students are pretty generous."

Mephisto nodded, listening. The look of suspicion slowly vanished, replaced by something that was either a leer or a smile, D'Agosta couldn't be sure which. "Of course. Always nice to meet an ally in these dark days. Let's seal this meeting with some refreshments. We can talk afterwards."

He clapped his hands. "Chairs for our guests! And get that fire going! Tail Gunner, bring us some meat." A thin, short man D'Agosta had not seen before appeared out of the shadows and left the caboose. Another, who had been sitting cross-legged on the floor, struggled to his feet and, moving with glacial slowness, piled wood on the fire and poked it into life. *It's already too damn hot in here,* D'Agosta thought as he felt the sweat trickle down the inside of his greasy shirt.

An enormous, heavily muscled man came in with two packing crates, which he set in front of Mephisto's chair. "Gentlemen, please," Mephisto said with mock gravity, gesturing at the crates.

D'Agosta settled himself gingerly on the packing crate as the man called Tail Gunner returned, carrying something wet and dripping in a piece of old newspaper. He dropped it beside the fire, and D'Agosta felt his stomach seize up involuntarily: inside was an enormous rat, its head half crushed, paws still twitching rhythmically as if to some internal beat.

"Excellent!" cried Mephisto. "Fresh caught, as you can see." He turned his piercing eyes on Pendergast. "You *do* eat track rabbit, don't you?"

"Of course," Pendergast replied.

D'Agosta noticed that the heavily muscled man was now standing directly behind them. It began to dawn on him that they were about to undergo a test they had better not fail.

Reaching out, Mephisto took the carcass in one hand and a long metal roasting spit in the other. Holding the rat beneath its front haunches, Mephisto deftly threaded the skewer from anus to head, then set it over the fire to roast. D'Agosta watched in horrified fascination as the hair immediately sizzled and caught fire, and the rat gave one final convulsive spasm. A moment later the entire animal flared up, sending a plume of acrid smoke toward the roof of the caboose. It died down again, the tail withering into a blackened corkscrew.

Mephisto watched the rat for a moment. Then he plucked it from the fire, pulled a knife out of his coat, and scraped the remaining hair off the skin. Piercing the belly to release the cooking gases, he returned it to the flame, this time at a higher elevation.

"It takes skill," he said, "to cook *le grand souris en brochette*."

D'Agosta waited, acutely aware that all eyes were on him and Pendergast. He did not want to imagine what would happen if he betrayed the slightest hint of disgust.

Minutes passed in silence as the rat sizzled. Mephisto rotated the rack, then looked at Pendergast. "How do you like yours?" he asked. "I prefer mine rare."

"Suits me," Pendergast said, as placidly as if he were being offered toast points at Tavern on the Green.

It's just an animal, D'Agosta thought in desperation. *Eating it won't kill me. Which is more than I can say for these guys.*

Mephisto sighed in ill-concealed anticipation. "Look done to you?"

"Let's eat," said Pendergast, rubbing his hands together.

D'Agosta said nothing.

"This calls for alcohol!" cried Mephisto. Almost immediately a half-empty bottle of Night Train appeared. Mephisto eyed it with disgust.

"These are guests!" he said, tossing the bottle aside. "Bring something suitable!" Shortly, a mossy bottle of Cold Duck and three plastic glasses arrived. Mephisto removed the metal skewer and slid the cooked rat onto the newspaper.

"You do the honors," he said, handing it to Pendergast.

D'Agosta struggled with a sudden sense of panic. What was Pendergast supposed to do? He watched with mingled horror and relief as Pendergast, without hesitation, raised the rat and put his lips to the gash in its flank. There was a sharp sucking sound as the rodent was eviscerated. D'Agosta felt his gorge rise.

Licking his lips, Pendergast set the newspaper and its burden in front of their host.

"Excellent," he said simply.

Mephisto nodded. "Interesting technique."

"Hardly." Pendergast shrugged. "They spread a lot of rat poison around the Columbia service tunnels. You can always tell by tasting the liver whether it's safe to eat."

A broad, and genuine, smile spread across Mephisto's face. "I'll remember that," he said. Taking the knife, he cut several strips of meat from one haunch and handed them to D'Agosta.

The moment had come. Out of the corner of his eye, D'Agosta saw the hulking figure behind them grow tense. Squeezing his eyelids closed, he attacked the meat with feigned gusto, stuffing everything into his mouth at once, chewing furiously and swallowing the strips almost before he had a chance to taste them. He grinned through his agony, wrestling with the horrible feeling of nausea that swept across his gut.

"Bravo!" said Mephisto, watching. "A true gourmand!"

The level of tension in the air decreased palpably. As D'Agosta sat back on his packing crate, putting a protective hand over his stomach, the silence in the room gave way to low laughter and whispered conversation.

"You'll forgive my suspicion," Mephisto said. "There was a time when life underground was much more open and trusting. If you are who you say you are, you know that already. But these are difficult times."

Mephisto poured them each a glass of wine, then raised his own in a toast. He sliced off several more cuts of meat and passed them to Pendergast, then demolished the rest of the rat himself.

"Let me introduce my Lieutenants," Mephisto said. He waved at the hulking figure that stood behind them. "This is Little Harry. Got into horse pretty young. Took to petty thievery to support the habit. One thing led to another, and he ended up in Attica. They taught him quite a lot there. When he got out, he couldn't find a job. Luckily, he wandered below and joined our community before he could fall back into bad habits."

Mephisto pointed at the slow-moving figure by the fire. "That's Boy Alice. Used to teach English at a Connecticut prep school. Things went sour. He lost his job, got divorced, ran out of money, began hitting the bottle. He gravitated to the shelters and soup kitchens. That's where he heard about us. As for Tail Gunner, he got back from 'Nam only to find that the country he'd defended didn't want anything to do with him."

Mephisto wiped his mouth on the newspaper. "That's more than you need to know," he said. "We've left the past behind, as you must have. So you're here about the killings?"

Pendergast nodded. "Three of our people have been missing since last week, and the rest are getting concerned. We heard your call for alliance against the Wrinklers. The headless killers."

"Word is getting around. Two days ago I heard from the Philosopher. Know of him?"

Pendergast hesitated for just a second. "No," he replied.

Mephisto's eyes narrowed. "Odd," he said. "He's my counterpart, leader of the communities beneath Grand Central."

"Perhaps some day we shall meet," Pendergast said. "For now, I need to take word back, reassurances for my people. What can you tell me about the killings and the killers?"

"They started almost a year ago," Mephisto replied in a silky hiss. "First was Joe Atcitty. We found his body dumped outside the Blockhouse, head gone. Next, Dark Annie disappeared. Then Master Sergeant. It went on and on. Some we found. Most we didn't. Later, we got word from the Manders that deep activity had been detected."

Pendergast frowned. "Manders?"

Again, Mephisto shot a suspicious glance toward him. "Never heard of the Manders?" He cackled. "You ought to stretch your legs more, get out, see the neighborhood, *Mayor* Whitey. The Manders live below us. Never come up, never use lights. Like salamanders. *Versteht?* They said there were signs of movement *below* them." His voice dropped to a whisper. "They said the Devil's Attic had been colonized."

D'Agosta looked questioningly at Pendergast. But the FBI agent merely nodded. "The lowest level of the city," he said, as if to himself.

"The very lowest," Mephisto replied.

"Have you been down there?" Pendergast asked with deliberate casualness.

Mephisto flashed him a look as if to imply even he wasn't that crazy.

"But you think these people are behind the killings?"

"I don't think it. I *know* it. They're beneath us, right now." Mephisto smiled grimly. "But I'm not sure I'd use the word *people*."

"What do you mean?" Pendergast said, the casualness gone from his voice.

"Rumor," Mephisto said very quietly. "They say they're called Wrinklers for a reason."

"Which is—?"

Mephisto did not answer.

Pendergast sat back on his crate. "So what can we do?"

"What can we do?" The smile vanished from Mephisto's face. "We can wake up this city, that's what we can do! We can show them that it won't just be the mole people, the invisible people, who die!"

"And if we do that?" Pendergast asked. "What can the city do about these Wrinklers?"

Mephisto thought a moment. "Like any infestation. Get them where they live."

"Easier said than done."

Mephisto's hard, glittery gaze landed on the FBI agent. "You got a better idea, Whitey?" he hissed.

Pendergast was silent. "Not yet," he said at last.

24

Robert Willson, librarian at the New York Historical Society, looked at the other occupant of the map room with irritation. Odd-looking guy: somber black suit, pale cat's eyes, blond-white hair combed severely back from a high forehead. Annoying, too. Annoying as hell. He'd been there all afternoon, making demands and throwing the maps askew. Every time Willson turned back to his computer to resume work on his own pet project—the definitive monograph on Zuñi fetishes—the man would be up, asking more questions.

As if on cue, the man got out of his chair and glided over noiselessly. "Pardon?" he said in his polite but insistent mint-julep drawl.

Willson glanced up from the screen. "Yes?" he snapped.

"I hate to trouble you again, but it's my understanding that the Vaux and Olmstead plans for Central Park called for canals to drain the Central Park swamps. I wonder if I could look at those plans?"

Willson compressed his lips. "Those plans were rejected by the Parks Commission," he replied. "They've been lost. A tragedy." He turned back to his screen, hoping the man would take the hint. The real tragedy would be if he didn't get back to his monograph.

"I see," the visitor said, not taking the hint at all. "Then tell me, how *were* the swamps drained?"

Willson sat back in his chair exasperatedly. "I should have thought it was common knowledge. The old Eighty-sixth Street aqueduct was used."

"And there are plans for the operation?"

"Yes," said Willson.

"May I see them?"

With a sigh, Willson got up and made his way through the heavy door back into the stacks. It was, of course, in its usual mess. The room managed to be both vast and claustrophobic, metal shelves reaching two stories into the gloom, tottering with rolled maps and moldering blueprints. Willson could almost feel the dust settling on his bald scalp as he scanned the arcane lists of numbers. His nose began to itch. He found the correct location, pulled the ancient maps and carried them back to the cramped reading room. *Why do people always request the heaviest maps,* he wondered to himself as he emerged from the stacks.

"Here they are," Willson said, placing them on the mahogany counter. He watched as the man took them over to his desk and began looking them over, jotting notes and making sketches in a small leather-bound notebook. *He's got money,* Willson thought sourly. *No professor could afford a suit like that.*

A heavenly quiet descended on the map room. At last, he could get some work done. Bringing some yellowed reference photographs out of his desk, Willson began making changes to his chapter on clan imagery.

Within minutes, he felt the visitor standing behind him again. Willson looked up again silently.

The man nodded at one of Willson's photographs. It showed a nondescript stone carved in an abstract representation of an animal, a small piece of sinew holding a flint point to its back. "I think you'll find that particular fetish, which I see you've labeled as a puma, is in fact a grizzly bear," the man said.

Willson looked at the pale face and the faint smile, wondering if this was some kind of a joke. "Cushing, who collected this fetish in 1883, specifically identified it as puma clan," he replied. "You can check the reference yourself." Everybody was an expert these days.

"The grizzly fetish," the man continued undeterred, "always has a spearpoint strapped to its back, as this one does. The puma fetish has an arrowhead."

Willson straightened up. "Just what is the difference, may I ask?"

"You kill a puma with a bow and arrow. To kill a grizzly, you must use a spear."

Willson was silent.

"Cushing was wrong on occasion," the man added gently.

Willson shuffled his manuscript together and laid it aside. "Frankly, I would prefer to trust Cushing over someone..." He left the sentence unfinished. "The library will be closing in one hour," he added.

"In that case," the man said, "I wonder if I could see the plates from the 1956 Upper West Side Natural Gas Pipeline Survey."

Willson compressed his lips. "Which ones?"

"All of them, if you please."

This was too much. "I'm sorry," Willson said crisply. "It's against the rules. Patrons are allowed only ten maps at a time from the same series." He glared at the visitor triumphantly.

But the man seemed oblivious, lost in thought. Suddenly, he looked back at the librarian.

"Robert Willson," he said, pointing at the nameplate. "Now I remember why your name is familiar."

"You do?" Willson asked uncertainly.

"Indeed. Aren't you the one who gave the excellent paper on mirage stones at the Navajo Studies Conference in Window Rock last year?"

"Why, yes, I did," Willson said.

"I thought so. I wasn't able to be there myself, but I read the proceedings. I've made something of a private study of southwestern religious imagery." The visitor paused. "Nothing as serious as yours, of course."

Willson cleared his throat. "I suppose one cannot spend thirty years in such study," he said as modestly as possible, "without one's name becoming known."

The visitor smiled. "It's an honor to make your acquaintance. My name is Pendergast."

Willson extended his hand and encountered an unpleasantly limp handshake. He prided himself on the firmness of his own.

"It's gratifying to see you continuing your studies," the man named Pendergast said. "Ignorance of southwestern culture is so profound."

"It is," Willson agreed wholeheartedly. He felt a peculiar sense of pride. Nobody had taken the least interest in his work before, let alone been able to talk about it intelligibly. Of course, this Pendergast was obviously misinformed about Indian fetishes, but...

"I'd love to discuss this further," Pendergast said, "but I fear I've taken up enough of your time."

"Not at all," Willson replied. "What was that you'd asked to see? The '56 Survey?"

Pendergast nodded. "There was one other item, if I may. I understand there was a survey of existing tunnels done in the 1920s for the proposed Interborough Rapid Transit system. Is that correct?"

Willson's face fell. "But there are sixty maps in that series..." His voice trailed off.

"I see," Pendergast said. "It's against the rules, then." He looked crestfallen.

Suddenly, Willson smiled. "I won't tell if you won't," he said, pleased at his own recklessness. "And don't worry about closing time. I'll be here late, working on my monograph. Rules were made to be broken, right?"

Ten minutes later, he emerged from the gloom of the storage room, pushing an overloaded cart across the worn floorboards.

25

Smithback walked into the cavernous entryway of the Four Seasons, eager to leave the heat and stench and noise of Park Avenue behind. He approached the four-square bar with measured step. He'd sat here many times before, looking enviously across the room, past the Picasso hanging, toward the unattainable paradise beyond. This time, however, he did not dally at the bar, but continued toward the maître d'. A quickly mentioned name was all it took, and now he, Smithback, was himself walking down that corridor of dreams toward the exclusive restaurant beyond.

Every table in the Pool Room was filled, yet the space seemed quiet and calm somehow, muted by its own vastness. He threaded his way past captains of industry, publishing moguls, and robber barons to one of the prized tables near the fountain. There, already seated, was Mrs. Wisher.

"Mr. Smithback," she said. "Thank you for coming. Please sit down."

Smithback took the indicated chair across the table, glancing about as he did so. This promised to be an interesting lunch, and he hoped he had time to enjoy it fully. He'd barely started to write up his big story, and press time was 6:00 P.M.

"Would you care for a glass of Amarone?" Mrs. Wisher asked, indicating the bottle beside the table. She was crisply dressed in a saffron-colored blouse and pleated skirt.

"Please," Smith replied, meeting her gaze. He felt much more at ease than the last time he'd spoken to her: sitting primly in her darkened apartment, a copy of the *Post* lying beside her like a silent accusation. His "Angel of Central Park South" obituary, the *Post's* reward offer, and his favorable coverage on the Grand Army Plaza rally made him feel confident of a warmer reception.

Mrs. Wisher nodded to the wine steward, waited until the man had poured a glass for the journalist and departed, then leaned almost imperceptibly forward.

"Mr. Smithback, you're undoubtedly wondering why I asked you to join me for lunch."

"It had occurred to me." Smithback tasted the wine, found it excellent.

"I won't waste any time sporting with your intelligence, then. Certain events are about to happen in this city. And I'd like you to document them."

Smithback put his wine glass down. "Me?"

The corners of Mrs. Wisher's mouth turned up slightly in what might have been a smile. "Ah. I thought you would be surprised. But you see, Mr. Smithback, I've done some research on you since our last meeting. And I read your book on the Museum murders."

"You bought a copy?" Smithback asked hopefully.

"The Amsterdam Avenue branch of the public library had one. It made very interesting reading. I had no idea you were so directly involved with almost every aspect of that event."

Smithback's eyes darted quickly toward her face, but he could detect no trace of sarcasm in her expression.

"I also read your article on our rally," Mrs. Wisher continued. "It had a positive tone that I found lacking in some of the other press coverage." She waved her hand. "Besides, I really have you to thank for what's happened."

"You do?" Smithback asked a little nervously.

Mrs. Wisher nodded. "It was you who convinced me that the only way to get the city's attention was to dig a spur into its flank. Remember your comment? 'People in this town don't pay attention to something unless you slap them in the face with it.' Had it not been for you, I might still be in my drawing room, writing letters to the mayor, instead of putting my sorrow to good use."

Smithback nodded. The not-so-merry widow had a point.

"Since that rally, our movement has spread dramatically," Mrs. Wisher said. "We've hit a common nerve. People are coming together—people of power and influence. But our message belongs just as much to the common man, the man on the street. And that's the person you can reach with your paper."

Although Smithback did not like to be reminded that he wrote for the common man, he kept his expression even. Besides, he'd seen it for himself: by the time the rally had ended, there'd been plenty of them around, drinking, heckling, hoping for action.

"And so this is what I propose." Mrs. Wisher placed her small, neatly manicured fingernails on the linen tablecloth. "I will give you privileged access to every event planned by Take Back Our City. Many of these actions will be intentionally unannounced; the press, like the police, will learn of them too late to make any real difference. You, however, will be brought into my circle. You will know what to expect, and when to expect it. You can accompany me directly, if you like. And then you can slap your readers in the face with it."

Smithback struggled to keep from betraying his excitement. *This is too good to be true,* he thought.

"I imagine you'd like to publish another book," Mrs. Wisher went on. "Once the Take Back Our City campaign reaches a successful conclusion, you'd have my blessing on such a project. I'll make myself available for interviews. And Hiram Bennett, editor-in-chief of Cygnus House, is one of my closest friends. I think he'd be very interested in seeing such a manuscript."

Jesus, Smithback thought. *Hiram Bennett, Mister Publishing himself.* He could imagine the bidding war between Cygnus House and Stockbridge, the publishers of his Museum book. He'd get his agent to set up an auction, specify a floor of two hundred grand, no, make that two fifty, with ten percent topping privileges and—

"I ask one thing in return," Mrs. Wisher coolly interrupted his thoughts. "That from now on, you devote yourself to covering Take Back Our City. I want your newspaper articles, when they appear, to focus exclusively on our cause."

"What?" Smithback said abruptly. "Mrs. Wisher, I'm a crime reporter. I'm hired to turn in product on a regular basis." His visions of publishing fame quickly faded, replaced with the angry face of his editor, Arnold Murray, demanding copy.

Mrs. Wisher nodded. "I understand. And I think I can deliver you all the 'product' you could wish for within a few days. I'll give you details as soon as we've finalized our plans. Trust me, I think that you will find this relationship to be beneficial to us both."

Smithback thought quickly. In a couple of hours, he was due to file his story covering what he'd learned eavesdropping on the Museum conference. He'd delayed it already, hoping in vain to gain additional information. This was to be the story that got him his raise, the story to set that prick Bryce Harriman back on his heels.

But would it? The reward was getting a little stale, and no leads had panned out. His report on Mephisto hadn't excited the interest he'd thought it would. There was no clear proof that the death of the Medical Examiner, though suspiciously coincidental, was connected. And then, there were always the unpleasant consequences of Museum trespass to be considered.

But this Wisher story, on the other hand, could be just the dynamite he was looking for. His journalist's instincts told him it had the feel of a winner. He could call in sick, stall Murray for a day or two. When he got the final results, all would be forgiven.

He looked up. "Mrs. Wisher, you've got yourself a deal."

"Call me Anette," she said, her gaze drifting over his face for a moment before falling toward the menu at her elbow. "And now let's order, shall we? I'd suggest the coldwater scallops wrapped in lemon phyllo and caviar. The chef here does them excellently."

26

Hayward rounded the corner onto 72nd Street, then stopped, frowning in disbelief at the sand-colored building that loomed up in front of her. She checked her pocket for the scribbled address, then stared up again. There was no mistake. But the place looked more like a mansion out of a Charles Addams cartoon—magnified perhaps twenty times—than a Manhattan apartment building. The structure rose, stone upon layer of stone, nine generous stories into the air. Near its top, huge two-storey gables hung like eyebrows over the facade. The copper-trimmed slate roof above was encrusted with chimneys, spires, turrets, finials—everything but a widow's walk. *Or maybe arrow slits would be more appropriate,* Hayward thought. The Dakota, it was called. Strange name for a strange-looking place. She'd heard of the place, but had never seen it. Then again, she didn't get many excuses to visit the Upper West Side.

She walked toward the arched carriageway that bored into the southern flank of the building. The guard inside the adjoining sentry box took her name, then made a brief call.

"Southwest lobby," he said, hanging up and directing her through. She stepped past him toward the dark tunnel.

On the far side, the archway opened into a large interior courtyard. Hayward stopped for a moment, staring at the bronze fountains, thinking that the genteel, almost secretive hush seemed absurdly out of place on the west side of Manhattan. Then she turned right and headed for the nearest corner of the courtyard. She stepped through the narrow lobby and into the elevator, stabbing the button with a slender finger.

The elevator rose slowly, opening at last into a small rectangular space. Stepping out, she saw that on the far side a single door had been set into the dark polished wood. The elevator whispered shut and began to descend, leaving Hayward in blackness. For a moment, she wondered if she was on the wrong floor. There was a slight rustle, and her right hand moved instinctively toward her service piece.

"Sergeant Hayward. Excellent. Please come in." Even in the dark, Hayward would have recognized the accent, the bourbon-and-buttermilk voice. But the far door had opened and Agent Pendergast was standing just within, his slim, unmistakable figure silhouetted by the soft light of the room beyond.

Hayward stepped inside and Pendergast shut the door behind her. Though the room was not especially large, its high ceiling gave it a sense of formal grandeur. Hayward looked around curiously. Three of the walls were painted a deep rose, edged above and below in black molding. Light came from behind what appeared to be wafer-thin pieces of agate, framed in scallop-shaped bronze fixtures set well above eye level. The fourth wall was covered in black marble. Across the entire face of the marble, a thin sheet of water fell like a stream of glass from ceiling to floor, gurgling silently into the grill that ran along its base. A few small leather sofas were placed about the room, their bases hidden by the thick nap of the carpet. The only decoration consisted of a few paintings and several twisted plants, scattered here and there on lacquer tables. The room was fastidiously clean, without a smudge or a particle of dust. Though she knew there must be other doors leading into the interior of the apartment, their outlines were too well concealed for her to make them out.

"Sit anywhere, Sergeant Hayward," Pendergast said. "May I offer you refreshment of some kind?"

"No thanks," Hayward replied, selecting the seat closest to the door and letting the soft black leather creep luxuriously up around her. She stared at the painting on the nearest wall, an impressionist landscape of haystacks and pink-tinged sunlight that seemed somehow familiar. "Nice place. Though the building's kind of weird."

"We tenants would prefer to call it eccentric," Pendergast said. "But many would have agreed with you over the years, I suppose. The Dakota, so named because when it was built in 1884, this part of town seemed as remote as Indian Territory. Still, it has a solidity, a kind of permanence, that I like. Built on bedrock, walls almost thirty inches thick at ground level. But you didn't come here to listen to a lecture on architecture. Actually, I'm grateful you came at all."

"You kidding?" Hayward asked. "And pass up a chance to tour Agent Pendergast's crib? You're kind of a legend among the rank and file these days. As if you didn't know."

"How reassuring," Pendergast replied, slipping into a chair. "But this is the extent of the tour, I'm afraid. I rarely entertain visitors. Still, it seemed the best place for our chat."

"And why's that?" Hayward asked as she looked around. Then her eyes lighted on the closest of the lacquered tables. "Hey!" she pointed. "That's a bonsai plant. A miniature tree. My *sensei* at the karate *dojo* has a couple of them."

"*Ginkgo biloba*," Pendergast said. "The Maidenhair. It's the only remaining member of a tree family common in prehistory. And to your right is a group planting of dwarf trident maples. I'm especially proud of their natural look. The trees in that planting all change color at different times in the fall. From the first tree to the last, that construction took me nine years. Your *sensei* could no doubt tell you that the secret to group plantings is to add bonsai in odd numbers at a time, up to a point where counting the trunks demands concentration. Then you're done."

"Nine *years*?" Hayward repeated. "Guess you got a lot of free time on your hands."

"Not really. Bonsai is one of my passions. It is an art that is never finished. And I find its blend of natural and artificial aesthetics intoxicating." He crossed one leg over the other, his black-suited form almost invisible against the dark leather, and waved one hand dismissively. "But stop encouraging me. A moment ago, you asked why I thought this the best place to talk. It's because I wish to learn more about the underground homeless."

Hayward was silent.

"You've worked with them," Pendergast continued. "You've *studied* them. You are an expert on the subject."

"Nobody else thinks so."

"If they gave the matter any thought, they would. In any case, I can understand why you're sensitive about your thesis. And it seemed to me you might be more comfortable discussing it off duty, someplace far away from headquarters or the station house."

The man had a point, Hayward thought. This strange, soothing room, with its quiet waterfall and stark beauty, seemed about as far from headquarters as the moon. Sitting back in the intoxicating softness of the chair, she felt her natural wariness draining away. She thought about taking off her bulky gun belt but decided she was too comfortable to move.

"I've been down twice," Pendergast said. "The first time merely to test my disguise and do some simple reconnaissance, and the second time to find Mephisto, the homeless leader. But when I found him, I discovered I'd underestimated a couple of things. The depth of his convictions. And the size of his following."

"Nobody knows, exactly, how many live belowground," Hayward said. "The only thing you can be sure of is the number's bigger than you expect. As for Mephisto, he's probably the most famous mayor down there. His community's the biggest. Actually, I heard it's several communities: a core community of troubled Vietnam vets and sixties relics, with others joining after the headless murders started. The deeper tunnels below Central Park are crawling with him and his pals."

"What surprised me was the variety I encountered," Pendergast went on. "I expected to find one flawed personality type predominating, perhaps two. But instead I found an entire cross section of humanity."

"Not all homeless go below," Hayward said. "But the ones afraid of the shelters, the ones that hate the soup kitchens and subway gratings, the loners, the cult freaks—they tend to go down. First to the subway tunnels. Then farther. Believe me, there're lots of places to hide."

Pendergast nodded. "Even on my first trip, I was astonished at the vastness. I felt like Lewis and Clark, setting out to explore unmapped territory."

"You don't know the half of it. There's two thousand miles of abandoned or half-dug tunnels, and another five thousand miles still in use. Underground chambers, sealed up and forgotten." Hayward shrugged. "And you hear stories. Like about bomb shelters, secretly built by the Pentagon in the fifties to protect Wall Street types. Some of them are still stocked with running water, electricity, canned food. Engine rooms filled with abandoned machinery, ancient sewers made from wooden pipes. An entire freakin' lost world."

Pendergast sat forward in his chair. "Sergeant Hayward," he said quietly. "Have you heard of the Devil's Attic?"

Hayward nodded. "Yeah. I've heard of it."

"Can you tell me where it is, or how I can locate it?"

There was a long silence while she thought. "No. One or two of the homeless mentioned it during rousts. But you hear so much crap down there, you tune most of it out. I always thought it was bullshit."

"Is there anybody I can talk to who might know more?"

Hayward shifted slightly. "You might talk to Al Diamond," she said, her eyes drifting again toward the picture of the haystacks. Amazing, she thought, how a couple of thick dabs of paint could capture an image so clearly. "He's an engineer for the PA, a real authority on underground structures. They always call him in when a deep main breaks, or when a new gas tunnel has to be bored." She paused. "Haven't seen him around for a while, though. Maybe he bought the farm."

"Excuse me?"

"Died, I mean."

There was a silence, broken only by the soft hush of the waterfall. "If the killers have colonized some secret space underground, the sheer number of homeless will make our own job extremely difficult," Pendergast said at last.

Hayward took her eyes from the picture of the haystack and fastened them on the FBI agent. "It gets worse," she said.

"What do you mean?"

"Autumn's only a few weeks away. That's when the homeless really start streaming underground, anticipating winter. If you're right about these killers, you know what that means."

"No, I don't," Pendergast said. "Why don't you tell me?"

"Hunting season," Hayward said, and shifted her gaze back to the painting.

27

The length of grimy industrial avenue ended in an embarkment of riprap, half tumbling into the murky depths of the East River. Beyond lay a panoramic view of Roosevelt Island and the 59th Street Bridge. Across the river, the thin gray strip of the FDR Drive wound its way up past the United Nations and the luxurious Sutton Place co-ops. *Nice view,* thought D'Agosta as he stepped out of the unmarked cruiser. *Nice view, lousy neighborhood.*

The August sun slanted into the avenue, softening the puddles of tar and coaxing waves of shimmering heat from the pavement. Loosening his collar, D'Agosta once again checked the address the Museum personnel office had given him: 11-46 94th Avenue, Long Island City. He glanced at the nearby buildings, wondering if there was some mistake. This sure as hell didn't look like a residential neighborhood. The street was lined with old warehouses and abandoned factories. Even though it was noon, the place was almost deserted, the only sign of life a shabby panel truck pulling out of a loading bay at the far end of the block. D'Agosta shook his head. *Another frigging dead end.* Leave it to Waxie to saddle him with what, in Waxie's opinion, was the assignment of lowest priority.

The door to 11-46 was of thick metal, dented and scarred, and covered in perhaps ten coats of black paint. Like everything else on the block, it looked like the entrance to an empty warehouse. D'Agosta rang the ancient buzzer and then, hearing nothing, pounded heavily on the door. Silence.

He waited a few minutes, then ducked into a narrow alley along one side of the building. Making his way through crumbling rolls of tar paper, D'Agosta approached a window of wired glass, webbed with cracks and almost opaque with dust. Climbing onto the tarpaper, he rubbed a hole clean with his tie and looked in.

As his eyes adjusted to the dim interior, he made out a vast empty space. Faint bars of light striped across the stained cement floor. At the far end was a staircase leading up to what must once have been the office of the line boss. Otherwise, nothing.

There was a sudden movement in the alley, and D'Agosta turned to see a man coming at him fast, a long kitchen knife shining wickedly in one hand. Reflexively, D'Agosta leapt for the ground, pulling his service piece as he did so. The man stared at the gun in surprise, stopping short. He gathered himself to flee.

"Halt!" D'Agosta barked. "Police officer!"

The man turned back again. Inexplicably, a look of amusement came over his features.

"A cop!" he cried sarcastically. "Fancy that, a cop in these parts!"

He continued to stand there, grinning. He was the strangest-looking person D'Agosta had ever seen: a shaved head, painted green; a wispy goatee; tiny, Trotskyesque glasses; a shirt made out of something like hairy burlap; ancient, red Keds sneakers.

"Drop the knife," said D'Agosta.

"Hey, it's okay," the man said. "I thought you were a burglar."

"I said, drop the damn knife."

The grin disappeared from the man's face. He tossed the knife onto the ground between them.

D'Agosta kicked it aside. "Now turn around, slowly, and put your hands on the wall. Spread your feet wide."

"What is this, Communist China?" the man objected.

"Do it," D'Agosta said.

The man obeyed, grumbling, and D'Agosta patted him down, finding nothing more than a wallet. He flipped it open. The driver's license showed an address next door.

D'Agosta holstered his gun and handed the man his wallet. "You know, Mr. Kirtsema, I could've shot you back there."

"Hey, but I didn't *know* you were a cop. I thought you were trying to break in." The man stepped away from the wall, wiping his hands together. "You don't know how many times I've been robbed. You guys don't even bother to respond anymore. You're the first cop I've seen around here in months, and—"

D'Agosta waved him silent. "Just be more careful. Besides, you don't know squat about handling a knife. If I was a real burglar, you'd probably be dead right now."

The man rubbed his nose, mumbling something incomprehensible.

"You live next door?" D'Agosta asked. He could not get over the fact that this man had painted his entire scalp green. He tried not to stare at it.

The man nodded.

"How long?"

"About three years. I used to have a loft in Soho, but I got evicted. This is the only place I found where I can do my work without being bothered."

"And what kind of work is that?"

"It's hard to explain." The man grew suddenly guarded. "Why should I tell you?"

D'Agosta dug into his pocket, flashed his badge and ID.

The man looked at the badge. "Homicide, eh? Someone murdered around here?"

"No. Can we go inside and talk for a moment?"

The man looked at him suspiciously. "Is this a search? Aren't you supposed to have a warrant?"

D'Agosta swallowed his annoyance. "It's voluntary. I want to ask you a few questions about the man who lived in this warehouse. Kawakita."

"Was that his name? Now there was a weird guy. Seriously weird." Leading D'Agosta out of the alley, the man named Kirtsema unlocked his own black metal door. Stepping inside, D'Agosta found himself inside another vast warehouse, painted bone white. Along the walls were a number of oddly shaped metal cans filled with trash. A dead palm tree stood in one corner. In the middle of the room, D'Agosta could see countless black strings, hung from the ceiling in clumps. It felt like some kind of nightmarish moon-forest. In the far corner he could see a cot, sink, exposed toilet, and hot plate. No other amenities were visible.

"So what's this?" D'Agosta asked, fingering the strings.

"My God, don't tangle them!" Kirtsema almost knocked D'Agosta aside in his rush to repair the damage.

"They're never supposed to *touch*," he said in a wounded tone as he fussed with the strings.

D'Agosta stepped back. "What is this, some kind of experiment?"

"No. It's an artificial environment, a reproduction of the primeval jungle that we all evolved in, translated to New York City."

D'Agosta looked at the strings in disbelief. "So this is art? Who looks at it?"

"It's *conceptual* art," Kirtsema explained impatiently. "Nobody looks at it. It's not meant to be seen. It is sufficient that it *exists*. The strings never touch, just as we human beings never touch, never really interact. We are alone. And this whole world is unseen, just as we float through the cosmos unseen. As Derrida said, 'Art is that which is not art,' which means—"

"Did you know if his first name was Gregory?"

"Jacques. *Jacques* Derrida. Not Gregory."

"I mean the man who lived next door."

"Like I said, I didn't even know his name. I avoided him like the plague. Guess you're here because of the complaints."

"Complaints?"

"Yeah. I called, again and again. After the first couple of times, nobody came." He blinked. "No, wait. You're Homicide. Did he kill somebody?"

Without answering, D'Agosta took a notebook out of a coat pocket. "Tell me about him."

"He moved in two years ago, maybe a little less. At first, he seemed pretty quiet. Then these trucks began pulling up, and all kinds of boxes and crates started going inside. That's when the noise started. Always at night. Hammering. Thuds. Loud popping noises. And the smell..." Kirtsema wrinkled his nose in disgust. "Like something acrid burning. He'd painted the inside of the windows black, but one of them got broken somehow and I got a look inside before it was repaired." He grinned. "It was a strange-looking setup. I could see microscopes, big glass beakers boiling and boiling, gray metal boxes with lights on them, aquaria."

"Aquaria?"

"One aquarium after another, rows upon rows. Big things, full of algae. Obviously, he was a scientist of some kind." Kirtsema pronounced the word with distaste. "A dissector, a reductionist. I don't like that way of looking at the world. I am a holist, Sergeant."

"I see."

"Then one day the power company came around. Said they had to hook up some special heavy-duty lines to his place, or something. And they turned off my power for two days. Two days! But try complaining to Con Ed. Dehumanized bureaucrats."

"Did he have any visitors?" D'Agosta asked. "Any friends?"

"Visitors!" Kirtsema snorted. "That was the last straw. People began arriving. Always at night. They had this way of knocking, like some kind of signal. That was when I first called the cops. I knew something seriously weird was happening there. I thought maybe it was drugs. The cops came, said there was nothing illegal going on, and left again." He shook his head bitterly at the memory.

"It went on like that. I kept calling the cops, complaining about the noise and the smell, but after the second visit they wouldn't come anymore. And then one day, maybe a year ago, the guy appeared at my door. Just showed up, no warning or anything, about eleven o'clock at night."

"What did he want?" D'Agosta asked.

"Don't know. I think he wanted to ask me why I'd called the cops on him. All I know is, he gave me the willies. It was September, almost as hot as it is now, but he had on a bulky coat with a big hood. He stood back in the shadows, and I couldn't see his face. He just stood there, in the darkness, and asked if he could come in. I said no, of course. Sergeant, it was all I could do not to shut the door in his face."

"Lieutenant," corrected D'Agosta absently, scribbling in his notebook.

"Whatever. I don't put stock in labels. *Human being* is the only label worth anything." The green dome bobbed in emphasis.

D'Agosta was still scribbling. This didn't sound like the Greg Kawakita he'd met once in Frock's office, after the disaster at the *Superstition* exhibition opening. He racked his brains, trying to remember what he could about the scientist.

"Can you describe his voice?" he asked.

"Yes. Very low, and with a lisp."

D'Agosta frowned. "Any accent?"

"Don't think so. But it was such a strong lisp I couldn't really tell. Sounded almost Castilian, except it was English instead of Spanish."

D'Agosta made a mental note to ask Pendergast what the hell 'Castilian' was. "When did he leave, and why?" he asked.

"A couple of weeks after he knocked on my door. Maybe October. One night I heard two big eighteen-wheelers pull up. That wasn't so unusual. But this time, they were loading stuff out of that place, not into it. When I got up at noon, the place was totally empty. They'd even washed the black paint off the inside of the windows."

"This was at noon?" D'Agosta asked.

"My normal sleep period is five to noon. I am not a slave to the physical rotations of the earth-sun-moon system, Sergeant."

"Did you notice anything on the trucks? A logo, say, or the name of a firm?"

Kirtsema went silent, thinking. "Yes," he said finally. "Scientific Precision Moving."

D'Agosta looked at the middle-aged man with a green scalp. "You sure?"

"Absolutely."

D'Agosta believed him. With his looks, the guy wouldn't be worth shit on a witness stand, but he was pretty damn observant. Or maybe just nosy. "Anything else you want to add?" he said.

The green dome bobbed again. "Yes. Right after he arrived all the streetlights went out, and they never seemed to be able to fix them. They're *still* out. I think he had something to do with that, though I don't know what. I called Con Ed about that, too, but as usual the faceless corporate robots never did anything. Of course, try forgetting to pay your bill one time, and—"

"Thanks for your help, Mr. Kirtsema," D'Agosta interrupted. "Call if anything else comes to mind." He closed the notebook, stuck it in his pocket, and turned to leave.

At the door, he paused. "You said you'd been robbed several times. What did they take? There doesn't seem to be much worth lifting in here." He glanced around the warehouse again.

"Ideas, Sergeant!" Kirtsema said, head back, chin raised. "Material objects mean nothing. But ideas are priceless. Look around you. Have you ever seen so many brilliant ideas?"

28

Vent Stack Twelve rose like a nightmare chimney above the 38th Street entrance to the Lincoln Tunnel, a two-hundred-foot spire of brick and rusting metal.

Near the top of the enormous stack, a small metal observation chamber clung, barnaclelike, to the side of the orange wall. From his vantage point on the narrow access ladder, Pendergast could make out the chamber far above his head. The ladder had been bolted to the river side of the vent stack, and in several places the bolts had pulled free of their moorings. As he climbed, he could see the traffic through the corrugations in the iron steps, wrestling its way into the tunnel thirty yards beneath his feet.

The ladder fell into shadow as he approached the underside of the observation chamber. Looking up, Pendergast noticed a hatch set into the chamber's underside. It had a circular handle, like the watertight door of a submarine, and the words PORT OF NEW YORK AUTHORITY had been stamped into it. The roar of the vent stack was like the shriek of a jet engine, and Pendergast had to bang several times on the hatch before it was raised by the person inside.

Pendergast climbed into the tiny metal room and straightened his suit while the occupant—a small, wiry man dressed in a plaid shirt and coveralls—closed the hatch. Three sides of the observation chamber looked down over the Hudson, the approaches to the Lincoln Tunnel, and the massive power plant that sucked foul air out of the tunnel and channeled it up the vent stacks. Craning his neck, Pendergast could make out the spinning turbines of the tunnel's filtration system rumbling directly beneath them.

The man stepped away from the hatch and moved to a stool behind a small draftsman's table. There was no other chair in the tiny, cramped chamber. Pendergast watched as the man looked at him and moved his mouth as if speaking. But no sound was audible over the shriek of the huge stack vent beside them.

"What?" Pendergast shouted, moving closer. The floor hatch did little to keep out either the noise or the traffic fumes wafting up from below.

"ID," the man replied. "They said you'd have some ID."

Pendergast reached into his jacket pocket and showed his FBI identification to the man, who examined it carefully.

"Mr. Albert Diamond, correct?" Pendergast said.

"Al," the man said with a careless gesture. "What ya need?"

"I hear you're the authority on underground New York," Pendergast said. "You're the engineer who's consulted on everything from the building of a new subway tunnel to the repair of a gas main."

Diamond stared at Pendergast. One cheek began to bulge as his tongue made a slow traverse of his lower molars. "Guess that's true," he replied at last.

"When were you last underground?"

Diamond raised one fist, opened it wide once, twice, closed it again.

"Ten?" Pendergast said. "Ten months?"

Diamond shook his head.

"Years?"

Diamond nodded.

"Why so long?"

"Got tired. Requested this instead."

"Requested? Interesting choice of assignment. About as far away from the underground as one could get without actually being airborne. Intentional?"

Diamond shrugged, neither agreeing nor contradicting.

"I need some information," Pendergast shouted. It was simply too loud in the observation chamber for any kind of small talk.

Diamond nodded, the bulge in his cheek slowly rising as the investigation moved to the upper molars.

"Tell me about the Devil's Attic."

The bulge froze in position. After a few moments, Diamond shifted on the stool, but said nothing.

Pendergast continued. "I'm told there's a level of tunnels underneath Central Park. Unusually deep tunnels. I've heard the region referred to as the Devil's Attic. But there are no records of such a place in existence, at least by that name."

After a long moment, Diamond looked down. "Devil's Attic?" he repeated, as if with great reluctance.

"Do you know of such a place?"

Diamond reached into his coveralls and drew out a small flask of something that was not water. He took a long pull, then returned the flask without offering it to Pendergast. He said something that was inaudible over the shriek of the exhaust stack.

"What?" Pendergast cried, moving still closer.

"I said, yeah, I know of it."

"Tell me about it, please."

Diamond looked away from Pendergast, his eyes gazing over the river toward the New Jersey shore.

"Those rich bastards," he said.

"I'm sorry?"

"Those rich bastards. Didn't want to rub shoulders with the working class."

"Rich bastards?" Pendergast asked.

"You know. Astor. Rockefeller. Morgan. And the rest. Built those tunnels over a century ago."

"I don't understand."

"Railroad tunnels," Diamond burst out irritably. "They were building a private railcar line. Came down from Pelham, under the Park, beneath the Knickerbocker Hotel, the Fifth Avenue parkfront mansions. Fancy private stations and waiting rooms. The whole nine yards."

"But why so deep?"

For the first time, Diamond grinned. "Geology. Had to go deeper than the existing train lines and early subway tunnels, of course. But right below was a layer of shitstone."

"I beg your pardon?" Pendergast yelled.

"Rotten Precambrian siltstone. We call it shitstone. You can run water and sewer lines through shitstone, but not a railroad tunnel. So they had to go deeper. Your Devil's Attic is thirty stories underground."

"But why?"

Diamond looked at the FBI agent in disbelief. "Why? Why do you think? Those fancy pants didn't want to share any sidings or signals with regular train lines. With those deep tunnels, they could go straight out of the city, come up around Croton, and be on their way. No delays, no mixing with the common folk."

"That doesn't explain why there is no record of their existence."

"Cost a fortune to build. And not all of it came from the pockets of the oil barons. They called in favors from City Hall." Diamond tapped the side of his nose. "That kind of construction you don't document."

"Why were they abandoned?"

"Impossible to maintain. Beneath most of the sewer and storm drains like they were, you could never keep them dry. Then there was methane buildup, carbon monoxide buildup, you name it."

Pendergast nodded. "Heavy gases, seeking the lowest level."

"They spent millions on those damn tunnels. Never finished the line. They were only open for two years before the flood of ninety-eight overwhelmed the pumps and half-filled everything with sewage. So they bricked everything up. Didn't even pull out the machinery or nothing."

Diamond fell silent, and the chamber filled once again with the roar of the vent stack.

"Are there any maps of these tunnels?" Pendergast asked after a moment.

Diamond rolled his eyes. "Maps? I looked for maps for twenty years. Those maps don't exist. I learned what I learned by talking to a few old-timers."

"Have you been down there?" Pendergast asked.

Diamond twitched noticeably. Then, after a long moment, he nodded silently.

"Could you diagram them for me?"

Diamond was silent.

Pendergast moved closer. "Any little thing you could do would be appreciated." His hand seemed merely to smooth the lapel of his jacket, but suddenly a hundred-dollar bill flared between two of the slender fingers, arching in the engineer's direction.

Diamond stared at the bill, as if deliberating. Finally, he took it, rolled it into a ball, and crammed it into a pocket. Then, turning to the drafting table, he began sketching deftly on a piece of yellow graph paper. An intricate system of tunnels began to take shape.

"Best I can do," he said, straightening up after a few minutes. "That's the approach I used to get inside. A lot of the stuff south of the Park has been filled with concrete, and the tunnels to the north collapsed years ago. You'll have to find your way down to the Bottleneck first. Take Feeder Tunnel 18 down from where it intersects the old 'Twenty-four water main."

"The Bottleneck?" Pendergast asked.

Diamond nodded, scratching his nose with a dirty finger. "There's a vein of granite running through the bedrock deep beneath the Park. Super hard stuff. To save time and dynamite, the old pipe jockeys just blasted one massive hole in it and funneled everything through. The Astor Tunnels are directly below. As far as I know, that's the only way to get inside them from the south—unless you got a wetsuit, of course."

Pendergast accepted the paper, looking it over carefully. "Thank you, Mr. Diamond. Is there any chance you'd be willing to return and make a more careful survey of the Devil's Attic? For adequate remuneration, of course."

Diamond took a long drink from the flask. "All the money in the world wouldn't get me down there again."

Pendergast inclined his head.

"Another thing," Diamond said. "Don't call it the Devil's Attic, all right? That's mole talk. They're the Astor Tunnels."

"Astor Tunnels?"

"Yeah. They were Mrs. Astor's idea. The story goes that she got her husband to build the first private station beneath her Fifth Avenue mansion. That's how it all got started."

"Where did the name 'Devil's Attic' come from?" Pendergast asked.

Diamond grinned mirthlessly. "I don't know. But think about it. Imagine tunnels thirty stories underground. Walls tiled in big murals. Imagine waiting rooms, stuffed to the gills with mirrors, sofas, fancy stained glass. Imagine hydraulic elevators with parquet flooring and velvet curtains. Now think of what all that would look like after being doused in raw sewage, then sealed up for a century." He sat back and stared at Pendergast. "I don't know about you. But to me, it would look like the attic of Hell itself."

29

The West Side railyard lay in a wide depression on the westernmost reaches of Manhattan, out of sight and practically invisible to the millions of New Yorkers who lived and worked nearby, its seventy-four acres the largest piece of undeveloped land on the island outside Central Park. Once a bustling hub of turn-of-the-century commerce, the railyard now lay fallow: rusted tracks sunken among burdock and ailanthus trees, ancient sidings rotting and forgotten, abandoned warehouses sagging and covered with graffiti.

For twenty years the piece of ground had been the subject of development plans, lawsuits, political manipulations, and bankruptcies. The tenants of the warehouses had gradually abandoned their leases and left, to be replaced by vandals, arsonists, and the homeless. In one corner of the railyard lay a small, bedraggled shantytown of plywood, cardboard, and tin. Alongside were a few pathetic kitchen gardens of straggly peas and squash run riot.

Margo stood amidst a plot of fire-scorched piles of rubble, sandwiched between two abandoned railyard buildings. The warehouse occupying the plot had burned four months earlier, and it had burned hotly and thoroughly. The structure had been reduced to a blackened I-beam framework and some low cinder-block stem walls. Beneath her feet, the cement pad was hip deep in rubble and burned shingles. The remains of several long metal tables stood in one corner of the lot, covered with smashed equipment and melted glass. She looked around, peering through the late afternoon shadows that knitted themselves across the sunken ground. There were several hulks that had once been large machines, housed in metal cabinets; the cabinets had melted and the inner workings lay exposed, masses of twisted wire and ruined circuit boards. The acrid stench of burned plastic and tar clung stubbornly to everything.

D'Agosta appeared at her side. "Whaddaya think?" he asked.

She shook her head. "Are you sure this was Greg's last known address?"

"Confirmed it with the moving company. The warehouse burned about the time of his death, so it's doubtful he moved anywhere else. But he used an alias with Con Ed and New York Telephone, so we can't be certain."

"An alias?" Margo continued to look around. "I wonder if he died before or after this place burned."

"Not as much as I wonder," D'Agosta replied.

"It looks like this was some kind of laboratory."

D'Agosta nodded. "Even I could have guessed that. This guy Kawakita was a scientist. Just like you."

"Not quite. Greg was more involved with genetics and evolutionary biology. My specialty is anthropological pharmacology."

"Whatever." D'Agosta hiked up his pants. "Question is, what kind of lab is it?"

"Hard to say. I'd need to learn more about those machines in the corner. And I'd have to map out the melted glass on these tables, try to re-create what the setups might have been."

D'Agosta looked at her. "Well?"

"Well, what?"

"You wanna take it on?"

Margo returned the Lieutenant's gaze. "Why me? You must have specialists in the department that—"

"They're not interested," D'Agosta interrupted. "It ranks right below jaywalking on their list of priorities."

Margo frowned in surprise.

"The powers that be don't give a damn about Kawakita or what he was doing before he was killed. They think he was just a random victim. Just like they think Brambell was a random victim."

"But you don't? You think he was involved in these murders somehow?"

D'Agosta pulled a handkerchief out of his pocket and mopped his brow. "Hell, I don't know. I just feel this guy Kawakita was up to something, and I'd like to know what it was. You knew him, right?"

"Yes," Margo said.

"I only met him once, when Frock had that good-bye party for Pendergast. What was he like?"

Margo thought a moment. "He was brilliant. An excellent scientist."

"What about his personality?"

"He wasn't the nicest person in the Museum," Margo said carefully. "He was—well, a little ruthless, I guess you could say. I felt he was the kind of person who would perhaps step over the line to advance his career. He didn't associate much with the rest of us, and didn't seem to trust anybody who might..." She stopped.

"Yeah?"

"Is this necessary? I hate to talk about someone who isn't around to defend himself."

"That's usually the best time. Was he the kind of guy to get involved in any criminal activity?"

"Absolutely not. I didn't always agree with his ethics— he was one of those scientists who held science above human values—but he was no criminal." She hesitated. "He tried to reach me awhile back. Maybe a month or so before he died."

D'Agosta looked at her curiously. "Any idea why? It doesn't seem like you two were exactly friends."

"Not close friends. But we were colleagues. If he was in some kind of trouble—" A shadow crossed her face. "Maybe I could have done something about it. Instead of just ignoring the call."

"Guess you'll never know. But anyway, if you'd take the time to poke around, try to get some ideas of what he was doing here, I'd appreciate it."

Margo hesitated, and D'Agosta gave her a closer look. "Who knows?" he said in a quieter tone. "Maybe it'll help lay some of those inner demons to rest."

Nice choice of words, Margo thought. Still, she knew he meant well. *Lieutenant D'Agosta, pop psychologist. Next thing you know, he'll be telling me that looking over this site will help give me* closure.

She glanced over the ruined site for a long minute. "Okay, Lieutenant," she said at last.

"Want me to get a photographer down here, take some pictures?"

"Maybe later. For now, I'd rather just make a few sketches."

"Sure thing." D'Agosta seemed restless.

"You go on," Margo said. "You don't need to hang around."

"No way," D'Agosta said. "Not after Brambell."

"Lieutenant—"

"I've got to collect some of the ashes anyway, to test for trace accelerants. I'll stay out of your way." He stood truculently, unmoving.

Margo sighed, pulled a sketchbook out of her carryall, and once again turned her attention to the ruined lab. It was a dreary place, surrounding her in silent accusation. *You could have done something. Greg tried to reach you. Perhaps it didn't have to end like this.*

She shook her head, scattering the guilty thoughts. They wouldn't be of any help. Besides, if any place held the clues to explain what happened to Greg, this place would. And maybe the only way to get out of this nightmare was for her just to lower her head and go straight through. Anyway, it got her out of the Forensic Anthropology lab, which had started to look like a charnel house. The Bitterman corpse had arrived from NYME Wednesday afternoon, bringing a fresh set of questions along with it. The scoring on the neck bones of the still-fleshed corpse pointed to decapitation by some kind of rough, primitive knife. The killer—or killers—had been rushed in their grisly task.

She quickly mapped out the rough outlines of the lab, sketching in the dimensions of the walls, the location of the tables, and the placement of the slaglike heaps of ruined equipment. Every laboratory had a flow to it, depending on what kind of work was being done. While the equipment might indicate the general kind of research, the flow itself would give clues to the specific application.

The rough outlines completed, Margo moved to the tables themselves. Being metal, they had withstood the heat of the fire relatively well. She sketched out a rectangle to indicate each tabletop, then began noting the melted beakers, titration tubes, volumetric flasks, and other items still unidentifiable. It was a complex, multilayered setup: clearly, some kind of high-level biochemistry had been going on. But what?

She paused for a moment, breathing in the mingled scents of burnt electrical insulation and the saline breeze off the Hudson. Then she turned her attention to the melted machinery. It was expensive stuff, judging from the brushed stainless-steel cabinetry and the remains of flat panel and vacuum fluorescent displays.

Margo tackled the largest machine first. Its metal casing had slumped in the heat, the innards detached. She gave it a light kick, shrinking back as it fell with a loud crash. She suddenly felt aware of how alone they were. Beyond the railyards and across the river, the sun hung low over the New Jersey Palisades. She could hear the cry of seagulls as they wheeled over the rotting stumps of old piers rising from the Hudson's shore. Beyond the railyards, a cheerful summer afternoon was ending. Yet here, in this sunken, abandoned place, no cheer came. She glanced at D'Agosta, who had collected his samples and was standing in the late sun, arms crossed, staring out at the Hudson. Now she was glad he'd insisted on staying.

She bent over the machine, smiling inwardly at her nervousness. Turning over the pieces of scorched and discolored metal, she eventually found the faceplate she was searching for. Rubbing it free of soot, she made out the words WESTERLY GENETICS EQUIPMENT, along with a WGE logo. Beneath, on the bezel, was a stamped serial number and the words WGE INTEGRATED DNA ANALYZER-SEQUENCER. She jotted the information down on her sketchpad.

In a far corner was heaped a small pile of shattered, melted machinery that looked different from the rest. Margo examined it, carefully turning over each piece and laying it out, trying to figure out what it was. It seemed to be a rather complex organic chem synthesis setup, complete with fractionation and distillation apparatus, diffusion gradients, and low-voltage electrical nodes. Toward the bottom, where things were less damaged by the heat, she found the broken pieces of several Erlenmeyer flasks. Judging by the words on their frosted labels, most were normal lab chemicals. One fragmentary label, however, she did not immediately recognize: ACTIVATED 7-DEHYDROCHOLE...

She turned the piece over. Damn, the chemical name had a familiar ring to it. At last, she dropped the piece into her carryall. No doubt it would be listed in the organic chem encyclopedia back at the lab.

Beside the machine were the remains of a thin notebook, burned through except for a few carbonized pages. As she picked it up curiously, it began to crumble in her hands. Carefully, she picked up the charred pieces, slid them carefully into a Ziploc bag, and stowed it in her carryall.

Within fifteen minutes, she had managed to identify enough of the other machines to be certain of one thing: this had once been a world-class genetics laboratory. Margo worked with similar machines on a daily basis, and she knew enough to estimate the cost of this ruined lab at over half a million dollars.

She stepped back. *Where had Kawakita gotten the money to fund this kind of lab? And what the hell could he have been up to?*

As she moved across the cement pad, making notations in her sketchbook, something odd caught her eye. Among the piles of rubble and melted glass, she made out what looked like five large puddles of mud, baked to a cementlike consistency by the fire. Around them were sprinkles of gravel.

Curious, she bent over to examine the rubble more closely. There was a small metal object, about the size of her fist, embedded in the nearest puddle. Pulling a penknife from her carryall, she pried out the object and scraped off the crust that clung to it like cement. Beneath the mud she could make out Minne Arium Suppl. Turning the object over and over in her hands, she realized what it was: an aquarium pump.

She stood up, looking down at the five similar heaps of rubble lined up beneath the remaining skeleton of a wall. The gravel, the broken glass... these must have been aquaria. Huge, too, judging by the size of the puddles. But aquaria filled with mud? It didn't make sense.

Kneeling, she took her penknife and worked it into the closest dried mass. It came away in pieces, like concrete. Picking up one of the larger pieces and turning it over, Margo was surprised to see what looked like the roots and partial stem of a plant, preserved from burning by the protective mud coating. Cursing the clumsiness of the penknife, she carefully worked the plant loose from the mud and held it up to the fading light.

Suddenly, she dropped the plant and jerked her hand back, as if burned. After a moment, she picked it up again and examined it more closely, her heart suddenly racing. *It's not possible,* she thought.

She knew this plant—knew it well. The tough, fibrous stem, the bizarrely knotted roots, brought back searing memories: sitting in the deserted Genetics lab at the Museum, face glued to the eyepiece of a microscope, mere hours before the disastrous opening of the *Superstition* exhibition. It was the rare Amazonian plant that the Mbwun creature had craved so desperately. The same plant Whittlesey had inadvertently used as packing material in the fateful crate of relics sent to the Museum from the Upper Xingu almost a decade before. The plant was now supposed to be extinct: its original habitat had been wiped out, and all remaining vestiges of it at the Museum had been destroyed by the authorities after the Mbwun creature—the Museum Beast— was finally killed.

Margo stood up again, brushing soot from her knees. Greg Kawakita had somehow gotten his hands on this plant and had been growing it in these massive aquaria.

But why?

A sudden, horrible thought struck her. As quickly as it had come, she brushed it aside. Surely, there was no second Mbwun creature that Greg had been feeding.

Or was there?

"Lieutenant?" she asked. "Do you know what this is?"

He came over. "Not a clue," he replied.

"*Liliceae mbwunensis*. The Mbwun plant."

"You're shitting me, right?"

Margo shook her head slowly. "I wish I were."

They stood, unmoving, as the sun sank below the Palisades, gilding the distant buildings across the river in a halo of oblique light. She looked again at the plant in her hand, preparing to place it in her carryall, and noticed something that she had missed before.

At the end of the root base, she could make out a small graft scar along the xylem, a long double-V in the dim light. A graft scar like that, she knew, meant one of only two things. A common hybrid experiment.

Or a very sophisticated genetic engineering experiment.

30

Hayward pushed the door open brusquely, her cheeks still full of lunch.

"Captain Waxie just called," she said, swallowing the tuna fish. "Wants you down in the IU right away. They got him."

D'Agosta looked up from placing the final pins in a missing-persons map that replaced the one taken by Waxie. "Got who?"

"*Him*. The copycat killer, of course." She raised her eyebrows.

"No shit." D'Agosta was at the door in a second, pulling his suit jacket off the hanger and shrugging into it.

"Caught him in the Ramble," Hayward said as they walked through the office pool toward the elevator bank. "Somebody on stakeout heard a commotion, went to check it out. The guy had just knifed a vagrant and was preparing to cut off his head."

"How'd they know that?"

Hayward shrugged. "Ask Captain Waxie."

"And the knife?"

"Homemade job. Real rough. Just what they were looking for." She didn't sound convinced.

The elevator doors opened to reveal Pendergast. Seeing D'Agosta and Hayward about to step in, he raised his eyebrows quizzically.

"The killer's in the IU," D'Agosta said. "Waxie wants me down there."

"Indeed?" The FBI agent stepped back and pressed the button for the second floor. "Well, let's head down there by all means. I'm curious to see exactly what kind of fish angler Waxie has landed."

The Interrogation Unit of One Police Plaza was a grim series of gray-colored rooms with cinder-block walls and heavy metal doors. The cop on desk duty buzzed them through, directing them to the observation area of room nine. Inside, Waxie was lounging in a chair, looking through the one-way glass into the interrogation cell. He glanced up when he heard them enter, frowned when he saw Pendergast, grunted at D'Agosta, and ignored Hayward.

"Is he talking?" D'Agosta said.

Waxie grunted again. "Oh, yeah. Talking is all he's doing. But so far we've only heard a load of shit. Calls himself Jeffrey; won't give anything else. We'll get the real story out of him soon, though. Meanwhile, thought you might like to ask him a few questions." In his triumph, Waxie was generous, brimming with smug self-confidence.

Looking through the glass, D'Agosta could see an unkempt, wild-eyed man. The rapid, silent movements of the suspect's mouth were in almost humorous contrast with his stiff, unmoving body.

"This is the guy?" D'Agosta said in disbelief.

"That's him."

D'Agosta kept looking through the glass. "Looks kind of small to have done so much damage."

Waxie's mouth set in a defensive frown. "Maybe he got sand kicked in his face one too many times."

D'Agosta leaned forward and pressed the mike button. Instantly, a torrent of curses spewed from the speaker above the one-way window. D'Agosta listened for a moment, then snapped the mike button off.

"What about the murder weapon?" he asked.

Waxie shrugged. "It's a handmade thing, a piece of steel sunk into a wooden shank. The handle's been wrapped in cloth, gauze, something like that. Too bloody to tell; we'll have to wait until forensics gets done with it."

"Steel," Pendergast said.

"Steel," Waxie replied.

"Not stone."

"I said, it was steel. Take a look for yourself."

"We will," D'Agosta said, stepping away from the window. "But for now, let's see what this guy has to say." He headed for the door, Pendergast gliding behind him like a silent spirit.

Number nine looked like countless interrogation rooms in countless police stations across the country. A scarred wooden table sat in the middle of the stark space. On the far side of the table, the prisoner sat in a straight-backed chair, arms cuffed behind his back. A single detective sat in one of several chairs on the table's near side, enduring the verbal abuse with complete disinterest as he manned the tape recorder. Police officers, armed and in uniform, faced each other from across the room. Two huge black-and-white blowups hung on the side walls. One showed the torn and broken body of Nicholas Bitterman, lying on the men's room floor inside Belvedere Castle. The other was the now-famous *Post* photo of Pamela Wisher. A video camera was fixed in one corner of the ceiling, dispassionately recording the proceedings.

D'Agosta took a seat at the table, inhaling the familiar blend of sweat, damp socks, and fear. Waxie followed him in, settling his bulk carefully into an adjoining chair. Hayward stood next to the closest uniformed officer. Pendergast closed the door, then leaned against it, the crisp black arms of his suit folded casually, one over the other.

The prisoner had stopped shouting when the door opened. Now he glared at the new arrivals through a greasy lock of hair. His eyes lighted on Hayward, lingered for a moment, then moved on.

"What the hell you looking at?" he said at last to D'Agosta.

"Don't know," D'Agosta replied. "You want to tell me about it?"

"Piss off."

D'Agosta sighed. "You understand your rights?"

The prisoner grinned, exposing small, filthy teeth. "That fat mother next to you read them to me. I don't need no lawyer to hold my hand."

"You watch your mouth," Waxie snapped, flushing an angry crimson.

"No, fat boy, you watch yours. *And* your fat ass." He cackled with laughter. Hayward didn't bother to suppress a smirk.

D'Agosta wondered if this was how they had been carrying on before he got there. "So what happened in the park?" he asked.

"You want a list? For firstly, he was in my sleeping spot. For secondly, he hissed at me, like a snake out of Egypt. For thirdly, he lacked the blessings of God. For fourthly, he—"

Waxie waved his hand. "We get the picture. Tell us about the others."

Jeffrey said nothing.

"Come on," Waxie pushed. "Who else?"

"Plenty," came the reply at last. "Nobody disses me and gets away with it." He leaned forward. "Better watch out, fat boy, case I carve a piece of blubber off *you*."

D'Agosta placed a restraining hand on Waxie. "So who else you done?" he asked quickly.

"Oh, they know me. They know Jeffrey, the cherub cat. I'm on my way."

"What about Pamela Wisher?" Waxie broke in. "Don't deny it, Jeffrey."

The seams at the corners of the prisoner's muddy eyes thickened. "I don't deny it. The scumbags disrespected me, all of them. They deserved it."

"And what'd you do with the heads?" Waxie asked breathlessly.

"Heads?" Jeffrey asked. To D'Agosta, he seemed to falter slightly.

"You're in too deep now; don't start denying."

"Heads? I ate their heads is what I did."

Waxie cast a triumphant gaze toward D'Agosta. "What about the guy at Belvedere Castle, Nick Bitterman? Tell me about him."

"That was a good one. That mother had no respect. Hypocrite, miser. He was the adversary." He rocked back and forth.

"Adversary?" D'Agosta asked, frowning.

"The prince of adversaries."

"Yes," said Pendergast sympathetically. "You must counteract the powers of darkness." They were the first words he'd spoken since entering.

The prisoner rocked more vigorously. "Yes, yes."

"With your electrical skin."

Suddenly, the rocking stopped.

"And your glaring eyes," Pendergast continued. Then he pushed himself away from the door and came forward slowly, looking directly at the suspect.

Jeffrey stared hard at Pendergast. "Who are you?" he breathed.

Pendergast was silent for a moment. "Kit Smart," he said at last, without removing his eyes from Jeffrey.

To D'Agosta, the change that came over the prisoner was shocking. The color seemed to drain from his face in an instant. He looked at Pendergast, mouth working silently. Then, with a shriek, he forced himself backwards with such force that the chair tipped over and crashed to the floor. Hayward and the two police guards sprang to subdue the struggling figure.

"Jesus, Pendergast, what the hell did you say to him?" Waxie said over the screams, hoisting himself to his feet.

"The right thing, apparently." Pendergast glanced at Hayward. "Please give this fellow every comfort. I think we can let Captain Waxie take over from here."

"So who is that guy?" D'Agosta asked as the elevator carried them back up toward the Homicide Division.

"I'm not sure what his real name is," Pendergast replied, smoothing his tie. "But it isn't Jeffrey. And he's not the person we're looking for."

"Tell Waxie that."

Pendergast glanced mildly at D'Agosta. "What we saw, Lieutenant, was a classic case of paranoid schizophrenia, aggravated by multiple personality disorder. You noticed how the man seemed to weave in and out of two personas? There was the blustering tough guy, no doubt as unconvincing to you as to me. Then there was the killer visionary—infinitely more dangerous. Did you hear? 'For secondly, he hissed at me, like a snake out of Egypt.' Or 'Jeffrey, the cherub cat'."

"Of course I heard it. The guy was talking like somebody just handed him the Ten Commandments or something."

"Or something. You're right, his ravings had the structure and cadence of written speech. This occurred to me, also. At that point, I recognized he was quoting from the old poem *Jubilate Agno*, by Christopher Smart."

"Never heard of it."

Pendergast smile faintly. "It's a fairly obscure work by a fairly obscure writer. It is undeniably powerful in its strange vision, however; you should read it. The author, Smart, wrote it while he himself was half-insane in a debtor's prison. In any case, there's a long passage in the poem in which Smart describes his cat, Jeoffry, whom Smart believed to be some kind of chrysalis creature undergoing a physical conversion."

"If you say so. But what does all this have to do with our vocal friend back there?"

"Obviously, the poor fellow identifies himself with the cat in the poem."

"The *cat*?" D'Agosta asked incredulously.

"Why not? Kit Smart—the real Kit Smart—certainly did. It's an extremely powerful image of metamorphosis. I feel sure this poor fellow was once an academician, or a failed poet, before the creeping descent into madness began. He killed one man, true enough—but only when his path was crossed at the wrong time. As for the rest..." Pendergast waved his hand. "There are many indications this man is not our true target."

"Like the photographs," D'Agosta said. All good interrogators knew that no killer could keep his eyes from photographs of his victims or artifacts from the crime scene. Yet, as far as D'Agosta could tell, Jeffrey had never moved his eyes to either picture.

"Exactly." The elevator doors whispered open, and the two made their way through the hubbub toward D'Agosta's office. "Or the fact that this murder, as Waxie describes it, has none of the elements of the *blitzkrieg* attacks suffered by the other victims. In any case, once I recognized his neurotic identification with the poem, it was easy enough to goad his madness to the surface."

Pendergast closed the office door and waited until D'Agosta was seated before continuing. "But let's put this irritating business behind us. Have you had any luck on that cross-correlation I requested?"

"DP just delivered it this morning." D'Agosta thumbed through a tall sheaf of miniprinter output. "Let's see. Eighty-five percent of the victims were male. And ninety-two percent were residents of Manhattan, including transients."

"I'm primarily interested in things that *all* the victims had in common."

"Gotcha." There was a pause. "All had last names beginning with letters other than *I, S, U, V, X,* and *Z.*"

Pendergast's mouth twitched in what might have been a faint smile.

"All were older than twelve and younger than fifty-six. None of the victims were born in November."

"Goon."

"I think that's it." D'Agosta flipped some more pages. "Oh, here's something else. We ran the data through SMUD, checking for various traits associated with serial murderers. The only common thread it found was that none of the murders were committed during a full moon."

Pendergast sat up. "Indeed? That's worth remembering. Anything else?"

"No, that's it."

"Thank you." He sank back in the chair. "Still, it's precious little. Information is what we need, Vincent, hard facts. And that's why I can't wait any longer."

D'Agosta looked at him, uncomprehending. Then he frowned. "You're not going down again."

"Indeed I am. If Captain Waxie continues to insist this man is the killer, then the extra patrols will be called off. Vigilance will fade. Creating an atmosphere that can only make additional killings easier."

"Where will you go?" D'Agosta asked.

"To the Devil's Attic."

D'Agosta snorted. "Come on, Pendergast. You don't even know if such a place exists, let alone how to get there. You've got nothing but the word of that hobo."

"I believe Mephisto's word to be reliable," Pendergast replied. "And in any case, I have considerably more than just his word. I've spoken with a city engineer named Al Diamond. He explained that the so-called Devil's Attic is in reality a series of tunnels, constructed by New York's wealthiest families before the turn of the century. They were intended as a private rail line, but abandoned after only a few years. And I've been able to reconstruct a rough approximation of the route of these tunnels." Taking a marker from the desk, Pendergast moved the missing person's map. He set the point of the marker down at the intersection of Park and 45th, drew a line over to Fifth, up to Grand Army Plaza, then diagonally across Central Park and north up Central Park West. Then he stepped back, looking at D'Agosta bemusedly.

D'Agosta stared at the map. Except for a few locations in the Park, almost all the white and red pins were clustered along the lines Pendergast had drawn.

"Holy shit," he breathed.

"You could say that," Pendergast said. "Diamond also pointed out that the sections of tunnels to the south and north of the Park have been sealed off. So it's beneath the Park that I go."

D'Agosta reached into his desk for a cigar. "I'm coming along."

"Sorry, Vincent. You're essential up here, now that the rest of the force is about to let down its guard. And I need you to work with Margo Green to determine the precise nature of Kawakita's movements. We haven't yet heard the last of his involvement in all this. In any case, this time around my goal will be stealth. It's an extremely dangerous trip. Two of us would double the chances of our being discovered." He replaced the marker cap with a snap of his finger. "However, if you could spare Sergeant Hayward's expertise for a few hours, I could use some help in my preparations."

Scowling, D'Agosta put the cigar down. "Christ, Pendergast—that's a long trip down. You'll be gone overnight."

"More than that, I'm afraid." The FBI agent put the marker back on the desk. "If you don't hear from me within seventy-two hours..." He paused. Then, suddenly, he smiled and grasped D'Agosta's hand. "A rescue mission would be foolish."

"What about food?"

Pendergast feigned surprise. "Have you forgotten the delicacy of track rabbit *au vin*, spit-roasted over an open fire?"

D'Agosta grimaced, and Pendergast smiled reassuringly. "Fear not, Lieutenant. I'll be well provisioned. Food, maps, all I need."

"It's like the journey to the center of the earth," D'Agosta said, shaking his head.

"Indeed. I do feel a bit like an explorer setting out into parts unknown, peopled by unknown tribes. Odd to think it exists directly beneath our feet. *Qui ci sono dei mostri,* my friend. Let us hope I avoid *i mostri.* Friend Hayward will see me off."

Pendergast stood motionless a moment, apparently lost in thought. Then, with a final nod at D'Agosta, he swept out of the office and into the corridor beyond, the silk nap of his black suit shining dully under the fluorescent lights, the last of the great explorers.

31

Pendergast walked swiftly up the broad steps toward the entrance of the New York Public Library, a large leather-and-canvas valise in one hand. Behind him, Hayward stopped to stare at the huge marble lions that flanked the stairway.

"You needn't look so worried, Sergeant," Pendergast said. "They've already had their afternoon feeding." Despite the warmth of the day, he was wearing a tightly buttoned olive duster that reached almost to his ankles.

Inside, the marble entrance hall was dim and pleasantly cool. Pendergast spoke quietly to a guard, showed his ID, asked a few questions. Then he nodded for Hayward to follow him through a doorway underneath the sweeping double staircase.

"Sergeant Hayward, you know underground Manhattan better than any of us," Pendergast said as they stepped into a small, leather-lined elevator. "You've already given me invaluable advice. Any last words?"

The elevator began lurching downward. "Yes," Hayward replied. "Don't go."

Pendergast smiled thinly. "I'm afraid that isn't an option. Only firsthand reconnaissance will prove whether or not the Astor Tunnels are really the source of these killings."

"Then take me with you," Hayward said immediately.

Pendergast shook his head. "Believe me, I wish I could. But my aim this time is stealth. Two bodies would make an unacceptable noise signature."

The elevator stopped at the lowest level, 3-B, and they stepped out into a dark corridor. "Then watch your butt," Hayward said. "Most of the moles go down there to escape from confrontation, not start it. But there are plenty of predators. Drugs and alcohol only make things worse. Remember that they can see better, they can hear better. And they know the tunnels. Any way you look at it, you're at a disadvantage."

"True," Pendergast said. "So I'll do what I can to even the odds." He stopped in front of an ancient door, opened it with a key, and ushered Hayward inside. The room beyond was stacked, floor to ceiling, with metal racks filled with ancient books. The passageways between the racks were barely twenty inches across. The smell of dust and mildew was almost overpowering.

"What are we doing here, anyway?" Hayward asked as she followed Pendergast through the stacks.

"Of all the structures I examined," Pendergast said, "this building had the best plans and the clearest access to the Astor Tunnels. I still have a long descent ahead, and I'm going down somewhat south of my final destination, but it seemed prudent to minimize the risks." He stopped a moment, looking around. "Ah," he said, nodding down one of the narrow rows. "This must be it."

He unlocked another, much smaller door in the far wall and led Hayward down a staircase to a cramped little room with an unfinished floor. "Directly beneath us is an access tube," he said. "It was begun in 1925 as part of a pneumatic system to deliver books to a storage outbuilding. The project was abandoned during the Depression and never resumed. However, it should allow me to access a main feeder tunnel."

Pendergast set down the valise, inspected the floor with a flashlight, then brushed the dust away from an ancient trapdoor.

He lifted it with Hayward's help, exposing a slender black tube lined with tiles. Poking the flashlight down into the darkness, he looked around for a few moments. Apparently satisfied, he straightened up, unbuttoning the long duster as he did so.

Hayward's eyes narrowed in surprise. Beneath the duster, the FBI agent was wearing a set of military fatigues in broken gray-and-black pattern. The zippers and buckles were plastic, with a matte black finish.

Pendergast smiled. "Unusual camos, aren't they?" he said. "Note the gray tones instead of the usual sepia. Designed for use in blackout conditions." He knelt in front of the valise, unfastening and opening it wide. From one compartment, he removed a tube of military-issue blackout, which he began applying to his face and hands. Next, he removed a rolled piece of felt. As Pendergast checked it, Hayward noticed several pockets had been sewed into its inside edge.

"A pocket disguise kit," Pendergast said. "Safety razor, towelettes, mirror, spirit gum. My intent this time is to avoid detection. I don't wish to meet anybody or anything. But I'll bring this along, just in case." He stuffed the tube of grease paint into one of the pockets, then rolled up the kit and placed it inside his shirt. Reaching into the valise, he removed a short-barreled pistol whose dull finish reminded Hayward more of plastic than metal.

"What's that?" she asked curiously.

Pendergast turned it over in his hands. "It's an experimental 9-millimeter, created by Anschluss GMBH. It fires a T-round composite bullet of ceramic and Teflon."

"Planning on going hunting?"

"You may have heard about my encounter with the Mbwun beast," Pendergast replied. "That experience taught me that one should always be prepared. This little handgun could send a bullet through an elephant. Lengthwise."

"An offensive weapon," Hayward replied. "In more ways than one."

"I'll take that as a sign of approval," Pendergast said. "Of course, defense will be at least as important as offense. I have my own armor." He pulled back the fatigues to expose a bulletproof vest. Reaching into the valise again, he removed a black skullcap made of Kevlar, which he snugged onto his head. As Hayward watched, Pendergast removed a water purifying kit and several other articles, placing them in various pockets. Finally, he pulled out two carefully sealed plastic bags. Inside were strips of something that looked like black shoe leather.

"Pemmican," he said.

"What?"

"Filet mignon, cut into strips and dried, then pounded with berries, fruits, and nuts. It has all the vitamins, minerals, and protein a man needs. And it is surprisingly edible. Nobody has yet invented a better expedition food than Native Americans. Lewis and Clark lived on it for months."

"Well, I guess you're provisioned, anyway," Hayward said, shaking her head. "Provided you don't get lost."

Pendergast unzipped the top of his fatigues, displaying the inner lining. "Perhaps my most vital possession: maps. Like the fliers of World War Two, I've traced them on my flight jacket, so to speak." He nodded at the complicated set of lines, tunnels, and levels that had been drawn on the cream-colored lining in a precise hand.

He zipped up the camos and then, as if remembering something, dug in his pockets and handed a set of keys to Hayward. "I meant to tape these to prevent any jingling. You'd better hold them for me." From another pocket he removed his wallet and FBI identification, which he also passed to the Sergeant. "Please give these to Lieutenant D'Agosta. I won't be needing them below."

He ran his hands quickly over his clothes, as if to reassure himself that everything was in place. Then he turned once again toward the trapdoor and lowered himself gingerly into the tube.

"I appreciate your taking care of this for me," he said, nodding at the valise.

"No problem," Hayward replied. "Send me a postcard."

The trapdoor shut over the dank, black tube, and Hayward sealed it with a quick twirl of her wrist.

32

Margo stared at the titration, scarcely blinking. As each clear drop trembled and fell into the solution, she waited expectantly for a color change. The sound of Frock's low breathing behind her—as he, too, stared at the apparatus—reminded her that she was unconsciously holding her breath.

Suddenly the solution blossomed a bright yellow color. Margo turned the glass stopcock, stopping the flow of solution, and recorded the level on the graduated cylinder.

She took a step back, aware that an unpleasantly familiar feeling was settling over her: a sense of unease, even dread. Standing motionless, she remembered the drama that had played out in another laboratory, a mere hundred feet down the hall and eighteen months into the past. It had been just the two of them that time as well: crowded around Greg Kawakita's genetic extrapolator, watching as the program listed the physical attributes of the creature that would come to be known as Mbwun, the Museum Beast.

She remembered almost cursing Julian Whittlesey, the scientist whose expedition had been lost in the depths of the Amazon. Whittlesey, who had inadvertently used a certain aquatic plant as packing fibers for the specimens he'd sent back to the Museum.

Unknown to Whittlesey—unknown to all of them—the Mbwun beast had been addicted to the plant. It needed the hormones in the plant in order to survive. And when its own habitat was destroyed, the beast went in search of the only remaining source of the plant: the packing fibers in the crates. But by a supreme irony, the crates were later locked in the Museum's secure area, forcing the creature to go after the closest substitute to the plant hormones it could find: the hypothalamus of the human brain.

As Margo stared at the yellow solution, she realized that she was feeling something else besides dread: dissatisfaction. There was something strange here, something unexplained. She had felt the same way after the carcass of the Mbwun beast had been taken away following the slaughter of the *Superstition* exhibition's opening night. Taken away in a van with government plates and never seen again. Though she'd never wanted to admit it, she'd always sensed, somehow, that they'd never gotten to the bottom of the story, never really understood what Mbwun was. At the time, she'd hoped to see autopsy results, a pathology report— something that could explain how the beast had known to come to the Museum in the first place. Or why the creature showed such a high proportion of human genes. Something, anything, that could bring the story to a close; even, perhaps, lay her own nightmares to rest.

She realized now that Frock's own theory of Mbwun being an evolutionary aberration had never completely convinced her. Against her will, she forced herself to think back to those few moments she'd actually seen the beast: charging down the darkened hallway toward herself and Pendergast, triumph in its feral eyes. To her, it had looked more like a hybrid than an aberration. But a hybrid of what?

The sound of Frock shifting in his wheelchair chased her thoughts away. "Let's try it once again," he said. "To be sure."

"I'm already sure," Margo replied.

"My dear," Frock said with a smile, "you are too young to be sure of anything. Remember, all experimental results must be reproducible. I don't mean to disappoint you, but I fear that this will all turn out to be a waste of time better spent examining the Bitterman corpse."

Margo began setting up the titration again, swallowing her irritation. At the rate they were going, they wouldn't have results on her finds at Kawakita's ruined lab for weeks. Frock was famous for the care and precision of his scientific experiments, and he seemed—as usual—supremely unaware that time was of the essence. But then, like most great scientists, he was self-absorbed, much more interested in his own work and his own theories than anyone else's. She remembered the conferences they'd had while he was her dissertation advisor, in which he would tell one story after another about his adventures in Africa, South America, or Australia, in the days before he became crippled—devoting more time to his own tales than to discussing her research.

They had been working for hours on titrations and linear regression programs, trying to coax some kind of results out of the plant fibers she'd found at the site. Margo watched the solution, massaging the small of her back. D'Agosta had been certain there was some kind of psychoactive drug in the fibers. But so far they had found nothing to support that theory. *If only we'd kept some of the original plant fibers,* Margo thought, *we could do cross-comparison studies.* But the CDC had demanded that all traces of the original fibers be destroyed. They'd even insisted on incinerating her handbag, which she'd once used to transport some of the fibers.

That was another thing. If all the remaining fibers had been destroyed, how had Greg Kawakita obtained some of his own? How had he managed to grow them? And above all else: *why?*

And then there was the mystery of the flask at his lab marked ACTIVATED 7-DEHYDROCHOLE. The missing piece was obviously *sterol*: she'd looked it up, and had to laugh at her own stupidity. Of course she knew at once why it sounded so familiar—it was the most common form of vitamin D_3. Once she had that figured out, it didn't take long to see that the organic chem equipment in Kawakita's lab had been a little setup hastily improvised for synthesizing vitamin D. But why?

The solution turned yellow, and she marked the level: exactly the same, as she knew it would be. Frock, putting away some equipment on the far side of the lab, took no notice. She hesitated a moment, deciding what to do next. Then she moved to the stereozoom, where she carefully teased yet another small fiber from their rapidly dwindling sample.

Frock rumbled over as she manipulated the microscope stage. "It's seven o'clock, Margo," he said gently. "Forgive me, but I think you've been working too hard. May I suggest we break for the evening?"

Margo smiled. "I'm almost done, Dr. Frock. I'd like to do one last thing, then I'll call it a day."

"Ah. And what might that be?"

"I thought I'd just freeze-fracture a specimen and get a ten-angstrom SEM image."

Frock frowned. "Toward what end?"

Margo stared at the specimen, a tiny dot on the glass stage. "I'm not really sure. When we first studied this plant, we knew it carried a reovirus of some kind. A virus that coded for both human and animal proteins. I wanted to see if this virus might be the source of the drug."

A low rumble shook Frock's capacious front, finally erupting as a chuckle. "Margo, I would say it is definitely time for a break," he said. "This is wild speculation."

"Perhaps," Margo said. "But I'd prefer to call it a hunch."

Frock looked at her a moment, then sighed deeply. "As you wish," he said. "But I, for one, need my rest. I'll be at Morristown Memorial tomorrow, enduring that annual battery of tests they seem to force on you in retirement. See you Wednesday morning, my dear."

Margo said good-bye, watching as Frock wheeled himself out into the corridor. She was beginning to realize that the famous scientist did not enjoy being crossed. When she'd been his graduate student, timid and compliant, he'd always been utterly charming, the soul of gentility. But now that Frock was emeritus and she was a curator in her own right, expressing her own ideas, he sometimes seemed less than pleased with the new assertiveness.

She brushed the tiny sample into a specimen well and carried it to the freeze-fracture machine. Inside the machine, it would be encased in a small plastic block, frozen to nearly absolute zero, and cleaved in two. Then the scanning electron microscope would make an extremely high-resolution picture of the fractured surface. Frock was right, of course: under normal circumstances, a procedure such as this would have no bearing on their research. She'd called it a hunch, but in reality it was for lack of anything else to try.

Soon, a green light appeared on the cryogenic machine. Handling the block with an electronic cradle, Margo moved it onto the cleaving stage. The diamond cleaver descended with a smooth motion, there was a faint click, and the block separated. Placing one of the halves in the SEM, she carefully adjusted the mount, scanning controls, and electron beam. In a few minutes, a crisp black and white image appeared on the adjoining screen.

Staring at it, Margo felt her blood run cold.

As expected, she could make out small hexagonal particles: the reovirus that Kawakita's extrapolation program had originally detected in the plant fibers eighteen months earlier. But here, it existed in an unbelievably high concentration: the plant organelles were literally packed with it. And surrounding the particles were large vacuoles that held some kind of crystallized secretion—that could only come from the reovirus itself.

She breathed out slowly. The high concentrations, the crystallized secretions, could mean only one thing: this plant, *Liliceae mbwunensis,* was only a carrier. The *virus* made the drug. And the reason they couldn't find traces of the drug was because the drug was encapsulated inside the vacuoles.

Well then, she thought. The answer was simple. Isolate the reovirus, grow it in a medium, and see what drug it produces.

Kawakita must have thought of this.

Perhaps Kawakita hadn't been trying to genetically engineer the plant at all. Perhaps he was genetically engineering the *virus.* If that were the case...

Margo sat down, her mind working furiously. At last, things seemed to be dovetailing: the old research and the new; the viral matter and its host plant; Mbwun; the fibers. But it still didn't explain why Kawakita had left the Museum to do this. And it didn't explain how the Mbwun creature could have come all that distance from the Amazon rain forest, in search of the plants that the Whittlesey expedition had...

Whittlesey.

In an instant she was on her feet, hand pressed to her mouth, the lab chair clattering to the linoleum floor.

Suddenly, everything had become perfectly, terrifyingly clear.

33

This time, when Smithback was shown into the eighteenth-floor foyer of Nine Central Park South, he noticed immediately that the windows of the vast drawing room beyond had been thrown wide. Sunlight streamed in, gilding the sofas and rosewood tables, turning what had once seemed like a funeral parlor into a blaze of warmth and brilliance.

Anette Wisher was sitting at a glass-topped table on the balcony, wearing a fashionable straw sun hat and dark glasses. She turned to him, smiled slightly, and motioned him to take a seat. Smithback did so, glancing admiringly at the vast green carpet of Central Park, unrolling itself northward to 110th Street.

"Bring Mr. Smithback some tea," Mrs. Wisher said to the maid who had shown him in.

"Call me Bill, please," Smithback said, shaking the proffered hand. He couldn't help noticing that, even in the bright unforgiving light of the summer sun, Mrs. Wisher's skin looked remarkably free from the ravages of time. It had a youthful resiliency, creamy and smooth without the flabby softness of age.

"I appreciate the patience you've shown," she said, withdrawing her hand. "I think you'll agree it's about to be rewarded. We've decided on a course of action, and, as promised,

I wanted you to be the first to know. Of course, it's to be kept a secret."

Smithback accepted the tea, drinking in the faint expensive aroma of jasmine. He felt a warm glow, sitting in this lovely apartment, with all of Manhattan spread out below him, drinking tea with the one woman every journalist in the city wanted to interview. It even made up for being scooped so humiliatingly by that smug bastard Bryce Harriman.

"The Grand Army Plaza rally was so successful we've decided to push Take Back Our City into a new phase," Mrs. Wisher said.

Smithback nodded.

"Our plan is quite simple, really. All future actions will be unannounced. Each will take place on a grander scale. And for every new murder that is committed, our people will descend on police headquarters, demanding an end to the outrage." She raised one hand, smoothing a stray wisp of hair. "But I don't expect we shall have to wait long to see some real changes."

"And why's that?" Smithback asked eagerly.

"At six o'clock tomorrow evening, our people will gather outside St. Patrick's Cathedral. Believe me, the group you saw at Grand Army Plaza will seem minuscule by comparison. We mean to show this city we are deadly serious. We will move up Fifth Avenue, across Central Park South, and then north on Central Park West, stopping for a candlelight vigil at the site of every murder. Then we shall converge on the Great Lawn in Central Park for a final midnight prayer."

She shook her head. "I'm afraid the government of this city still hasn't gotten the message. But when they see midtown Manhattan immobilized by countless voters, all demanding action—they *will* get the message, mark my words."

"And the mayor?" Smithback asked.

"The mayor may well show up again. Politicians of his ilk can never resist a crowd. When he does, I plan to tell him that this is his last chance. If he fails us again, we are ready to mount a recall campaign. And when we're finished with him, he won't be able to get a job as dogcatcher in Akron, Ohio." A wintry smile crossed her lips. "I'll expect you to quote me on that, at the appropriate time."

Smithback couldn't help smiling himself. This was going to be absolutely perfect.

34

It was almost complete.

He stepped into the humid darkness of the Temple, running his fingers lightly along the cool orbs that made up the walls, caressing the organic surfaces, the hollows and swells. It was right that it should be built here: so like what had come before in that other place, yet so unlike. He turned and settled into the throne they had crafted for him, feeling the rough leathery surface of the seat and the slight give of the lashed members, hearing the faint creak of sinew and bone, his senses alive as never before. It would soon be complete. As he, now, was complete.

They had toiled long and hard for him, their leader and master. They loved and feared him, as was his due, and now they would worship him. He closed his eyes and inhaled the thick, fragrant air that eddied about him like a fog. In times past he would have been repelled by the reek of the Temple, but that was before he'd acquired the gift of sensory acuteness. The plant had given him that, as it had given him so much else. Now, everything was different. The smell was like a vista to him, ever shifting, painted in every imaginable color, here bright and clean, there dark and mysterious. There were mountains and canyons and deserts of scent, oceans and skies, rivers and meadows, a magnificent panorama of fragrance, indescribable in human language. It rendered the world of sight flat, ugly, sterile by comparison.

He savored his triumph. Where the other had failed, *he* had succeeded. Where the other had withered in fear and doubt, *he* had grown in strength, and courage. The other had been unable to discover the flaw that was hidden in the formula. *He* had not only found the flaw, but had taken the next step and perfected the glorious plant and the secret payload it contained. The other had underestimated the Children's desperate thirst for ritual, for ceremony. *He* had not. He alone understood the ultimate meaning.

This was the true manifestation of his life's work—how galling to think he had never realized it before! It was he, and no other, who had the power, the intellect, and the will to carry it through. He alone could cleanse the world and guide it into its future.

The world! As he murmured the word aloud, he could feel that pathetic world so far above him, pressing down upon the sanctuary of his Temple. He saw everything so clearly now. It was an overpopulated world, teeming with insectlike swarms that had no purpose, no meaning, and no value, their ugly little lives churning like the manic pistons of some senseless machine. They were above him always, dropping their dung, mating, giving birth, dying, tied to the slaving meat-wheel of human existence. How easy—and how inevitable—that it should all be swept aside, all of it, as one kicks open an anthill and grinds the soft white pupae underfoot. Then the New World could come: so fresh, so various, and so full of dreams.

35

"Where are the others?" Margo asked as D'Agosta entered the small Anthropology conference room.

"They're not coming," D'Agosta said, hiking up his trouser legs and sitting down. "Scheduling." Then he caught Margo's glance and gave his head a disgusted shake. "Ah, what the hell. If you want to know the truth, they're not interested. That guy Waxie, who you saw at Brambell's presentation? He's in charge of the case now. And he believes he's already got his man."

"What do you mean, already got his man?" Margo asked.

"Some nut they found in the park. He's a murderer, all right, but he's not the killer we're looking for. At least, Pendergast doesn't think so."

"And Pendergast?"

"He's on a little business trip." D'Agosta smiled, as if at some private joke. "So whatcha got?"

"I'll start at the beginning." Margo took a deep breath. "It's ten years ago, okay? There's an expedition to the Amazon Basin. It's headed by a Museum scientist named Julian Whittlesey. There are personality conflicts, and the team splits up. For various reasons, nobody makes it back alive. But several boxes of relics are shipped to the Museum. One of them includes a hideous figurine, packed in some fibrous material."

D'Agosta nodded. So far, it was ancient history.

"What they didn't know was that the figurine was a representation of a savage, indigenous creature. And that the packing material was a local plant essential to the diet of this creature. Soon after, the creature's home environment is destroyed in the local government's search for mineral deposits. So this monster—this Mbwun—follows the only remaining fibers. All the way from the Amazon Basin, to Belem, to New York City. It survives in the Museum basement, eating feral animals and consuming this plant, to which it seems addicted."

D'Agosta nodded again.

"Well," said Margo, "I don't buy it. I used to, but I don't anymore."

D'Agosta raised an eyebrow. "What about it don't you buy, exactly?"

"Think about it, Lieutenant. How could a wild animal—even an extremely intelligent one—make its way from the Amazon Basin to New York City in search of a few cases full of fibers? That's a hell of a long way from its habitat."

"You're not telling me anything we didn't already know when that beast was destroyed. There was no other interpretation then, and I sure can't see any other one now. Mbwun was here. I felt the thing *breathe* on me, for Chrissakes. If it didn't come from the Amazon, then where?"

"Good question." said Margo. "What if Mbwun was originally from New York and was simply coming home?"

There was a brief silence. "Coming home?" D'Agosta said, mystified.

"Yes. What if Mbwun was not an animal at all, but a human being? What if he was *Whittlesey*?"

This time, the silence was much longer. D'Agosta looked at Margo. Great shape or no, she must be near dead from exhaustion, working nonstop on those corpses. And Brambell getting murdered like that, and then her discovering that one of the corpses she'd been picking over belonged to a former coworker. A coworker she already felt guilty about having dropped out of touch with... How could he have been so stupid, so selfish, bringing her in on a job like this, knowing how much the original Museum murders had upset her? "Listen," he began. "Dr. Green, I think you'd better—"

Margo held up her hand. "I know, I know, it sounds crazy. But it's not, I swear it's not. My lab assistant is working on several more tests as we speak, just to verify my findings. So let me finish. Mbwun had an astonishingly high percentage of human DNA. We had one of the claws sequenced, remember? We found intact strings of perfect human DNA, many thousands of base pairs long. That's no evolutionary aberration. Also, Pendergast found some items of Whittlesey's in the creature's lair, remember? And don't forget that the creature killed everyone it came in contact with except one person: Ian Cuthbert. Why? Cuthbert had once been a close friend of Whittlesey's. And then, Whittlesey's body was never found..."

D'Agosta's jaw set. This was insane. Pushing the chair back, he began to rise.

"Let me finish," Margo said quietly.

D'Agosta returned her level gaze. Something about the look in her eyes made him sit down again.

"Lieutenant," she continued, "I know how this sounds. But you *must* listen. We made a terrible mistake. I'm as much to blame as anybody else. We never put the final pieces of the puzzle together. But somebody did. *Greg Kawakita* did."

She placed an 8" x 10" blowup of a microscopic image on the table. "This plant contains a reovirus."

"We already knew that."

"But what we overlooked is that these reoviruses have a unique ability: they can inject foreign DNA into the host cell. And they produce a drug. I ran some additional tests on the fibers this evening, after I made this discovery. They carry genetic

241

material—reptilian DNA—which is inserted into the human host when the plant is eaten. And that DNA, in turn, initiates a *physical* transformation. Somehow—I don't know how or why—Whittlesey must have ingested the plant while on the expedition. He underwent a morphological change. *He became Mbwun.* Once the change was complete, he needed a steady diet of the drug in the plants. And when the local supply was destroyed, Whittlesey knew that more could be found in the Museum. He knew, because he'd sent them the plants here, as packing fibers in the crates. So he returned to the crates. It was only when he was cut off from the supply of fibers that he began killing human beings. See, the hypothalamus of the human brain contains a hormone similar to the plants—"

"Wait. You're saying that eating this plant turns you into some kind of monster?" D'Agosta asked incredulously.

Margo nodded. "And now I know what Greg had to do with this. He figured everything out, then dropped out of sight to pursue some plan of his own." She unrolled a large diagram on the conference table. "Here's a map of his laboratory, or as much of it as I could reconstruct. This list in the corner inventories all the equipment I could identify. Even at wholesale prices, it all must have cost in excess of eight hundred thousand dollars."

Despite himself, D'Agosta whistled. "Drug money."

"That's exactly right, Lieutenant. The only purpose of such a lab would be some very sophisticated production-level genetic engineering. I emphasize the word *production.*"

"Late last year, there were rumors about a new drug on the street," D'Agosta said, "called glaze. Very rare, very expensive, with an amazing rush. Haven't heard much about it recently, though."

Margo placed a finger on the diagram. "There are three stages to genetic engineering. The first is to map the DNA of an organism. That's what these machines along the north wall did. Combined, they made up a massive sequencing operation. This first one controls the polymerase chain reaction, which replicates the DNA so it can be sequenced. This one sequences the DNA. Then this machine, here, was a Cambridge Systems NAD-1. We have one downstairs. It's a highly specialized supercomputer that uses gallium arsenide CPUs and vector processing to analyze sequencing results. Then here, along the south wall, were the melted remains of a series of aquaria. Kawakita was growing the Mbwun plant in large quantities to supply raw material for this operation. And here was an Ap-Gel viral production facility for incubating and culturing viruses."

There was a deathly silence. D'Agosta mopped his brow and felt around in his pocket for the reassuring shape of his cigar. Despite himself, he was starting to believe.

"Kawakita was using this equipment to *remove* genes from the plant virus." Margo placed some more pictures on the table. "These are SEM micrographs. They show that he was removing the reptilian genes. Why? Because he was obviously trying to negate the *physical* effects of the drug."

"What does Frock think of all this?"

As he asked the question, D'Agosta thought he saw a momentary flush move across Margo's features. "I haven't had the chance to tell him yet. But I know he'll be skeptical. He's still wedded to his fractal evolution theory. This may sound crazy, Lieutenant, but the fact is there are many substances in nature— hormones, for instance—that cause startling transformations like this. It's not as bizarre or unusual as it sounds. There's a hormone called BSTH which turns a caterpillar into a butterfly. There's another called resotropin-x. When a tadpole gets a dose of that, it turns into a frog in a matter of days. That's what's happening here, I'm sure of it. Only now, we're talking about changing a human being."

She paused. "There's something else."

"Isn't this enough?"

Margo dug into her carryall and pulled out some small scraps of burned paper, sandwiched between pieces of clear plastic. "I found what looked like Kawakita's lab journal among the ashes.

These were the only sheets with any legible writing on them."
She brought out more photographs. "I had the scraps enlarged.
This first one is from the middle of the notebook. It's some kind
of a list."

D'Agosta peered at the photograph. He could make out a few
scribbled words along the left edge of the badly burned page:
wysoccan, dung-loving blue foot. Then, nearer the bottom: green
cloud, gunpowder, lotus heart.

"Mean anything to you?" D'Agosta asked, scribbling the
words into his notebook.

"Just the gunpowder," Margo replied. "Although something
tells me I ought to recognize more of it." She handed him another
photograph. "There's another one that seems to be fragments of
code for his extrapolation program. Then there's a longer one."
D'Agosta scanned the offered fragment.

> *...can't live with the knowledge of what I've... How could
> I, while concentrating on... ignore the mental effects that...
> but the other one grows more eager by the day. I need the
> time to...*

"Sounds like he was getting a conscience, there toward the end,"
D'Agosta said, handing back the card. "But what was it, exactly,
that he did?"

"I'm getting to that," Margo replied. "Notice he talks
here about the mental effects of glaze as something he hadn't
considered. And did you catch that reference to 'the other one'?
I still haven't figured that part out." She reached for another
card. "Then there's this. I think it came from the last page
of the journal. As you can see, besides a lot of numbers and
calculations, there are only three completely legible words, with
a period between them: 'irreversible. Thyoxin might...'"

D'Agosta looked at her questioningly.

"I looked it up. Thyoxin is an experimental herbicide, highly
potent, for removing algae from lakes. If Greg was growing this

plant, what would he want with thyoxin? Or with vitamin D, which he was also apparently synthesizing? There's still a lot I haven't figured out."

"I'll mention it to Pendergast, just in case he has any ideas." D'Agosta stared at the photographs a moment, then pushed them aside. "So tell me, Dr. Green," he went on, "I'm not quite there yet. Just what exactly was Kawakita trying to do with all this apparatus of his?"

"He was probably trying to tame the drug by subtracting the reptilian genes from the Mbwun plant virus."

"Tame?"

"I think he was trying to create a drug that didn't cause the grotesque physical changes. To make the user more alert, stronger, faster, able to see better in the dark. You know, the kind of hypersensory abilities Mbwun had. But without the side effects."

Margo began rolling up the diagram. "I'd need to test tissue samples from Kawakita's corpse to be sure. But I think we'll find traces of the Mbwun drug, substantially altered. And I think that the drug itself will be found to have some kind of narcotic side effect."

"You mean Kawakita was taking it *himself*?"

"I'm certain of it. But he must have screwed up in some way. He must not have refined it or purified it properly. And the deformation that we saw in his skeleton was the result."

D'Agosta wiped his brow again. God, he needed that cigar. "Just a minute," he said. "Kawakita was a smart guy. He wouldn't just take a dangerous drug for the hell of it, to see what would happen. No way."

"You're right, Lieutenant. And perhaps that's where the guilt comes in. See, he wouldn't have taken the drug himself right away. He would have tested it first."

"Oh," D'Agosta said. There was a long silence, and then he added, "Oh, shit."

36

Bill Trumbull felt great. The market was up sixteen points for the day, nearly a hundred for the week, with no end in sight. At twenty-five, he was already pulling down a hundred large a year. Wouldn't his classmates at Babson shit when they heard that at the reunion next week. Most of them had gone on to crummy management jobs, lucky to be making fifty.

Trumbull and his friends pushed through the turnstiles and entered the platform of the Fulton Street subway station, chattering and hooting. It was past midnight, and they'd put away a fine dinner at the Seaport, as well as a lot of microbrewed beer, and had talked endlessly about how rich they were all becoming. Now they were in an uproarious mood, chortling about the dork who had just joined the training program and wouldn't last a month.

Trumbull felt a puff of stale wind and heard the familiar distant rumble as two tiny headlights appeared on the track. He would be home in half an hour. He felt a momentary annoyance at how far uptown he lived—98th Street and Third Avenue— and at how long it took to get home from Wall Street. Maybe it was time to move, get a loft downtown, or a nice two-bedroom in the low Sixties. While a Soho address wasn't too bad, an East

Side address was still better. Balcony on a high floor, king-sized bed, cream carpeting, chrome and glass.

"... So she says, 'Honey, can *I* borrow seventy dollars?'" Everyone roared salaciously as the punch line was delivered, and instinctively Trumbull laughed along with them.

The rumble grew into a deafening roar as the express train pulled into the station. One of the group nudged Trumbull playfully toward the edge of the platform, and he leaned back out of the way of the approaching train. It came to a halt with a great shriek of brakes, and they piled into one of the cars.

Trumbull lurched into a seat as they pulled out of the station, looking around in annoyance. The car's air-conditioning wasn't working and all the windows were open, letting in the stale, damp smell of the tracks and the deafening noise of the train. It was hot as hell. He loosened his tie further. He was beginning to feel logy, and a mild but persistent pain was gathering at his temples. He glanced at his watch: they had to be back at the office in six hours. He sighed and leaned back. The train rocketed through the tunnel, swaying, making so much noise it was impossible to speak. Trumbull closed his eyes.

At 14th Street, several of the guys got off to catch trains for Penn Station. They grasped his hand, punched his shoulder, and were gone. More got off at Grand Central, leaving only Trumbull and Jim Kolb, a bond trader who worked one floor below. Trumbull didn't particularly like Kolb. He closed his eyes again, exhaling wearily as the train dove deeper into the earth, following the express track.

Vaguely, Trumbull was aware of the train pulling into the 59th Street station, the doors opening, closing, the express plunging back into the darkness, gathering speed for the thirty-block run to 86th. *One more stop,* he thought drowsily.

Suddenly, the train lurched, then slowed, screeching to a halt. A long moment passed. Jostled awake, Trumbull sat in gathering irritation, listening to the tickings and creakings of the motionless car.

"Screw it," said Kolb loudly. "Screw the Lexington Avenue Number Four." He looked around for a response, getting none from the two other half-asleep riders. Then he elbowed Trumbull, who managed a wan smile as he thought about what a loser Kolb was.

Trumbull glanced down the car. He saw a cute-looking waitress and one black kid, wearing a bulky overcoat and knitted cap despite the hundred-degree interior of the train. Although the youth appeared to be sleeping, Trumbull eyed him warily. *Probably coming back from a hard night's mugging,* he thought. He felt in his pocket for his penknife. Nobody was going to take his wallet, even if there was no money left in it.

There was a sudden crackle of static and a raspy voice came over the PA system: *Attention passengzweesh therlalignal problem reshorkwix hortly.*

"Yeah, right, tell me another one," Kolb said disgustedly.

"Huh?"

"It's what they always say. A signal problem. We should be moving shortly. In their dreams."

Trumbull crossed his arms, closing his eyes again. His headache was getting worse, and the heat felt like a suffocating blanket.

"To think they charge a buck fifty to make us sit in this sweatshop," Kolb said. "Maybe next time we should hire a limo."

Trumbull nodded vaguely and checked his watch. Twelve forty-five.

"No wonder people jump the turnstile," Kolb was saying.

Trumbull nodded again, wondering how he could make Kolb shut up. He heard a noise outside the car and glanced idly at the window. There was a dim form in the humid darkness, approaching up the adjoining track. Some MTA repairman, no doubt. *Maybe he's just doing late night track repairs,* Trumbull thought, watching idly as the figure came closer. Hope swelled, then ebbed. *But if there's something wrong with the train, shit, we could be down here until—*

Suddenly it passed by his window, soundlessly, a figure in white. Trumbull sat up like a shot. It was no track worker, but a woman: a woman in a long dress, running and stumbling down the tracks. He watched her retreating back through the open windows. Just as she disappeared into the gloom, he noticed that the woman's back was splattered with something that glistened black in the reflected light of the stalled train.

"Did you see that?" he asked Kolb.

Kolb glanced up. "See what?"

"A woman running along the tracks."

Kolb grinned. "One too many, Billy boy?"

Trumbull stood up and thrust his head out the window, squinting down the tracks in the direction the figure had gone. Nothing. As he ducked back into the car, he realized nobody else had noticed anything.

What was going on here? A mugging? He looked back out the window but the woman was gone, the tunnel once again quiet and empty.

"This is getting to be a lot longer than 'shortly,'" Kolb groused, tapping his two-toned Rolex.

Trumbull's head was pounding now. God knows he'd had enough to drink to be seeing things. Third time this week he'd gotten hammered. Maybe he shouldn't go out so much. He must have seen a track worker carrying something on his back. Or her back. Some of them were women these days, after all. He glanced through the coupling doors into the next car, but it was equally peaceful, its sole occupant staring vacantly into space. If anything had happened, it would have been announced on the PA.

He sat down, closed his eyes, and concentrated on making the pain in his head go away. Most of the time, he didn't mind riding the subway. It was a fast trip, and the clattering tracks and flashing lights kept a person distracted. But at times like this—idled without explanation, in the overheated darkness—it was hard not to think about just how deep under the earth the express track ran, or the mile of blackness that lay between him and the next stop...

At first, it sounded like a distant train, screeching into a station. But then, as Trumbull listened, he realized what the sound was: a distant, drawn-out scream, strangely distorted by the echoing tunnel, wafting faintly through the windows.

"What the hell—?" Kolb said, sitting forward. The youth's eyes popped open, and the late-night waitress suddenly became alert.

There was an electric silence while everyone waited, listening. No other sound came.

"Christ, Bill, you hear that?" Kolb asked.

Trumbull said nothing. There had been a robbery, maybe a murder. Or—perhaps worse—a gang, working its way down the stalled train. It was every subway rider's worst nightmare.

"They never tell you anything," Kolb said, glancing nervously at the loudspeaker. "Maybe someone should check it out."

"Be my guest," Trumbull said.

"A man's scream," Kolb added. "It was a *man* screaming, I swear it."

Trumbull glanced out the window again. This time he could make out another figure moving along the far track, walking with a strange rolling motion, almost a limp, as it approached them.

"There's somebody coming," he said.

"Ask him what's going on."

Trumbull moved to the window. "Hey! Hey, you!"

In the dimness beyond the train, he saw the figure stop.

"What's going on?" Trumbull called out. "Did someone get hurt?"

The figure began moving forward again. Trumbull watched as it went to the head of the next car forward, then climbed up onto the coupling and disappeared.

"I hate these TA assholes," Kolb said. "Bastards make forty grand a year and don't do shit."

Trumbull walked to the front, looking through the window into the next car forward. Its lone occupant was still there, now reading a paperback book. Everything was quiet once more.

"What do you see?" Kolb whined.

Trumbull returned to his seat. "Nothing," he said. "Maybe it was just some transit worker yelling to a buddy."

"I wish they'd just get *moving*," the waitress suddenly said, her voice tight with nerves. The youth in the heavy coat was slumped motionless in his seat, hands shoved in pockets. *I'll bet he's got his hand on a gun,* thought Trumbull, uncertain whether the thought made him anxious or relieved.

The lights blinked out in the forward car.

"Oh, shit," Kolb said.

A loud thump came from the darkened car, causing the train to shudder as if something heavy had been slammed against it. The thump was followed by a strange sighing sound. Trumbull thought of air being released from a wet balloon.

"What was that?" the waitress asked.

"I'm getting the hell out of here," Kolb said. "Come on, Trumbull. The Fifty-ninth Street station can't be more than a couple blocks back."

"I'm staying right here."

"Then you're an idiot," said Kolb. "You think I'm just gonna wait here for some gang to come busting through that door?"

Trumbull shook his aching head. The thing to do was stay put and stay calm. If you got up and called attention to yourself, the only thing you did was make yourself a mark.

There was another sound from the dark car, like rain pelting against metal.

Cautiously, Trumbull leaned forward, looking ahead toward the darkened car. Immediately, he saw that the window was splattered from the inside with something like paint. Thick paint, running down the window in black clots.

"What is it?" Kolb cried.

Some kids were vandalizing the car, splashing paint around. At least, it looked like paint, red paint. Maybe it *was* time to get the hell out, and before he had even articulated the thought he was up and running for the rear door of the car.

"Billy!" Kolb was on his feet following.

Behind him, Trumbull heard something slamming against the forward door, the shuffling patter of many feet, and then the sudden screaming of the waitress. Without stopping or looking back, he grabbed the handle and twisted it, throwing the sliding door open. He jumped across the coupling and wrenched open the door to the rearward car, Kolb right behind him, muttering "shit, shit, shit," in a dull monody.

Trumbull had just enough time to notice that the last car was empty before the lights went out in the entire train. He glanced about wildly. The only illumination came from the faint, infrequent lights of the tunnel, and the distant yellow glow of the 59th Street station.

He stopped and turned to Kolb. "Let's pry open the rear door."

At that moment the sound of a gunshot echoed crazily from the car they'd just left. As the shot died away, Trumbull thought he could hear the faint sobbing of the waitress end abruptly.

"They cut his throat!" Kolb screamed, glancing over his shoulder.

"Shut up," Trumbull hissed. No matter what sound reached his ears, he wasn't looking back. He ran to the far door and grasped the rubber flanges, trying to pry them apart. "Help me!" he cried.

Kolb grabbed the other flange, the tears streaming down his face.

"*Pull, for Chrissakes!*"

There was a sigh of air and the door gave way, flooding the car with a suffocating, earthy odor. Before he could move, Trumbull felt himself shoved aside by Kolb, who jammed through the opening and leapt onto the tracks. Trumbull tensed himself for the leap, then froze. Several figures were coming into focus out of the darkness of the tunnel ahead of them, shambling toward Kolb. Trumbull opened his mouth, then closed it again, swaying weakly in disbelief. There was something horribly wrong, something unutterably *foreign,* about the way the figures moved. He watched as Kolb was surrounded. One of the figures grabbed Kolb's hair, jerking his head back, while a second pinioned his arms. Kolb struggled soundlessly in jerky pantomime. A third stepped forward from the dim shadows, and, with a strangely delicate movement, flicked his hand across Kolb's throat. Immediately, a hose of blood jetted in the direction of the train.

Trumbull shrank back in terror, falling to the floor and then scrambling to his knees, momentarily disoriented. He glanced back desperately at the car from which they'd run. In the darkness, he could see two figures crouched over the prone body of the waitress, working busily around her head...

Trumbull felt an indescribable desperation suddenly pierce his gut. He turned and leapt out of the emergency door, stumbling onto the tracks, running past the figures hovering over Kolb, racing for the dim far light of the station. Dinner and beer came up together in a rush, decorating his legs as he ran. He heard sounds of pursuit starting up behind him, crunching and thudding footfalls. A sob escaped his lips.

Then two more figures stepped out ahead of him on the tracks, cloaked and hooded, silhouetted against the distant light of the station. Trumbull stopped short as they began to move, loping toward him with a terrible speed. Behind him, the sounds of pursuit grew closer. A strange lethargy was turning his limbs to stone, and he felt his reason begin to give way. In a few seconds he'd be caught, just like Kolb...

And then, in the brief flash of a signal light, he caught a glimpse of one of the faces.

A single thought, clear and quite unmistakable, came to him through the haze of a night which had suddenly turned to nightmare. He realized what he had to do. Quickly, he scanned the tracks beneath him, located the yellow warning stapes and the bright clean rail, and thrust his foot beneath the shoe guard as the world dissolved in a flash of miraculous brilliance.

37

D'Agosta tried to think of Yankee Stadium: the white orb of cowhide soaring through the blue July sky, the smell of grass newly ripped by a slide, the outfielder slamming into the wall, glove upraised. It was his form of transcendental meditation, a way to shut off the outside world and collect his thoughts. Especially useful when everything had gone totally to shit.

He kept his eyes shut a moment longer, trying to forget the sounds of the telephones, the slamming doors, the frantic secretaries. Somewhere, he knew, Waxie was rushing around like a turkey in heat. Thank God he wasn't within squawking distance. *Guess he isn't so sure about old Jeffrey anymore,* he thought. It brought no consolation.

With a sigh, D'Agosta forced his thoughts back to the strange figure of Alberta Muñoz, sole survivor of the subway massacre.

He had arrived just as she was being brought up an emergency exit at 66th Street on a stretcher: hands folded in her lap, pleasant vacant expression on her face, plump and motherly, her smooth brown skin in stark contrast to the sheets around her. God only knew how she'd managed to hide: she had not uttered a sound. The train itself had been turned into a temporary morgue: seven civilians and two TA workers dead, five with smashed skulls and throats cut to the backbone, three others with their heads completely missing, one electrocuted by the third rail. D'Agosta could almost smell the lawyers circling.

Mrs. Muñoz was now up at St. Luke's in psychiatric seclusion. Waxie had hollered and pounded and threatened, but the admitting doctor was unyielding: no interviews until at least six that morning.

Three heads missing. The trails of blood were picked up immediately, but the hemoluminesence team was having a tough time in the labyrinth of wet tunnels. D'Agosta went over the setup once more in his head. Someone had cut a signal wire just beyond the 59th Street station, causing an immediate halting of all East Side express trains between 14th and 125th, leaving the one train trapped in the long approach to 86th Street. There they had waited, in ambush.

The whole setup took intelligence and planning, and perhaps an inside knowledge of the system. So far, no clear footprints had been found, but D'Agosta estimated there had been at least six of them. Six, but no more than ten. A well-planned, well-coordinated attack.

But why?

The SOC team had determined that the electrocuted man probably stepped on the third rail deliberately. D'Agosta wondered just what a man would have to see in order to do something like that. Whatever it was, Alberta Muñoz might have seen it, too. He *had* to talk to her before Waxie got there and ruined everything.

"D'Agosta!" a familiar voice bellowed, as if on cue. "What, are you frigging *asleep*?"

He slowly opened his eyes, silently regarding the quivering, red face.

"Forgive me for interrupting your beauty rest," Waxie continued, "but we've got a tiny little crisis on our hands here—"

D'Agosta sat up. He looked around the office, spotted his jacket on the back of a chair, grabbed it and began sliding one hand into an armhole.

"You hearing me, D'Agosta?" Waxie shouted.

He pushed past the Captain and walked into the hallway. Hayward was standing by the situation desk checking an incoming fax. D'Agosta caught her eye and motioned her toward the elevator.

"Where the hell are you going now?" Waxie said, following them to the elevator. "You deaf or something? I said, we got a crisis—"

"It's your crisis," D'Agosta snapped. "You deal with it. I've got things to do."

As the elevator doors closed, D'Agosta placed a cigar in his mouth and turned to face Hayward.

"St. Luke's?" she asked. He nodded in response.

A minute later, the elevator doors chimed open on the wide tiled lobby. D'Agosta began to step out, then stopped. Beyond the glass doors, he could see a crowd of people, fists thrust in the air. It had tripled in size since he'd arrived at One Police Plaza at 2:00 A.M. That rich woman, Wisher, was standing on the hood of a squad car, speaking animatedly into a bullhorn. The media was there in force: he could see the pop of flash guns, the assembled machinery of television crews.

Hayward put a hand on his forearm. "Sure you don't want to take a black-and-white from the basement motor pool?" she asked.

D'Agosta looked at her. "Good idea," he said, stepping back into the elevator.

The admitting doctor kept them waiting on plastic chairs in the staff cafeteria for forty-five minutes. He was young, grim, and dead tired.

"I was told that Captain had no interviews until six," he said in a thin, angry voice.

D'Agosta stood up and took the doctor's hand. "I'm Lieutenant D'Agosta, and this is Sergeant Hayward. Pleased to meet you, Dr. Wasserman."

The doctor grunted and withdrew his hand.

"Doctor, I just want to say up front that we don't want to do anything that will cause harm to Mrs. Muñoz."

The doctor nodded.

"And you're to be the only judge of that," D'Agosta added.

The doctor said nothing.

"I also realize that a certain Captain Waxie was up here causing trouble. Perhaps he even threatened you."

Wasserman suddenly exploded. "In all my years working this emergency room, I've never been treated quite like that bastard treated me."

Hayward snickered. "Join the club," she said.

The doctor shot her a surprised look, then relaxed slightly.

"Doctor, there were at least six, probably ten, men involved in this massacre," D'Agosta said. "I believe they're the same individuals who killed Pamela Wisher, Nicholas Bitterman, and many others. I also believe they may be roaming the subway tunnels as we speak. It may be that the only living person who can identify them is Mrs. Muñoz. If you really feel that my questioning Mrs. Muñoz now will be harmful, I'll accept that. I just hope you'll consider that other lives might hang in the balance."

The doctor stared at him for a long time. At last, he managed a wan smile. "Very well, Lieutenant. On three conditions. I must be present. You must be gentle in your questioning. And you must end the interview as soon as I request it."

D'Agosta nodded.

"I'm afraid you'll be wasting your time. She's suffering from shock and the early symptoms of post-traumatic stress syndrome."

"Understood, Doctor."

"Good. From what we can tell, Mrs. Muñoz is from a small town in central Mexico. She works as a child-care domestic for an Upper East Side family. We know she speaks English. Beyond that, not much."

Mrs. Muñoz lay in the hospital bed in exactly the same position she'd lain on the crime scene stretcher: arms folded, eyes staring vacantly into the far distance. The room smelled of glycerine soap and rubbing alcohol. Hayward took up a position outside in case Waxie showed up prematurely, while D'Agosta and the doctor took seats on either side of the bed. They sat for a moment, motionless. Then, wordlessly, Wasserman took her hand.

D'Agosta removed his wallet. Sliding out a picture, he held it in front of the woman's face.

"This is my daughter, Isabella," said D'Agosta. "Two years old. Isn't she beautiful?"

He held the photo, patiently, until at last the woman's eyes flickered toward it. The doctor frowned.

"Do you have any children?" D'Agosta asked, replacing the photo. Mrs. Muñoz looked at him. There was a long silence.

"Mrs. Muñoz," D'Agosta said, "I know you're in this country illegally."

The woman quickly turned away. The doctor shot D'Agosta a warning look.

"I also know a lot of people have made you promises they haven't kept. But I'm going to make you a promise that I swear on my daughter's picture I will keep. If you help me, I'll see to it that you get your green card."

The woman did not respond. D'Agosta took out another picture and held it up. "Mrs. Muñoz?"

For a long moment, the woman remained motionless. Then her eyes strayed toward the picture. Something relaxed inside D'Agosta.

"This is Pamela Wisher when she was two years old. The same age as my daughter."

Mrs. Muñoz took the picture. "An angel," she whispered.

"She was killed by the same people who attacked your subway train." He spoke gently but rapidly. "Mrs. Muñoz, please help me to find these terrible people. I don't want them to kill anyone else."

A tear trickled down Mrs. Muñoz's face. Her lips twitched. "*Ojos...*"

"I'm sorry?" D'Agosta said.

"Eyes..."

There was another pause while Mrs. Muñoz's lips worked silently. "They came, silently... lizard's eyes, devil's eyes." A sob escaped her.

D'Agosta opened his mouth to speak, but a look from Wasserman restrained him.

"Eyes... *cuchillos de pedernal*... faces like the devil..."

"How so?"

"Old faces, *viejos*..."

She covered her face with her hands and let out a great groaning cry.

Wasserman stood up, gesturing at D'Agosta. "That's enough," he said. "Out."

"But what did she—?"

"Out *now*," the doctor said.

In the corridor, D'Agosta reached for his notebook, quickly spelling out the Spanish phrases as best he could.

"What's that?" Hayward asked, peering curiously around his shoulder.

"Spanish," said D'Agosta.

Hayward frowned. "That isn't like any Spanish I ever saw."

D'Agosta looked at her sharply. "Don't tell me you *habla Español* on top of everything else."

Hayward looked at him, one eyebrow raised. "You can't always roust in English. And just what is that crack supposed to mean?"

D'Agosta shoved the notebook into her hand. "Just figure out what it says."

Hayward began examining it intently, moving her lips. After a few moments, she moved to the nurse's station and picked up a phone.

Wasserman came out, closing the door quietly behind him. "Lieutenant, that was... well, unorthodox, to say the least. But in the end I think it may prove beneficial. Thank you."

"Don't thank me," D'Agosta replied. "Just get her on her feet again. There are a lot more questions I'll need to ask her down the road."

Hayward had hung up the phone and was walking back toward them. "This is the best that Jorge and I could do," she said, handing the notebook back.

D'Agosta looked at the jottings, frowning. "Knives of flint?"

Hayward shrugged. "Can't even be sure it's what she said. But it's our best guess."

"Thanks," D'Agosta said, thrusting the notebook into his pocket and walking away quickly. A moment later he stopped, as if recollecting something. "Doctor," he said, "Captain Waxie will probably be here in the next hour or so."

A black look crossed Wasserman's features.

"But I assume Mrs. Muñoz is too exhausted to see anybody. Am I right? If the Captain gives you any trouble, refer him to me."

For the first time, Wasserman broke into a smile.

38

When Margo arrived at the Anthropology conference room around ten that morning, it was obvious that the meeting had already been underway for some time. The small conference table in the center of the lab was cluttered with coffee cups, napkins, half-eaten croissants, and breakfast wrappings. In addition to Frock, Waxie, and D'Agosta, Margo was surprised to see Chief Horlocker, the heavy braid on his collar and hat looking out of place among all the equipment. Resentment hung in the air like a heavy pall.

"You expect us to believe that the killers are *living* in those Astor Tunnels of yours?" Waxie was saying to D'Agosta. At the sound of her entrance, he turned with a frown. "Glad you could make it," he grumbled.

Hearing this, Frock looked up, then rolled back to make room for her at the table, a relieved look on his face. "Margo! At last. Perhaps you can clear things up. Lieutenant D'Agosta here has been making some unusual claims about your discovery at Greg's lab. He tells me you've been doing some, ah, additional research in my absence. If I didn't know you as well as I do, my dear, I'd think that—"

"Excuse me!" D'Agosta said loudly. In the abrupt silence, he looked around at Horlocker, Waxie, and Frock in turn.

"I'd like Dr. Green to review her findings," he said in a quieter tone.

Margo took a seat at the table, surprised when Horlocker made no response. Something had happened, and, though she couldn't be sure, it seemed obvious that it had to do with the subway massacre the night before. She considered apologizing for her lateness and explaining that she'd remained at her lab until three that morning, but decided against it. For all she knew, Jen, her lab assistant, was still at work down the hall.

"Just a minute," Waxie began. "I was saying that—"

Horlocker turned to him. "Waxie, shut up. Dr. Green, I think you'd better tell us exactly what you've been doing and what you've discovered."

Margo took a deep breath. "I don't know what Lieutenant D'Agosta has told you already," she began, "so I'll be brief. You know that the badly deformed skeleton we found belongs to Gregory Kawakita, a former curator here at the Museum. He and I were both graduate assistants. After leaving the Museum, Greg apparently ran a series of clandestine laboratories, the last one being down in the West Side railyards. My examination of the site turned up evidence that, before his death, Greg was manufacturing a genetically engineered version of *Liliceae mbwunensis*."

"And that's the plant the Museum Beast needed to survive?" Horlocker asked. Margo listened for a sarcastic edge to his voice, but could not detect one.

"Yes," she replied. "But I now believe that this plant was more than just a food source for the beast. If I'm right, the plant contains a reovirus that causes morphological change in any creature that ingests it."

"Come again?" Waxie said.

"It causes gross physical alteration. Whittlesey, the leader of the expedition that sent the plants back to the Museum, must have ingested some himself—perhaps unwittingly, or perhaps against his will. We'll never know the details. But it seems clear now that the Museum Beast was, in fact, Julian Whittlesey."

There was a sharp intake of breath from Frock. Nobody else spoke.

"I know this is difficult to believe," Margo said. "It certainly wasn't the conclusion we came to after the beast was destroyed. We thought the creature was simply some evolutionary aberration that needed the plants to survive. We assumed that, when its own ecological niche was destroyed, it followed the only remaining plants back to the Museum. They'd been used as packing fibers for the artifacts that were crated up and shipped back to New York. Then later, when the beast couldn't get the plants, it ate the nearest available substitute: the human hypothalamus, which contains many of the same hormones found in the plant.

"But I now think we were wrong. The beast was a grossly malformed Whittlesey. I also think Kawakita stumbled on the true answer. He must have found a few specimens of the plant and begun altering them genetically. I guess he believed he'd been able to rid the plant of its negative effects."

"Tell them about the drug," D'Agosta said.

"Kawakita had been producing the plant in large quantities," Margo said. "I believe that a rare designer drug—didn't I hear you call it 'glaze'?—is derived from it, though I can't be sure. It probably has potent narcotic or hallucinatory properties in addition to its viral payload. Kawakita must have been selling it to a select group of users, probably to raise money for more research. But he was also testing the effectiveness of his work. Clearly, he ingested the plant himself at some point. That's what accounts for the bizarre malformations to his skeletal structure."

"But if this drug, or plant, or whatever, has such terrible side effects, why would this Kawakita take it himself?" Horlocker asked.

Margo frowned. "I don't know," she said. "He must have continued perfecting new strains. I assume he felt he'd bred out the negative elements of the drug. And he must have seen some beneficial aspect to it. I'm conducting tests on the plants I found in his laboratory. We've introduced them into various test animals, including white mice and some protozoans. My lab assistant, Jennifer Lake, is going over the results now."

"Why wasn't I informed—?" Waxie began.

D'Agosta rounded on him. "When you finally get around to checking your inbox and listening to your messages, you'll find that you were informed of every goddamn step."

Horlocker held up his hand. "Enough. Lieutenant, we all know that mistakes have been made. We'll leave the recriminations for later."

D'Agosta sat back. Margo had never seen him so angry. It was almost as if he blamed everyone in the room—himself included—for the subway tragedy.

"Right now, we've got an unbelievably serious situation on our hands," Horlocker continued. "The mayor's on my back, screaming for action. And now, with this massacre, the governor's joined in." He wiped his brow with a damp handkerchief. "All right. According to Dr. Green here, we're dealing with a group of drug addicts, supplied by this scientist, Kawakita. Only now, Kawakita is dead. Maybe their supplies have run out, or maybe they've gone wild. They're living deep underground in these Astor Tunnels D'Agosta was describing, abandoned long ago because of flooding. And they're going mad with need. When they can't get the drug, they're forced to eat the human brain. Just like the Mbwun beast. Hence, all the recent killings." He looked around, glaring. "Supporting evidence?"

"The Mbwun plants we found at Kawakita's lab site," Margo said.

"The bulk of the killings parallel the route of the Astor Tunnels," D'Agosta added. "Pendergast showed that."

"Circumstantial," Waxie snorted.

"How about testimony of countless homeless, all stating the Devil's Attic has been colonized?" Margo said.

"You'd trust a bunch of bums and drug addicts?" Waxie asked.

"Why the hell would they lie?" Margo demanded. "And who's in a better position to know the truth than they are?"

"Very well!" The Chief raised his hand. "In the face of the evidence, we're forced to agree. No other leads have panned out. And the powers that be in this city want immediate action. Not tomorrow, or the next day, but right now."

Frock cleared his throat quietly. It was the first sound he'd made in some time.

"Professor?" Horlocker said.

Frock rolled forward slowly. "Forgive my skepticism, but I find this a little too fantastic," he began. "It all seems too much an extrapolation from the facts. Since I wasn't involved in the most recent tests, I can't speak with authority, of course." He looked at Margo with mild reproof. "But the simplest explanation is usually the correct one."

"And what *pray tell* is the simple explanation?" D'Agosta broke in.

Frock moved his gaze to the Lieutenant. "I beg your pardon," he said icily.

Horlocker turned to D'Agosta. "Stow it, Vincent."

"Perhaps Kawakita *was* working with the Mbwun plant. And I see no reason to doubt Margo when she says that our own assumptions of eighteen months ago were a trifle hasty. But where is the evidence of a drug, or of the distribution of a drug?" Frock spread his hands.

"Jesus, Frock, he had a stream of visitors out at his lab in Long Island City—"

Frock turned another cool stare at D'Agosta. "I daresay *you* have visitors at your apartment in *Queens*"—the distaste in his voice was evident—"but that doesn't mean you're a drug peddler. Kawakita's activities, however professionally reprehensible, do not have any bearing on what I think is probably a gang of youths on a homicidal rampage. Kawakita was a victim like the rest. I fail to see the connection."

"Then how do you explain Kawakita's deformities?"

"Very well, he was making this drug, and perhaps he *was* taking it. In deference to Margo, I'll go even further and say—without any proof, of course—that perhaps this drug does cause certain physical changes in the user. But I have yet to see one iota of evidence that he was distributing it, or that his, ah, clients are responsible for these killings. And the idea that the Mbwun creature was once Julian Whittlesey... come now. It goes directly against evolutionary theory."

Your evolutionary theory, Margo thought.

Horlocker passed a weary hand over his brow and pushed litter and papers away from a map that was lying across the table. "Your objections are noted, Dr. Frock. But it no longer matters exactly *who* these people are. We know what they do and we have a good idea where they live. All that's left now is to take action."

D'Agosta shook his head. "I think it's too soon. I know every minute counts, but we're still in the dark about too many things. I was in the Museum of Natural History, remember. I *saw* the Mbwun creature. If these drug users have even a trace of that thing's abilities..." He shrugged. "You saw the slides of Kawakita's skeleton. I just don't think we should move until we know what we're dealing with. Pendergast went down for his own reconnaissance over forty-eight hours ago. I think we should wait until he returns."

Frock looked up in surprise, and Horlocker snorted. "Pendergast? I don't like the man and I *never* liked his methods. He has no jurisdiction here. And frankly, if he went down there alone, that's his lookout. He's probably history by now. We've got the firepower to do whatever needs to be done."

Waxie nodded vigorously.

D'Agosta looked dubious. "At the most, I'd propose some kind of containment effort until we get more information from Pendergast. Just give me twenty-four hours, sir."

"*Containment* effort," Horlocker repeated sarcastically, looking around the room. "You can't have it both ways, D'Agosta. Didn't you hear me? The mayor is screaming for action. He doesn't want containment. We've run out of time." He turned to his assistant. "Get the mayor's office on the phone. And locate Jack Masters."

"Personally," Frock said, "I'm of the same opinion as D'Agosta. We shouldn't be precipitous—"

"The decision's made, Frock," Horlocker snapped, returning his attention to the map.

Frock flushed a deep crimson. Then he spun his wheelchair away from the table and rolled toward the door. "I'm going to take a turn around the Museum," he said to nobody in particular. "I can see my usefulness here has ended."

Margo began to rise, but D'Agosta placed a restraining hand on her arm. She watched the door close with regret. Frock had been a visionary, the one person most instrumental in her own choice of careers. Yet now she could only feel pity for the great scientist who'd grown so set in his ways. *How much less painful,* she thought, *if only he'd been allowed to enjoy his retirement in peace.*

39

Pendergast stood on a small metal catwalk, watching the mass of sewage moving sluggishly four feet below him. It glowed faintly green and surreal in the artificial phosphor of the VisnyTek night-vision goggles. The smell of methane gas was dangerously strong, and every few minutes he reached inside his jacket for a whiff of pure oxygen from a hidden mouthpiece.

The catwalk was bedecked with rotten strips of paper and other, less identifiable things that had caught in the metal slats during the last rainstorm. With every step, Pendergast's feet sunk into puffy mounds of rust that coated the metal like fungus. He moved quickly, examining the slimy walls, looking for the thick metal door that signified the final descent to the Astor Tunnels. Every twenty steps, he removed a small canister from a pocket and sprayed two dots on the wall: markers for long-wavelength light. The dots, invisible to the human eye, glowed a ghostly white when the VisnyTeks were in infrared mode. This would help him to find his way back. Especially if—for whatever reason—he was in a hurry.

Ahead, Pendergast could now make out the faint outlines of the metal door, plated with rivets and heavy with a crust of calcite and oxides. A massive lock hung from its faceplate, frozen by time. Pendergast dug into his jacket, removed a small metal tool, and flicked it on. The high whine of a diamond blade sang down the sewer line, and a stream of sparks flickered into the darkness. In seconds the lock fell onto the catwalk. Pendergast examined the rusted hinges, then positioned the small blade and cut through the three sets of door pins.

He replaced the saw and gave the door a long, appraising glance. Then, grasping the faceplate with both hands, he jerked it toward him. There was a sudden shriek of metal and the door came away, falling off the catwalk and landing with a splash in the water below. On the far side of the door was a dark hole, leading down into unguessable depths. Pendergast switched on the goggles' infrared LED and peered down the hole, wiping the dust from his latex gloves. Nothing.

He played a thin Kevlar rope down into the darkness, fixing the end to an iron bolt. Then, taking a nylon-webbed Swiss seat from his pack, he stepped gingerly into it, locked on a carabiner with a motorized brake bar, and stepped into the well, sliding quickly to the bottom.

His boots landed in a soft, yielding surface. Pendergast unhooked the Swiss seat and tucked his gear away, then did a slow scan with the VisnyTeks. The tunnel was so hot that everything was burned to white. He adjusted the amplitude and slowly the room swam into view, illuminated in a monochromatic landscape of pale green.

He was standing in a long, monotonous tunnel. The muck on the ground was about six inches deep and thick as axle grease. Completing the visual sweep, he pulled open his camos and consulted the diagrams inside. If the map was correct, he was in a service tunnel, close to the main line. Perhaps a quarter of a mile down the passage lay the remains of the Crystal Pavilion, the private waiting area deep beneath the long-forgotten Knickerbocker Hotel, which once stood on the corner of Fifth Avenue and Central Park South. It was the largest of the waiting areas, larger than the platforms beneath the Waldorf and the great Fifth Avenue mansions. If there was a central hub of the Devil's Attic, he would find it within the Crystal Pavilion.

Pendergast moved carefully down the tunnel. The smell of methane and the stench of decay were dizzying; nevertheless, he breathed deeply through his nose, aware of a certain goatish odor he remembered all too well from the darkened Museum subbasement eighteen months before.

The service tunnel merged with another and made a slow bend toward the main line. Pendergast glanced downwards and froze. There in the sludge was a trail of footprints. Bare footprints, apparently fresh. They headed down the track toward the main line.

Taking a long whiff of oxygen, Pendergast bent to examine the track more closely. Allowing for the elasticity of the sludge, the footprints looked normal, if a little broad and squat. Then he noticed the way the toes narrowed to thick points—more like talons than toenails. There were certain depressions in the muck between the toe imprints that suggested webbing.

Pendergast straightened up. It was all true, then. The Wrinklers were real.

He hesitated a moment, taking another hit from the mouthpiece. Then he moved down the service tube, following the tracks, keeping near the wall. When he reached the main junction, he paused for a moment, listened, then spun quickly around the corner into the Weaver stance, gun thrust forward.

Nothing.

The footprints now joined a second, well-traveled path down the center of the main line. Pendergast knelt and examined the trail. It was made of many tracks, mostly bare feet, a few shoes or boots. Some of the feet were extremely broad, almost spadelike. Others looked normal.

Many, many individuals had traveled this trail.

After another careful reconnaissance, he started forward again, passing several side tunnels as he went. Footpaths ran out of these tunnels, converging with the main path. It was almost, Pendergast thought, like the web of tracks one found when hunting in Botswana or Namibia: animals, converging on a watering hole—or a lair.

A large structure loomed ahead. If Al Diamond was correct, this was the remains of the Crystal Pavilion. As Pendergast moved closer, he could make out a long railway platform, its sides layered with the muck of innumerable floods. Carefully, he followed the herd path up onto the platform and looked around, making sure to keep his back against the nearest wall.

The VisnyTek goggles showed, in pitiless greens, a scene of fantastic decay. Gaslight fixtures, once beautiful, now empty and skeletal, hung from the cracked tile mosaics that adorned the walls, and a mosaic ceiling displaying the twelve figures of the zodiac covered the ceiling.

At the rear of the platform, the herd path converged beneath a low archway. Pendergast moved forward, then stopped abruptly. From the other side of the archway came a hot breeze, carrying an unmistakable smell. Reaching into his pack, he felt for the military-issue argon flash lamp, found it, and drew it out. The flash was powerful enough to blind a person temporarily, even in the bright midday sun; the drawback was that it took seven seconds to recharge and the charge pack held enough juice for only a dozen flashes. Taking another whiff of oxygen, he thrust the flash forward with one hand, aimed his gun into the blackness with the other, and stepped beneath the archway.

The night-vision goggles bloomed into static as they tried to resolve the vast space that lay beyond. As best Pendergast could tell, he was in a large, circular room. Far above his head, the remains of an enormous crystal chandelier, filthy and askew, dangled from the groined ceiling. Bits of material that looked like seaweed hung from its still-graceful curves. The ceiling was a great dome, tiled in mirrors that were now shattered and webbed, hovering above him like a ruined, glittering sky. Although he could not make out the center of the large space, Pendergast saw a series of stone steps, placed at irregular intervals, leading ahead into the darkness. The muddy footprints followed these steps. In the center was some kind of structure: an information kiosk, perhaps, or ancient refreshment area.

The walls of the room curved away from him into the distance, pillared in Doric columns of crumbling plaster. Between the nearest columns was an enormous tiled mural: trees, a quiet lake with a beaver dam and beaver, mountains, and an approaching thunderstorm were all depicted in ruined complexity. The decayed condition of the mural and its shattered tiles would have reminded Pendergast of Pompeii, were it not for the furious sea of dried mud and filth that had swept up along its lower edges. Broad streaks of ordure, like a giant's fingerpainting, ran crazily up the walls. Along the crown of the mural, Pendergast could make out the name *ASTOR* in complex tilework. He smiled; Astor had originally made his fortune in beaver pelts. This had indeed been a private sanctuary for a few very rich families.

The next bay contained another great mural, this one depicting a steam locomotive crossing a river gorge, pulling a line of hopper and tank cars and framed by snow-capped peaks. The name *VANDERBILT* was tiled above it—a man who made his fortune in railroads. In front of the mural lay an ancient ottoman, its arms askew and its back broken, mildewed stuffing pouring from the rent pillows. Farther along, a niche marked *ROCKEFELLER* depicted an oil refinery in a bucolic setting, surrounded by farms, the distillation columns tinged by the sunset.

Pendergast took a step into the large space. He watched the rows of columns recede into darkness, the grand names of the Gilded Age glowing in his goggles: Vanderbilt, Morgan, Jesup, others too faint to make out. He moved slowly, watching for any movement. At the far side of the room, a corridor marked TO HOTEL led to two ornate elevators, their brass doors wide open and stained with verdigris, the cars inside in complete devastation, cables draped along the floor like iron snakes. Inset into a nearby wall between two shattered mirrors was a mahogany schedule board, warped and rotten with worm holes.

Though the bottom of the board had fallen away, he could make out the lettering across the top:

WEEKENDS IN SEASON

Dest.	Time
Pocantico Hills	10:14
Cold Spring	10:42
Hyde Park	11:3

Beside the timetable was a small waiting area of disintegrating chairs and sofas. Amidst them, Pendergast saw what had once been a Bösendorfer concert grand. The floods had rotted and then stripped most of the wood away, leaving a massive metal frame, keyboard, and wild nest of broken strings: a musical skeleton, now silent.

Pendergast turned toward the center of the room and listened. The silence was broken only by the distant sound of dripping water; he glanced around and saw a stream of shivering drops falling from the ceiling. He began moving forward, scanning in the direction of the archway and platform for a flash of white in the goggles that would indicate something warmer than the surrounding environment. Nothing.

The goatish smell became stronger.

As the shape in the center began resolving itself in the green haze of his goggles, Pendergast realized it was too low and squat to be a kiosk. Now he could see that it was a crudely made structure: a hut of smooth white stones with only a partial roof, apparently unfinished, surrounded by low platforms and pedestals. Moving still closer, he could see that what he had thought were stones were actually skulls.

Pendergast stopped and took several breaths of the cleansing oxygen. The entire hut had been constructed of human skulls, anterior sides facing outward. Ragged holes yawned through their backs, glowing eerily green in his goggles. He counted the skulls from floor to roof, then did a rough estimation of the diameter; a quick calculation told him that the circular wall of the hut was formed of roughly four hundred and fifty skulls. Hair and scalp fragments showed that most, if not all, of the skulls were fresh.

Pendergast circled to the front of the hut, then waited outside the entrance for several minutes, motionless. The tracks ended here—thousands of them—in a mad jumble of prints around the opening. Above it, he could see three ideographs, painted in some dark liquid:

There was no sound, no movement. Taking a deep breath, he crouched, then spun toward the inside.

The hut was deserted. Ceremonial clay goblets, at least a hundred or more, had been placed on the floor along the inside wall. Outside the entrance stood a simple stone offering table, perhaps four feet high and two in diameter. It was surrounded with a fence made out of what appeared to be human long-bones, lashed with rawhide. Some odd-looking metal parts had been arranged on the table and covered with rotting flowers, as if part of a shrine. Pendergast picked up one of the parts and examined it in surprise. It was a flat piece of metal with a worn rubber handle. The other, equally mundane items provided no further clues. He slipped a few of the smallest into his pocket.

Suddenly, a flash of white registered in his goggles. Quickly, he dropped to a kneeling position behind the table. All seemed quiet, and he wondered if he had been mistaken. Occasionally the goggles could be fooled by thermal layers in the air.

But there it was again: a shape, human—or nearly—loping through the archway from the platform beyond, a white blob leaving an infrared track on his field of view. It appeared to be clutching something to its chest as it ran toward him.

In the thick dark, Pendergast silently raised his gun in one hand, his flash apparatus in the other, and waited.

40

Margo sat back in the flimsy institutional chair, massaging her temples lightly with her fingertips. After Frock's departure, the meeting had quickly degenerated into disagreement. Horlocker left the room for several minutes to speak privately with the mayor. He returned with a city engineer named Hausmann. Now, Jack Masters, head of NYPD's Tactical Response Unit, was also on the phone. But so far they had made little progress toward any course of action.

"Look," came the voice of Masters, tinny and distorted, through the speakerphone. "It's taken my people almost half an hour just to verify the existence of these Astor Tunnels. How can we insert a team?"

"Send several teams, then," Horlocker snapped. "Try different entrance points. Use a wave approach, so we know at least one team will make penetration."

"Sir, you can't even tell me the number or condition of the, well, whatever you call them. And the terrain is unfamiliar. The tunnel system beneath Manhattan is so complex, my men would be compromised. There are too many unknowns, too many ambush points."

"There's always the Bottleneck," said Hausmann, the City Engineer, chewing fretfully on the end of his pen.

"The what?" Horlocker replied.

"The Bottleneck," said the engineer. "All the piping in that quadrant has to go through a single large blast hole, maybe three hundred feet down. The Astor Tunnels are below that somewhere."

"There you go," Horlocker said into the speakerphone. "We could seal it off and proceed from there. Right?"

There was a pause. "I suppose so, sir."

"So we could trap them."

"Maybe." Masters sounded dubious even through the speakerphone. "But what then? We couldn't lay siege. And we couldn't very well go in and root them out. It would be a stalemate. We need more time to grid the route."

Margo glanced at D'Agosta, looking on disgustedly. It was what he'd been recommending from the beginning.

Horlocker pounded on the table. "Goddammit, we don't *have* time! I've got the governor and the mayor breathing down my neck. They've authorized me to take any action necessary to stop these killings. And I plan to do just that."

Now that Horlocker had made up his mind, his determination, his impatience, was remarkable. Margo wondered just what it was the mayor had said in their telephone conversation that had so put the fear of God into the Police Chief.

Hausmann, the engineer, removed his pen from his mouth long enough to speak. "How can we be sure these creatures live in the Astor Tunnels, anyway? I mean, underground Manhattan's a large place."

Horlocker turned toward Margo. She cleared her throat, aware of being put on the spot.

"From what I understand," she said, "there are a lot of underground homeless throughout the tunnels. If there were a concentration of these creatures elsewhere, the homeless would know about it. Like we said earlier, there's no reason to doubt the word of this Mephisto. Besides, if the creatures have any of the characteristics of the Mbwun beast, they'll shun light. The deeper their nest, the better. Of course," she added quickly, "Pendergast's report will—"

"Thank you," Horlocker said, stepping hard on her final words. "Okay, Masters? You've got the brief."

The door swung open suddenly, the squeaking of rubber wheels announcing Frock's return. Margo looked up slowly, almost afraid to see the expression on the old scientist's face.

"I think I owe everyone here an apology," he said simply, wheeling up to the table. "As I went through the Museum's halls just now, I did my best to look at things objectively. And on reflection, I'm afraid I may well have been wrong. It's difficult to admit it, even to myself. But I suppose the theory advanced by Margo best fits the facts." He turned toward Margo. "Please forgive me, my dear. I'm a tiresome old man, overly fond of his pet theories. Especially when it comes to evolution." He smiled wanly.

"How noble," Horlocker said. "But leave the soul-searching for later."

"We need better maps," the voice of Masters continued, "and more information about the hostiles' habits."

"Damn it!" Horlocker cried. "Aren't you hearing me? We don't have time for a geological survey here! Waxie, what's your take on this?"

There was a silence.

Frock eyed Waxie, who was staring out the window as if hoping to see the much-needed answer spray painted across Central Park's Great Lawn. The Captain frowned, but no words came.

"The first two victims," Frock said, still eyeing Waxie, "appear to have been washed out in a storm."

"So they were nice and clean when we found them," Horlocker growled. "Good. So what?"

"The gnaw marks on these victims don't show signs of hurried work," Frock continued. "It would appear the creatures had plenty of time to do their work unmolested. That would imply the bodies were near, or perhaps in, their lair at the time the marks were made. There are numerous analogs in nature."

"Yeah?"

"If a few victims can be flooded out by a storm, what would it take to flood the lair itself?"

"That's it!" Waxie cried, turning from the window in triumph. "We'll drown the bastards!"

"That's crazy," said D'Agosta.

"No, it isn't," Waxie said, pointing excitedly out the window. "The Reservoir's got to drain out through the storm system, right? And when the storm drains get overloaded, doesn't the overflow go into the Astor Tunnels? Wasn't that why you said they were abandoned?"

There was a short silence. Horlocker turned toward the engineer with a quizzical look, who nodded. "It's true. The Reservoir can be dumped directly into the storm drain and sewage system."

"Is it feasible?" Horlocker asked.

Hausmann thought a moment. "I'll have to check with Duffy to be sure. But there are upward of two thousand acre feet of water in the reservoir, at least. That's ninety million cubic feet. If even a fraction of that water—say, thirty percent—were suddenly released into the sewer system, it would completely overwhelm it. And as I understand it, the overflow would go into the Astor Tunnels, then on into the Hudson."

Waxie nodded triumphantly. "Exactly!"

"Seems like a pretty drastic step to me," D'Agosta said.

"Drastic?" Horlocker repeated. "Excuse me, Lieutenant, but we just had the better part of a subway train massacred last night. These things are out for blood, and it's getting worse, fast. Maybe you'd prefer to walk up and give them a summons, or something. But that just won't do the trick. I've got most of Albany on my back, demanding action. This way"—he waved his hand in the direction of the window and the Reservoir beyond—"we can get them where they *live*."

"But how do we know exactly where all this water's going to go?" D'Agosta asked.

Hausmann turned to D'Agosta. "We have a pretty good idea. The way the Bottleneck works, the flow will be confined to the very lowest level of the Central Park quadrant. The overflow shunts will direct the water straight down through the Bottleneck into the deepest storm drains and the Astor Tunnels, which in turn drain into the West Side Laterals and finally into the Hudson."

"Pendergast did say that the tunnels south and north of the Park had been sealed off years before," D'Agosta said, almost as if to himself.

Horlocker looked around, a smile creasing his features. To Margo, it looked awkward, as if Horlocker didn't use those particular muscles very often. "They'll be trapped beneath this Bottleneck, swept away and drowned. Objections, anybody?"

"You'd have to make sure all the creatures were down there when you let the Reservoir go," said Margo.

Horlocker's smile faded. "Shit. And how the hell can we do that?"

D'Agosta shrugged. "One of the patterns we found was that no killings occurred during a full moon."

"That makes sense," Margo replied. "If these creatures are like Mbwun, they hate light. They probably remain below during the full moon."

"What about all the homeless living down there, under the Park?" D'Agosta asked.

Horlocker snorted. "Didn't you hear Hausmann? The water will go straight to the lowest levels beneath the city. We've heard the homeless shun that area. Besides, the Wrinklers would have killed any that wandered too deep."

Hausmann nodded. "We'll plan a limited operation that wouldn't flood anything but the Astor Tunnels."

"And any moles that might be camping out in the path of the descending water?" D'Agosta persisted.

Horlocker sighed. "Ah, shit. To be on the safe side, I guess we'd better roust them out of the Central Park quadrant and put them in shelters." He straightened. "In fact, we could kill two birds with one stone—and maybe even get that Wisher woman off our backs, to boot." He turned to Waxie. "Now this is what I call a plan," he said. "Nicely done."

Waxie blushed and nodded.

"It's a hell of a big place down there," D'Agosta said, "and those homeless people aren't going to go willingly."

"D'Agosta?" Horlocker snapped. "I don't want to hear you whining any more about why it can't be done. For Chrissakes, how many homeless are we talking about below Central Park? A hundred?"

"There's a lot more than—"

"If you've got a better idea," Horlocker interrupted, "let's hear it. Otherwise, stow it." He turned to Waxie. "Tonight's the full moon. We can't afford to wait another month: we'll have to do it now." He leaned toward the speakerphone. "Masters, I want all underground spaces in the vicinity of Central Park cleared of homeless before midnight. Every damn tunnel, from Fifty-ninth Street to One Hundred-tenth, and from Central Park West to Fifth Avenue. A night in the shelters will do the moles good. Get the Port Authority, the MTA, anyone you need. And get me the Mayor, I'll need to brief him on our plan of action, get the rubber stamp."

"You'll need some ex-TA cops down there," D'Agosta said. "They've done rousting details; they'll know what to expect."

"I disagree," Waxie said immediately. "Those moles are dangerous. A group of them almost killed us just a couple of days ago. We want real cops."

"Real cops," D'Agosta repeated. In a louder tone he added, "Then at least take Sergeant Hayward."

"Forget it," Waxie said. "She'll just be in the way."

"Just shows how much you know," D'Agosta snapped. "The most valuable resource you had, Waxie, and you never bothered to tap her potential. She knows more than anyone about the underground homeless. You hear me? More than *anyone*. Believe me, you'll need her expertise on a roust of this size."

Horlocker sighed. "Masters, make sure to include this Sergeant Hayward on the field trip. Waxie, contact what's his name?— Duffy?—at the Water Authority. I want those valves opened at midnight." He looked around. "We'd better move this down to Police Plaza. Professor Frock, we could use your assistance."

Margo watched as Frock, despite himself, beamed with pleasure at feeling useful. "Thank you for that. But I think I'll go home and rest first, if I may. This business has quite exhausted me." He smiled at Horlocker, winked at Margo, and rolled out the door.

Margo watched him go. *Nobody else will ever have any idea how much effort it cost him to admit he was wrong*, she thought.

D'Agosta began following Horlocker and Waxie into the corridor. Then he stopped and turned back to Margo. "Thoughts?" he asked.

Margo shook her head, bringing herself back. "I don't know. I understand there's no time to waste. But I can't help remembering what happened when..." She hesitated. "I just wish Pendergast was here," she said at last.

The phone rang, and she moved to answer it. "Margo Green here." She listened for a long moment, then hung up.

"You'd better go on ahead," she said to D'Agosta. "That was my lab assistant. She wants me downstairs right away."

41

Smithback pushed aside one man in a seersucker suit and dug his elbow into another, trying to force his way through the thickening mob. He'd badly underestimated just how long it would take him to get here; the crowd was jammed solidly for almost three blocks' worth of Fifth Avenue real estate, and more were arriving every minute. Already, he'd missed Wisher's opening speech in front of the cathedral. Now he wanted to reach the first candlelight vigil before the crowd began moving again.

"Watch it, asshole," a young man brayed loudly, removing a silver hip flask from his lips just long enough to speak.

"Go suck on a long bond," Smithback retorted over his shoulder as he straggled forward. He could hear policemen now beginning to work the edges of the crowd, trying ineffectually to clear the avenue. Several news crews had arrived, and Smithback could see cameramen climbing onto the roofs of their vans, craning for a good shot. It seemed that the wealth and power concentrated in the first rally had now been joined by a much larger, much younger crew. And they had all taken the city by surprise.

"Hey! Smithback!" Turning, the journalist made out Clarence Kozinsky, a *Post* reporter on the Wall Street beat. "Can you believe this? Word spread like lightning."

"Guess my article did the trick," Smithback said proudly.

Kozinsky shook his head. "Hate to disappoint you, pal, but your article only hit the streets half an hour ago. They didn't want to take the chance of alerting the cops too early. Word got passed in late afternoon over the services. You know, brokers' wires, the NYSE network, Quotron, LEXIS, all the rest. Seems the boys downtown have really taken to this whole Wisher thing. They think she's the answer to all their white-bread problems." He snickered. "It's not just about crime anymore. Don't ask me how it happened. But the talk in all the bars is that she's got twice the balls the Mayor has. They think she's gonna cut welfare, clean up the homeless, put a republican back in the White House, bring the Dodgers back to Brooklyn, all at once."

Smithback looked around. "I didn't know there were so many financial types in the whole world, let alone Manhattan."

Kozinsky snickered again. "Everybody assumes that Wall Street types are all retro-yuppie drones in boring suits with two point five children, a house in the suburbs, and treadmill, cookie-cutter existences. Nobody remembers the place has a whole sleazy underbelly, too. You got your mere exchange floor runners, bond strippers, interest-rate swappers, pork-belly traders, boiler-room operators, money launderers, you name it. And we're not exactly talking upper crust here. We're talking some real Archie Bunker types. Besides, it isn't just Wall Street anymore. Word's going out by pager, network, and broadcast fax now. The back offices of banks and insurance companies everywhere are coming to join the party."

Ahead, between the rows of heads, Smithback made out Mrs. Wisher. Saying a hasty good-bye to Kozinsky, he pushed his way forward. Mrs. Wisher was standing in the stately shadow of Bergdorf Goodman, flanked by a Catholic priest, an Episcopalian minister, and a rabbi, in front of a three-foot pile of fresh flowers and cards. An effete-looking, long-haired young man wearing a pinstripe suit and thick violet socks stood mournfully to one side. Smithback recognized the hangdog face as that of the

Viscount Adair, Pamela Wisher's boyfriend. Mrs. Wisher looked spare and dignified, her light hair pulled severely back and her face without makeup. As he switched on his tape recorder and thrust it forward, Smithback couldn't help thinking that she was a born leader.

Mrs. Wisher stood silently, head bowed, for a long moment. Then she turned toward the assembled crowd, adjusting a wireless microphone. She cleared her throat dramatically.

"Citizens of New York!" she cried. As a hush fell over the crowd, Smithback looked around, startled by the clarity and volume of her voice. He made out several people scattered strategically through the crowd, holding portable speakers on metal poles. Despite the spontaneous look of the march, Mrs. Wisher and her people had clearly thought things out in great detail.

When the silence was complete, she resumed in a quieter voice. "We are here to remember Mary Ann Cappiletti, who was mugged and shot to death at this spot on March 14. Let us pray."

Between her sentences, Smithback could hear the police bullhorns more clearly now, ordering the crowd to disperse. Mounted police had arrived only to find the crowd too heavy for them to move in safely, and their horses pranced at the fringes in frustration. Smithback knew that Mrs. Wisher had deliberately not sought a parade permit this time in order to cause maximum surprise and consternation at City Hall. Like Kozinsky had said, announcing the march over the private services made for an efficient system of communication. It also had the advantage of bypassing law enforcement, the general media, and municipal government, who only got wind of the event when it was too late to stop it.

"It's been a long time," Mrs. Wisher was saying, "a very long time since a child could walk in New York City without fear. But now, even adults are afraid. We're afraid to walk the streets, to stroll through the park... to ride the subway."

An angry murmur rose at this reference to the recent massacre. Smithback added his own voice to the crowd's, knowing that Mrs. Wisher had probably never hung from a strap in her life.

"Tonight!" she cried suddenly, eyes glittering as she surveyed the crowd. "Tonight we will change all that. And we will start by taking back Central Park. At midnight we will stand, unafraid, on the Great Lawn!"

A roar rose from the crowd, growing in intensity until the pressure of it seemed almost to constrict Smithback's chest. He turned off his cassette recorder and stuffed it into his pocket; it couldn't handle the noise, and besides, he wouldn't need any help remembering this event. He knew that, by now, other journalists would have arrived in force, national as well as local. But he, Smithback, was the only journalist with exclusive access to Anette Wisher, the only reporter provided with details of the march. Not long before, a special afternoon edition of the *Post* had begun appearing on newsstands. It included an insert that displayed maps of the march and listed all the stopping points at which the murder victims would be memorialized. Smithback felt a flush of pride. He could see that many people in the crowd had a copy of the insert in their hands. Kozinski didn't know everything. He, Smithback, had helped spread the word far and wide. Newsstand sales would no doubt go through the roof, and it was the best kind of circulation—not just working class types, but a good smattering of affluent, influential people who normally read the *Times*. Let that dweeb Harriman explain this particular phenomenon to his fossilized, dung-encrusted editor.

The sun had fallen behind the towers and minarets of Central Park West, and a warm summer evening was gathering in the air. Mrs. Wisher lit a small candle, then nodded to the clergymen to do the same.

"Friends," she said, holding the candle above her head, "let our small lights, and our small voices, unite into one raging bonfire and one unmistakable roar. We have but one goal, a goal that cannot be ignored or resisted: to *take back our city*!"

As the crowd took up the chant, Mrs. Wisher moved forward into Grand Army Plaza. With a final shove, Smithback forced himself past the front row and into the small entourage. It was like being inside the eye of a hurricane.

Mrs. Wisher turned toward him. "I'm delighted you could make it, Bill," she said, as calmly as if Smithback were attending a tea party.

"Delighted to be here," Smithback replied, grinning widely in return.

As they moved slowly past the Plaza Hotel and onto Central Park South, Smithback turned back to watch the great mass of people swinging in behind them, like some vast serpent sliding its bulk along the boundaries of the park. Now he could see more people ahead of them as well, flowing out from Sixth and Seventh Avenues, coming down to join them from the west. There was a healthy scattering of old-monied blue bloods in the crowd, sedate and gray. But Smithback could see growing masses of the young men Kozinsky had been talking about—bond salesmen, bank AVPs, brawny-looking commodity traders—drinking, whistling, cheering, and looking as if they were spoiling for action. He remembered how little it had taken to rouse them into throwing bottles at the mayor, and he wondered just how much control Wisher could exert on the crowd if things got ugly.

The drivers of the vehicles along Central Park South had given up honking and had left their vehicles to watch or join the throng, but a vast caterwauling of horns was still rising from the direction of Columbus Circle. Smithback breathed deeply, drinking in the chaos like fine wine. *There's something unbelievably bracing about mob action,* he thought.

A young man hustled up to Mrs. Wisher. "It's the mayor," he panted, holding out a cellular phone.

Tucking the microphone into her purse, Mrs. Wisher took the phone. "Yes?" she said coolly, without breaking stride. There was a long silence. "I'm sorry you feel that way, but the time for permits is long past. You don't seem to realize this city is in an emergency. And we're putting you on notice. This is your final chance to bring peace to our streets." There was a pause while she listened, placing a hand over her free ear to shut out the noise of the crowd. "I'm grieved to hear that the march is hindering your policemen. And I'm pleased to know that the Chief of Police is mounting some operation of his own. But let me ask you a question. Where were your policemen when my Pamela was murdered? Where were your—"

She listened impatiently. "No. Absolutely not. The city is drowning in crime and you are threatening *me* with a citation? If you have nothing else to say, I'll hang up. We're rather busy here."

She handed the phone back to her assistant. "If he calls again, tell him I'm engaged."

She turned to Smithback, slipping one hand into his arm. "This next stop is the site where my daughter was killed. I need to be strong for this, Bill. You'll help me, won't you?"

Smithback licked his lips. "Yes, ma'am," he replied.

42

D'Agosta followed Margo down a dusty, poorly lit hall on the first floor of the Museum. Once part of an ancient exhibit, the hall had been sealed from public view for years, and was now used primarily as overflow storage space for the mammalian collection. Various stuffed beasts, in postures of attack or defense, lined both sides of the narrow corridor. D'Agosta nearly snagged his jacket on the claw of a rearing grizzly. He found himself keeping his arms close to his sides to avoid brushing against the rest of the moldering specimens.

As they rounded a corner into a cul-de-sac, D'Agosta saw a huge stuffed elephant dead ahead, its much-repaired gray skin tattering and flaking. Beneath its massive belly, hidden in shadow, was the two-story metal door of a freight elevator.

"We gotta make this quick," he said as Margo pressed the elevator button. "One Police Plaza has been mobilizing all afternoon. Looks like they're getting ready to storm the Normandy beaches. Besides that, there's some kind of surprise rally by Take Back Our City forming along Fifth Avenue." There was a smell in the air that reminded him of certain summer crime scenes he'd visited.

"The preparation lab is just down the hall," Margo said, watching as D'Agosta's nose wrinkled. "They must be macerating a specimen."

"Right," said D'Agosta. He glanced up at the huge elephant overhead. "Where are the tusks?"

"That's Jumbo, P. T. Barnum's old showpiece. He was hit by a freight train in Ontario and his tusks were shattered. Barnum ground them up, made gelatin out of them, and served it at Jumbo's memorial dinner."

"Resourceful." D'Agosta slid a cigar into his mouth. Nobody could complain about a little smoke with a reek like this.

"Sorry," said Margo, grinning sheepishly. "No smoking. Possibility of methane in the air."

D'Agosta put the cigar back in his pocket as the elevator door slid open. Methane. Now there was something to think about.

They stepped out into a sweltering basement corridor lined with steam pipes and enormous packing crates. One of the crates was open, exposing, the knobby end of a black bone, big as a tree limb. *Must be a dinosaur,* D'Agosta thought. He struggled to control a feeling of apprehension as he remembered the last time he'd been in the Museum's basement.

"We tested the drug on several organisms," Margo said, walking into a room whose bright neon lights stood in sharp contrast to the dingy corridor outside. In one corner, a lab worker was bending over an oscilloscope. "Lab mice, *E. coli* bacteria, blue-green algae, and several single-celled animals. The mice are in here."

D'Agosta peered into the small holding area, then stepped back quickly. "Jesus." The white walls of the stacked cages were flecked with blood. Torn bodies of dead mice littered the floors of the cage, shrouded in their own entrails.

Margo peered into the cages. "You can see that of the four mice originally placed in each cage, only one remains alive."

"Why didn't you put them all in separate cages?" D'Agosta asked.

Margo glanced up at him. "Leaving them together was the whole point. I wanted to examine behavioral as well as physical changes."

"Looks like things got a little out of hand."

Margo nodded. "All of these mice were fed the Mbwun lily, and all became massively infected by the reovirus. It's highly unusual for a virus that affects humans also to affect mice. Normally, they're very host-specific. Now watch this."

As Margo approached the topmost cage, the surviving mouse leapt at her, hissing, clinging to the wire, its long yellow incisors knitting the air. Margo stepped back.

"Charming," said D'Agosta. "They fought to the death, didn't they?"

Margo nodded. "The most surprising thing is that this mouse was badly wounded in the fight. But look at how thoroughly its cuts have healed. And if you check the other cages, you'll see the same phenomenon. The drug must have some powerful rejuvenative or healing properties. The light probably makes them irritable, but we already know that the drug makes one sensitive to light. In fact, Jen left one of the lights on and by morning the protozoan colony directly beneath it had died."

She stared at the cages for a moment. "There's something else I'd like to show you," she said at last. "Jen, can you give me a hand here?"

With the lab assistant's help, Margo slid a divider across the topmost cage, trapping the live mouse on one side. Then she deftly removed the remains of the dead mice with a long pair of forceps and dropped them into a Pyrex basin.

"Let's take a quick look," she said, carrying the pieces into the main lab and placing them on the stage of a wide-angle stereozoom. She peered through the eyepieces, probing the remains with a scapula. As D'Agosta looked on, she sliced open the back of a head, peeled the skin and fur away from the skull, and examined it carefully. Next, she cut open a section of spinal cord and peered closely at the vertebrae.

"As you can see, it looks normal," she said, straightening up. "Except for the rejuvenative qualities, it seems the primary changes are behavioral, not morphological. At least, that's the case in this species. It's too early to be sure, but perhaps Kawakita did succeed in taming the drug in the end."

"Yeah," D'Agosta added. "After it was too late."

"That's what's been puzzling me. Kawakita must have taken the drug *before* it reached this stage of development. Why would he take such a risk, trying the drug on himself? Even after testing it on other people, he couldn't have been sure. It wasn't like him to act so rashly."

"Arrogance," said D'Agosta.

"Arrogance doesn't explain turning yourself into a guinea pig. Kawakita was a careful scientist, almost to a fault. It just doesn't seem in character."

"Some of the most unlikely people become addicts," D'Agosta said. "I see it all the time. Doctors. Nurses. Even police officers."

"Maybe." Margo sounded unconvinced. "Anyway, over here are the bacteria and the protozoans we inoculated with the reovirus. Strangely enough, they all tested negative: the amoebas, paramecia, rotifers, everything. Except for this one." She had open an incubator, exposing rows of Petri dishes covered with purple agar. Glossy, dime-sized welts in each dish of agar indicated growing colonies of protozoans.

She removed a dish. "This is *B. meresgerii,* a single-celled animal that lives in the ocean, growing in shallow water on the surface of kelp and seaweed. It usually feeds on plankton. I like to use them because they're relatively docile, and they're exceptionally sensitive to chemicals."

She carefully dragged a wire loop through the colony of single-celled animals. Smearing the loop on a glass slide, she seated the slide on the microscope tray, adjusted the focus, then stepped away so D'Agosta could take a look.

Peering into the eyepiece, D'Agosta couldn't see anything at first. Then he made out a number of round, clear blobs, waving their cilia frantically against a gridded background.

"I thought you said they were docile," he said, still staring.

"They usually are."

Suddenly, D'Agosta realized that the frenzied maneuvering was not random at all: the creatures were attacking each other, ripping at each other's external membranes and thrusting themselves into the breaches they created.

"And I thought you said they ate plankton."

"Again, they normally do," Margo replied. She looked at him. "Creepy, isn't it?"

"You got that right." D'Agosta backed away, inwardly surprised at how the ferocity of these tiny creatures somehow made him feel squeamish.

"I thought you'd want to see this." Margo stepped up to the microscope and took another look herself. "Because if they plan on—"

She paused, stiffening, as if glued to the eyepiece.

"What is it?" D'Agosta asked.

For a long minute, Margo didn't respond. "That's odd," she murmured at last. She turned to her lab assistant. "Jen, will you stain some of these with eosinophil? And I want a radioactive tracer done to find out which are the original members of the colony."

Motioning D'Agosta to wait, Margo helped the lab assistant prepare the tracer, finally placing the entire treated colony under the stereozoom. She peered into the microscope for what seemed to D'Agosta like an eternity. At last she straightened up, scratched some equations into her notebook, then peered into the stereozoom once again. D'Agosta could hear her counting something to herself.

"These protozoa," she said at last, "have a normal life span of about sixteen hours. They've been in here thirty-six. *B. meresgerii*, when incubated at thirty-seven degrees Celsius, divides once every eight hours. So"—she pointed to a differential equation in her notebook—"after thirty-six hours, you should see a ratio of about seven to nine dead to live protozoa."

"And—?" D'Agosta asked.

"I just did a rough count and found the ratio is only half that."

"Which means?"

"Which means the *B. meresgerii* are either dividing at a lower rate, or..."

She put her eye back to the microscope and D'Agosta could hear the whispered counting again. She straightened up again, this time more slowly.

"The dividing rate is normal," she said, in a low voice.

D'Agosta fingered the cigar in his breast pocket. "Which means?"

"They're living fifty percent longer," she said flatly.

D'Agosta looked at her a moment. "There's Kawakita's motive," he said quietly.

There was a soft knock at the door. Before Margo could answer, Pendergast glided in, nodding to them both. He was once again attired in a crisp black suit, and his face, though a little drawn and tired, betrayed no sign of his recent journeys beyond a small scrape above the left eyebrow.

"Pendergast!" D'Agosta said. "About time."

"Indeed," said the FBI agent. "I had a feeling you'd be here, too, Vincent. Sorry to have been out of touch so long. It was a somewhat more arduous journey than I had imagined. I would have been here to report my encounter half an hour earlier, but I felt a shower and change of clothes to be rather essential."

"Encounter?" Margo asked incredulously. "You saw them?"

Pendergast nodded. "I did, and much else besides. But first, please bring me up to date on events aboveground. I heard about the subway tragedy, of course, and I saw the troops in blue, massing as if for Runnymede. But there's obviously much that I've missed."

He listened intently as Margo and D'Agosta explained about

the true nature of glaze, about Whittlesey and Kawakita, and about the plan to flush out the Astor Tunnels. He did not interrupt except to ask a few questions while Margo was sketching out the results of her experiments.

"This is fascinating," he said at last. "Fascinating, and extremely unsettling." He took a seat at a nearby lab table, crossing one thin leg over the other. "There are disturbing parallels here to my own investigations. You see, there is a gathering point, deep in the Astor Tunnels. It's located in the remains of what was once the Crystal Pavilion, the private train station beneath the defunct Knickerbocker Hotel. In the center of the Pavilion I found a curious hut, built entirely of human skulls. Countless footprints converged on this hut. Nearby was what appeared to be an offering table, along with a variety of artifacts. While I was examining it, one of the creatures approached out of the darkness."

"What did it look like?" Margo asked almost reluctantly.

Pendergast frowned. "Difficult to tell. I never came that close, and the NVD I was wearing does not resolve well at distance. It looked human, or close to it. But its gait was... well, it was *off* somehow." The FBI agent seemed uncharacteristically at a loss for words. "It squatted forward in an unnatural way as it ran, cradling something that I believe was meant as another addition to the hut. I blinded it with a flash and fired, but the sudden brilliance overloaded the goggles, and by the time I could see again the thing was gone."

"Was it hit?" D'Agosta asked.

"I believe so. Some blood spoor was evident. But by that point, I was somewhat anxious to return to the surface." He looked at Margo, one eyebrow raised. "I would imagine that some of the creatures are more deformed than others. In any case, there are three things we can be sure of. They are fast. They can see in the dark. And they are completely malevolent."

"And they live in the Astor Tunnels." Margo shivered. "All under the influence of glaze. With Kawakita dead and the plants gone, they're probably mad with need."

"It would seem so," Pendergast said.

"And this hut you describe was probably the site where Kawakita dispensed the drug," Margo continued. "At least toward the end, when things were getting out of hand. But it all sounds almost ceremonial."

Pendergast nodded. "Precisely. Over the entrance to the hut I noticed Japanese ideographs translating roughly to 'Abode of the Unsymmetrical.' That is one of the names used to describe a Japanese tea room."

D'Agosta frowned. "Tea room? I don't understand."

"Neither did I, at first. But the more I thought about it, the more I realized what Kawakita must have done. The *roji*, or series of steps placed at irregular intervals in front of the hut. The lack of ornamentation. The simple, unfinished sanctuary. These are all elements of the Tea Ceremony."

"He must have distributed the plant by steeping it in water, like tea," Margo said. "But why go to all that trouble, unless..." She paused. "Unless the ritual itself—"

"My own thought exactly," Pendergast said. "As time went on, Kawakita must have had increasing difficulty controlling the creatures. At some point, he abandoned selling the drug and realized he simply had to *provide* it. Kawakita was also trained as an anthropologist, correct? He must have understood the settling, the *taming*, influence of ritual and ceremony."

"So he created a distribution ritual," Margo said. "Shamans in primitive cultures often use such ceremonies to institute order, preserve their power."

"And he chose the Tea Ceremony as the basis," Pendergast said. "Whether reverently or irreverently, we'll never know. Though I would guess it was a cynical addition on his part, considering his other borrowings. Remember the burned notes you found in Kawakita's lab?"

"I have them right here," D'Agosta said, pulling out his notebook, flipping pages, then handing it to Pendergast.

"Ah, yes. Green cloud, gunpowder, lotus heart. These are green teas of varying rarity." Pendergast pointed to D'Agosta's notebook. "And this: 'dung-loving blue foot.' Strike a chord, Dr. Green?"

"It should, but it doesn't."

Pendergast's lips twitched in a slight smile. "It is not one substance, but two. What members of the Route 666 community would no doubt label 'shrooms'."

"Of course!" Margo snapped her fingers. "*Caerulipes* and *coprophilia*."

"You lost me," D'Agosta said.

"The blue-foot *Psilocybe* and the dung-loving *Psilocybe*," Margo said, turning to the Lieutenant. "Two of the most potent hallucinogenic mushrooms there are."

"And this other item, wysoccan," Pendergast murmured. "If memory serves, that was a ritual drink used by the Algonquin Indians during coming-of-age ceremonies. It contained significant amounts of scopolamine. Jimsonweed. A very nasty hallucinogen, causing deep narcosis."

"So you think this is a laundry list?" D'Agosta asked.

"Perhaps. Perhaps Kawakita wanted to modify his brew in some way, making the drug users more docile."

"If you're right, and Kawakita wanted to keep the glaze users under control, then why this hut of skulls?" Margo asked. "It seems to me building something like that would have the opposite, inciting effect."

"True enough," Pendergast said. "There is still a large piece missing from this puzzle."

"A hut, built entirely of human skulls," Margo mused. "You know, I've heard of that before. I think there was a mention of something like that in Whittlesey's journal."

Pendergast looked at her speculatively. "Really? Interesting."

"Let's check the archive. We can use the terminal in my office."

★

The rays of the late afternoon sun shone through the lone window of Margo's cramped office, cloaking papers and books in a mantle of gold. As Pendergast and D'Agosta looked on, Margo sat down at her desk, pulled the keyboard toward her, and began to type.

"The Museum got a grant last year to scan all its field notebooks and similar documents into a database," she said. "With any luck, we'll find the journal here."

She initiated a search on three words: *Whittlesey, hut,* and *skulls.* The name of a single document appeared on the screen. Margo quickly called it up, then scrolled ahead to the penultimate entry. As she read the words, coldly impersonal on the computer screen, she was irresistibly reminded of the events of eighteen months before: sitting in a darkened Museum office with Bill Smithback, looking over the journalist's shoulder as he paged eagerly through the moldy notebook.

...Crocker, Carlos, and I press on. Almost immediately, stopped to repack crate. Specimen jar had broken inside. While I repacked, Crocker wandered off trail, came upon ruined hut in the center of a small clearing. It appeared to be made entirely from human skulls, pegged with human longbones set jacal-fashion into the ground. Ragged holes cut through back of each skull. Small offering table in the center of the hut, made from longbones lashed with sinew. We found the figurine, along with some oddly carved pieces of wood, on table. But I get ahead of myself. We brought gear down to investigate, reopened crate, retrieved toolbag—before we could investigate hut, old native woman wandered out from brush, staggering— sick or drunk, impossible to tell—pointed to crate, wailing loudly...

"That's enough," Margo said more abruptly than she meant to, clearing the screen. The last thing she needed now was another reminder of the contents of that nightmare crate.

"Very curious," Pendergast said. "Perhaps we need to sum up what we know so far." He paused a moment, poised to tick off the items on his slender fingers. "Kawakita refined the drug known as glaze, tested it on others, then used an improved version on himself. The unfortunate users, deformed by the drug and increasingly shy of light, went underground. Growing feral, they began preying on the subterranean homeless. Now, in the wake of Kawakita's death and loss of the glaze supply, their predations have become bolder."

"And we know Kawakita's own motive for taking the drug," Margo said. "The drug seems to have a rejuvenating ability, even the ability to extend one's lifespan. The underground creatures were given an earlier version of the drug he gave himself. And it seems he continued to perfect the drug even *after* he began taking it. The creatures in my lab show no physical abnormalities at all. But even his most refined drug has negative effects: look how aggressive and homicidal it made the mice and even the protozoa."

"But that still leaves three questions," D'Agosta said suddenly. They turned to look at him.

"First, why did these things kill him? Because it sure seems obvious to me that's what happened."

"Perhaps they were growing ungovernable," Pendergast said.

"Or they became hostile to him, seeing him as the cause of their troubles," Margo added. "Or perhaps there was a power play between him and one of the creatures. Remember what he wrote in his notebook: 'The other one grows more eager by the day.'"

"Second, what about that other mention in his notebook: the herbicide, thyoxin? That doesn't seem to fit anywhere. Or the vitamin D you said he was synthesizing?"

"And don't forget Kawakita also wrote the word *irreversible* in his notebook," Pendergast said. "Perhaps he ultimately realized that he could not undo what he had done."

"And that might account for the remorse he seemed to show in his notebook," Margo said. "Apparently, he concentrated on ridding the drug of its physical changes. But in the process, he ignored what his new strain might do to the mind."

"Third, and last," D'Agosta continued, "what the hell was the point of rebuilding this hut of skulls mentioned in Whittlesey's journal?"

At this, everyone was silent.

At last, Pendergast sighed. "You're right, Vincent. I find the purpose of that hut incomprehensible. As incomprehensible as the odd pieces of metal I found on its offering table." Pendergast removed the small items from his jacket pocket and spread them on Margo's worktable. D'Agosta picked them up immediately, examining them closely. "Could they just be pieces of garbage?" he asked. Pendergast shook his head. "They were carefully, even lovingly arranged," he said. "Like relics in a reliquary."

"A what?"

"A reliquary. Something used to display revered objects."

"Well, they don't look reverential to me. They look like the pieces to a dashboard. Or some appliance, maybe." D'Agosta turned to Margo. "Any ideas?"

Margo stood up from the computer terminal and walked over to the worktable. She picked up a piece, studied it a moment, then put it down. "This could be anything," she said, picking up another, a tube of metal with one end encased in gray rubber.

"Anything," Pendergast agreed. "But I sense, Dr. Green, that when we know what they are—and why they were lying enshrined on a stone platform, thirty stories below New York City—we'll have the key to this puzzle."

43

Hayward shouldered the riot gear, adjusted the lantern visor strapped around her head, and glanced across the mass of blue milling around the lower concourse of the 59th Street station. She was supposed to find Squad Five, led by a Lieutenant Miller, but the vast space was in chaos, everyone trying to find everyone else and consequently finding nobody.

She saw Chief Horlocker arrive, fresh from mustering the squads that were assembling at the 81st Street station under the Museum. Horlocker took up a position on the far side of the concourse next to Tactical Head Jack Masters, a thin, sour-looking man. Master's long arms, which usually hung down by his side like an ape's, were now gyrating as he talked to a group of lieutenants, slapping a series of maps, tracing out imaginary lines. Horlocker stood by, nodding, holding a pointing device like a swagger stick, occasionally tapping it on the map to emphasize a particularly salient point. As Hayward watched, Horlocker dismissed the lieutenants and Masters picked up a bullhorn.

"Attention!" he barked in a rasping voice. "Are the squads assembled?" It reminded Hayward of Girl Scout camp.

A rumbling murmur that might have been "No" arose.

"Squad One here, then," Masters said, pointing toward the front. "Squad Two, assemble at the downtown level." He continued through the squads, assigning them various sections of the concourse. Hayward headed for the Squad Five assembly point. As she arrived, Lieutenant Miller was spreading out a large diagram of his own squad's area of responsibility shaded in blue. Miller was wearing a light gray assault uniform whose loose folds could not conceal a generous load of adipose tissue.

"I don't want no heroics, no confrontations," Miller was saying. "Okay? It's basically a traffic cop assignment, nothing fancy. If there's any resistance, you've got your mask and your tear gas. Don't fart around; show them you mean business. But I don't expect any trouble. Do your job right, and we'll be out of here in an hour."

Hayward opened her mouth, then restrained herself. It seemed to her that using tear gas in underground tunnels might be a little tricky. Once, years before the Transit Police merged with the regular force, someone at headquarters had suggested using gas to quell a disturbance. The rank and file almost revolted. Tear gas was bad enough on the surface, but it was murderous belowground. And she could see that their detail covered the deeper subway and maintenance tunnels beneath Columbus Circle station.

Miller swiveled his head, the dark glasses around his neck swinging from a Day-Glo chord. "Remember, most of these moles are wigged out on some shit or other, maybe weakened by too much juice," he barked. "Show them some authority and they'll fall in line. Just move 'em up and out like cattle, if you know what I mean. Once you get them started, they'll keep going. Head them toward this central point here, beneath the number two turnaround. That's the staging point for squads four through six. Once the squads have reassembled, we'll move the moles up to the parkside subway exit, here."

"Lieutenant Miller?" Hayward said, unable to keep silent any longer.

The Lieutenant looked at her.

"I used to roust some of those tunnels, and I know these guys. They're not going to move along as easily as you think they are."

Miller's eyes widened, as if seeing her for the first time. "You?" he asked in disbelief. "A rouster?"

"Yes, sir," Hayward said, thinking she'd give the next guy who asked her that a swift kick in the balls.

"Jesus," said Miller, shaking his head.

There was a silence as the other cops looked at Hayward.

"Any other ex-TAs here?" Miller asked, looking around. Another officer raised his hand. Hayward quickly took in the obvious features: tall, black, built like a tank.

"Name?" Miller barked.

"Carlin," the heavyset man drawled.

"Any others?" Miller asked. There was a silence.

"Good."

"Us ex-Transit Police, we know those tunnels," Carlin said in a mild voice. "Too bad they didn't think to enlist more of us for this picnic. Sir."

"Carlin?" Miller said. "You got your gas, you got your stick, you got your piece. So don't wet your pants. And when I want your opinion again, I'll ask for it." Miller looked around. "There are too many goddamn bodies in here. This action calls for a small, elite group. But what the Chief wants, the Chief gets."

Hayward glanced around herself, estimating there were perhaps a hundred officers in the room. "There're at least three hundred homeless beneath Columbus Circle alone," she said evenly.

"Oh? And when did you last count them?" Miller asked.

Hayward said nothing.

"There's one in every group," Miller muttered to no one in particular. "Now listen up. This is a tactical operation, and we've got to be tight and obey orders. Is that understood?"

There were a few nods. Carlin caught Hayward's eye and rolled his own briefly toward the ceiling, indicating his opinion of Miller.

"All right, partner up," Miller snapped, rolling up the chart.

Hayward turned toward Carlin, and he nodded in return. "How you doing?" he asked. Hayward noticed her first impression of the officer as overweight was wrong: he was strongly built, cut like a weight lifter, not an ounce of fat anywhere. "What was your beat before the merge?"

"I had the tour under Penn Station. The name's Hayward." Out of the corner of her eye, she could see a derisive look cross Miller's face: Carlin and the broad.

"This is really a man's job," Miller said, still looking at Hayward. "There's always the chance things could turn a little ugly. We won't hold it against you if—"

"With Sergeant Carlin here," Hayward interrupted, "there's enough *man* for the both of us." She swept her eyes appraisingly across Carlin's massive frame, then looked pointedly at Miller's stomach.

Several cops erupted into laughter, and Miller frowned. "I'll find something in the rear for you two."

"Officers of the law!" Horlocker's voice suddenly barked through the bullhorn. "We have less than four hours to clear the homeless from the areas beneath and surrounding Central Park. Keep in mind that precisely at midnight, millions of gallons of water will be released from the reservoir into the storm drain system. We'll be channeling the flow precisely. But there's no guarantee that a couple of wandering homeless won't get caught in the downward rush of water. So it's imperative that your work be done, and everyone within the clear zone evacuated well before the deadline. *Everyone.* This is not a temporary evacuation. We're going to use this unique opportunity to clear out, once and for all, the underground homeless from these areas. Now, you have your assignments, and you have team leaders who've been chosen for their experience. There is no reason why these assignments cannot be completed with an hour or two to spare.

"We've made arrangements to provide these people with food and shelter for the night. Explain this to them, as necessary. From the exit points marked on your maps, buses will take them to shelters in Manhattan and the other boroughs. We don't expect resistance. But if there is resistance, you have your orders."

He looked around at the assembled group for a moment, then raised the bullhorn again.

"Your fellow officers in the northern sections have been fully briefed and will begin their operations simultaneously with your own. I want everyone moving together. Remember, once underground, your radios will be of limited use. You may be able to communicate with each other and nearby team leaders, but aboveground communication will be intermittent at best. So keep to the plan, keep to the schedule, and do your part."

He stepped forward. "And now, men, let's do some good!"

The ranks of uniformed officers straightened up as Horlocker walked through them, clapping some on the back, dispensing encouraging words. As he was passing Hayward, he stopped, frowning. "You're Hayward, right? D'Agosta's girl?"

D'Agosta's girl, my ass. "I work with D'Agosta, sir," she said out loud.

Horlocker nodded. "Well, get to it, then."

"Hey, sir, I think you'd better..." Hayward began, but an aide had run up to Horlocker's side, babbling something about a rally in Central Park growing much larger than expected, and the Chief moved away quickly. Miller shot her a warning look.

As Horlocker left the concourse with a retinue of aides, Masters picked up the bullhorn. "Move out by squad!" he barked.

Miller turned to the group with a lopsided grin. "Okay, men. Let's bag some moles."

44

Captain Waxie stepped out of the ancient puddingstone Central Park precinct station and huffed along the path that angled northward into the wooded gloom. On his left was a uniformed officer from the station. On his right was Stan Duffy, the city's Chief Engineer of Hydraulics. Already, Duffy was trotting ahead, looking back at them impatiently.

"Slow it down a bit," Waxie said, panting. "This isn't a marathon."

"I don't like being in the Park this late," Duffy replied in a high, reedy voice. "Especially with all these murders going on. You were supposed to be at the station half an hour ago."

"Everything north of Forty-second is messed up," Waxie said. "Gridlocked beyond belief. It's all that Wisher woman's fault. There's some kind of march, formed out of nowhere." He shook his head. They'd jammed up Central Park West and South, and stragglers were still wandering up Fifth Avenue, causing all kinds of chaos. They didn't even have a damn permit. And she'd given no warning. If he were mayor, he would have clapped them all in jail.

Now the bandshell loomed ahead to their right: empty and silent, festooned with impossibly dense graffiti, a haven for muggers. Duffy glanced at it nervously, hurrying past.

The three angled around the pond, following the East Drive. In the distance, beyond the shadowy borders of the Park, Waxie could hear yelling, cheering, the sounds of horns and motors. He glanced at his watch: eight-thirty. The plans called for initiating the drainage sequence by eight forty-five. He trotted a little faster. They were barely going to make it.

The Central Park Reservoir Gauging Station was housed in an old stone building a quarter mile south of the Reservoir. Now, Waxie could see the building looming through the trees, a single light glowing through a dirty window, the letters CPRGS chiseled on the doorway lintel. He slowed to a walk while Duffy unlocked the heavy metal door. It swung inwards to reveal an old, stone room sparsely decorated with map tables and dusty, long-forgotten hydrometric instruments. In one corner, in dramatic juxtaposition to the rest of the equipment, sat a computer workstation, along with several monitors, printers, and strange-looking peripherals.

Once they were inside, Duffy closed and locked the door carefully, then went over to the console. "I've never done this before," he said nervously, reaching under a desk and removing a manual that weighed at least fifteen pounds.

"Don't crap out on us now," Waxie said.

Duffy swiveled a yellow eye in his direction. For a moment, he looked as if he were going to say something. Instead, he paged through the manual for a few minutes, then turned to the keyboard and began to type. A series of commands appeared on the larger of the monitors.

"How does this thing work?" Waxie asked, shifting from one foot to the other. The intense humidity of the room made his joints ache.

"It's fairly simple," Duffy said. "Water from the lower Catskills is gravity fed into the Central Park Reservoir. That Reservoir may look big, but it holds only about three days' worth of water for Manhattan. It's really more of a holding tank, used to smooth out rises and dips in demand."

He tapped at the keys. "This monitoring system is programmed to anticipate those rises and dips, and it adjusts the flow into the Reservoir accordingly. It can open and close gates as far away as Storm King Mountain, a hundred miles away. The program looks back over twenty years of water use, factors in the latest weather forecasts, and makes demand estimates."

Safe in his locked chamber, Duffy was warming to his subject. "At times there are departures from the estimate, of course. When demand is less than expected, and too much water flows toward the Reservoir, the computer opens the Main Shunt and bleeds the excess into the storm drain and sewer system. When demand is unexpectedly high, the Main Shunt is closed and additional upstream gates are opened to increase the flow."

"Really?" Waxie said. He'd lost interest after the second sentence.

"I'm going to do a manual override, which means I'm going to open the gates upstream *and* open the Main Shunt. Water will pour into the Reservoir and drain immediately into the sewer system. It's a simple and elegant solution. All I have to do is program the system to release twenty million cubic feet—that's about a hundred million gallons—at midnight, then revert back to automatic mode upon completion."

"So the Reservoir isn't going to go dry?" Waxie asked.

Duffy smiled indulgently. "Really, Captain. We don't want to create a water emergency. Believe me, this can be done with the most minimal impact on the water supply. I doubt we'll see the level in the Reservoir drop more than ten feet. It's an incredible system, really. Hard to believe it was designed over a century ago by engineers who anticipated even the needs of today." The smile faded. "Even so, nothing on this scale has ever been done before. Are you sure you really want to do this? All the valves opening at once... well, all I can say is it's going to make one heck of a surf."

"You heard the man," Waxie said, rubbing his bulbous nose with his thumb. "Just make sure it works."

"Oh, it'll work," Duffy replied.

Waxie laid a hand on his shoulder. "Of course it will," he said. "Because if it doesn't, you're going to find yourself a junior sluice gate operator in the Lower Hudson sewage treatment plant."

Duffy laughed nervously. "*Really,* Captain," he repeated. "There's no need for threats." He resumed his typing while Waxie paced the room. The uniformed cop stood soberly by the door, watching the proceedings disinterestedly.

"How long will it take to dump the water?" Waxie asked at last.

"About eight minutes."

Waxie grunted. "Eight minutes to dump a hundred million gallons?"

"As I understand it, you want the water dumped as quickly as possible, to fill up the lowest tunnels under Central Park and sweep them clean, right?"

Waxie nodded.

"Eight minutes represents the system at one hundred percent flow. Of course, it will take almost three hours for the hydraulics to get in position. Then it will simply be a matter of draining water *from* the Reservoir, at the same time that we bring new water *into* the Reservoir from the upstate aqueducts. That should keep the Reservoir's water level from dropping excessively. It has to be done just right, because if the flow coming into the reservoir is greater than the flow going out... well, that means a major flood in Central Park."

"Then I hope to hell you understand what you're doing. I want this thing to proceed on schedule, *no* delays, *no* glitches."

The sound of typing slowed.

"Stop worrying," Duffy said, his finger poised on a key. "There won't be any delays. Just don't change your mind. Because once I press this key, the hydraulics take over. I can't stop it. You see—"

"Just hit the damn key," Waxie said impatiently.

Duffy pressed it with a melodramatic flourish. Then he turned to face Waxie. "It's done," he said. "Now, only a miracle can stop the flow. And in case you hadn't heard, they don't allow miracles in New York City."

45

D'Agosta gazed at the small pile of rubber and chromed parts, picked one up, then dropped it again in disgust. "It's the damnedest thing I've ever seen," he said. "Could these have been left there by accident?"

"I assure you, Vincent," Pendergast said, "they were carefully arranged on the altar, almost as if they were some kind of offering." There was a silence while he paced restlessly across the lab. "There's another thing I'm uneasy about. Kawakita was the one who was growing the lily in tanks, after all. Why would they kill him *and* burn the lab? Why would they destroy their only source of the drug? The one thing an addict is most terrified of is losing his connection. And the lab was burned deliberately. You said there were trace accelerants in the ashes."

"Unless they were growing it somewhere else," D'Agosta said, fingering his breast pocket absently.

"Go ahead and light up," Margo said.

D'Agosta eyed her. "Really?"

Margo smiled and nodded. "Just this once. But don't tell Director Merriam."

D'Agosta brightened. "It'll be our secret." He slipped the cigar out, jabbed a pencil into its head, and moved to the lone window, lifting the sash wide. He lit up and puffed the clouds of smoke contentedly out over Central Park.

I wish I had a vice I enjoyed half as much as that, Margo thought as she watched idly.

"I considered the possibility of an alternate supply," Pendergast was saying. "And I kept my eyes open for signs of an underground garden. But there was no evidence of one. Such a lily farm would require still water and fresh air. I can't imagine where they could be hiding it underground."

D'Agosta blew another stream of blue smoke out the window, resting his elbows on the windowsill. "Look at that mess," he said, nodding southward. "Horlocker's going to have kittens when he sees that."

Margo walked to the window and let her gaze fall over the rich green mantle of Central Park, shadowy and mysterious beneath the pink of the western sunset. To her right, along Central Park South, she could hear the faint sound of countless horns. A great mass of marchers was moving into Grand Army Plaza with the slow flow of molasses.

"That's some march," she said.

"You're damn right it is," D'Agosta said. "And those people vote."

"I hope Dr. Frock's car service didn't get stuck in all that on his way home," she murmured. "He hates crowds."

She let her eyes drift northward, over the Sheep Meadow and the Bethesda fountain, toward the placid oval of the Reservoir. At midnight, that calm body of water would let loose twenty million cubic feet of death into the lowest levels of Manhattan. She felt a sudden pang for the Wrinklers caught below. It wasn't exactly due process. But then her mind drifted back to the bloody mouse cages, to the sudden viciousness of the *B. meresgerii*. It was a deadly drug; one that increased a thousand-fold the natural aggressiveness that evolution had built into almost all living creatures. And Kawakita, infected himself, believed the process to be irreversible...

"I'm glad we're up here and not down there," D'Agosta murmured, puffing meditatively.

Margo nodded. She could see, out of the corner of her eye, Pendergast pacing the room behind her, picking up things, putting them down again.

When the sun next rises over the Park, Margo thought, *the Reservoir will be twenty million cubic feet lighter.* Her eyes rested on the surface of the water, its hint of internal light reflecting the oranges, reds, and greens of the sunset. It was a beautiful scene, its quiet tranquility in stark contrast to the marching and the frantic horns twenty blocks to the south.

Then she frowned. *I've never seen a green sunset before.*

She strained to make out the darkening surface of water rapidly disappearing into shadow. In the dying glow she could clearly see dull patches of green on the surface of the water. A strange and awful thought had crept unbidden into her mind. *Still water and fresh air...*

It's impossible, she thought. *Someone surely would have noticed. Or would they?*

She turned from the window and glanced at Pendergast. He caught her eye, saw the look in it, and ceased his pacing.

"Margo?" he asked, arching an eyebrow.

She said nothing, and Pendergast followed her gaze out toward the Reservoir, stared for a moment, then stiffened visibly. When he looked back at her, she could see the same dawning realization in his own eyes.

"I think we'd better take a look," Pendergast said quietly.

The Central Park Reservoir was separated from the surrounding jogging path by a tall chain-link fence. D'Agosta grasped the base of the fence and tugged it violently from the ground. With Pendergast and D'Agosta close behind, Margo scrambled down the gravel service path to the water's edge, wading out to a patch of small, oddly shaped lily pads, terrifying in their familiarity.

She tore the closest one from the group and held it up, water dripping from its pulpy roots.

"*Liliceae mbwunensis*," she said. "They're growing it in the Reservoir. That's how Kawakita planned to solve his supply problem. Aquariums are limited. So not only did he engineer the drug, but he was *also* hybridizing the plant to grow in a temperate climate."

"There's your alternative source," D'Agosta said, still puffing on the cigar.

Pendergast waded in after her, his hands sweeping the dark waters, ripping up plants and examining them in the twilight. Several joggers stopped abruptly in their robotic courses around the water, staring wide-eyed at the bizarre sight: a young woman in a lab coat, an overweight man with a cigar glowing like a firebrand in his mouth, and a tall, strikingly blond man in an expensively tailored black suit, standing up to their chests in the Manhattan drinking supply.

Pendergast held up one of the plants, a large nut-brown pod hanging from its stem. The pod had curled open. "They're going to seed," Pendergast said quietly. "Flushing the Reservoir will simply dump this plant and its deadly cargo into the Hudson River—and into the ocean."

There was a silence, punctuated only by the distant cacophony of horns.

"But this thing can't grow in saltwater," Pendergast continued. "Can it, Dr. Green?"

"No, of course not. The salinity..." A sudden terrible thought burned its way through Margo's consciousness. "Oh, Jesus. How stupid of me."

Pendergast turned toward her, eyebrows raised.

"The *salinity*," she repeated.

"I'm afraid I don't understand," Pendergast replied.

"The only single-celled animal affected by the viral drug was *B. meresgerii*," Margo continued slowly. "There's one difference between *B. meresgerii* and the other organisms we tested with the drug. The agar plates for *B. meresgerii* were saline plates. *B. meresgerii* is a marine organism. It lives in a saline environment."

"So?" asked D'Agosta.

"It's a common way to activate a virus. Just add a small amount of saline solution to the viral culture. In the cold, fresh reservoir water, the plant stays dormant. But when those seeds hit the saltwater, it'll activate the virus. And dump the drug into the ecosystem."

"The Hudson," said Pendergast, "is tidal all the way up past Manhattan."

Margo dropped the plant and took a step back. "We saw what the drug did to just one microscopic organism. If it's released into the ocean, God knows what the end result would be. The marine ecology could be totally disrupted. And the food chain is dependent on the oceans."

"Hold on," said D'Agosta. "The ocean's a pretty big place."

"The ocean distributes many seeds of freshwater and land-growing plants," Margo said. "Who knows what plants and animals the virus will colonize and multiply in? And if the plant propagates in the ocean—or if the seeds find their way into estuaries and wetlands—it won't make any difference."

Pendergast waded out of the water and slung the plant over his shoulder, its bulbous, knotted roots staining the narrow line of his shoulders.

"We've got three hours," he said.

PART 3

HUT OF SKULLS

It can be illustrative to view the various stratum of subterranean New York society in the same way one would view a geologic cross section, or a food chain showing devolvement from predator to prey. Highest on the chain are those who inhabit a twilight world between the underground and the surface; who visit soup kitchens, welfare offices, or even places of employment by day, only to return to the tunnels by night to drink or sleep. Next come the long-term, habitual, or pathologically homeless persons who simply prefer the dark, warm filth of the underground to the sunlit, often freezing filth of the city streets. Below them—often literally—are the multiple substance abusers and criminals who use the subway and railroad tunnels as havens or hideaways. At the bottom of the cross section are the dysfunctional souls for whom normal life "topside" has simply become too complex or painful to bear; they shun the homeless shelters and flee to dark places of their own. And of course there are other, less categorizable, groups that exist on the fringes of these main strata of underground society: predators, hard-core criminals, visionaries, the insane. This latter category comprises a growing percentage of the homeless, primarily due to the abrupt court-ordered closures of many state mental institutions in recent years.

All human beings have the propensity to organize themselves into communities for protection, defense, and social interaction. The homeless—even the deepest, most alienated "moles"—are no exception. Those who have chosen to live in perpetual darkness belowground will still form their own societies and communities. Of course, *society* itself is a misleading term when dealing with the underground population. Society implies regularity and order; underground living is, by definition, disordered and entropic. Alliances, groups, communities come together and dissolve with the fluidity of mercury. In a place where life is short, often brutal, and always without natural light, the trappings and niceties of civilized society can fall away like so much ash under the least pressure of wind.

L. Hayward, *Caste and Society Beneath Manhattan*
(forthcoming)

46

Hayward peered down the abandoned subway tunnel, toward the flashlights that played like emergency beacons across the low ceilings and wet stone walls. The Plexiglas riot shield felt bulky and heavy against her shoulder. To her right, she could sense Officer Carlin's alert, calm presence next to her in the dark. He seemed to know his stuff. He'd know that the worst thing you could be belowground was cocky. The moles wanted to be left alone. And the only thing that inflamed them more than the sight of one policeman was the sight of many policemen, bent on rousting and eviction.

At the front, where Miller was, there was lots of laughter and tough talk. Squad Five had already rousted two groups of upper-level homeless, fringe dwellers who had fled upstairs in terror before the thirty-strong phalanx of cops. Now they were all feeling like hot shit. Hayward shook her head. They had yet to encounter any hard-core mole people. And that was strange. There should have been a lot more homeless in the subway tunnels beneath Columbus Circle. Hayward had noticed several smoldering fires, recently abandoned. That meant the moles had gone to ground. Not surprising, with all the racket everyone was making.

The squad continued down the tunnel, pausing occasionally while Miller ordered small teams off to explore alcoves and side passages. Hayward watched as the groups came swaggering back out of the dark, empty-handed, kicking aside garbage, holding their riot shields at their sides. The air was foul with ammoniac vapors. Even though they were already deeper than ordinary rousting parties ever went, the atmosphere of a field trip had not yet dissipated, and nobody was complaining. *Wait until they begin to breathe hard,* she thought.

The spur tunnel came to an abrupt end and the squad proceeded, single file, down a metal staircase to the next level. Nobody seemed to know just where this Mephisto hung out, or the extent of the Route 666 community, the primary target of their roust. But nobody seemed to be worried about it. "Oh, he'll come out of his hole," Miller had said. "If we don't find him, the gas will."

As she followed the rattling, jostling group, Hayward had the unpleasant sensation she was sinking into hot, fetid water. The staircase came out in a half-finished tunnel. Ancient water pipes, weeping with humidity, lined the rough-hewn rock walls. Ahead of her, the laughter tapered off into whispers and grunts.

"Watch your step," Hayward said, pointing her flashlight downwards. The floor of the tunnel was peppered with narrow boreholes.

"Hate to trip over one of those," Carlin said, his large head made even larger by the heavy helmet he wore. He kicked a pebble into the closest borehole, then listened until a faint rattle came reverberating up. "Must have fallen a hundred feet," he said. "Hollow down there, too, by the sound of it."

"Look at this," Hayward said under her breath, shining her light on the rotting wooden pipes.

"A hundred years old if they're a day," Carlin replied. "I think—"

Hayward put a restraining hand on his arm. A soft tapping was sounding in the heavy darkness of the tunnel.

A flurry of whispers filtered back from the head of the squad. As Hayward listened, the tapping sped up, then slowed down, following its own secret cadence.

"Who's there?" Miller cried out.

The faint sound was joined by another, deeper tapping, and then another, until the entire tunnel seemed filled with an infernal symphony of noise. "What the hell is it?" Miller asked. He drew his weapon and pointed it down the beam of his flashlight. "Police officers. Come out, now!"

The tapping echoed on as if in mocking response, but nobody stepped into the flashlight beams.

"Jones and McMahon, take your group ahead a hundred yards," Miller barked. "Stanislaw, Fredericks, check the rear."

Hayward waited as the short details disappeared into the darkness, returning empty-handed a few minutes later.

"Don't tell me there's nothing!" Miller shouted in response to the shrugged shoulders. "Somebody's making that sound."

The tapping tapered off to a single, faint ditty.

Hayward took a step forward. "It's the moles, banging on the pipes—"

Miller frowned. "Hayward, stow it."

Hayward could see that she had the attention of the others.

"That's how they communicate with each other, sir," Carlin said mildly.

Miller turned, his face dark and unreadable in the blackness of the tunnel.

"They know we're here," Hayward said. "I think they're warning the nearby communities. Sending out word they're under attack."

"Sure," said Miller. "You telepathic, Sergeant?"

"Read Morse, Lieutenant?" Hayward challenged.

Miller paused, uncertain. Then he guffawed loudly. "Hayward here thinks the natives are restless." There was some brief, half-hearted laughter. The single tapping continued.

"So what's it saying now?" Miller asked, sarcastically.

Hayward listened. "They've mobilized."

There was a long silence, and then Miller said loudly, "What a load of horseshit." He turned to the group. "Forward on the double! We've wasted enough time as it is."

As Hayward opened her mouth to protest, there was a soft thudding sound nearby. One of the men in the front ranks staggered back, groaning loudly and dropping his shield. A large rock bounced toward Hayward's feet.

"Formation!" Miller barked. "Bring your shields up!"

A dozen flashlight beams swept the blackness around them, probing alcoves and ancient ceilings. Carlin approached the injured policeman. "You okay?" he asked.

The cop, McMahon, nodded, breathing heavily. "Bastard got me in the stomach. My vest took the worst of it."

"Show yourselves!" Miller shouted.

Two more rocks came winging out of the darkness, flitting through the flashlight beams like cave bats. One rocketed into the dust of the tunnel floor, and the other struck a glancing blow off Miller's riot shield. There was a roar as the Lieutenant discharged his shotgun, the rubber pellets slapping off the rough ceiling.

Hayward listened as the sound reverberated down the tunnels, finally dying into silence. The men were looking around restlessly, stepping from one foot to the other, already jumpy. This was no way to work a roust of this size.

"Where the hell are they?" Miller said to no one in particular.

Taking a deep breath, Hayward stepped forward. "Lieutenant, we'd better move *right now*—"

Suddenly the air was full of missiles: bottles, rocks, and dirt came pelting out of the darkness ahead of them, a rain of garbage. The officers ducked, pulling their shields up to protect their faces.

"Shit!" came a frantic cry. "Those bastards are throwing shit!"

"Get organized, men!" Miller cried. "Give me a line!"

As Hayward turned, looking for Carlin, she heard a nearby voice say, "Oh, my sweet Lord," in a disbelieving whisper. She spun around to a sight that weakened her knees: a ragged, filthy army of homeless was boiling out of the dark tunnel from *behind* them in a well-planned ambush. In the lambent glow of the flashlights it was impossible to get a good count, but to Hayward it seemed there must be hundreds: screaming with rage, brandishing angle irons and pieces of rebar.

"Back!" Miller cried, aiming at the mob. "Fall back and fire!" A fusillade of shots rang out, brief but impossibly loud in the confines of the tunnel. Hayward thought she could hear the slap of rubber bullets on flesh: several of the figures in the front rank fell, squealing in pain and tearing at their rags, thinking they'd been shot.

"Off the pigs!" a tall, dirty mole with matted white hair and feral eyes cried out, and the crowd surged forward again. Hayward saw Miller retreat into the confused group of officers, barking contradictory commands. More shots rang out, but the flashlights were flickering wildly off the walls and ceiling and there was no way to get a bead. The moles were screaming, a wild, ululating cry that raised the hairs on the back of her neck.

"Oh, shit," Hayward said in disbelief as she watched the mob surge through the flickering darkness and collide with the phalanx of police officers.

"The other side!" she heard a cop cry out. "They're coming from the other side!"

There was a sound of shattering glass, and a flickering darkness descended, punctuated occasionally by muzzle flashes as more rubber bullets were fired, mingling with strange screams and cries. Hayward stood rooted in place amidst the chaos, disoriented by the lack of light, trying to get her bearings.

Suddenly, she felt a greasy arm snake up between her shoulder blades. Immediately, her paralysis evaporated: dropping her shield and throwing her weight forward, she flipped the assailant over her shoulder, then stomped his abdomen viciously with a booted foot. She heard the man's howl of pain rise above the hoarse screeching and the firing of the guns. Another figure came at her, rushing out of the blackness, and instinctively she assumed a defensive posture: low, weight on the back leg, left arm vertical before her face. She feinted, chopping with the left arm, then floored him with a roundhouse kick.

"Holy shit," came Carlin's appreciative voice, as he waded in beside her.

The darkness was now absolute. They were finished unless they could get some light. Quickly, Hayward fumbled at her belt, found an emergency flare, and yanked its firing string. The length of tunnel was bathed in an eerie orange light. Hayward looked around at the struggling figures in amazement. They were walled in on both sides by huge numbers of moles. There was a pop and a burst of light beside her: at least Carlin had the presence of mind to follow her example.

Hayward held the flare aloft, scanning the melee, looking for a way to organize the men. Miller was nowhere to be seen. Picking up her shield and pulling her "ugly stick" from the leather scabbard, Hayward took some tentative steps forward. Two moles rushed forward, but judicious blows of her baton drove them back. Carlin, she saw, was beside her, a massive, intimidating presence in the dark, guarding her flank with his own baton and riot shield. Hayward knew that most of the underground homeless were malnourished or weakened by drug abuse. Though the flares had temporarily eroded the moles' advantage, the greatest danger remained their superiority of numbers.

Now other police officers were rallying around them, forming a line against one wall of the tunnel with their shields. Hayward could see the number of moles that had come up from behind was relatively small, and they were massing with the main group. The bulk of the police were re-forming on the far side of the mob, which was retreating back into the dark recess of the tunnel toward the stairway, screeching and throwing rocks. The only way out was to flank the mob, driving them up to the next level in the process.

"Follow me!" she yelled. "Drive them toward the exit!" She led the officers toward the right flank of the mob, dodging rocks and bottles as she ran. The homeless surged back into the tunnel and Hayward fired over their heads, breaking their ranks. The rain of debris slowed as the mob began to run out of projectiles. The screaming and cursing continued fitfully, but their morale seemed to be broken, and Hayward watched with relief as the mob scrabbled back in disorder.

She took a moment to catch her breath and size up the situation. Two cops were lying on the filthy floor of the tunnel, one cradling his head, the other apparently knocked senseless. "Carlin!" she called, nodding at the wounded men.

Suddenly, there was a loud commotion in the retreating ranks of the mob. Hayward held the flare high, craning her neck for the source of the disturbance. There was Miller, marooned on the far side of the large group of moles. He must have fled back down the tunnel during the first attack, and been caught by the second ambush.

Hayward heard a pop, saw a cloud of smoke, sickly green in the fitful glow of the flare. Miller, panicked, must have gone for the tear gas.

Christ, that's the last thing we need. "Masks!" she cried aloud. The gas billowed toward them in slow, lazy rolls, spreading along the floor like a poison carpet. Hayward fumbled with her mask, snugging the Velcro tight.

Miller ducked out of the cloud, looking like an alien apparition in his mask. "Gas them!" came his muffled yell.

"No!" Hayward began to protest. "Not here! We've got two men down!"

She stepped forward as Miller, ignoring her, grabbed a canister from the belt of a nearby officer, popped the pin, and threw it toward the mob. Hayward watched one or two other canisters fly as the panicked men followed Miller's example. There were more dull popping sounds, and the crowd of moles disappeared into the roiling clouds of smoke. Hayward could hear Miller directing other officers to drop their canisters down the boreholes that dotted the floor of the tunnel. "Smoke the bastards out," Miller was saying. "If any more are hiding below, we'll flush them with these."

Carlin looked up from the prone body of the policeman. "Stop, goddammit!" he roared.

The clouds of gas were rising slowly now, spreading their vapor throughout the tunnel. All around, cops were kneeling, dropping canisters down the boreholes. Hayward could see the homeless streaming up the staircase, trying to get away from the gas. "Time's up!" Miller yelled, his high-pitched voice breaking. "We've gotta get out of here!" Most of the policemen needed no more encouragement, and vanished into the clouds of gas.

Hayward fought her way back toward Carlin, once again bending over the prone figure with McMahon. The other casualty was sitting up now, holding his gut and retching. The gas was creeping toward them.

"Let's back them up a bit," Hayward said. "We can't put a mask on this guy while he's puking." The conscious cop stood up slowly, swaying and holding his head. She led the officer away while Carlin and McMahon carried the unconscious man to a safer spot in the tunnel.

"Wake up, buddy," Carlin said, patting his cheek, bending forward to examine the nasty gash across the man's forehead. The roiling green wall of tear gas was coming closer.

The man's eyes fluttered open.

"You okay?"

"Shit," the man said, trying to sit up.

"Can you think straight?" Carlin asked. "What's your name?"

"Beal," came the muffled reply.

The gas was almost on them. Carlin reached down and unstrapped the mask from the man's service belt. "I'm gonna put this on you now, okay?"

The man named Beal nodded vacantly. Carlin strapped on the mask and turned the D-valve. Then he helped him carefully to his feet.

"I can't walk," Beal said through the mask.

"Lean on us," Carlin said. "We'll get you out of here." The cloud had now enveloped them, a strange greenish fog lit by the flickering of the dying flares. They moved forward slowly, half-dragging the man along, until they reached Hayward, who was adjusting the gas mask around the head of the other wounded policeman. "Let's go," she said.

They moved carefully through the tear gas. The surrounding area was deserted; the homeless had fled the gas and Miller, leading the group of officers, had followed behind them. Hayward tried her radio, but she was unable to raise anybody through the dense static. In the far distance, they could hear coughs and curses as the stragglers hiding in the warren of tunnels below were forced to the surface by the gas. Now she could make out the staircase. The airflow was slowly spreading the tear gas through the tunnels and up to the next level, filling their escape route. But Hayward also knew it would drive the rest of the moles to the surface. She sure as hell didn't want to be around when they came out.

As they reached the stairs, Beal suddenly doubled up, retching into the mask. Turning quickly from the other man, Hayward tore Beal's mask off. The officer's head sagged forward, then whipped back as the gas hit him. His limbs stiffened and he thrashed about, tearing himself from their grasp and collapsing to the ground, clutching at his face.

"We gotta move, now!" McMahon cried.

"You go," said Hayward. "I'm not gonna leave this man here."

McMahon stood there indecisively. Carlin glared at him. Finally, McMahon scowled. "Okay, I'm with you."

With McMahon's help, Hayward lifted the gasping Beal to his feet. She nuzzled her mask close to the man's ear. "Either you walk," she said quietly, "or we all drown. It's as simple as that, good buddy."

47

The NYPD's crisis control center had been brought on-line for the drainage operation. As Margo entered, trotting behind Pendergast and D'Agosta, she noticed several banks of communications equipment still sitting on dollies. Uniformed officers were standing over benches overflowing with grid maps. Heavy wires, wound with electrical tape, snaked across the floor in thick black rivulets.

Horlocker and Waxie sat at a long table, their backs to the communications gear. Even from the door Margo could see that their faces were slick with sweat. A small man with a brushy little mustache sat at a computer terminal nearby.

"What's this?" Horlocker asked as they arrived. "The ladies' visiting committee?"

"Sir," D'Agosta said, "you can't drain the Reservoir."

Horlocker tilted his head. "D'Agosta, I don't got time for you right now. I've got my hands full, dealing with the Wisher rally on top of this shit. And meanwhile the roust of the century is taking place underground. I've got the force spread thin as a pancake. So just write me a letter, okay?" He paused. "What, you guys been swimming?"

"The Reservoir," Pendergast said, stepping forward, "is loaded with deadly lilies. It's the plant the Mbwun beast needed to survive. The plant that Kawakita derived his drug from. And it's ready to go to seed." He unshouldered the muddy plant and slapped it onto the table. "There it is. Riddled with glaze. Now we know where they've been growing their supply."

"What the hell?" Horlocker said. "Get that goddamn thing off my desk."

Waxie broke in. "Hey, D'Agosta, you just finished convincing us that your little green monsters in the sewers needed to be flushed out. So now we're doing it, and you want to change your mind? Forget it."

D'Agosta stared distastefully at Waxie's bulging, sweating neckline. "You sorry sack of shit. It was your idea to drain the goddamn Reservoir in the first place."

"Now listen, Lieutenant, you watch—"

Pendergast held up his hands. "Gentlemen, please." He turned to Horlocker. "There will be plenty of blame to apportion at some later time. The problem now is that, once those seeds hit saltwater, the reovirus that carries the drug will be activated." His lips twitched briefly. "Dr. Green's experiments show this drug capable of affecting a wide variety of life-forms, from unicellular organisms all the way up the food chain to man. Would you care to be the one responsible for global ecological disaster?"

"This is nothing but a big load of—" Waxie began to blurt.

Horlocker laid a hand on his sleeve, then glanced at the large plant soiling the papers littering the command desk. "Doesn't look that dangerous to me," he said.

"There's no doubt," Margo said. "It's *Liliceae mbwunensis*. And it's carrying a genetically engineered modification of the Mbwun reovirus."

Horlocker looked from the plant to Margo, then back to the plant again.

"I can understand your uncertainty," Pendergast said calmly. "A lot has happened since this morning's meeting. All I ask is twenty-four hours. Dr. Green here will run the necessary tests. We'll bring you proof that this plant is loaded with the drug. And we'll bring you proof that exposure to saltwater will release the reovirus into the ecosystem. I know we're right. But if we're wrong, I'll withdraw from the case and you can drain the Reservoir at your leisure."

"You should have withdrawn on day one." Waxie sniffed. "You're FBI. This isn't even your jurisdiction!"

"Now that we know the manufacture and distribution of a drug is involved, I could make it my jurisdiction," Pendergast said evenly. "And very quickly. Would that satisfy you?"

"Just a minute, now," said Horlocker, darting a cold look in Waxie's direction. "There's no need for that. But why not just pour in a good dose of weed killer?"

"Offhand, I can't think of any herbicides that could reliably kill all the plants without harming the millions of Manhattan residents who rely on this water," Pendergast said. "Can you, Dr. Green?"

"Only thyoxin," she said, pausing to think. "But that would take twenty-four hours, maybe forty-eight, to do the job. It's very slow acting." Then she frowned. *Thyoxin. That word came up recently, I'm sure of it. But where?* And then she remembered: it was one of the fragmentary words in Kawakita's burned notebook.

"Well, we'd better pour it in anyway." Horlocker rolled his eyes. "I'll have to alert the EPA. Jesus, this is turning into one hell of a screwup." Margo watched him glance at the frightened-looking man at the nearby workstation, who was still hunched over his monitor, an exaggerated look of concentration on his face.

"Stan!"

The man jerked up.

"Stan, I guess you'd better abort the drainage sequence," Horlocker said with a sigh. "At least until we get this figured out. Waxie, get Masters on the horn. Tell him to proceed with clearing the tunnels, but let him know we're going to need to keep the homeless on ice an extra twenty-four hours."

Margo watched as the man's face grew paler.

Horlocker turned back to the engineer. "You heard me, Duffy?" he asked.

"I can't do that, sir," the man named Duffy said in the smallest of voices.

There was a silence.

"What?" Pendergast demanded.

Looking at the expression on Pendergast's face, Margo felt a stab of fear. She'd assumed their only problem lay in convincing Horlocker.

"Whaddaya mean?" Horlocker exploded. "Just tell the computer to shut it down."

"It doesn't work that way," Duffy said. "As I explained to Captain Waxie here, once the sequence is initiated, everything is gravity-fed. Countless tons of water are moving through the system. The hydraulics are all automatic, and—"

Horlocker slammed his hand down on the table. "What the hell are you talking about?"

"I can't stop it with the computer," came the strangled response.

"He never said anything about that to *me*," Waxie whined. "I swear—"

Horlocker silenced him with a savage look. Lowering his voice, he turned back to the engineer. "I don't want to hear what you *can't* do. Just tell me what you *can* do."

"Well," Duffy said reluctantly, "someone could go underneath the Main Shunt and turn off the valves manually. But it would be a dangerous operation. I don't think those manual workings have been used since the automated system went online. That's at least a dozen years. And forget stopping the Reservoir inflow. We've already got eight-foot aqueduct pipe bringing down millions of cubic feet from upstate. Even if you succeed in closing those valves manually, you couldn't stop the water. When it enters the Reservoir from the north, it'll raise the level over the banks. Everything will just pour into Central Park and—"

"I don't care if you create Lake Ed Koch. Take Waxie, get the men you need, and do it."

"But sir," Waxie said, eyes wide, "I think it would be better if..." his voice trailed off.

Duffy's small moist hands were working busily at nothing. "It's very difficult to get down there," he babbled. "It's directly beneath the Reservoir, suspended under the valve works, and there's rushing water and someone might get hurt—"

"Duffy?" Horlocker interrupted. "Get the hell *out* of here and shut those valves. Understand?"

"Yes," Duffy said, his face paler than ever.

Horlocker turned toward Waxie. "You started it. You stop it. Any questions?"

"Yes, sir," Waxie said.

"What?"

"I mean, no, sir."

There was a silence. Nobody moved.

"Get your asses moving, then!" Horlocker roared.

Margo stepped aside as Waxie lurched to his feet and followed Duffy reluctantly out the door.

48

The entrance to the Whine Cellar—one of a new breed of swank basement clubs that had begun sprouting up around Manhattan over the last year—was little more than a narrow Art Deco doorway, placed like an afterthought in the lower left corner of the Hampshire House facade. From his vantage point beside the door, Smithback could make out a sea of heads, stretching east and west down the avenue street, punctuated by the ancient gingko trees that lined the entrance to Central Park. Many people were bowed in silent reverence. Others—young men in rolled-up white cotton shirts mostly, with their ties tugged down—were drinking beer out of paper sacks and high-fiving each other. In the second row, he noticed a girl holding up a poster reading PAMELA, WE WILL NEVER FORGET. A tear rolled slowly down one cheek. Smithback couldn't help but notice that in her other hand, the girl held a copy of his recent article. While a hush had fallen over the closest rows, in the distance Smithback could hear the shouts and yells of marchers, mingling with the even more distant crackle of bullhorns, wail of sirens, and honking of car horns.

Beside him, Mrs. Wisher was now placing a candle beside the large portrait of her daughter. Her hand was steady, but the flame flickered wildly in the cool night breeze. The silence deepened as she knelt in private prayer. Then she stood and moved toward a tall bank of flowers, allowing a series of friends to move forward in turn and place their own candles next to hers. A minute went by, then another. Mrs. Wisher took a final look at the photograph, now encircled by a bracelet of candles. For a moment she seemed to stagger, and Smithback quickly caught her arm. She looked at him, blinking in surprise, as if she had suddenly forgotten her purpose. Then her eyes lost their faraway look; her grip grew briefly firm, almost painful; and easing off his arm, she turned to face the crowd.

"I want to express my sorrow," she said clearly, "to all mothers who have lost children to crime, to murder, to the sickness that has gripped this city and this country. That is all."

A number of television cameras had managed to squeeze toward the front of the crowd, but Mrs. Wisher simply raised her head defiantly. "To Central Park West!" she cried. "And the Great Lawn!"

Smithback stayed close to her as the crowd surged westward, propelled as if by its own internal engine. Despite all the drinking by some of the younger marchers, everything seemed under control. It was almost as if the crowd was conscious of participating in an unforgettable event. They passed Seventh Avenue: an unbroken string of red brake lights, motionless, receding almost to the limits of vision. The sound of police whistles and horns was now one long continuous wail, a steady background noise that came from all directions. Smithback dropped back a moment to consult the *Post* timetable, treading on the handmade shoes of the Viscount Adair as he did so. Almost nine-thirty. Right on schedule. Three more stops, all along Central Park West. Then they'd turn into the Park for the final midnight vigil.

As they made the grand sweep around Columbus Circle, Smithback glanced down Broadway, a wide gash of gray between the unbroken rows of buildings. The police had moved more quickly here, and he could see that the road was barricaded and deserted as far south as Times Square, looking strangely vacant, the pavement shining black beneath countless street lamps. A few cops and squad cars were manning the far end; the rest of the police force was probably still mobilizing, scrambling to find ways to control traffic and keep the march from growing even larger. Maybe that's why more of them weren't on the scene yet. He shook his head, amazed at how this one diminutive woman had brought all of Midtown to a virtual standstill. There was no way they could ignore her after this. And no way they could ignore his articles, for that matter. Already, he'd mapped everything out. First, an in-depth report of the event, written literally at the right hand of Mrs. Wisher, but naturally with his own special slant. Then a series of profiles, interviews, and puff pieces, leading up to his book. Figure half a million bucks in royalties for domestic hardcover sales, perhaps twice that for the paperback, and with foreign rights bringing in at least—

His calculations were interrupted by a strange rumbling noise. It stopped, then came again, so deep it seemed more vibration than sound. The noise level around him dropped for a moment: apparently, others had heard it, too. Suddenly, two blocks down the long empty length of Broadway, Smithback saw a manhole cover lift from the asphalt and fall back onto the street. A cloud of what appeared to be steam drifted skyward; then an impossibly dirty man clambered up, sneezing and coughing in the glare of the streetlight, filthy rags of clothes fluttering loosely around his limbs. For a moment, Smithback thought it was Tail Gunner, the haunted-looking man that had taken him to Mephisto. Then another figure emerged from the manhole, blood flowing freely from a cut on his temple; another followed him, then another.

There was an audible intake of breath at Smithback's side. He turned and saw that Mrs. Wisher had faltered, staring in the direction of the wild-looking men. He quickly drew alongside her.

"What is this?" she said, almost in a whisper.

Suddenly, another manhole cover popped free closer to the march, and a series of gaunt figures clambered out, disoriented and coughing. Smithback stared in disbelief at the bedraggled group, unable to tell age or even sex beneath the matted hair and crusted dirt. Some held pipes or ragged pieces of rebar; others carried bats and broken police batons. One was wearing what looked like a brand-new police cap. The crowd of marchers nearest Broadway had stopped and were staring at the spectacle. Smithback could hear a low undercurrent of sound: worried muttering from the older, elegantly dressed people, scoffs and hoots of derision from the young white-collar turks and desk jockeys. A cloud of green mist sighed out of the IRT station beneath the Circle, and more homeless emerged, scurrying up the steps. As additional bodies clambered out of manholes and the subway, a ragged army began to form, looks of blinking bewilderment quickly turning to hostility.

One of the ragged men stepped forward, glaring at the front rank of marchers. Then he opened his mouth in an inarticulate roar of frustration and rage, a long piece of rebar held over his head like a staff.

A great cry arose from the throats of the homeless, who raised their hands in answer. Smithback could see that every hand held something—rocks, chunks of cement, pieces of iron. Many had cuts and bruises. It looked like they were preparing for a battle— or had just come from one.

What the hell is this? Smithback thought. *Where have all these guys come from?* For a moment he wondered if it was some kind of organized mass-scale robbery. Then he remembered what Mephisto had told him as he'd crouched down there in the dark: we will find other ways to make our voices heard. *Not now,* he thought. *This is the worst possible time.*

A wisp of smoke drifted closer, and several of the nearest marchers began to choke and gasp. In an instant, Smithback's eyes began to sting painfully, and he realized that what he'd thought was steam was actually tear gas. Farther down the empty stretch of Broadway, Smithback saw what looked like a small group of policemen—their blue uniforms torn and grimy—stumble up a subway staircase, then stagger in the direction of the distant squad cars. *Shit, something big's happened down there,* he thought.

"Where's Mephisto?" one of the homeless yelled out.

Another voice rose up. "I heard he was paddied!"

The mob grew increasingly agitated. "Goddamn cops!" someone shouted. "I bet they beat his ass!"

"What are these scumbags doing, anyway?" Smithback heard a young voice behind him ask.

"Don't know," came an answer. "Too late at night to cash a welfare check." There was scattered laughter and hooting.

"Mephisto!" The chant began to rise among the ragged crowd before them. "Where's Mephisto?"

"The mothers probably murdered him!"

There was a sudden commotion among the Wisher marchers on the side of the street nearest the Park, and Smithback turned to see a large subway grating being forced open, and more homeless boiling up from below.

"Murdered!" one of the ragged army was screaming. "The bastards murdered him!"

The man who had stepped to the front pumped his rebar. "They won't get away with it! Not this time, they won't!"

He held up his arms. "*The mothers gassed us!*" he cried.

The tattered mob screamed wildly in response.

"They destroyed our homes!"

Another roar came from the mob.

"*Now we'll destroy theirs!*" He flung the piece of rebar at the glass facade of a nearby bank branch. There was a splintering crash as it burst through the window and fell into the lobby. An alarm began to whine, quickly drowned out in the ocean of noise.

"Hey!" somebody beside Smithback yelled out. "Did you see what that asshole did?"

The homeless mob, screaming, poured a rain of missiles toward the buildings lining Broadway. Smithback, glancing up and down the avenue, watched as more and more homeless persons rose from manholes, vents, and subway exits, filling Broadway and Central Park West with their incoherent rage. Over their cries, he could make out the faint, insistent blatting of emergency vehicles. The dark pavement glittered brightly with countless shards of broken glass.

He jumped in surprise as he heard Mrs. Wisher's amplified voice ring out. She had taken the microphone and turned to address the marchers. "Do you see this?" she cried, her voice echoing off the tall facades and rolling into the dark, silent Park beyond. "These people are intent on destroying the very thing we're here to preserve!"

Angry cries began to arise from around her. Smithback looked around. He could see large groups of older marchers—Mrs. Wisher's original followers—talking amongst themselves, pointing back toward Fifth Avenue or Central Park West, moving hurriedly away from the approaching confrontation. Others—the younger, brusquer element—were shouting angrily, moving toward the front.

The television cameras were milling around, some focused on Mrs. Wisher, others on the homeless mob now moving up the street, scooping up fresh projectiles from trash cans and Dumpsters, shouting their anger and defiance.

Mrs. Wisher looked across the sea of marchers, stretching out her hands briefly, then drawing them together as if to rally the group behind her banner. "Look at this rabble! Are we going to let this happen, tonight, of all nights?" She gazed across the crowd, half questioningly, half imploringly, as a tense silence gathered. The front lines of homeless paused in their rampage, startled by the booming, omnipresent sound of her voice, echoing from a dozen loudspeakers.

"No way!" slurred a young voice.

With mingled awe and dread, Smithback watched as, very slowly, Mrs. Wisher raised one arm above her head. Then, with commanding deliberation, she brought it down, pointing a manicured finger directly at the swelling lines of homeless. "These are the people that would destroy our city!" Though her voice was steady, Smithback sensed a ragged edge of hysteria.

"Look at these bums!" screamed a young man, pushing through the front rank of marchers. A noisy group began to form a knot behind him, ten feet from the now-silent ranks of the homeless. "Get a job, asshole!" he shouted at the leader.

The ranks of mole people fell into a deathly, ominous silence.

"You think I work my ass off and pay taxes just to give you a free ride?" he screeched.

An angry murmur swept through the crowd of homeless.

"Why don't you do something for your country, instead of just living off it?" the man screamed, taking a step toward the leader and spitting on the ground. "Homeless piece of shit."

A roar of approval rose from the marchers.

A homeless man stepped forward, waving the ruined stump of what had been his left arm. "Look what I did for my country!" he shrieked, voice breaking. "I gave *everything*." The stump flapped back and forth and he turned toward the young man, face distorted with rage. "Chu Lai, ever heard of it?" The mole people pressed forward, an angry buzz rising fast.

Smithback glanced at Mrs. Wisher. Her face was still set in a hard, cold mask, as she stared at the homeless. He realized, with growing disbelief, that she really believed these people were the enemy.

"Kiss my ass, welfare bloodsucker!" a drunken voice yelled.

"Go mug a liberal!" shouted a beefy young man, to a burst of raucous laughter.

"They killed my brother!" one of the moles, a tall, skinny man, said angrily. "Fragged for his country, Phon Mak Hill, August 2, 1969." He stepped forward, raising his middle finger in a violent gesture at the beefy man. "You can *have* your damn country, asswipe."

"Too bad they didn't finish the job and blow *your* ass off, too!" the drunken man yelled back. "One less scumbag roaming the streets!"

A bottle whipped out of the seething crowd of homeless and struck the young man solidly on the head. He staggered backward, legs crumpling, as he raised his hands toward the blood streaming from his forehead.

It was as if the rally suddenly exploded. With an inarticulate roar, the young men surged toward the homeless. Smithback looked around wildly. The older marchers had disappeared, leaving behind a wild and drunken element. He felt himself engulfed as the younger marchers rushed forward with angry yells, moving directly toward the line of homeless. Spun around and temporarily disoriented, he looked about in panic for Mrs. Wisher and her entourage, but they too had vanished.

Struggling, he was borne along on the tide. Over the shouting of the mob, he could now hear the sickening sound of wood hitting bone and fists smacking flesh. Cries of pain and rage began to mix with the yells. There was a sudden heavy blow across his shoulders and he dropped to his knees, instinctively shielding his head. Out of the corner of one eye he saw his recorder skidding across the pavement, kicked aside, and then crushed by running feet. He tried to rise, but then ducked down again as a chunk of concrete came hurtling in his direction. It was astonishing how quickly chaos engulfed the darkened streets.

Who or what had forced the homeless to the surface in such huge groups was anyone's guess; Smithback only knew that, suddenly, each side saw the other as the incarnation of evil. Mob mentality had taken over.

He rose to his knees and looked about wildly, staggering as he was jostled and shoved from countless directions. The march had disintegrated. However, his story was still salvageable; perhaps more than just salvageable, if this riot was as big as he thought it was. But he needed to get away from the mob, gain some high ground where he could get perspective on the situation. Quickly, he looked north, toward the Park. Over the sea of raised fists and sticks he could see the bronze statue of Shakespeare, gazing down placidly on the chaos. Keeping low, he began pushing his way toward it. A wide-eyed homeless person bore down on him, screaming and raising an empty beer bottle threateningly. Instinctively he lashed out with his fist and the figure dropped, clutching its stomach. With surprise, Smithback saw that it was a woman. "Sorry, ma'am," he mumbled as he scuttled away.

Glass and debris crunched beneath his feet as he made his way across Central Park South. He shoved a drunk aside, pushed past a group of screaming young men in expensive but torn suits, and gained the far sidewalk.

Here, on the fringes, it was quieter. Avoiding the pigeon lime, he clambered onto the base of the statue and grabbed the lower fold of Shakespeare's garment. Then he hoisted himself up the arm, onto the open bronze book, and atop the Bard's wide shoulders.

It was an awe-inspiring sight. The melee had spread several blocks down Broadway and Central Park South. More homeless were still streaming up from Columbus Circle subway station, and from gratings and vent shafts along the edge of the Park. He hadn't known there were that many homeless people in the entire world, or that many drunken young yuppies, for that matter. He could now see the older marchers, the main guard of Take Back Our City, streaming in well-ordered ranks toward Amsterdam Avenue, moving as far from the melee as possible, desperately trying to flag down cabs. Around him, knots of brawling people were coalescing and dissolving. He stared in horrified fascination at the flying missiles, the fistfights, and stick battles. There were a number of people down now—unconscious or perhaps worse. Blood was mingling with the glass, concrete, and debris littering the street. At the same time, much of the riot consisted of screaming, shoving, and posturing groups of people—a lot of bark but no bite. Squads of police were now at last making inroads into the crowd, but there were not enough of them, and already the riot was moving into the Park where it would be much harder to control. *Where are all the cops?* Smithback thought again.

Despite his horror and revulsion, a certain secret part of Smithback felt a surging elation: what a story this was going to be. His eyes strained against the darkness, trying to imprint the images on his brain, already writing the lead in his head. The homeless mob now seemed to be gaining the upper hand, screaming in righteous anger, pushing the throngs of marchers back into the southern fringes of the Park. Though many of the moles were no doubt weakened by hand-to-mouth lives, they obviously knew a lot more about street fighting than their opponents. A number of television cameras had been smashed by the mob, and the remaining crews were hanging back in a protective phalanx, spotlights glaring out of the darkness. Others hung over the rooftops of nearby buildings with long lenses, bathing the rioters in eerie white light.

A patch of blue nearby caught his attention. He glanced down to see a tight group of policemen battling their way through the crowd, batons flashing. At the center of the group was a scared-looking civilian with a bushy moustache and a fat, sweaty guy Smithback recognized as Captain Waxie.

Smithback watched, intrigued, as the group forced its way past the rioters. Something was strange here. Then he realized what it was: these cops were doing nothing to stop the fighting or control the crowd. Instead, they seemed to be protecting the two men in the middle, Waxie and the other guy. As he watched, the knot of policemen gained the curb and jogged through a stone gate into the Park. They were obviously on a mission of some sort or other: they were heading someplace special in a hurry.

But what mission, Smithback thought, *could be more important than stopping this riot?*

He remained for a few moments, poised stiffly on Shakespeare's shoulders, in an agony of indecision. Then, very quickly, he slipped off the statue, vaulted the low stone wall, and ran after the group into the enfolding darkness of Central Park.

49

D'Agosta removed the unlit cigar from his mouth, picked a piece of tobacco off his tongue, and examined the sodden end with distaste. Margo watched as he patted his pockets for a match, then, finding none, caught her eye and raised his eyebrows in a silent question. She shook her head no. D'Agosta turned toward Horlocker, began to open his mouth, then obviously thought better of it. The Chief had a portable radio plastered to one ear, and he didn't look happy.

"Mizner?" he was shouting. "Mizner! You copy?"

There was a faint, lengthy squawking that Margo assumed must be Mizner.

"Just subdue and arrest the—" Horlocker began.

More faint squawking.

"Five *hundred*? From underground? Look, Mizner, don't give me this shit. Why aren't they on the buses?"

Horlocker stopped again to listen. From the corner of her eye, she noticed Pendergast sitting on the edge of a table, leaning against a mobile radio unit, seemingly engrossed in an issue of the *Policeman's Gazette*.

"Riot control, tear gas, I don't give a rat's ass *how* you do it... marchers? What do you mean, they're fighting with the *marchers*?" He lowered the phone, looked at it as if in disbelief, then raised it to his other ear. "No, for Chrissakes, don't use gas anywhere near the marchers. Look, we got most of the Twentieth and Twenty-second underground, the Thirty-first is manning the checkpoints, Uptown is laid wide open as a... no, forget it, tell Perillo I want a wildfire meeting with all the deputy chiefs in five minutes. Bring in staff from the outer boroughs, off duty, meter cops, whatever. We need more manpower applied to that spot, you hear me?"

He punched the phone angrily and grabbed at another on the desk in front of him. "Curtis, get the Governor's office on the phone. The evac went south, and some of the underground homeless we were clearing from the area around the Park are rioting. They've run straight into that big march on Central Park South. We'll have to call in the Guard. Then contact Masters, we're going to need a Tactical helicopter, just in case. Have him get the assault vehicles from the Lexington Avenue armory. No, forget that, they may not be able to make it through. Contact the Park substation instead. I'll call the Mayor myself."

He hung up the phone, more slowly this time. A single bead of sweat was making its slow traverse down a forehead that had gone from red to gray in a matter of moments. Horlocker looked around the command center, seemingly blind to the scurrying cops, the transmitters crackling on countless bands. To Margo, he looked like a man whose entire world had suddenly imploded.

Pendergast carefully folded the *Gazette* and placed it on the table beside him. Then he leaned forward, smoothing his pale blond hair with the fingers of his right hand.

"I've been thinking," he began, almost casually.

Uh-oh, Margo thought.

Pendergast glided forward until he stood directly in front of the Chief. "I've been thinking that this situation is simply too dangerous to leave in the hands of one man."

Horlocker closed his eyes for a minute. Then, as if making a tremendous effort, he raised them to Pendergast's placid face.

"Just what the hell are you talking about?" he asked.

"We're relying on Squire Waxie to manually shut the Reservoir valves and stop the drainage process."

"So?"

Pendergast put a finger to his lip, as if he was about to whisper a secret. "Not to be indelicate about this, but Captain Waxie has not proven himself to be—well, the most reliable of errand boys. If he fails, the catastrophe will be complete. The Mbwun lilies will be shunted through the Astor Tunnels and out to the open sea. Once exposed to salinity, the reovirus will be unleashed. It could alter the ecology of the oceans significantly."

"More than that," Margo heard herself blurt. "It could insert itself into the food chain, and from there..." She fell silent.

"I've heard this story before," Horlocker said. "It doesn't get any better the second time around. What's your point?"

"What we in the Bureau call a redundant solution," Pendergast said.

Horlocker opened his mouth to speak just as a uniformed officer signaled from a comm desk. "Captain Waxie for you, sir. I'll patch him through on the open line."

Horlocker picked up the phone again. "Waxie, what's your status?" He stopped to listen. "Speak up, I can't hear you. The *what*? What do you mean, you're not sure? Well, take care of it, goddammit! Look, put Duffy on. Waxie, you hear me? You're breaking up. Waxie? *Waxie!*"

He slammed the phone into its cradle with a shattering crash. "Get Waxie back on the horn!" he yelled.

"May I continue?" Pendergast asked. "If what I just heard is any indication, time is short. So I'll be brief. If Waxie fails and the Reservoir is drained, we must have a backup plan in place to prevent the plants from escaping into the Hudson."

"How the hell are we going to do that?" D'Agosta asked. "It's nearly ten o'clock. The Reservoir is scheduled to dump in just over two hours."

"Can we just stop the plants from escaping somehow?" Margo asked. "Place filters over the exit pipes, or something?"

"An interesting thought, Dr. Green," Pendergast said, glancing toward her with his pale eyes. He paused briefly. "I'd imagine that 5-micron filters would be sufficient. But where would we find them manufactured to the proper dimensions? And what about the tolerances required to withstand the tremendous water pressure? And how could we be certain we had located every exit?" He shook his head. "I'm afraid the only solution that time allows is to seal the exits from the Astor Tunnels with high explosive. I've studied the maps. A dozen charges of C-4, accurately placed, should be sufficient."

Horlocker swiveled himself toward Pendergast. "You're crazy," he said matter-of-factly.

There was a sudden commotion at the entrance to the center, and Margo looked over to see a group of policemen half running, half stumbling in from the concourse beyond. Their uniforms were disheveled and muddy, and one of the officers had a nasty cut on his forehead. In their midst, struggling wildly, was an incredibly dirty man wearing a ragged corduroy suit. His long gray hair was matted and streaked with dirt and blood. A large turquoise necklace hung from his neck, and a heavily stained beard hung down to his handcuffed wrists.

"We got the ringleader!" one of the cops panted as they tugged the struggling man toward the Chief.

D'Agosta stared incredulously. "It's Mephisto!" he cried.

"Oh?" Horlocker said sarcastically. "A friend of yours?"

"Merely a social acquaintance," Pendergast replied.

Margo watched as the man named Mephisto stared from D'Agosta to Pendergast. Suddenly, the piercing eyes flooded with recognition, and his face turned dark.

"You!" he hissed. "*Whitey!* You were spies. Traitors! Pigs!" He struggled with a sudden, terrible strength, breaking free of his captors for a moment only to be tackled to the floor and pinned again. He grappled and strained, raising his manacled hands. "Judas!" he spat in Pendergast's direction.

"Frigging lunatic," Horlocker said, looking toward the group wrestling on the tiled floor.

"Hardly," Pendergast replied. "Would you act any differently if somebody had just gassed you and driven you out of your home?"

Mephisto lunged again.

"Hold him, for Chrissakes," Horlocker snapped, stepping out of reach. Then he turned back to Pendergast. "Now, let me see if I understand this," he said with insulting sweetness, the parody of a father humoring a foolish son. "You want to blow up the Astor Tunnels. Do I have it right?"

"Not the tunnels so much as the exits from the tunnels," Pendergast replied, oblivious to the sarcasm. "It is critical that we stop any water draining from the Reservoir from reaching the open ocean. But perhaps we can accomplish both ends: cleanse the Astor Tunnels of their inhabitants while preventing the reovirus from escaping. All we have to do is hold the water for forty-eight hours and let the herbicide do its work."

Out of the corner of her eye, Margo watched as Mephisto went still.

"We can send in a team of divers up the spillways from the river," Pendergast went on. "The route to the Astor outflow is relatively straightforward."

Horlocker shook his head.

"I've studied the system carefully. When the Astor Tunnels fill, the overflow will channel into the West Side Lateral. That's what we'll have to block with explosives."

"I don't believe this," Horlocker said, lowering his head and resting it on the knuckles of one hand.

"But then again, that may not be enough," Pendergast went on, paying no attention to Horlocker now, thinking out loud. "To be certain, we'd also need to seal the Devil's Attic from *above,* as well. The charts show that the Bottleneck and its drainage tubes are a closed system all the way up to the Reservoir, so all we have to do to keep the water trapped inside is to seal any escape routes immediately below it. That will also prevent the creatures from riding out the flood in an air pocket somewhere."

Horlocker looked blank. Pendergast found a scrap of paper and swiftly drew a diagram. "Don't you see?" he asked. "The water will pass through the Bottleneck, here. The second team will descend from the surface and block any exit paths directly beneath the Bottleneck. Several levels deeper is the Devil's Attic and the spillways that vent to the river. The SEAL team will set their charges in the spillways." He looked up. "The water will be trapped in the Astor Tunnels. There will be no escape for the Wrinklers. None."

A low wheeze escaped from the manacled figure, raising the hairs on Margo's neck.

"I'll have to lead the second team, of course," Pendergast went on calmly. "They'll need a guide, and I've already been down once before. I've got a crude map, and I've studied the city plans for the works closer to the surface. I'd go by myself, but it will take several men to carry the plastique."

"It won't work, Judas," Mephisto rasped. "You'll never make it down to the Devil's Attic in time."

Horlocker suddenly looked up, slamming his fist to the table. "I've heard enough," he snapped. "Playtime's over. Pendergast, I've got a crisis on my hands. So get out."

"Only *I* know the tunnels well enough to get you in and out before midnight," Mephisto hissed, staring intently at Pendergast.

Pendergast returned the gaze, a speculative expression on his face. "You're probably correct," he replied at last.

"Enough," Horlocker snapped at the group of officers who had brought Mephisto in. "Get him downtown. We'll deal with him once the dust has settled."

"And what would be in it for you?" Pendergast asked Mephisto.

"Room to live. Freedom from harassment. The grievances of my people redressed."

Pendergast gazed at Mephisto almost meditatively, his expression unreadable.

"I *said,* get the man the hell out," Horlocker roared.

The cops pulled Mephisto to his feet and began to drag him toward the exit.

"Stay where you are," Pendergast said. His voice was low, but the tone was so commanding the officers instinctively stopped in their tracks.

Horlocker turned, a vein pulsing in his temple. "What's this?" he said, almost in a whisper.

"Chief Horlocker, I'm taking custody of this individual, under the authority vested in me as a federal agent of the United States government."

"You're bullshitting me," Horlocker replied.

"Pendergast!" Margo hissed. "We've got barely two hours."

The agent nodded, then addressed Horlocker. "I'd like to stay and bandy civilities, but I'm afraid I've run out of time," he said. "Vincent, please get the handcuff key from these gentlemen."

Pendergast turned toward the knot of policemen. "You, there. Release this man into my custody."

"Don't do it!" Horlocker shouted.

"Sir," one of the officers said, "you can't fight the Feds, sir."

Pendergast approached the bedraggled figure, now standing beside D'Agosta and rubbing his manacled wrists. "Mr. Mephisto," he said in a low voice, "I don't know what role you played in today's events, and I can't guarantee your personal freedom. But if you help me now, perhaps we can rid this city of the killers that have been preying on your community. And I will give my personal guarantee that your demands for homeless rights will be given a fair hearing." He held out his hand.

Mephisto's eyes narrowed. "You lied once," he hissed.

"It was the only way I could make contact with you," said Pendergast, continuing to hold out his hand. "This isn't a fight between the haves and have-nots. If it was once, it isn't anymore. If we fail now, we all go down: Park Avenue and Route 666 alike."

There was a long pause. At last, Mephisto nodded silently.

"How touching," said Horlocker. "I hope you all drown in shit."

50

Smithback peered through the rusting steel grid of the catwalk floor, down into the brick-lined shaft that ran away into vertiginous darkness beneath his feet. He could hear Waxie and the rest—far below him—but he couldn't see what they were up to. Once again, he fervently hoped that this wouldn't turn into a wild-goose chase. But he'd followed Waxie all this way; he might as well stick around and see just what the hell was up.

He moved forward cautiously, trying to catch a glimpse of the five men below him. The rotten catwalk hung down from the underside of a gigantic bowl of pitted metal, moving in a long gentle arc toward a vertical shaft that seemed to head for the center of the earth itself. The catwalk sagged with his every movement. Reaching a vertical ladder, he craned his neck out into the chill space and looked downward. A bank of floodlights shone into the shaft, but even their power was inadequate to penetrate deeply into the gloom. A tiny thread of water came from a crack in the vault above and spiraled down through empty space, disappearing silently into the darkness. There was a pinging noise coming from above, like the creaking of a submarine hull under pressure. A steady rush of cold, fresh air blew up from the shaft and stirred the hair on his forehead.

In his wildest dreams, Smithback could not have imagined that such a strange, antique space existed beneath the Central Park Reservoir. He knew that the enormous metal ceiling above him must actually be the drainage basin at the lowest level of the Reservoir, where its earthen bed met the complex tangle of storm drains and feeder tunnels. He tried not to think of the vast bulb of water hanging directly over his head.

He could see the team in the dim spaces below him now, standing on a small platform abutting the ladder. Smithback could vaguely make out a complicated tangle of iron pipes, wheels, and valves, looking like some infernal machine out of an Industrial Age nightmare. The ladder was slimy with condensation, and the tiny platform far below him had no railing. Smithback took a step down the ladder, then thought better of it and retreated. *As good a vantage point as any,* he thought, curling up on the catwalk. From here, he could see everything that went on, but remain virtually invisible himself.

Flashlights were licking across the brick walls far below him, and the policemen's voices, rumbled and distorted, floated up to him. He recognized Waxie's basso profundo from the evening he'd spent in the Museum's projection booth. The fat cop seemed to be speaking into his radio. Now he put his radio away and turned to the nervous-looking man in shirt sleeves. They seemed to be arguing bitterly about something.

"You little liar," Waxie was saying, "you *never* told me that you couldn't reverse the flood."

"I did, I *did*," came a high-pitched whine in response. "You even *said* you didn't want it reversible. I wish I'd had a tape recorder, because—"

"Shut up. Are these the valves?"

"They're here, at the back."

There was a silence, then the groaning protest of metal as the men shifted position.

"Is this platform safe?" came Waxie's voice from deep within the pit.

"How should I know?" the high-pitched voice replied. "When they computerized the system, they stopped maintaining—"

"All right, all right. Just do what you have to do, Duffy, and let's get out of here."

Smithback inched his nose farther into space and peered down. He could see the man named Duffy examining the nest of valves. "We have to turn all these off," came his voice. "It closes the Main Shunt manually. That way, when the computer directs the Reservoir to drain, the shunt gates will open, but these manual valves will contain the water. Works on the siphon principle. If it works at all. Like I said, it's never been tried."

"Great. Maybe you'll win the Nobel Prize. Now do it."

Do what? Smithback wondered. It sounded as if they were trying to prevent the Reservoir from being drained. The thought of millions of cubic feet of water thundering down from above was enough to swivel his eyes toward the exit far over his head. *But why? Computer glitch of some kind?* Whatever it was, it didn't sound worth leaving the biggest riot in a hundred years for. Smithback's heart began to sink; this was definitely not where the real story was.

"Help me turn this," Duffy said.

"You heard him," Waxie snapped at the policemen. From his perch, Smithback could see two of the tiny figures gripping a large iron wheel. There was a faint grunting. "It ain't moving," one of the policemen announced.

The man named Duffy bent closer, inspecting. "Somebody's been messing around here!" he cried, pointing. "Look at this! The shaft's been packed with lead. And over here, these valves have been broken off. Recently, too, by the looks of it."

"Don't give me any of your bullshit, Duffy."

"Look for yourself. This thing is shot to hell."

There was a silence. "Shit on a stick," came Waxie's fretful voice. "Can you fix it?"

"Sure we can. If we had twenty-four hours. And acetylene torches, an arc welder, new valve stems, and maybe a dozen other parts that haven't been manufactured since the turn of the century."

"That isn't good enough. If we can't stop that shunt from opening manually, we're screwed. You got us into this fix, Duffy. You'd damn well better get us out."

"To hell with you, Captain!" the shrill voice of Duffy echoed up. "I've had all I'm going to take. You're a stupid, rude human being. Oh, yes, I forgot: fat, too."

"That's going in my report, Duffy."

"Then be sure you put in the part about being fat, because—"

There was an abrupt silence.

"You smell that?" asked one of the policemen on the ladder.

"What the hell is it?" came another voice.

Smithback sniffed the cool, moist air, but could smell nothing but damp brick and mildew. "Let's get the hell out of here," Waxie said, grabbing the ladder and hoisting himself up the rungs.

"Just a minute!" came the voice of Duffy. "What about the valve?"

"You just told me it couldn't be fixed," Waxie said without looking down.

Smithback heard a faint rattling sound from the deeper darkness of the pit.

"What was that?" Duffy asked, his voice cracking.

"Are you coming?" Waxie yelled, hauling his ungainly body up the ladder, one rung at a time.

As Smithback watched, Duffy took a look over the platform edge, hesitating. Then he turned back and began to scramble up the ladder behind Waxie, followed by the uniformed policemen. Smithback realized that in five minutes, they'd reach the catwalk. By then he'd have to be gone, making that long crawl back up the gangway and out of sight. And with jack shit to show for his pains. He turned to go, hoping he hadn't missed the rest of the riot, wondering where Mrs. Wisher was by now. *Jesus, what a bad call,* he thought ruefully. *Can't believe my instincts let me down.* With his luck, that prick Bryce Harriman was already...

A sound echoed up from below: the protesting squeal of rusty hinges, the loud booming of an iron grating being slammed.

"What was that?" Smithback heard Waxie yelp.

Smithback turned back and looked down the ladder. He could see the figures on the ladder below him, suddenly motionless. Waxie's last question was still echoing and rumbling, dying away in the shaft. There was silence. And into the silence came the sound of scrabbling on iron rungs, mingled with strange grunts and wheezes that raised the hairs on Smithback's nape.

Flashlight beams played downwards from the group on the ladder, revealing nothing.

"Who is it?" Waxie cried again, peering down.

"There're some people coming up the ladder," one of the policemen said.

"We're police officers!" Waxie yelled, his voice suddenly shrill.

There was no answer.

"Identify yourselves!"

"They're still coming," the policeman said.

"There's that smell again," came another voice, and suddenly it hit Smithback like a hammer: an overripe, goatish odor that brought back like a physical blow the nightmare hours he'd spent in the bowels of the Museum, eighteen months before.

"Unholster your weapons!" Waxie yelled in a panicky voice.

Now Smithback could see them: dark shapes moving quickly up the ladder from the depths, wearing hoods and dark cloaks that billowed behind them in the updraft.

"You hear me down there?" Waxie cried. "Stop and identify yourselves!" He twisted his thick form on the ladder and looked down at the officers. "You men, wait here. Find out their business. If they're trespassers, give them citations." He turned and began scrambling desperately up the ladder again, Duffy at his heels.

As Smithback watched, the strange figures passed the platform and approached the stationary cops. There was a pause, then what to Smithback appeared to be a struggle, the dim light making it look oddly like a graceful ballet. The illusion vanished with the roar of a 9-millimeter, deafening in the confined space, rolling up and down the brick shaft like thunder. Then the echoes were drowned out by a scream, and Smithback saw the lowest policeman detach from the ladder and plunge into the shaft, one of the figures still clinging to him. The attenuated screams of the officer echoed up from the pit, slowly vanishing into nothing.

"Stop them!" Waxie cried over his shoulder, toiling up the ladder. "Don't let them come!"

As Smithback watched in frozen horror, the shapes came ever more swiftly, the metal ladder clattering and groaning under their weight. The second cop fired wildly at the figures, then he was grabbed by the leg and yanked with horrible strength from the ladder rung. He hurtled downwards, firing his revolver again and again, the muzzle flashing as he pin-wheeled into the darkness. The third policeman turned and began climbing with panicky speed.

The dark figures were swarming upward now, two rungs at a time, climbing with long, loping movements. One of the figures passed through the beam of a spotlight, giving Smithback a glimpse of something thick and moist shining briefly in the reflected glow. Then the lead figure caught up with the policeman and made a wide, slashing movement across the back of the retreating man's legs. He screamed and twisted on the ladder. The figure pulled himself level with the officer, then began tearing at his face and throat while the rest of the hooded figures scrambled past.

Smithback tried to move but seemed unable to tear his gaze away from the spectacle beneath him. In his panic to climb the ladder, Waxie had slipped and was clutching to one side, trying to gain a purchase with his scrabbling feet. Duffy was coming up quickly beneath him, but several of the dark figures were right behind.

"It's got my leg!" Duffy screamed. There were unmistakable sounds of thrashing and kicking. "Oh, my God, help me!" The hysterical voice echoed and reechoed crazily through the dim space.

As Smithback watched, Duffy shook himself free with a strength born of terror and scrambled up the ladder past the struggling Waxie.

"No! No!" Waxie yelled in desperation, trying to kick away the grasping hands of the closest figure and knocking back its hood in the process. Smithback jerked his head back instinctively at the sight, but not before his brain had registered something out of his worst nightmare, worse for being vague in the dim light: narrow lizard's pupils, thick wet lips, great creases and folds of extra skin. It suddenly dawned on him that these must be the Wrinklers Mephisto had referred to. Now he knew why.

The sight broke Smithback's paralysis, and he began scrambling up the catwalk. Behind him, he could hear Waxie firing his service piece—there was a roar of pain that almost turned Smithback's limbs to jelly—two more quick shots in rapid succession—then Waxie's rising, blubbering scream of anguish, suddenly truncated to a horrifying wet gurgle.

Smithback half ran, half scuttled up the catwalk, trying to keep the sense of overwhelming fear from paralyzing him once again. Behind him, he could hear Duffy—God, he hoped it was Duffy—sobbing and scrambling up the iron rungs. *I've got a good head start,* he thought; the figures still had nearly one hundred feet of ladder to climb. For a moment, he considered going back to help Duffy, but it was the work of an instant to realize there was nothing he could do. *Just give me the luxury of living to regret running away,* he thought hysterically, *and I won't ask for anything, ever ever again.*

But as he approached the stone steps leading to the surface, and the faint sweet circle of moonlit sky appeared above him, he saw with sudden horror bulky figures looming forward, blotting out the stars. Now they were descending—oh, God—toward him. He dropped back to the catwalk, desperately looking around at the brick walls, at the curve of the shaftway as it ran down toward the pit. To one side of the catwalk lay the entrance to an access tunnel: an ancient stone archway, rimed in crystallized lime, like hoarfrost. The figures were closing in fast now. Smithback leapt for the archway, passed beneath it, and entered a low tunnel. Feeble lightbulbs dotted its ceiling at infrequent intervals. He plunged forward, running with desperate abandon, realizing even as he did so that the tunnel angled in precisely the direction he did not want to go: down, ever down.

51

The FBI agent on duty in Armory Division was leaning back, nose deep in a copy of *Soldier of Fortune,* his chair precariously balanced on its rear two legs. Over the top of the magazine, Margo could see his eyes widen at their approach. Probably he wasn't used to seeing an impossibly ratty, wild-eyed man with an unkempt beard, wandering around the basement of the FBI's Federal Plaza headquarters with a young woman and pudgy man in tow. She watched as the eyes suddenly narrowed, the nostrils flaring. *Must have caught wind of Mephisto, as well,* Margo thought.

"Just what the hell can I do for you *gentlemen?*" the guard asked, lowering the magazine and easing the chair forward slowly.

"They're with me," Pendergast said briskly, coming forward and flashing his identification. But the man had caught sight of him and bounded to his feet already, the magazine skidding across the floor.

"I'll need to sign for some ordnance," Pendergast said.

"Of course, right away, sir," the agent babbled, unlocking the upper and lower locks of the metal door behind him and swinging it open.

Margo stepped into the large room beyond. Row upon row of wooden cabinets rose in ordered procession toward the low ceiling. "What is all this stuff?" she asked as they followed Pendergast down the nearest aisle.

"Emergency supplies," came the answer. "Rations, medical supplies, bottled water, food supplements, blankets and bedding, spare parts for the essential systems, fuel."

"You got enough shit to withstand a siege in here," D'Agosta muttered.

"That's exactly the point, Lieutenant," Pendergast said, approaching a small metal door in the far wall, punching in a code, and flinging it open. Beyond lay a narrow corridor. Rows of stainless steel lockers flanked both sides, Plexiglas labels engraved on their fronts. Entering the room, Margo stopped to look at a few of the closest labels: M-16/XM-148, CAR-15/SM-177E2, KEVLAR S-M, KEVLAR L-XXL.

"The cop and his toys," Mephisto said.

Pendergast moved quickly down the aisle, then stopped at a locker, wrenched it open, and removed three masks of clear plastic, attached to small canisters of oxygen. Keeping one for himself, he tossed the others to D'Agosta and Mephisto.

"Just in case you feel like gassing a few more underground residents on our way down?" Mephisto said, catching it awkwardly in his manacled hands. "I've heard we make good sport."

Pendergast stopped and turned toward the homeless man. "I know you feel your people were ill-used by the police," he said quietly. "As it happens, I agree with you. You'll simply have to take my word when I say I had nothing to do with it."

"Two-faced Janus speaks again. Mayor of Grant's Tomb, sure. I should've known it was a crock of shit."

"It was your own paranoia and isolation that made my ruse necessary," Pendergast said, opening additional lockers and removing a head-mounted flash unit, several pairs of goggles with long eye-stalks Margo guessed were night-vision devices, and some long yellow canisters she didn't recognize. "I don't, and never did, look upon you as an enemy."

"Then take these cuffs off."

"Don't do it," D'Agosta warned.

Pendergast paused in the act of removing several K-bar knives from the locker. Then he dug into the breast pocket of his black suit, stepped forward, and released the cuffs with a quick turn of his wrist. Mephisto flung them contemptuously down the narrow corridor.

"Planning on whittling while you're below, *Whitey*?" he asked. "Those little Special Forces penknives you've got there won't do you much good against the Wrinklers. Except maybe tickle them some."

"It is my hope we won't meet up with any inhabitants of the Astor Tunnels," Pendergast said, snugging a pair of handguns into the waist of his pants, his head buried in the locker. "But I've already learned that it pays to be prepared."

"Well, enjoy your turkey shoot, FBI man. Afterwards, we can stop by Route 666 for tea and biscuits, have a nice chin-wag, maybe get your trophies stuffed."

As Margo watched, Pendergast stepped back from the locker. Then he moved slowly toward Mephisto. "What can I do, *exactly*, to impress on you the seriousness of this situation?" he asked, his face inches from that of the underground leader. He spoke softly, yet there was a subtle edge to his voice that seemed somehow menacing.

Mephisto took a step backward. "If that's what you want, you're going to have to trust me."

"If I didn't," Pendergast replied, "I wouldn't have removed your handcuffs."

"Then prove it." Mephisto said, quickly recovering his nerve. "Give me a piece. One of those nice shiny Stoners I saw in that locker back there. Or at least a 12-gauge. If you guys get greased, I want a fighting chance to survive."

"Pendergast, don't be crazy," D'Agosta said. "This guy's bent. Today's the first time he's seen daylight since George Bush was president, for Chrissakes."

"How quickly can you get us to the Astor Tunnels?" Pendergast asked.

"Ninety minutes, maybe. If you don't mind getting your feet wet on the way down."

There was a silence. "You seem to know your weapons. Do you have any experience?"

"Seventh Infantry, I-Corps. Wounded for the greater glory of the U.S. of frigging A. in the Iron Triangle." As Margo watched with disgusted fascination, Mephisto unbuckled his filthy pants and dropped them, exposing a puckered scar that ran across his abdomen and down his thigh, ending in a large knot of scar tissue. "Had to restuff me before they could get me onto the stretcher," he said, with a lopsided grin.

Pendergast paused for a long moment. Then he turned, opened another locker, and removed two automatic weapons, slinging one over his right arm and tossing the other to D'Agosta. Then he withdrew a case of buckshot and a stubby-looking pump-action shotgun. He closed the locker, turned, and passed the weapon to Mephisto.

"Don't let me down, soldier," he said, his hand still on the barrel.

Mephisto pulled the gun from Pendergast and pumped the magazine, saying nothing.

Margo had begun to notice a troublesome pattern: Pendergast had been removing plenty of equipment, but none of it was finding its way to her. "Hold on a minute," she said. "What about me? Where's my gear?"

"I'm afraid you're not coming," Pendergast said, dragging bulletproof vests from the locker and checking their sizes.

"Who the hell says I'm not?" Margo said. "Because I'm a woman?"

"Dr. Green, please. You know very well it has nothing to do with that. You're not experienced in this kind of police action." Pendergast began digging into another locker. "Here, Vincent, take charge of these, will you?"

"M-26 fragmentation grenades," D'Agosta said, handling them gingerly. "You've got enough firepower in here to invade China, pal."

"Not experienced?" Margo echoed, ignoring D'Agosta. "I was the one who saved your ass back there in the Museum, remember? If it wasn't for me, you'd have been Mbwun droppings long ago."

"I would be the first to admit it, Dr. Green," Pendergast replied as he shrugged into a backpack equipped with a long hose and a strange hooded nozzle.

"Don't tell me that's a flamethrower," D'Agosta asked. "ABT FastFire, if I'm not mistaken," Mephisto said. "When I was a grunt, we called the jelly they sprayed purple haze. The sadistic weapon of a morally bankrupt republic." He looked speculatively into one of the open lockers.

"I'm an anthropologist," Margo said. "I know these creatures better than *anyone*. You're going to need my expertise."

"Not enough to endanger your life," said Pendergast. "Dr. Frock's an anthropologist, too. Shall we wheel him down with us and get his learned opinion on the matter?"

"I was the one who discovered all this. Remember?" Margo realized she was raising her voice.

"She's right," said D'Agosta. "We wouldn't be here if it weren't for her."

"That still doesn't give us the right to involve her further," Pendergast replied. "Besides, she's never been belowground, and she's not a police officer."

"Look!" Margo shouted. "Forget my expertise. Forget the help I've given you in the past. I'm an expert shot. D'Agosta here can testify. And I'm not going to slow you down, either. If anything, you'll be panting to keep up with *me*. It comes down to this: if you get in trouble down there, every extra body you've got is going to count."

Pendergast turned his pale eyes toward her, and Margo could feel the keen force of his stare as it almost seemed to probe her thoughts. "Why exactly do you need this, Dr. Green?" he asked.

"Because—" Margo stopped suddenly, wondering why, in fact, she wanted to descend to that netherworld. It would be so much easier to wish them well, step out of the building, walk home, order dinner from the Thai restaurant on the corner, and crack open that Thackeray novel she'd been meaning to start for the last month.

Then she realized it was not a question of wanting. Eighteen months before, she had stared into the face of Mbwun, seen her reflection in its feral red eyes. Together, she and Pendergast had killed the beast. And she'd thought it was over. They all did. Now she knew better.

"A couple of months ago," she said, "Greg Kawakita tried to contact me. I never bothered to follow up. If I had, maybe all of this could have been avoided." She paused. "I need to see this thing finished."

Pendergast continued to gaze at her appraisingly.

"You brought me back into this, goddammit!" Margo said, rounding on D'Agosta. "It's the last thing I wanted. But now that I'm here, I need to see it through."

"She's right about that, too," D'Agosta said. "I did bring her into the investigation."

Pendergast put his hands on Margo's shoulders in an uncharacteristically physical gesture. "Margo, please," he said quietly. "Try to understand. Back at the Museum, there was no choice. We were already trapped inside with Mbwun. This is different. We're walking knowingly *into* danger. You're a civilian. I'm sorry, but there it is."

"For once, I agree with Mayor Whitey." Mephisto looked at Margo. "You seem like a person of integrity. That means you're out of place in company like this. So let them get their own official asses killed."

Pendergast looked at Margo a moment longer. Then, dropping his hands, he turned toward Mephisto. "What's our route?" he asked.

"The Lexington line, under Bloomingdale's," came the response. "There's an abandoned shaft, about a quarter mile north on the express track. Heads straight into the Park, then angles down toward the Bottleneck."

"Christ," D'Agosta said. "Maybe that's how the Wrinklers ambushed that train."

"Maybe." Pendergast fell silent a moment, as if lost in thought. "We'll need to draw the explosives from C section," he continued abruptly, moving toward the door. "Let's go. We've got less than two hours."

"Come on, Margo," D'Agosta said over his shoulder as he jogged after Pendergast. "We'll see you out."

Margo stood motionless, watching the three move quickly toward the outer door of the armory. "Shit!" she cried in a frustrated rage, throwing her carryall to the floor and giving the nearest locker a vicious kick. Then she sank to the floor and put her head in her hands.

52

Snow checked the oversized wall clock. The narrow hands behind the protective metal cage read 10:15 P.M. His eyes traveled across the empty squad room, past the extra tanks and regulators, the torn flippers and oversized masks. His gaze came to rest at last on the mountain of paperwork atop the desk in front of him, and he winced inwardly. Here he was, supposedly recovering from a bacterial infection of the lungs. But he, and the rest of the NYPD dive team, knew that he was actually in the doghouse. The Dive Sergeant had taken him aside, told him what a great job he'd done, but Snow hadn't believed it. Even the fact that the skeletons he'd discovered had been the start of a big police investigation didn't make any real difference. The fact was he'd lost it, lost it on his first dive. Even Fernandez didn't bother to tease him anymore.

He sighed, looking out the grimy window at the long-deserted dock and the dark oily water beyond, glittering in the restless night. The rest of the squad was out after a helicopter crash in the East River earlier in the evening. And there was something big going on in the city, too: his police radio had been squawking nonstop with talk of marches, riots, mobilizations, crowd-control measures. Seemed like the action was everywhere except in his own quiet little corner of the Brooklyn docks. And here he was, filling out reports.

He sighed, stapled some papers into a folder, closed it, and tossed it in the outgoing tray. Dead dog, removed from the Gowanus canal. Cause of death: gunshot wound; ownership unknown; case closed. He slid another folder off the pile: Randolf Rowell, jumper, Triborough Bridge, age 22. Suicide note found in pocket. Cause of death: drowning. Case closed.

As he dropped the file into the bin, he heard the diesel rumble of the launch as it nosed its way into the dock. Back early. The engine sounded different somehow, throatier, he thought. Maybe it needed a tune-up or something.

He heard running footfalls on the wooden dock and suddenly the door burst open: men in black wetsuits, no insignia, faces black and green with greasepaint. Twin haversacks of rubber and latex dangled around their necks.

"Where's the dive team?" barked the forward man, a hulking figure with a Texas accent.

"East River chopper crash," Snow said. "You the second squad?" He glanced out the window and was surprised to see, not a familiar blue-and-white police boat, but a powerful inboard V-bottom launch, lying low in the water and painted as dark as the men.

"All of them?" the man asked.

"All except me. Who are you?"

"We ain't your mother's long-lost nephews, darlin'," the man said. "We need someone who knows the shortest route into the West Side Lateral, and we need him now."

Snow felt an involuntary twinge. "Let me radio the Dive Sergeant—"

"No time. What about you?"

"Well, I know the flow grid around the Manhattan shoreline. That's part of Basic, every police diver has to—"

"Can you bring us in?" the man said brusquely, cutting him off.

"You want to get *in* the West Side Lateral? Most of the pipes are grilled, or too narrow for a—"

"Just answer the question: yes or no?"

"I think so," Snow said, his voice faltering a little.

"Your name?"

"Snow. Officer Snow."

"Get in the boat."

"But my tanks and suit—"

"We got everything you need. You can suit up on the launch."

Snow scrambled from his chair, following the men out onto the dock. It didn't seem to be an invitation he could refuse. "You still haven't told me who—"

The man paused, one foot on the gunwale of the launch. "Commander Rachlin, Patrol Leader, SEAL Team Blue Seven. Now get a wiggle on."

The helmsman gunned the launch out of the slip. "Mind your rudder," the Commander said, then gestured Snow closer. "Here's the op," he said, lifting a matted seat and pulling out a sheaf of waterproof maps from the storage space beneath. "There'll be four teams, two to each team." He glanced around. "Donovan!"

"Sir!" a man said, coming over. Even in the bulky suit, he looked thin and wiry. Snow could see nothing of his facial features behind the neoprene and greasepaint.

"Donovan, you and Snow here are buddying up."

There was a silence that Snow interpreted as disgust. "What's going on?" he asked.

"It's a UD job," Rachlin said.

"A what?"

The Commander looked at him sharply. "Underwater demolition. That's all you need to know."

"Is this connected with the headless murders?" Snow asked.

The Commander stared. "For a dumb-ass, tit-suckin', bath-tub-divin' tadpole of a *po*-lice diver, you ask a whole lot of questions, darlin'."

Snow said nothing. He didn't dare look at Donovan.

"We can chart our way in from this point," Rachlin said, unrolling one of the maps and tamping his thumb on a blue dot. "But the new treatment plant made these insertion areas here obsolete. So you're gonna get us in to that point."

Snow bent over the laminated map. At the top, in chiseled copperplate script, a legend read 1932 WEST SIDE STORM AND SEWER SURVEY, LOWER QUADRANT. Below was a labyrinth of faint intersecting lines. Somebody had placed three sets of dots beneath the western side of Central Park. He stared at the complex traceries, his mind racing. The Humboldt Kill was the easiest insertion point, but it was a hell of a long way in to the Lateral from there, with many twists and turns. Besides, he didn't want to go back there, ever, if he could help it. He tried to remember their training sessions, the long days on boats nosing up muddy canals. Where else did the West Side Lateral drain into?

"This isn't an essay question," Rachlin said quietly. "Hurry it up. We're on a tight schedule here."

Snow looked up. There was one route he knew of, a very direct route. *Well,* he thought, *they asked for it.* "The Lower Hudson Sewage Treatment Plant itself," he said. "We can go in through the main settling tank."

There was a silence, and Snow glanced around.

"Dive in goddamn *sewage*?" a very deep voice said.

The Commander turned. "You heard the man." He tossed a wetsuit toward Snow. "Now get your lovely little behind below and suit up. We've got to be clear and at the extraction point by six minutes to midnight."

53

Margo sat on the cold tile floor of the armory, inwardly fuming. She wasn't sure who she was more angry at: D'Agosta, for roping her into this mess to begin with; Pendergast, for refusing to take her along; or herself, for being unable just to let the whole thing drop. But that was something she simply couldn't do. It was clear to her now just how long a shadow the Museum murders—the terrifying final struggle in the Museum basement—had cast over her. It had robbed her of sleep, fractured her peace of mind. *And now this shit, on top of everything else...*

She knew Pendergast had been thinking of her safety, but she still could not contain the frustration of being left behind. *If it wasn't for me, they'd still be in the dark,* she thought. *I made the connection between Mbwun and Whittlesey. I figured out what really happened.* With a little more time, she might have even tied up the nagging, perplexing loose ends that still remained: what the rest of Kawakita's cryptic journal fragments meant, what he'd been doing with the thyoxin, why he'd been synthesizing vitamin D at his final laboratory.

Actually, the thyoxin made sense. The journal entries implied that, near the end, Kawakita had had a change of heart. Apparently, he'd realized his latest strains of glaze no longer twisted the body, but instead twisted the mind. Maybe he'd even learned of the environmental dangers posed by saltwater coming in contact with the plants. In any case, it seemed clear he'd decided to undo what he'd done, and rid the reservoir of *Liliceae Mbwunensis*. Perhaps the creatures themselves had learned of his intention. That could explain his death: obviously, the last thing they wanted was somebody meddling with their supply. But that still didn't explain what the hell he'd been doing with vitamin D. Could it have been necessary for the genetic sequencing? No, that wasn't possible...

Suddenly, Margo sat up, drawing in her breath sharply. *He was planning to kill off the plants, I'm sure of it*, she thought. *And he knew that put him in terrible danger. So the vitamin D wasn't for glaze production. It was for...*

Suddenly, she understood.

In an instant, she scrambled to her feet. There wasn't a moment to lose. Galvanized into action, she began yanking open locker drawers, spilling the contents into the narrow corridor, hastily grabbing at the items she needed, stuffing them into her carryall: oxygen mask, night-vision goggles, boxes of 9-millimeter hollow-point rounds for her semiautomatic pistol.

Breathing heavily, she ran to the door of the armory and looked out into the larger storage area. *It's got to be around here somewhere*, she thought. She began running along the rows of wooden cabinets, quickly scanning their Formica labels. Stopping abruptly, she opened one of the cabinets and took out three empty one-liter bottles equipped with sports-style squeeze caps. Placing them on the floor along with her carryall, she opened another cabinet and pulled out several gallon containers of distilled water. Then she ran down the rows, searching once again, muttering under her breath. Finally, she stopped and yanked open another cabinet door. It was filled with rows of jars containing pills and tablets. She feverishly scanned the labels, found what she wanted, and raced back to her carryall.

Kneeling, she opened the jars and upended them, making a small mountain of white pills on the tiled floor. "What's the concentration, Greg?" she found herself saying out loud. *No way of knowing: I'll have to guess high.* Using the bottom of one of the jars, she smashed the pills to powder, then scooped several handfuls into each of the liter bottles. She topped off the bottles with water, shook them vigorously, checked the suspension: a little coarse, perhaps, but there was no time for anything better. It would soon dissolve.

She stood up and grabbed her carryall, scattering the empty bottles noisily down the corridor.

"Who's there?" came a voice. Too late, she realized she'd forgotten about the guard on duty outside. Quickly, she stuffed the bottles into her carryall and slung it over her shoulder as she headed for the exit.

"Sorry," she said. "Daydreaming." She hoped she sounded sincere.

The guard frowned, putting his magazine aside. He began to stand up.

"Which way did Agent Pendergast go again?" she said hurriedly. "He mentioned something about C section."

Mentioning Pendergast's name had the desired effect; the guard sat back down in his chair. "Take Elevator Bank Four up two flights and make a left," he said.

Margo thanked him and hurried to the wall of elevators at the end of the corridor. She checked her watch as the doors closed, then cursed: no time. Savagely, she punched the button for the lobby. As the door opened, she gathered herself for a sprint. Then, noticing the numerous guards, she settled for walking quickly across the lobby, turning in her visitor's pass, and stepping out into the humid Manhattan night.

Outside, she sprinted toward the curb and the nearest taxi. "Fifty-ninth and Lex," she said, jumping in and slamming the door behind her.

"Okay, but it ain't gonna be a fast ride," the cabbie said. "There's some kind of march or riot or something going on near the Park; traffic's snarled up tighter than the hairs in a dog's asshole."

"Then do something about it," Margo said, tossing a twenty into the front seat.

The driver raced east, then swung north on First Avenue, dodging traffic at a breakneck pace. They made it as far as 47th Street before lurching to a stop. Ahead, Margo could see a veritable parking lot of cars and trucks, engines idling and horns blaring, six parallel lines of brake lights stretching unbroken down the dark thoroughfare. In an instant, she grabbed her carryall and tumbled out the door, sprinting northward through the pedestrian traffic.

Seven minutes later she reached the Bloomingdale's subway entrance. She took the steps downward two at a time, dodging the late-evening revelers as best she could. Her shoulder ached from the weight of the carryall. Over the noise of the engines and the frantic horns, she thought she could hear a strange, muffled roaring in the distance, like ten thousand people all yelling at once. Then she was underground and all sound was blotted out except the squealing of the trains. Fishing in her pocket for a token, she went through the turnstile and raced down the steps to the express track. A small crowd was already there, huddled near the lighted staircase.

"You see those guys?" a young woman with a Columbia T-shirt was saying. "What the heck was that thing on his back?"

"Probably rat poison," said her companion. "They grow 'em big down here, you know. Just last night, at the West Fourth Street Station, I saw one that must have been the size of a full grown—"

"Where'd they go?" Margo interrupted breathlessly.

"They just jumped on to the express tracks and ran uptown—"

Margo dashed to the north end of the platform. Ahead, she could see the subway tracks stretching into the darkness ahead.

Small, stagnant pools lay between the rails, shimmering a faint green in the lights of the infrequent switches. She looked back down the track quickly to ensure no train was approaching, then took a deep breath and jumped down onto the track.

"There goes another!" she heard someone shout behind her. Hoisting the carryall to a more comfortable position, she began to run, trying hard not to stumble on the gravel bed or the uneven surface of the railroad ties. She squinted ahead into the distance, trying vainly to make out shapes or silhouettes. She opened her mouth to shout Pendergast's name, then abruptly closed it again: it was farther up this very line, after all, that the subway massacre had occurred not so long before.

Even as the thought crossed her mind, she felt a puff of wind raise the hair at the back of her neck. She turned, and her heart sank: behind, in the darkness, she could see the circular red symbol of the number four express, distant but unmistakable.

She ran faster, gasping the dense and humid air into her lungs. The train would only stop a moment to load and unload passengers, then it would be off again, gaining speed as it raced toward her. Frantically, she looked around, searching for a workmen's cutout or some other place she could take shelter. But the tunnel stretched smooth and dark into the distance.

Behind her now she could hear the chimes of the closing doors, the hiss of air brakes, the whirring of the diesels as the train gathered speed. Wildly, she turned toward the only shelter available: the narrow gap between the northbound and southbound lanes. Stepping gingerly over the third rail, she cowered between rusting girders, trying to make herself thinner than the track switch that stood beside her like a dark sentinel.

The train neared, its whistle shrieking a deafening warning. Margo felt herself blown backward by the concussive blast of its passing, and stretched out her arms, grasping desperately at the girders to keep from sprawling onto the southbound tracks. The cars passed in a flash of bright windows, like a reel of cinema film trailing horizontally in front of her, and then it was receding northward, rocking slightly to the left and right, spitting a shower of sparks.

Coughing from the mushrooming clouds of dust, her ears ringing, Margo stepped back onto the tracks and looked quickly in both directions. Ahead, in the red glow of the receding train, she could make out three figures, emerging from a distant break in the tunnel wall.

"Pendergast!" she shouted. "Agent Pendergast, wait!"

The figures stopped, then turned to face her. As she sprinted forward, she could now make out the narrow features of the FBI agent, staring motionlessly in her direction.

"Dr. Green?" came the familiar drawl.

"Jesus Christ, Margo!" the voice of D'Agosta snapped angrily. "What the hell are you doing here? Pendergast told you—"

"Shut up and listen!" Margo hissed, coming to a stop before them. "I figured out what Kawakita was doing with the vitamin D he was synthesizing in his lab. It had nothing to do with the plant, or glaze, or anything. He was making a *weapon*."

Even in the dark, she could make out the disbelief on D'Agosta's features. Mephisto stood behind him, silent and watching, like a dark apparition.

"It's true," she panted. "We know the Wrinklers hate light. Correct? But it's more than hatred. They *fear* it. Light is deadly to them."

"I'm not sure I understand," Pendergast said. "It's not the light itself, actually. It's what the light *creates*. Sunlight falling on skin activates vitamin D. Right? If this were poisonous to the creatures, direct light would cause them great pain, even death. That's why some of my inoculated cultures died. They were left under the lamp overnight. And that might even explain how the Wrinklers got their name. Skin lacking in vitamin D tends to have a wrinkled, leathery appearance. And vitamin D deficiency causes osteomalacia, softening of the bones. Remember how Dr. Brambell said Kawakita's skeleton looked almost as if it had suffered a nightmarish case of scurvy? Well, it had."

"But this is all guesswork," D'Agosta said. "Where's the proof?"

"Why else would Kawakita have been synthesizing it?" Margo cried. "Remember, it was equally poisonous to him. He knew the creatures would be after him if he destroyed their plant supply. And then, lacking the drag, they would go on a killing rampage. No, he had to kill both the plants *and* the creatures."

Pendergast was nodding. "It appears to be the only possible explanation. But why have you come all this way to tell us about it?"

Margo slapped her carryall. "Because I've got three liters of vitamin D in solution, right here."

D'Agosta snorted. "So? We're not exactly short of firepower here."

"If there's as many of them down there as we think, you couldn't *carry* enough firepower to stop all of them," Margo said. "Remember what it took to bring down Mbwun?"

"Our intention is to avoid any encounters," Pendergast said.

"But you sure aren't taking any chances, with all those weapons you're toting," Margo replied. "Bullets may hurt them. But this"—she gestured at her pack—"gets them where they live."

Pendergast sighed. "Very well, Dr. Green," he said. "Pass it over. We'll divide the bottles among ourselves."

"No way," Margo said. "*I* carry the bottles. And I come along."

"Another train's coming," Mephisto interjected.

Pendergast was silent a moment. "I already explained that it's not—"

"I've come this far!" Margo said, hearing the anger and determination in her own words as she spoke. "There's no way in hell I'm going back now. And don't tell me again how dangerous it is. You want me to sign something indemnifying the authorities in case I scratch myself? Fine. Pass it over."

"That won't be necessary." Pendergast sighed deeply "Very well, Dr. Green. We can't waste any more time arguing. Mephisto, take us below."

54

Smithback froze in the tunnel, listening. There were the footsteps again, seemingly more distant this time. He breathed deeply several times, swallowing hard, trying to force his heart back down out of his throat. In the dark, he'd lost his way in the narrow passages. He was no longer even sure he was moving in the right direction. For all he knew, he'd turned himself around completely and was heading back toward the killers, whoever or whatever they were. Yet instinct told him he was still heading away from the scene of horrible butchery. The slick-walled passages still seemed to lead in only one direction: down.

The hideous creatures he had seen were the Wrinklers, he was sure of that. The ones Mephisto had been raving about, maybe the ones that had killed all those people in the subway. Wrinklers. In the space of a few minutes, they'd killed at least four men... Waxie's screams seemed to echo and reecho in his ears until he wasn't sure what was real and what was merely memory.

Then another, very real, sound intruded into his thoughts: the footsteps again, and very close. He twisted around in panic, looking for a place to run. Suddenly there was a bright light in his eyes, and behind it a figure loomed toward him. Smithback tensed for a fight he hoped would be mercifully short.

But then the figure shrank back, squealing in terror. The flashlight dropped to the floor and came rattling toward Smithback. With a flood of relief, the journalist recognized the bushy mustache belonging to Duffy, the fellow who'd been straggling up the ladder behind Waxie. He must have eluded his pursuers, God only knew how.

"Calm down!" Smithback whispered, grabbing the flashlight before it rolled away. "I'm a journalist; I saw it all happen."

Duffy was too frightened, or winded, to ask what Smithback was doing underneath the Central Park Reservoir. He sat on the brick floor of the tunnel, his sides heaving. Every few seconds he took a quick look into the blackness behind him.

"Know how to get out of here?" Smithback prodded.

"No," Duffy gasped. "Maybe. Come on, help me up."

"Name's Bill Smithback," Smithback whispered, reaching down and hoisting the trembling engineer to his feet.

"Stan Duffy," the engineer hiccuped.

"How'd you get away from those things?"

"I lost them back there in the overflow shunts," Duffy said. A large tear rolled slowly down his mud-streaked face.

"How come these tunnels only lead down, and not up?"

Duffy dabbed absently at his eyes with one sleeve. "We're in the secondary flow tunnels. In an emergency, water runs down both the main tube and these secondary tubes, right to the Bottleneck. It's a closed system. Everything around here has to go through the Bottleneck." He stopped, and his eyes widened, as if remembering something. Then he glanced at his watch. "We have to go!" he said. "We've got just ninety minutes!"

"Ninety minutes? Until what?" Smithback asked, playing the light ahead of them down the tunnel.

"The Reservoir's going to drain at midnight; there's no stopping it now. And when it does, it's going right down these tunnels."

"What?" Smithback breathed.

"They're trying to flush out the lowest levels, the Astor Tunnels, to get rid of the creatures. Or they were, anyway. Now they want to change their minds. But it's too late—"

"The Astor Tunnels?" Smithback asked. *Must be that Devil's Attic Mephisto was talking about.*

Duffy suddenly grabbed the flashlight and started running down the tunnel.

Smithback took off after him. The passage joined a larger one which continued downward, spiraling like a gigantic corkscrew. There was no light save for the wildly flailing beam of the flashlight. He tried to stay to the sides of the curving tunnel floor, avoiding the standing water that ran along its bottom. Though he wasn't sure why he bothered; Duffy was splashing straight down the center, making enough noise to raise the dead.

Moments later, Duffy stopped. "I heard them!" he shrieked as Smithback appeared by his side.

"I didn't hear anything," Smithback panted, looking around.

But Duffy was running again, and Smithback followed, panic ripping his heart, thoughts of a big story forgotten. A dark opening appeared at the side of the tunnel, and Duffy made for it. Smithback followed, and suddenly the ground opened up beneath his feet. In an instant, he was sliding uncontrollably down a slick wet chute. Duffy's wail came keening up from below as Smithback spun around, clawing at the slick surface. It was like every dream he'd ever had of falling, except even more horrible, inside a dank black runnel, unguessable depths beneath Manhattan. Suddenly there was a splash in front of him, and the next moment he too landed, hard, in about twenty inches of water.

He scrambled to his feet, aching in numerous places but glad to feel a firm surface under his feet. The floor of the tunnel seemed even, and the water smelled relatively fresh. Beside him, Duffy was wailing uncontrollably.

"Shut up," Smithback hissed at him. "You're going to draw those things right to us."

"Oh, my God," Duffy sobbed in the darkness. "This can't be happening, it can't. What are they? What—"

Smithback reached into the blackness, located Duffy's arm, and pulled the man toward him brusquely. "Shut *up*," he said, lips touching the engineer's ear.

The sobbing subsided to a soft hiccuping.

"Where's the flashlight?" Smithback whispered.

Sobbing was the only reply. But then a dim light switched on nearby. Miraculously, Duffy was still clutching it.

"Where are we?"

The hiccuping subsided.

"*Duffy!* Where are we?'"

There was a stifled sob. "I don't know. One of the spillover tubes, maybe."

"Any idea where it goes?"

There was a sniffle. "It bleeds off excess flow from the Reservoir. If we move downstream to the Bottleneck, maybe we can reach the lower drain system."

"And from there, how do we get out?" Smithback whispered.

Duffy hiccuped. "Don't know."

Smithback mopped his face again and said nothing, trying to roll the fear, the pain, and the shock into a little ball he could stuff down inside himself. He tried to think about his story. God, he'd be a made man with a story like this, following on the heels of the Museum Beast murders. And with luck, he'd still have the Wisher piece in his pocket. But first...

There was a splashing sound, its distance hard to gauge because of the echoes but clearly approaching. He leaned into the darkness, straining to hear.

"They're still after us!" Duffy yelped, inches from his eardrum.

Smithback grabbed the arm a second time. "Duffy, shut up and listen to me. We can't outrun them. We need to *lose* them. You know the system: you've got to tell me how."

Duffy struggled, making an unintelligible sound of fear.

Smithback squeezed harder. "Look, we're going to be all right if you just calm down and think."

Duffy seemed to relax, and Smithback could hear him breathing heavily. "All right," the engineer said. "The emergency spillovers have gauging stations at the bottom. Just before the Bottleneck. If that's where we are, maybe we can hide inside—"

"Let's go," Smithback hissed.

They splashed through the darkness, the flashlight beam jogging from wall to wall. The low tunnel took a turn, and a vast, ancient piece of machinery rose up before Smithback: a giant hollow screw, or something like it, placed horizontally on a bed of granite. Heavily rusted pipes protruded from either end, and a convoluted mass of pipes lay farther back, like coiled iron guts. At the base of the machine was a small railed platform. The main body of the stream ran down past the station, while a small side tunnel snaked its way into the blackness to their left. Taking the flashlight, Smithback grabbed the railing and swung himself up, then helped Duffy to a position beside him.

"Into the pipe," Smithback whispered. He pushed Duffy inside, then wriggled in himself, tossing the lighted flashlight into the stream before retreating into the darkness.

"Are you crazy? You just threw away—"

"It's plastic," Smithback said. "It'll float. I'm hoping they'll follow the light downstream."

They sat in absolute silence. The thick walls of the gauging machinery muffled the tunnel noise, but in a few minutes Smithback could tell that the splashing sounds had grown more distinct. The Wrinklers were approaching—swiftly, too, by the sound. Behind him, he could feel Duffy twitch, and he prayed the engineer would keep his head. The splashing became louder and now Smithback could hear them breathing, a heavy wheezing, like a winded horse. The splashing sounds drew alongside the gauging station, then stopped.

The foul goatish reek was thick now, and Smithback shut his eyes tightly. In the blackness to his rear, Duffy was trembling violently.

He heard splashes in the water outside the station as the things milled about. There was a low noise that sounded like snuffling, and Smithback froze, remembering the Mbwun beast's keen sense of smell. The splashing continued. Then—with an enormous feeling of relief—Smithback heard it begin to retreat. The things were continuing down the tunnel.

He breathed slowly and deeply, counting each breath. At thirty, he turned to Duffy. "Which way to the storm drains?"

"Out the far end," Duffy whispered.

"Let's go."

Carefully, they turned around within the cramped, fetid space and began wriggling their way toward the rear of the pipe. Duffy emerged at last into the open air. Smithback heard first one, then both, of the engineer's feet drop into the water, and was wriggling forward himself when a sudden piercing scream cut through the pitch black, and a spray too thick and warm to be water spattered his face. He backed frantically into the pipe.

"Help!" Duffy blurted suddenly. "No, please don't, you're gonna—Oh, God, that's my guts—Jesus, somebody get—"

The voice changed suddenly to a frenzied wet wheeze, then died beneath the heavy thrashing of water. Smithback, scrambling backward in mindless terror, heard a thudding sound like meat chopped with a cleaver, followed by the knuckle-crack of bones being wrenched from their sockets.

Smithback fell out the near end of the pipe, landed on his back in the stream, scrambled to his feet and ran blindly down the side tunnel, not hearing, not caring, not thinking about anything except running. He ran and ran, careening off the sides of the tunnel, scrabbling and thrashing down the endlessly forking paths, deeper and deeper into the dark bowels of the earth. The tunnel joined another, and another, each one larger than the last. Until, quite suddenly, he felt an arm, wet and horribly strong, slide around his neck, and a powerful hand clamp down simultaneously over his mouth.

55

Within an hour of its spontaneous flare-up, the riot along Central Park South had begun to sputter fitfully. Well before 11:00 P.M., most of the initial rioters had spent their anger along with their energy. Those who had been hurt were helped to the sidelines. Shouting, insults, and threats began to replace fists, clubs, and stones. However, a hard central core of violence continued. As people left the scene, bruised or exhausted, others arrived: some curious, some angry, some drunk and spoiling for a fight. Television reports waxed lurid and hysterical. Word traveled like an electric spark through the island: up First and Second Avenues, where young Republicans gathered in singles bars to jeer and hoot at the liberal President; along St. Mark's Place and into the Marxist corners of the East Village; over fax lines and telephone lines. As word spread, so did the rumors. Some said that the homeless and those that tried to help them were being massacred in a police-instigated genocide. Others said that leftist radicals and criminal mobs were burning banks, shooting citizens, and looting businesses uptown. Those that answered this call to action ran into—sometimes brutally—the last pockets of homeless that were still streaming to the surface, emerging here and there around Central Park, fleeing the trapped and spreading tear gas.

The original vanguard of Take Back Our City—the Brahmins of New York wealth and influence—had quickly retreated from the scene. Most had returned to their townhouses and duplexes in dismay. Others had massed toward the Great Lawn, assuming the police would quickly quell the rioting and hoping that the final vigil would go on as planned. But as the police shored up their line and began to hem in the rioters, the fighting itself also retreated deeper into the Park, moving ever closer to the Lawn and the Reservoir that lay beyond. The darkness of the Park, the thick woods, the tangle of undergrowth, and the maze of paths all made efforts at riot control difficult and slow.

The police moved against the rioters with caution. Already spread too thin by the massive rousting operation, much of the force was late on the scene of the riot. The police brass was all too keenly aware that influential people might still be among the milling throng, and the idea of gassing or clubbing a member of the New York elite was not something the politically conscious mayor would allow. In addition, a large body of officers had to be dispatched to patrol the adjoining areas of the city, where sporadic looting and vandalism was now being reported. And in the backs of everyone's minds lay the unspoken, but dreaded, spectacle of the Crown Heights riot of a few years before, which had gone on for three days before finally drawing to an uneasy close.

Hayward watched as the emergency medical crew rolled Beal into the waiting ambulance. The back legs of the stretcher folded up as the officer was slid inside. Beal groaned, then raised a hand toward his bandaged head.

"Careful," Hayward snapped to the paramedic. She put a hand on one of the rear doors and leaned inside. "How you doing?" she asked.

"Been better," Beal said with a weak smile.

Hayward nodded. "You'll be fine." She turned to go.

"Sergeant?" Beal said. Hayward paused. "That bastard Miller would have left me there to find my own way out. Or to drown, maybe. I think I owe you guys my life."

"Forget it," Hayward said. "It's part of the job. Right?"

"Maybe," Beal said. "But anyway, I won't forget. Thanks."

Hayward left Beal with the paramedic and walked around to the driver's seat. "What's the news?" she asked.

"What do you want to hear?" the driver asked, scribbling on a log sheet. "Gold futures? The international situation?"

"Take your act to the Poconos," she replied. "I'm talking about *this*." And she waved her hand along Central Park West.

A surreal quiet lay over the dark scene. Except for emergency vehicles and the police cars stationed at every other cross street, there was no traffic on the immediate blocks. Pools of darkness dotted the avenue; a mere handful of streetlights remained unbroken, sizzling and sputtering. The broad avenue was dotted with chunks of concrete, broken glass, and trash. Farther to the south, Hayward noticed, the flashing lights grew much more numerous.

"Where you been?" the driver asked. "Unless you spent the last hour at the center of the earth, it was pretty hard to miss the action around here."

"You're not that far wrong," she said. "We've been clearing out the homeless underneath the Park. There was resistance. This guy got wounded, and it took us a long time to extract him. We were pretty deep underground, and we didn't want to jostle him too much. Okay? We came up five minutes ago at the Seventy-second Street station, only to find a ghost town around here."

"Clearing out the homeless?" the driver asked. "So you're the ones responsible."

Hayward frowned. "For what?"

The ambulance driver tapped his ear, then pointed eastward, as if that was the only answer necessary.

Hayward stopped to listen. Over the squawk of the ambulance scanner and the distant pulse of the city, she could make out sounds floating from the dark interior of Central Park: the angry buzz of bullhorns, shouts, screams, the whine of sirens.

"You know that Take Back Our City march?" the driver asked. "The unannounced one that was going along Central Park South?"

"Heard something about it," Hayward said.

"Yeah. Well, suddenly all these homeless started pouring up from underground. Kinda hostile, too. Apparently, you cops had been using them for baton practice. Started squabbling with the marchers. Before you know it, there was a full-blown confrontation. People just went nuts, I heard. Screaming, yelling, stomping on other people. Then the looting started up along the fringes. Took the cops an hour to get the situation under control. It *still* isn't under control, actually. But they've managed to confine everything to the Park."

The paramedic in the rear gave a signal, and the driver put the ambulance in gear and pulled away, flashing lights striping the limestone facades. Farther up Central Park West, Hayward could see curious people looking out from their windows, pointing into the Park. A few braver souls were standing on the pavement outside of lobbies, staying close to the protective presence of uniformed doormen. She gazed up at the huge Gothic shape of the Dakota, unharmed and seemingly aloof from the chaos, almost as if its narrow, stylized moat had repulsed an angry throng. She found her eyes traveling up the corner tower toward what must be Pendergast's windows. She wondered if he'd made it back from the Devil's Attic in one piece.

"Get Beal off okay?" she heard Carlin call out. His massive form emerged out of the distant shadows.

"Just now," she replied, turning toward him. "How about the other one?"

"Refused medical treatment," Carlin said. "Any sign of Miller?"

Hayward scowled. "He's probably in some Atlantic Avenue bar by now, sucking down beer and bragging about his exploits.

That's how it works, right? He'll get a promotion, and we'll get letters of caution for insubordination."

"Maybe other times it works that way," Carlin said with a knowing smile. "But not this time."

"What's that supposed to mean?" Hayward asked, then continued without giving Carlin time to answer: "No way to tell what Miller did or didn't do. Guess we'd better report in." She grabbed at her radio, snapping it on. But torrents of noise, static, and panic came pouring from every band.

...Moving toward the Great Lawn, we need more manpower to... Got eight of them but I can't hold them much longer, if that wagon doesn't come soon they'll just melt away into the dark... I called for a medevac thirty goddamn minutes ago; we got people hurt up here... Christ, they've gotta seal that southern quadrant; more keep coming in all the time... Hayward snapped the radio off and snugged it back into her belt, then motioned Carlin to follow her down to the squad car at the next corner. A police officer in riot gear stood beside it, vigilantly scanning the street, shotgun in hand.

"Where's command for this operation?" Hayward asked.

The policeman tipped up his face shield and looked at her. "There's a forward command post in the Castle," he said. "That's what dispatch says, anyway. Things are kinda disorganized right now, as if you couldn't tell."

"Belvedere Castle." Hayward turned toward Carlin. "We'd better head for it."

As they ran down Central Park West, Hayward was strangely reminded of her visit to a Hollywood back lot two years before. She remembered walking down the ersatz Manhattan street on which countless musicals and gangster films had been shot. She'd seen phony street lamps, shop fronts, fire hydrants... everything but people. At the time, common sense had told her that a mere hundred yards away were bustling, vibrant California streets. Yet the still emptiness of the lot had seemed almost spectral.

Tonight, Central Park West felt the same way. Though she could hear the distant honking of car horns and the whistle of sirens—and though she knew that, within the Park itself, police were massing to stop the rioting and confusion—this darkened avenue seemed ghostly and unreal. Only the occasional vigilant doorman, curious resident, or police checkpoint broke the atmosphere of a ghost street.

"Holy shit," Carlin muttered at her side. "Would you look at that." Hayward glanced up, and her reverie instantly dissolved.

It was like crossing a demilitarized zone from order into chaos. To the south, across 65th Street, they saw a sea of ruin. Lobby windows were smashed, awnings over elegant entrances were torn to shreds and flapping idly in the breeze. The police presence here was stronger, the blue-painted barricades omnipresent. Cars along the curbs were missing windows and windshields. A few blocks down, a police tow truck with flashing yellow lights was removing the smoking skeleton of a taxi.

"Looks like some pretty pissed off mole people came through here," Hayward murmured.

They cut across the street, angling toward the drive and heading into the Park. After the destruction they'd just passed, the narrow asphalt paths seemed quiet and deserted. But the smashed benches, overturned trash cans, and smoldering garbage bore mute testimony to what had taken place here not long before. And the noise that drifted toward them from the interior of the Park gave promise of even greater pandemonium to come.

Suddenly Hayward stopped short, motioning Carlin to do the same. Ahead in the dark she could make out a group of people— how many she could not be certain—swaggering in the direction of the Great Lawn. *Can't be cops,* she thought. *They're not wearing riot helmets, or even hats.* A noisy burst of hooting and cursing from the group confirmed her suspicion.

She moved forward quickly, running on the balls of her feet to minimize noise. At ten yards back she stopped. "Halt!" she said, hand on her service piece. "Police officers!"

The group came to a ragged stop, then turned back to look at her. Four, no, five men, youngish, dressed in sports jackets and polo shirts. Her eyes took in the visible weapons: two aluminum bats and what looked like a kitchen carving knife.

They stared at her, faces flushed, grins still on their youthful faces.

"Yeah?" one of them said, taking a step forward.

"Stop right there," Hayward said. The man stopped. "Now, why don't you boys tell me exactly where you're headed?"

The man in front scoffed at the stupidity of the question, indicating the interior of the Park with the merest jerk of his head.

"We're here to take care of business," came a voice from the group.

Hayward shook her head. "What's going on there is none of your business."

"The hell it isn't," the one in front snapped. "We've got friends there, getting the shit beat out of them by a bunch of goddamn bums. There's no way we're going to let that go on." He took another step forward.

"This is a police matter," Hayward said.

"The police haven't done jack shit," the man replied. "Look around. You've let this scum trash our city."

"We heard they killed twenty, thirty people already!" came the slurred voice of a man holding up a cellular phone. "Including Mrs. Wisher. They're trashing the city. They got bastards from the East Village and Soho to help them out. Goddamn NYU activists. Our friends need help."

"Got that?" said the one in front. "So get out of the way, lady." He took another step forward.

"You take another step and I'll part your hair with this," Hayward said, slipping her hand from her gun to her baton and sliding it smoothly from the belt ring. She felt Carlin tense beside her.

"Pretty easy for you to talk tough," the man said scornfully. "With a gun on your belt and a goddamn human refrigerator at your side."

"Think you can take all five of us?" said someone in the group.

"Maybe she thinks she can smother us all to death with those jugs of hers," said another. Several grins broke out.

Hayward took a deep breath, then replaced her baton. "Officer Carlin," she said, "please take twenty steps back."

Carlin remained motionless.

"Do it!" she snapped.

Carlin stared at her for a moment. Then, without turning or taking his eyes from the group, he began walking backward down the path they had come.

Hayward stepped deliberately up to the lead youth. "Now listen up," she said evenly, without taking her eyes off his. "I could take off my badge and my piece, and still kick all your sorry white-bread asses back to Scarsdale, or Greenwich, or wherever it is your mothers tuck you in at night. But I don't need to do that. See, if you refuse to follow my instructions to the letter, then your mothers won't be tucking you in this evening. They'll be waiting in line at Police Plaza tomorrow morning to make your bails. And all the money, or power, or influence in the world won't be able to remove the words *intent to commit felonious assault* from your police record. In this state, a person convicted of a felony can *never* practice law. They can *never* hold public office. And they can *never* get a license to trade securities. And your daddies aren't going to like that. Not one bit."

She paused a moment. "So drop your weapons," she said coolly.

There was a brief instant in which nobody moved.

"I said, *drop your weapons*!" she yelled at the top of her voice.

In the silence that followed, she heard the clink of an aluminum bat hitting asphalt. Then another. Then came a quieter sound: a steel blade dropping to the earth. She waited a long moment, then took a deliberate step backward.

"Officer Carlin," Hayward said quietly. In a moment, he was at her side.

"Shall I frisk them?" he asked.

Hayward shook her head. "Driver's licenses," she said to the group. "I want those, too. Drop them on the ground right there."

There was a brief pause. Then the youth in front dug a hand into his jacket pocket, removed his wallet, and let the plastic card flutter to the ground. The rest followed suit.

"You can pick them up tomorrow afternoon at One Police Plaza," she continued. "Ask for Sergeant Hayward. Now, I want you all to walk straight past me until you reach Central Park West. Then I want you to go your separate ways. Do not pass Go; do not collect two hundred dollars. Head straight home, and go to bed. Understand?"

There was another silence.

"*I can't hear you!*" Carlin's voice roared out, and the men jumped.

"We understand," came the chorused response.

"Then move out," Hayward said. The youths stood motionless, as if rooted to the spot.

"*Shake it!*" she barked. The group started up, silently, heads straight ahead, walking slowly at first, then faster, toward the west. Soon they had vanished into the darkness.

"Bunch of pricks," said Carlin. "You think twenty or thirty were really killed?"

Hayward snorted as she bent to pick up the weapons and licenses. "Hell, no. But if the rumors keep spreading, people like that are going to keep coming. And this situation will never get resolved." She handed him the bats with a sigh. "Come on. We might as well report in and see if we can help out tonight. Because tomorrow, you know we're going to get our butts reprimanded for what happened down in those tunnels."

"Not this time," Carlin replied, grinning slightly.

"You said that before." Hayward turned toward him. "Just what are you telling me, Carlin?"

"I'm telling you that this time, the righteous shall be rewarded. And it's the Millers of the world who will get hung out to dry."

"And just when did you acquire this gift of prophecy?"

"When I learned that our friend Beal, who you helped into the ambulance back there, is the son of one Steven X. Beal."

"Steven Beal, the state senator?" Hayward asked, eyes widening.

Carlin nodded. "He doesn't like people to know," he said. "Afraid people will think he's pulling influence to get an easy ride or something. But that crack on his head must have loosened his tongue a bit."

Hayward stood motionless a moment. Then, shaking her head, she turned back in the direction of the Great Lawn.

"Sergeant?" Carlin asked.

"Yes?"

"Why did you ask me to step away from those punks like that?"

Hayward paused. "I wanted to show them that I wasn't afraid. And that I meant business."

"Would you have?"

"Would I have what?"

"You know," Carlin gestured. "Kicked their asses back to Scarsdale, and all that."

Hayward looked at him, raising her chin slightly. "What do you think?"

"I think—" Carlin hesitated a moment. "I think you're one scary lady, Ms. Hayward."

56

As the launch sliced through the dark waters of the Hudson River, Snow suited up belowdecks, feeling the hull tremble with the muffled rumble of the big twin diesels. There was barely enough room to stand amongst the loran gear, geopositioning satellite units, sonar equipment, and arms lockers. He noted that it was a wetsuit, not the usual sealed drysuit the police team wore, and instantly regretted his suggestion to go in through the treatment plant. *Too late,* he thought, struggling with the suit. The boat lurched and he pitched forward, banging his head painfully against a bulkhead.

He rubbed his forehead with a curse. It hurt, all right. So he wasn't dreaming. He really was in a boat full of Navy SEALs, armed to the teeth, bound for God only knew what kind of mission. Fear and excitement surged through him simultaneously. This, he knew, meant a chance at redemption. Maybe his only chance. He'd make damn sure he didn't screw it up.

He adjusted the lantern visor, snugged on the last glove, and went topside. Commander Rachlin, who had gone forward and was speaking with the coxswain, turned at his approach. "Where the hell's your paint? And what took you?"

"The equipment is a little different from what I'm used to, sir."

"Well, you got from now until insertion to get used to it."

"Yes, sir."

Rachlin jerked his head toward Snow. "Donovan, get him fixed up."

Donovan came over and wordlessly began smearing black and green greasepaint across Snow's cheeks and forehead.

Rachlin motioned the rest of the team to gather round. "Now listen up," he said, unrolling a plastic map on one thigh. "We're going in via the main settling tank above the West Side Lateral. According to Snow here, it's the quickest way in." His finger traced a route on the map. "Once at the first riser, we'll follow our plotted course until we reach this place, here, where the tunnels branch. That's our rally point. Once we're in position, teams Alpha, Beta, and Gamma will each take one of these tunnels. I'll lead Alpha, and ride point. Snow and Donovan are Team Delta. They catch the milk run, staying in the rear and covering our asses. Questions?"

Snow had several, but he decided against asking any of them. His face burned from the rough strokes of Donovan's gloved hand, and the thick greasepaint smelled like rancid tallow.

The Commander nodded. "We'll go in, place the charges, and come out. Nice and simple, just like exercises at the 'phib base. The charges will seal off the lower drainage tunnels that feed into the Lateral. Another team is going down from the street, sealing access from above. Real pros, from the sound of it." The Commander made a snorting sound through his mask. "They told us to use NVDs. If you can believe that."

"NVDs?" Snow echoed.

"Night-vision devices, darlin'. But try wearing one over a wetsuit and mask." He spat over the side. "We're not afraid of the dark. And anything that wants to come take a piece of us, let them try. Still, I like to see what I'm blowin' away."

He stepped forward. "All right. Hastings, Clapton, Beecham, you catch AW duty this mission. I want one weapons carrier per team. Lorenzo, Campion, Donovan, carry the pyros. You'll be the candymen, along with myself. We've got redundant charges, so expect a heavy load. Now shoulder up."

Snow watched as the men slung automatic weapons over their shoulders. "What about me?" he heard himself asking.

Rachlin turned toward him. "I don't know. What about you?"

Snow paused. "I'd like to do something. To help, I mean."

Rachlin stared at him for a moment. Then a small smile appeared briefly on his lips. "Okay," he said. "You get to be chunk boy for this op."

"Chunk boy?" Snow asked.

"Chunk boy." The Commander nodded. "Beecham! Toss the kit over here." Rachlin caught the waterproof rubber duffel that was thrown to him, then placed it over Snow's neck. "That stays on until we reach the exit point," he muttered.

"I'll need a weapon, sir," Snow said.

"Get him something." Somebody thrust the butt of a harpoon gun into Snow's gut, and he quickly looped the strap over his shoulder. He thought he heard somebody sniggering quietly, but he ignored it. Snow had speared plenty of fish in the Sea of Cortez, but he'd never seen spears quite as long or as evil-looking as the ones that hung from the underbelly of this gun, fat explosive charges packed at their ends.

"Don't shoot any crocodiles," Donovan said. "They're endangered." It was the first time he'd spoken.

The throb of the engines grew deeper, and the boat eased up to a cement landing beneath the dark outline of the Lower Hudson Sewage Treatment Plant. Snow looked up at the enormous concrete structure with a sinking feeling. It was fully automated, supposedly state of the art, but he'd heard the facility had seen nothing but problems since going online almost five years before. He hoped to God he was right about going in through the main settling tanks.

"Think we ought to alert them that we're coming?" Snow asked.

Rachlin looked at him, faint amusement on his face. "Way ahead of you. Took care of things while you were belowdecks. They'll be expecting us."

A Jacob's ladder was thrown over the side, and the men quickly scrambled down to the landing. Snow looked around, orienting himself. He recognized the area from the Basic tour: the control room was not far off. The team followed him up a metal staircase, then past a large array of aeration and setting tanks. The smell of methane and sewage hung in the air like a mephitic fog. At the far end of the tanks, Snow stopped at a metal door, bright yellow against the monotonous gray of the facility, with painted red letters: DO NOT OPEN DOOR, ALARM WILL SOUND. Rachlin brushed Snow aside and kicked the door open, revealing a spare cement corridor blazing with white fluorescent light. A siren began, low and insistent.

"Move out," Rachlin said quietly.

Snow led them up a double flight of stairs, and onto a landing marked CONTROL. There was a set of doors on the landing, with a carded entry system set into the wall beside them. The Commander stood back, preparing to kick in the doors again. Then, reconsidering, he moved forward and nudged one with his hand. It swung open, unlocked.

Beyond was a vast room, flooded with light and full of the odor of treated sewage. Monitoring equipment and regulators lined the walls. In the center, a lone supervisor sat at the control station. He hung up the phone on his desk, his hair disheveled, blinking as if the telephone had roused him out of a sound sleep.

"Do you know who that was," he exclaimed, pointing at the phone. "Holy God, that was the Deputy Director of the—"

"Good," Rachlin replied. "Then I won't have to waste any time. We need you to shut down the main outflow propeller right now."

The man blinked at Rachlin as if seeing him for the first time. Then his gaze traveled down the line of SEALs, growing more wide-eyed as he went.

"Damn," he said almost reverently, staring at Snow's harpoon gun. "He wasn't kidding, was he?"

"Hurry up, now, darlin'," Rachlin drawled, "or we'll throw you in the tank and let your fat old carcass shut it down for us."

The man jumped to his feet, trotted over to a panel, and flipped several levers, "Five minutes is the most I can spare," he said over his shoulder as he moved toward another bank of controls. "Any longer, and everything west of Lenox Avenue will back up."

"Five minutes is all we'll need." Rachlin looked at his watch. "Get us to the settling tank."

Panting softly, the supervisor led the team back out to the landing, down one flight, and along a narrow corridor. At the far end, he opened a small access door and descended a spiral staircase of painted red metal. The staircase opened onto a small walkway that hung suspended a few feet above a foamy, roiling surface.

"You really going down in that?" the man asked, looking them over once again with the same expression of disbelief on his jowled face.

Snow looked down at the foamy, scum-laden surface, nose wrinkling involuntarily, regretting he'd been in the office that evening, and deeply regretting that he'd suggested this as an entry point. *First the Humboldt Kill, and now—*

"That's an affirmative," the Commander replied.

The man licked his lips. "You'll find the main feeder five feet below the surface, on the east side of the tank," he said. "Watch out for the propeller valve. I've turned it off, but the residual flow will still be turning the blades."

Rachlin nodded. "And the first riser is where exactly?"

"Three hundred twenty feet down the feeder," the supervisor said. "Keep to your left as the pipes divide."

"That's all we need to know," Rachlin said. "Get on upstairs, now, and fire everything back up as soon as you get there."

The man paused, still staring at the group.

"*Move!*" Rachlin barked, and the man scampered up the staircase.

Snow went first, falling backwards into the bubbling vat, followed by Donovan. When he gingerly opened his eyes, he was surprised at how clear the effluent was: thin, not treacly, and with the faintest milky cast. The others jumped in. He could feel the wetness creeping against his skin, and tried not to think about it.

Snow swam forward against the slight current. Ahead, he could see the stalled propellers of the outflow valve blocking the circular pipe beyond, the steel blades still turning slowly. He stopped and let Rachlin and the other teams catch up, until the seven SEALs were all hanging suspended beside them. Rachlin pointed to Snow, then made an exaggerated count with his fingers. At three, Snow and Donovan darted through the propellers. Alpha Team was next, then Beta, then Gamma.

Snow found himself within a massive stainless steel pipe, leading on into vast, dark depths.

The same creeping terror he'd felt in the mud of Humboldt Kill threatened to bubble once again to the surface, but he fought it back, slowing his breathing, mentally counting his heartbeats. No panic, not this time.

Rachlin and his partner swam through the blades, then Rachlin made a sharp gesture to Snow to continue. He quickly moved ahead, leading the other teams down the tunnel. Behind him, Snow heard the whine of a turbine, and the propeller began to pick up speed. The current around him quickened noticeably. No going back now, even if he wanted to.

The tunnel angled downward, forking once, then twice. Snow kept to the left each time. After what seemed like an eternity of swimming, the squad stopped at last beside the first vent riser, a narrow steel shaft barely wider than his shoulders. Rachlin indicated that he would take the lead from here. Following the SEALs, Snow swam downward, awash in bubbles from the preceding air tanks. After several yards, the Commander stopped the descent, then led them into a horizontal tube even narrower than the riser. Snow squeezed in behind Donovan, breathing hard as his tanks bounced from wall to wall in time to the motion of his swimming.

Suddenly, gleaming steel gave way to old iron pipe, covered with a spongy coating of rust. The passage of the previous divers swirled the effluent an opaque orange against Snow's mask. He struggled forward, feeling the reassuring turbulence from Donovan's unseen fins. They stopped briefly while Rachlin consulted his map with the aid of a submersible penlight. Then two more bends, another short rise, and Snow felt the surface of the water break around his head. They were in a huge ancient passageway, perhaps sixteen feet in diameter and full to half its depth in sluggishly flowing liquid. The Main Lateral.

"Snow and Donovan to the rear," came the muffled voice of Rachlin. "Stay on the surface but keep breathing tank air. This atmosphere's likely to be loaded with methane. Proceed in standard formation." The Commander quickly consulted a plastic map hooked to his suit, and then started forward.

The group spread out, swimming along the surface, tracing a circuitous route through the system of pipes. Snow prided himself on his ability as a distance swimmer, but he felt distinctly outclassed by the seven men moving easily through the water ahead of him.

The passageway opened at last into a large pentagonal chamber, yellow stalactites dripping water from the vaulted ceiling. Snow stared with amazement at a massive iron chain hanging from a metal eye cleat set in the vault's apex. A trickle of water ran down the chain, off a great rusted hook at its end, and dribbled into the pool. There was a cement landing streaked with rust. Three large, dry tunnels branched off from the walls of the chamber.

"Three Points," Rachlin said. "We'll use this as our rally base. The op should be a cakewalk, but we'll do it by the book. Follow strict challenge-and-reply procedures: proper response will be three even numbers. The rules of engagement are simple. Identify yourself, but shoot to kill any threat or hindrance to your work. Extraction point will be the One Hundred Twenty-fifth Street Canal." The Commander looked around. "All right, gentlemen, let's earn our MREs."

57

For a dreadful moment Margo thought they were under attack, and she turned instinctively, raising her weapon to the ready position, strangely reluctant to look at the thing Pendergast was struggling with. There was a whispered curse from D'Agosta. Squinting through the still-unfamiliar goggles, Margo realized Pendergast was grappling with a person, perhaps a homeless man who had evaded the police roust. He certainly looked the part: wet, caked in mud, apparently bleeding from some unseen wound.

"Shut off the light," Pendergast hissed. D'Agosta's flashlight beam struck her goggles, then winked out. The glowing vista seesawed violently as her goggles tried to compensate, corning back into focus as they stabilized. She drew her breath in sharply. There was something about the lanky features, the tousled hair, that was irresistibly familiar.

"Bill?" she asked in disbelief.

Pendergast had the man on the ground, hugging him almost protectively, murmuring words into one ear. After a moment, the man stopped struggling and went limp. Pendergast released him gently and stood up. Margo leaned in for a closer look. It was Smithback, all right.

"Give him a minute," Pendergast said.

"I don't believe it," D'Agosta growled. "What, you think he followed us down here?"

Pendergast shook his head. "No. Nobody followed us." He looked around at the confluence of tunnels above and below. "This is the Bottleneck, where all descending tunnels of the Central Park quadrant meet. He was being chased, apparently, and his path intersected ours. The question is, chased by whom? Or what?" He unshipped his flamethrower and glanced at D'Agosta. "You'd better be ready with the flash, Vincent."

Suddenly, Smithback lunged upwards, then fell back onto the mass of pipes and twenty-four-inch mains that made up the floor of the Bottleneck.

"They killed Duffy!" he cried. "Who are you? Help me, I can't see!"

Pocketing her weapon, Margo came forward and knelt at his side. The trip down from the subway tunnel—through noisome corridors and dark, echoing galleries that seemed incredibly out of place dozens of stories beneath Manhattan—had been like an endless dark dream. Seeing her friend race out of the darkness, petrified with fear and shock, only increased her sense of unreality.

"Bill," she said soothingly. "It's okay. It's Margo. Please keep quiet. We don't dare use lights, and there isn't a spare set of goggles. But we'll help you along."

Smithback blinked in her direction, pupils wide. "I want to get out of here!" he cried suddenly, struggling to his feet.

"What?" D'Agosta said sarcastically. "And miss your story?"

"You can't go back alone," Pendergast said, putting a restraining arm on his shoulder.

The struggle seemed to have exhausted Smithback, and he sagged forward. "What are you doing here?" he asked at last.

"I might ask you the same question," Pendergast replied. "Mephisto is leading us to the Astor Tunnels—the Devil's Attic.

There was a plan to drain the Reservoir and flood the creatures out."

"Captain Waxie's plan," D'Agosta added.

"But the Reservoir is full of the Mbwun lily. That's where the creatures were growing it. And we can't allow the plants to reach the open ocean. It's too late to stop the water dump, so a SEAL team was sent in from the river to seal the lowest spillway tunnels below. We're going to seal off the spaces *above* the Astor Tunnels to prevent any spillages. We'll bottle up the flow, keep it from escaping down into the river. If we succeed, it will back up to the Bottleneck here, but nowhere else."

Smithback remained unspeaking, his head bowed.

"We're well armed, and fully prepared for whatever's down there. We have maps. You'll be safer with us. Do you understand, William?"

Margo watched as Pendergast's mellifluous delivery worked its calming effect. Smithback's breathing seemed to slow, and finally he nodded almost imperceptibly.

"So what were *you* up to, anyway?" D'Agosta asked.

Pendergast made a restraining motion with one hand, but Smithback looked in the direction of the Lieutenant. "I followed Captain Waxie and a group of policemen underneath the Reservoir," he said quietly. "They were trying to shut off some valves. But they'd been sabotaged, or something. Then—" He stopped abruptly. "Then *they* came."

"Bill, don't," Margo interjected.

"I ran away," Smithback said, swallowing hard. "Duffy and I ran away. But they caught him in the gauging station. They—"

"That's enough," said Pendergast quietly. There was a silence. "Sabotage, did you say?"

Smithback nodded. "I heard Duffy say that somebody had been messing with the valves."

"That is troublesome. Troublesome indeed." There was a look on Pendergast's face that Margo had not seen before. "We'd better continue," he said, shouldering the flamethrower again.

"This Bottleneck is a perfect place for an ambush." He glanced around the dark tunnel. "Mephisto?" he whispered.

There was a stirring in the darkness, then Mephisto came forward, arms folded across his chest, a wide smirk on his whiskered lips.

"I was just enjoying this touching reunion," he said, in his silky hiss. "Now the merry band of adventurers is complete. Ho, scriblerian! I see you've descended farther than you dared venture on our first meeting. Grows on you, doesn't it?"

"Not especially," Smithback replied in a low voice.

"How nice, at least, to have one's own Boswell at hand." In the artificial light of the goggles, it seemed to Margo that Mephisto's eyes glittered gold and crimson as they surveyed the group. "Will you compose an epic poem on the event? The Mephistiad. In heroic couplets, please. That's assuming you live to tell the tale. I wonder which of us will survive, and which will leave their whitened bones to lie here, forever, in the tunnels beneath Manhattan?"

"Let's move on," Pendergast said.

"I see. *Whitey* here feels there has been enough talk. Perhaps he fears it will be *his* bones left to the rats."

"We need to set several series of charges directly below the Bottleneck," Pendergast said smoothly. "If we stand here listening to your empty posturing, we won't have time to exit before the Reservoir dumps. Then it will be your bones, as well as mine, that are left for the rats."

"Very well, very well!" Mephisto said. "Don't chafe." He turned and began clambering down a large, dark tube.

"No," Smithback said.

D'Agosta took a step toward the journalist. "Come on. I'll take your hand."

The vertical tube ended in a high-ceilinged tunnel, and they waited in the darkness while Pendergast set several sets of charges, then motioned them on. A few hundred yards down the tunnel, they arrived at a walkway that crossed a few feet above the level of the water. Margo felt grateful; the ankle-deep stream had been cold and foul.

"Well!" whispered Mephisto, climbing on the walkway. "Perhaps the Mayor of Grant's Tomb can finally dry out his wingtips."

"Perhaps the Hobo King can finally shut up," D'Agosta growled.

A delighted hiss came from Mephisto. "Hobo King. Charming. Perhaps I should go hunting track rabbits and leave you to do your own spelunking."

D'Agosta stiffened but held his tongue, and Mephisto led the way across the walkway into a crawl space beyond. Margo heard the roar of falling water in the distance, and soon the passage ended at a narrow waterfall. A narrow iron ladder, almost concealed by the ordure of many decades, descended into a vertical tunnel at the base of the falls.

They passed through the tunnel one at a time, dropping to an irregular bedrock floor beneath the confluence of two seventy-two-inch mains. The narrow boreholes of explosive drills lined the walls like the work of disorderly termites.

"*Nous sommes arrivés,*" said Mephisto, and for the first time Margo thought she could detect nervousness behind the bluster. "The Devil's Attic is directly beneath us."

Motioning them to stay put, Pendergast checked his maps and then vanished noiselessly into the ancient tunnel. As the seconds turned to minutes, Margo found herself ready to jump at every drop of water from the mossy ceiling, at every stifled sneeze or restless stirring. Once again, she questioned her own motives for coming along. It was becoming increasingly hard to ignore the fact that she was hundreds of feet underground, in an obscure and long-forgotten warren of service passageways, railroad tunnels, and other spaces even more obscure, with a lurking foe that at any moment might...

There was a movement in the dark beside her. "Dear Dr. Green," came the silky hiss of Mephisto. "I'm sorry you decided to join our little walkabout. But since you're here, maybe you can do me a favor. Please understand I have every intention of letting your friends here take all the risk. But if something unpleasant should happen, maybe you could deliver something for me." Margo felt a small envelope being thrust into her hand. Curiously, she began to lift it toward her goggles.

"No!" said Mephisto, catching her hand and thrusting it into her own pocket. "Plenty of time for that later. If necessary."

"Why me?" Margo asked.

"Who else?" came the hiss. "That slippery G-man, Pendergast? Or maybe the large economy model of our city's finest, standing over there? Or Smithback, the yellow journalist?"

There was a rapid footfall in the darkness, then Pendergast was back within the dim circle of their flashlights. "Excellent," he said as Mephisto melted from her side. "Up ahead is the catwalk where I made my own descent. The charges under the Bottleneck should take care of the main Reservoir flow to the south. Now we'll set the rest of the charges to block off any spillage from feeders beneath the north end of the Park." The matter-of-fact tone of his voice was more appropriate for a croquet party, Margo thought, than this nightmare stalk. But she was grateful for it.

Pendergast grasped the handle of the flamethrower, undipped the nozzle guard, and pressed the primer a few times. "I'll go first," he said. "Then Mephisto. I trust your instincts; let me know if you sense anything wrong or out of place."

"*Being* here is out of place," Mephisto said. "Ever since the Wrinklers arrived, this has been shunned ground."

"Margo, you'll be next," Pendergast continued. "Take care of Smithback. Vincent, I'd like you to cover the rear. There might be a conflict."

"Right," D'Agosta said.

"I'd like to help," Margo heard Smithback say softly.

Pendergast looked at him.

"I'm useless without a weapon," the writer explained, his voice unsteady but determined.

"Can you handle a gun?" Pendergast asked.

"Used to shoot skeet with a 16-gauge," Smithback said.

D'Agosta stifled a laugh. Pendergast pursed his lips a moment, as if calculating something. Then he unslung the other weapon from his shoulder and passed it over. "This is an M-79. It fires 40-millimeter high-explosive rounds. Be sure you've got a kill zone of at least one hundred feet before you use it. D'Agosta can describe to you how to reload as we go. I expect if action starts, there will be plenty of light for you to see with."

Smithback nodded.

"The thought of a journalist with a grenade launcher makes me very nervous," came D'Agosta's voice out of the darkness.

"We'll set the charges, then leave," Pendergast said. "Fire only as a last resort; the sound will bring the entire nest down upon us. Vincent, set the flash unit to strobe, and use it at the first sign of trouble. We'll blind them first, then fire. Be sure to remove your goggles first—the flash unit will overload them. We know they hate light, so once they know we're here, let's use it to our advantage." He turned. "Margo, just how sure are you about the vitamin D?"

"One hundred percent sure," she answered immediately. Then she paused. "Well, ninety-five percent, anyway."

"I see," the FBI agent replied. "Well, if there's a confrontation, you'd better use your pistol first."

Pendergast took a final look around, then began cautiously leading the group down the ancient tunnel. Margo could see D'Agosta leading the journalist forward, gripping his arm tightly. After about fifty yards, Pendergast raised his hand. One by one, they all stopped. Very slowly, he brought a warning finger to his lips. Reaching into a pocket of his jacket, he removed a lighter and held it close to the nozzle of the flamethrower. There was a puff, a flash of light, and a low hiss. A tiny blue pilot flame played around the end of the copper nozzle.

"Smores, anyone?" Mephisto murmured.

Margo breathed through her nose, struggling to stay calm. The air was heavy with the combined reek of methane and ammonia. And overlying them both was a faint goatish odor she knew only too well.

58

Snow leaned his aching back against the brick wall of the landing. Easing the fins from his feet, he laid them carefully along the wall, where the weights and tanks were being placed in neat rows. He thought about removing the rubber duffel at his side, then remembered what the Commander had said about not parting with it until the mission was over. The landing felt slimy beneath his neoprene booties. He removed his mouthpiece, wincing at the smell of the ambient air. His eyes stung, and he blinked several times. *Better get adjusted,* he thought, taking a hit of oxygen. From this point on, he knew, it would be on foot.

Around him, the SEALs were removing their masks and tanks, opening waterproof packs, readying gear. Commander Rachlin snapped on a flare and jammed it into a crack in the brick wall. It hissed and sputtered quietly, bathing the room in fitful red light. "Ready your comm sets. Emergency use only, on the private frequency. I want noise discipline enforced at all times. Remember, each team has a candyman carrying redundant charges. If for any reason one of the three forward teams is unable to carry out their mission, the other teams will cover."

He took another glance at his waterproof map, then rolled it tight and snugged it into the curve of his knife strap. "Delta," he said, speaking to Donovan, "you're failsafe. You hang back here at the rally point, provide loose cover to the rear. If any team fails in its objective, you fill in." He looked around. "Beta, take that tunnel. Gamma, the far tunnel. They'll end in vertical shaftways at about five hundred meters. That's where you'll place your charges. We meet back here no later than twenty-three-twenty hours. Any later, and we're not leaving."

Rachlin looked hard at Snow. "You all right, darlin'?"

Snow nodded.

The Commander nodded. "Let's go. Beecham, you're with me."

Snow watched the three teams disappear into the darkness, shadows bobbing against glistening walls, their booties squelching in the thick muck. The comm set felt awkward and foreign on his head. As the sounds faded away, swallowed by the darkness of the outflow tunnels, he felt a gathering sense of menace.

Donovan was exploring the cavern, examining the shorings and aged bricks. In a few minutes, he stepped noiselessly back toward the equipment cache, ghostly in the light of the flare.

"Smells like shit down here," he said at last, squatting down beside Snow.

Snow didn't bother to make the obvious reply.

"Not bad swimming, for a civ," the SEAL continued, adjusting his Webb belt. Apparently, Snow's performance in the tunnels had convinced Donovan it wouldn't be beneath his dignity to speak with him. "You're the guy that pulled the two bodies out of the Cloaca, aren't you?"

"Yeah," Snow replied defensively. He wondered what Donovan had heard.

"Crazy damn job, looking for dead bodies." Donovan laughed.

No crazier than killing Vietcong or packing explosives under some poor bastard's hull, Snow thought. Aloud, he said, "We don't just look for dead bodies. That day, we were actually looking for a cache of heroin somebody'd thrown off a bridge."

"Heroin, huh? Must've been some pretty messed-up fish down there for a while."

Snow ventured a laugh, but even to himself it sounded forced and awkward. *What the hell's the matter with you? Be cool, like Donovan.* "I'll bet the Cloaca hasn't seen a live fish for two hundred years."

"Got a point there," Donovan said, heaving himself to his feet again. "Man, I don't envy you. I'd rather do a week of PT than swim five minutes in this muck."

Snow saw the SEAL look at his harpoon gun with a smirk. "You'd best have a real weapon, just in case we have to go in." Donovan rummaged in one of the kit bags and pulled out a machine gun with a cruel-looking metal tube fixed to the underside of its barrel. "Ever fire an M-16 before?" he asked.

"The Tactical guys let us try some on the range during the Academy graduation picnic," Snow said.

A look of incredulity mixed with amusement crossed Donovan's features. "Is that right. The Academy graduation picnic. And I'll bet your mother made you a sack lunch." He tossed the rifle toward Snow, then reached into the bag and passed over some magazine pouches. "Those are 30-round clips. They'll empty in less then two seconds on full automatic, so keep your trigger finger light. Not exactly new technology, but tried and true." He passed over another pouch. "That forward trigger is for the XM-148. The grenade launcher attachment. Here are two 40-millimeter canister rounds, just in case you get ambitious."

"Donovan?" Snow had to ask. "What's a chunk boy?"

A long slow grin spread across the SEAL's painted face. "No harm in telling, I guess. It's the unlucky stiff who catches hi-mag duty for the operation."

"Hi-mag duty?" Snow was as much in the dark as he'd been before.

"White magnesium flares. Mandatory issue for all night ops, even stealth runs like this. Stupid-ass regulation, but that's the way it is. They're ultra, ultra bright. Twist off the top to arm the detonator, toss one a safe distance, and you've got half a million candlepower on impact. But they're not too stable, if you know what I mean. All it takes is one bullet in that bag, even something small like a .22, and boom! Chunk boy. If you know what I mean." He chuckled, then wandered off again.

Snow shifted position, trying to hold the bag as far from his torso as possible. Except for the fitful sputtering of the flare, there was silence for several minutes. Then Snow heard Donovan's low chuckle again. "Man, take a look at this! Can you believe some crazy bastard's been wandering around here? In bare feet, no less."

Putting the rifle aside, Snow stood up and came over for a look. A set of bare footprints tracked through the mud. Fresh, too: the mud around the edges was damp, not dry.

"Big mother," Donovan murmured. "Must be a size fourteen triple-E, at least." He laughed again.

Snow stared at the strangely broad footprint, the feeling of menace increasing. As Donovan's laughter subsided, Snow heard a distant rumble. "What was that?" he asked.

"What?" Donovan asked, kneeling and adjusting his H-harness.

"Isn't it too early to set off the charges?" Snow asked.

"I didn't hear anything."

"I did." Suddenly, Snow's heart was hammering in his rib-cage.

Donovan listened, but there was only silence. "Chill, sport," he said. "You're starting to hear things."

"I think we should check it with the Patrol Leader."

Donovan shook his head. "Yeah, and piss him off good." He glanced at his watch. "Strict noise discipline, remember? The op site isn't even a click away from here. They'll be back in ten minutes. Then we can get the hell out of this toilet." He spat fervently into the stagnant mud.

The flare guttered and died, plunging the vault into darkness.

"Shit," Donovan muttered. "Snow, hand me another from that ditty bag near your feet."

There was another rumble, which slowly resolved into the faint muffled staccato of gunfire. It seemed to shiver through the ancient walls, rising and falling like a distant storm.

In the dark, Snow could hear Donovan rise quickly to his feet, finger punching the comm set. "Team Alpha, Patrol Leader, do you read?" he hissed.

A mass of static came crackling over the frequency.

There was a rolling shudder in the ground. "That was a damn grenade," Donovan said. "Alpha! Beta! Come in!"

The ground shuddered again.

"Snow, get your weapon." Snow heard the long rattle of a well-oiled bolt being drawn back. "What a cluster-hump this is turning into. Alpha, do you *read*?"

"Five by five." Rachlin's voice came crackling over the comm set. "We've lost communications with Gamma. Stand by."

"Roger that," Donovan said.

There was a brief, tense silence, then the Commander's voice returned.

"Delta, Gamma must-have run into difficulties setting their charges. Handle the redundancy. We've already set our charges and will check Beta's status."

"Aye-aye." A light snapped on, and Donovan looked at Snow. "Let's move," he said. "We'll have to set Gamma's charges." Twisting the light into his shoulder snap, he set off at a lope, running low, his rifle held perpendicular to his chest. Taking a deep breath, Snow followed him into the tunnel. Glancing down, he noticed footprints in the flickering illumination—more prints here, crossing and crisscrossing in a crazed welter, too numerous to pick out the SEAL booties of Gamma team. He swallowed hard.

Within minutes, Donovan slowed at what looked like an old siding, surrounded by a mass of pylons. "Shouldn't be much farther," he muttered, switching off his light and listening carefully.

"Where are they?" Snow heard himself asking. He wasn't surprised when Donovan didn't bother to answer.

"We're back at the rally point," came the voice of Rachlin in his comm set. "I repeat: charges successfully set. Going to check on Beta now."

"Come on," Donovan said, moving forward again. Suddenly, he stopped.

"You smell that?" he whispered.

Snow opened his mouth, then closed it again as the stench hit him. He turned away instinctively. It was an overripe, earthy smell, its pungency overwhelming the stink of the drainage tunnel. And there was something else: the strangely sweet smell of a butcher's shop.

Donovan shook his head as if to clear it, then tensed to move forward again. At that moment, the comm unit buzzed in Snow's ear. There was a hiss, then Rachlin's voice suddenly came through: "... attack. Drop flares..."

Snow wondered if he'd heard right. Rachlin had spoken with abnormal calmness. Then there was a burst of static from the comm unit, and a rattle that sounded like gunfire.

"Alpha!" Donovan yelled. "You reading? Over."

"That's a rog," came Rachlin's voice. "We're under attack. Couldn't reach Beta. We're setting their charges now. Beecham, *there*!" There was a whump, then a terrific explosion. Emerging from the electronic snow were unintelligible sounds: shouting, perhaps a scream, yet somehow too deep and hoarse to be human. Again, the low rumble of gunfire came through the walls.

"Delta..." came Rachlin's voice over the roar of static, "... surrounded..."

"Surrounded?" Donovan shouted. "Surrounded by what? You need backup?"

There was more gunfire, then a massive roar.

"Alpha!" Donovan called. "Do you need backup?"

"My God, so many... Beecham, what the hell is that..." Rachlin's voice died in a roar of static. All at once, the sound stopped, and Snow—rooted in place in the close darkness—thought that perhaps his comm unit had gone dead. Then it emitted a hideous, coughing scream, so loud it seemed to come from beside him, followed by the rubbery noise of neoprene being torn.

"Alpha, come in!" Donovan turned to Snow. "This channel's still live. Commander, this is Delta, reply!"

There was a burble of static, followed by what to Snow seemed the sound of sucking mud, and then more static.

Donovan adjusted his comm unit unsuccessfully. He glanced at Snow. "Come on," he said, readying his weapon.

"Where?" Snow asked, shock and horror turning his mouth to sandpaper.

"We still have to set Gamma's charges."

"Are you crazy?" Snow whispered fiercely. "Didn't you hear that? We've got to get out of here *now*."

Donovan turned to look at him, his face hard. "We set Gamma team's charges, my friend." His voice was quiet, but it held unshakable determination, perhaps even an implicit threat. "We finish the op."

Snow swallowed. "But what about the Commander?"

Donovan was still looking at him. "First, we finish the op," he said.

Snow realized there-was no room for argument. Gripping the M-16 tightly, he followed the SEAL into the darkness. He could make out a fitful illumination ahead of them: light from around a bend in the tunnel, dancing off the brickwork of the far wall.

"Keep your weapon at the ready," came the murmured warning.

Snow moved cautiously around the curve, then stopped short. Ahead of him, the tunnel came to a sudden end. Iron rungs in the far wall led to the mouth of a large pipe set in the ceiling.

"Oh, Christ," Donovan groaned.

A single flare, sizzling in the muck of a far corner, cast a dim light over the scene. Snow looked around wildly, taking in the frightful details. The walls of the tunnel were scarred and raked with bullet marks. A deep bite had been taken out of one wall, its edges burned and sooty. Two dark forms lay sprawled about the mud beside the flare, packs and weapons strewn beside them in wild disarray. Feathers of cordite drifted through the dead air.

Donovan had already leapt toward the closest of the figures, as if to rouse it. Then he stepped back again quickly, and Snow caught a glimpse of a neoprene suit torn from neck to waist, a bloody stump where the head should have been.

"Campion, too," Donovan said grimly, looking at the other SEAL. "Jesus, what would do this?"

Snow shut his eyes a moment, taking short choppy breaths, trying to keep a hold on the thin edge of his control.

"Whoever they are, they must have gone up that way," Donovan said, indicating the pipe above their heads. "Snow, grab that magazine pouch."

Doing as he was told, Snow leaned forward and snatched the pouch. It almost slipped out of his hands, and looking down he saw it was slick with blood and matter.

"I'll set the charges here," Donovan said, pulling bricks of C-4 out of his own haversack. "Cover our exit."

Snow raised his weapon and turned his back on the SEAL, staring down toward the bend in the tunnel, flickering crazily in and out of sight in the lambent glow of the flare. His comm unit hissed briefly with the sound of static—or was it the sound of something heavy, dragging through the mud? Was that a soft, moist gibbering beneath the electrical cracklings and spittings?

The unit dropped into silence again. From the corner of his eye, he saw Donovan plunging the timer into the explosive, punching up a time. "Twenty-three fifty-five," he said. "That gives us almost half an hour to find the PL and get the hell out of here." He stooped, pulling the tags from the headless necks of his fallen comrades. "Move out," he said, picking up his weapon and shoving the dog tags inside his rubber vest.

As they began to move forward again, Snow heard a sudden scrabbling from behind, and a sound like a cough. He turned to see the forms of several figures clambering down from the pipe and dropping into the muck by the fallen SEALs. Snow saw, with a sense of eerie unreality, that they were cloaked and hooded.

"Let's go!" Donovan cried, racing toward the bend in the tunnel.

Snow followed him, panic driving his legs. They clattered down the ancient brick passage, racing from the horrible scene. As they rounded the curve, Donovan slipped in the mud and fell, tumbling head over heels in the murky gloom.

"Make a stand!" he shouted, grabbing for his weapon and snapping on a flare at the same time.

Snow turned to see the figures heading toward them, running low with a kind of sure-footedness. The brilliant flare light seemed to give them a momentary pause. Then they surged forward. There was something bestial about their scuttling that turned his blood to ice. His index finger eased forward, feeling for the trigger guard. A huge roar sounded beside him, and he realized Donovan had fired his grenade launcher. There was a flash of light, then the tunnel shook with the concussion. The weapon jerked and bucked in his hands and Snow realized that he was firing his own M-16 wildly, scattering bullets across the tunnel before them. He quickly took his finger off the trigger. Another figure rounded the bend, emerging from the smoke of the grenade into Snow's field of fire. He aimed and touched the trigger. Its head jerked back, and for a split second Snow had the image of an impossibly wrinkled and knobby face, features hidden within great folds of skin. Then there was another roar, and the horror disappeared in the flame and smoke of Donovan's grenade.

His gun was firing on an empty clip. Snow released his finger, ejected the clip, dug into his pocket for another, and slammed it home. They waited, poised to fire again, as the echoes gradually faded. No more figures came loping out of the smoke and the darkness.

Donovan took a deep breath. "Back to the rally point," he said.

They turned back down the tunnel, Donovan reaching up to snap on his flashlight. A thin red beam shot into the murk ahead of them. Snow followed, breathing hard. Ahead lay Three Points, and their gear, and the way out. He found he was thinking from moment to moment now, concentrating only on getting out, getting to the surface, because anything else would mean thinking of the horrors that had scuttled out toward them, and to think of those would mean...

He suddenly ploughed into Donovan's back. Staggering for a moment, he glanced around, trying to determine what had caused the SEAL to stop so suddenly.

Then he saw, in the beam of Donovan's light, a group of the creatures *ahead* of them: ten, perhaps a dozen, standing motionless in the thick atmosphere of the outflow tunnel. Several of them were holding things, things that dangled by what looked to Snow like dense threads. He peered more closely, in mingled fascination and horror. Then he looked away quickly.

"Mother of God," he breathed. "What do we do now?"

"We blow our way out," Donovan said quietly, raising his weapon.

59

Margo took a deep drag from the oxygen mask, then passed it to Smithback. The oxygen cleared her head immediately, and she glanced around. At the head of the group, Pendergast was placing bricks of plastic explosive around the base of an open hatchway. Each time he pulled another charge from his pack and dropped it in place, clouds of dust and fungus spore billowed up from the ground, obscuring his face momentarily. Behind her stood D'Agosta, weapon at the ready. Mephisto stood to one side, silent and motionless, his eyes red embers in the dark.

Pendergast shoved the detonators into the C-4, then set the time carefully, checking it against his own Patek Philippe. Then he retrieved his pack and rose silently, signaling it was time to move on to the next position. From the circles of his night-vision goggles to the base of his chin, Pendergast was a mask of light gray dust. His normally immaculate black suit was torn and muddied. Under other circumstances, he would have looked ridiculous. But Margo was in no mood to laugh.

The air was so bad she realized she had placed a hand protectively over her nose and mouth. She gave up and took another pull from the mask.

"Don't Bogart that oxygen," Smithback whispered. He smiled weakly, but his eyes remained grim and distant.

They moved down the narrow corridor, Margo now helping Smithback through the darkness. Huge iron rivets, spaced about ten feet apart, hung from the ceiling. After a couple of minutes, they stopped again while Pendergast consulted his plans, then took the charges from Margo's pack and placed them in a niche near the roof.

"Very good," he said. "One more series and we can head for the surface. We'll need to move quickly."

He started down the passage, then stopped abruptly.

"What is it?" Margo whispered, but Pendergast held up his hand for silence.

"Do you hear that?" he asked at last in a low tone.

Margo listened, but could hear nothing. The close, fetid atmosphere was like cotton wool, muffling all sound. But now she heard something: a dull thump, then another, like rolling thunder far beneath their feet.

"What is that?" she asked.

"I'm not sure," Pendergast murmured.

"It's not the SEALs, setting off their explosions?"

Pendergast shook his head. "Doesn't sound powerful enough to be plastique. Besides, it's too early." He listened a moment, frowning, then motioned them forward again. Margo followed close behind, leading Smithback as the passage rose, then fell, tracing a crazy course through the bedrock. She found herself wondering who could have constructed this passage, perhaps three dozen stories beneath the streets of Manhattan. She saw herself as in a vision, walking along Park Avenue, but the road appeared as just a thin skin of asphalt, covering a vast network of shafts, tunnels, galleries, and corridors, plunging deep into the earth, crawling like a wasp's nest with the activity of...

She gave her head a vicious shake and took another hit of the oxygen. As her thoughts cleared again, she realized that the muffled sound was still coming from somewhere beneath her feet. Now, however, it was different: it had a cadence, like the sound of a throbbing engine, rising and falling and rising again.

Pendergast stopped again. "Nobody speak above a whisper. Understood? Vincent, ready the flash."

Ahead of them, the tunnel ended in a large sheet of iron punctuated with more rivets. A single door stood open in the middle of the metal wall, and Pendergast glided through, flamethrower at the ready. The flaming tip darted from side to side, leaving a scribble of glowing tracks on Margo's goggles. In a moment, he turned and motioned the group to follow him.

As she stepped carefully into the enclosed space, Margo realized that the sound beneath her feet was the beating of drums, mingled with what sounded like a low, murmuring chant.

D'Agosta jostled her from behind as he stepped into the compartment, and she jumped forward with a sharp intake of air. She could see ancient brass levers and gears lining one wall, their broken dials encrusted with verdigris and dirt. A massive winch and several rusted generators stood in the far corner.

Pendergast moved swiftly to the center of the room and knelt by a large metal plate. "This was the central switching room for the Astor Tunnels. If I'm correct, we're directly above the Crystal Pavilion. It was the private waiting room below the old Knickerbocker Hotel. We should be able to see into the Pavilion below."

He waited until an absolute silence had descended on the group, then he slipped the corroded brackets from the plate and slid it carefully to one side. As Margo watched, a flickering light came streaming up, and the goatish odor—the old, familiar scent of nightmare—grew stronger. The sound of drumming and muffled chanting swelled. Pendergast peered down, the lambent glow from the Crystal Pavilion moving fitfully across his face. He stared for a long time, then stepped back slowly. "Vincent," he said, "I think perhaps you should take a look."

D'Agosta stepped forward, tilted up his goggles, and peered into the hole. Margo could see beads of sweat popping out on his brow in the faint light, and his hand unconsciously settled on the butt of his gun. He stepped back wordlessly.

Then Margo felt Smithback push himself forward. He stared, breathing loudly through his nose, hardly seeming to blink.

"Ah, the scriblerian in heat," whispered Mephisto sarcastically.

But Smithback did not look to Margo as if he was enjoying the view. His hands began to shake, first slightly, then almost uncontrollably. He allowed D'Agosta to pull him away from the viewplate, a look of horror frozen on his face.

Pendergast gestured to Margo. "Dr. Green, I'd like your opinion," he whispered.

She knelt by the hole, lifted her goggles, and peered down into the cavernous space. For a moment her mind couldn't quite grasp the image that was spread out beneath her. She found herself looking down through the remains of a shattered chandelier into the center of the vast space. She could make out the ruins of what had once been a room of great elegance: Doric columns, giant murals, and tattered velvet draperies contrasted with the mud and filth that coated the walls. Directly beneath her, in between the cracked candelabra arms and dangling crystals, she could make out the hut of skulls that Pendergast had described. A least a hundred hooded figures stamped and shuffled in front of the hut, swaying in ragged lines, murmuring a toneless, unintelligible chant. In the distance, the monotonous tattoo drummed on as more figures streamed in, taking their places, picking up the chant. Margo stared, blinked, stared again in mingled fascination and horror. There could be no doubt: these were the Wrinklers.

"It seems like some kind of ritual," she whispered.

"Indeed," Pendergast replied from the darkness beside her. "No doubt this is the other reason that people were never killed on the nights of the full moon. The ritual, whatever it is, is still in place. The question is, who or what is leading it, now that Kawakita has been killed?"

"It's quite possible there was some kind of coup d'état," Margo said. "In primitive societies, the shaman was often killed and replaced by a rival shaman, usually a dominant figure from within the group." She watched, intrigued despite the great fear and loathing she felt. "My God. If only Frock could see this."

"Yes," Pendergast replied. "If one of these creatures took Kawakita's place, killing him in the process, that could explain why the murders have grown more numerous and more vicious."

"Look at how they walk," Margo whispered. "Almost as if they were bowlegged. Could be incipient scurvy. If they can't take vitamin D into their systems, that would be a result."

Suddenly, there was a commotion, a chorus of guttural sound beyond Margo's field of vision. The group of Wrinklers shuffled apart. There was a low series of calls, and then Margo saw a figure, cloaked and hooded like the rest, being carried slowly into view in a sedan chair made of bone and twisted leather. As she watched, the procession approached the hut, incorporeal in the flickering light. The sedan chair was carried inside, and the swelling of the chant increased, reverberating through the chamber.

"Looks like the shaman's arrived," she said breathlessly. "The ceremony, whatever it is, could start at any moment."

"Hadn't we better get moving?" she heard D'Agosta mutter. "I hate to spoil this *National Geographic* moment, but there's about thirty pounds of high explosive down the hall, just waiting to go off."

"That's correct," Pendergast said. "And one last charge to set." He placed his hand on Margo's arm. "We must get moving, Dr. Green."

"Just a minute, please," she hissed. There was a sudden stir in the crowd below, and perhaps a dozen cloaked figures came into view, heading directly for the hut. At the entrance they knelt, arranging several small black objects in a semicircle. The chanting continued as a figure stepped out of the hut, bearing two burning torches.

Margo looked closer, trying to determine what the black things were. There were six of them, and from her vantage point, they looked like irregularly shaped rubber balls. Obviously, they were an integral part of the ceremony. The Chudzi tribe of Natal, she remembered, had used round stones, painted white and red, to symbolize the daily cycle of—

Then one of the figures tugged at the nearest object, the black rubber cowl sloughed away, and Margo took an instinctive step backward, smothering a groan of dismay.

Pendergast quickly moved to the opening and stared downwards for a long moment. Then he stood up and stepped away. "We've lost the SEAL team," he said.

Mephisto came forward, glancing down into the flickering space, his long tangle of beard given a Mephisthophelean tinge by the ruddy glow. "Now dearies, don't forget it's dangerous to swim after a heavy meal," he muttered to them.

"You think they set their charges before...?" D'Agosta's voice trailed off in the darkness.

"We'll just have to hope they did," Pendergast murmured, sliding the cover back into position. "Let's set the last charge and leave while there's still time. Keep in position. Remember, we're practically in their nest now. Exercise hypervigilance."

"Hypervigilance." Mephisto snorted.

Pendergast gazed toward the homeless leader in mild reproof. "We'll discuss your low opinion of me—and my own opinion of your taste in haute cuisine—some other time," he said, turning toward the exit.

They left through a passage on the far side of the housing and moved quickly along the passageway. After traveling about a hundred yards, Pendergast stopped short at a spot where a ragged-walled tunnel came up from below to join the main passageway. The drumming could be heard distinctly, issuing up from the narrow tube.

"Odd," the FBI agent said, gazing at the intersecting tunnel. "This access route isn't marked on my map. Well, it won't matter; the last charge should bring down this entire structure of drifts, in any case."

They moved forward again, arriving in a few minutes at the entrance to what looked like an old maintenance area. Massive rusted wheels were stacked against one wall, along with what looked to Margo like various types of signaling and switching equipment. A tin lunch box sat on a rotting table; inside, Margo could see the ancient, desiccated skeleton of a half-chicken. The whole place had the air of being abandoned in a hurry.

"God, what a spot," D'Agosta said. "Makes you wonder what the true story of these tunnels is."

"Or if anybody still knows it almost a century later," Pendergast said. He nodded toward a metal-banded door in a far corner, between stacks of dusty equipment. "That's the maintenance stairway leading down to the Astor Tunnels. Here's where we'll set the last charge." He pulled another brick of explosive from his bag, rolling it in the mud beneath his feet.

"What's that for?" D'Agosta asked. "Camouflage?"

"Exactly," came Pendergast's whispered reply as he molded the charge around the base of a cement pylon. "This is apparently a more heavily trafficked area." He nodded back down the tunnel in illustration.

"Jesus," Margo breathed. The floor of the passage they had just come down was lined with the tracks of countless bare feet. She dug for the mask and took a drag of oxygen. The humidity was close to one hundred percent. She took another deep breath from the mask, then offered it to Smithback.

"Thanks," he said, taking two slow hits. Margo watched as a dull gleam returned to his eyes. His hair hung limply over his forehead, and his shirt was torn and streaked with blood. *Poor Bill,* she thought. *He looks like something that just crawled out of a sewer. Come to think of it, that's not far wrong.*

"What was going on topside?" Margo asked, hoping to draw him out of his thoughts.

"All hell was breaking loose," the journalist replied, handing the mask back to her solemnly. "In the middle of Wisher's march, hundreds of mole people began popping up from underground.

Right there on Broadway. I heard somebody say the cops teargassed the tunnels under Fifty-ninth Street and the Park."

"*Mole* people, scriblerian?" Mephisto hissed. "Yes, we're mole people. We shun the light, not because of its warmth or its brightness, but because of what it shows us. Venality, and corruption, and countless useless worker ants running on treadmills. 'A crowd flowed over London Bridge, so many / I did not know death had undone so many.'"

"Stow it," D'Agosta snapped. "Just get me back to that venal, corrupt surface, and I promise you can crawl into the deepest shithole you can find and I'll never come looking for you, ever."

"While you two have been filling the air with strophe and antistrophe, I have set the final charge," Pendergast said, rubbing his hands and tossing away the now-empty munitions bag. "I'm surprised you haven't brought the entire foul nest down on us with your bickering. Now let's get out, as quickly as possible. We have less than thirty minutes." He led the way back out of the storage area.

Suddenly, he stopped. There was a brief silence.

"Vincent," Margo heard him whisper. "Are you ready?"

"I was born ready."

Pendergast checked the nozzle on the flamethrower. "If necessary, I'll flame, then we retreat. Wait for the flames to clear before advancing. This fires a fast, clean-burning mixture designed for close fighting, but the propellant clings to surfaces for several seconds before flaring out. Understood? Remove your goggles and get ready to close your eyes against the flash. Hold off until I signal. The rest of you, ready your weapons."

"What is it?" Margo whispered, pulling out the Glock and snapping off the safety. Then she smelt it: the foul reek of the creatures, hanging in the air like an apparition.

"We've got to get past that access vent," Pendergast whispered. "Let's go."

Then there was a sudden scrabbling in the tunnel ahead and beneath them. Pendergast brought his hand down and D'Agosta switched on the beam at low power. Margo saw, with dread, that a knot of cloaked creatures was scrambling up the passageway toward them. They moved with sickening speed. Suddenly, everything seemed to happen at once: Pendergast cried out, there was a sharp snap from D'Agosta's flashgun, and a white light of almost supernatural intensity burst through the tunnel, turning the dim black outlines of the rock to instantaneous color. There was a strange, drizzling roar, and a blue-orange flame shot from the flamethrower. Even though she was behind the FBI agent, Margo felt a terrific wave of heat cross her face. The stream hit the onrushing creatures with a loud popping sound and a firestorm of swirling sparks. For a moment the figures kept coming, and to Margo it looked as if the front ranks were wearing strange, blossoming robes of flame, which crisped and vanished into cinders. The flashgun winked out, but not before a terrible image of humped, misshapen bodies—swathed in burning flesh, falling forward, legs windmilling—imprinted itself on Margo's brain.

"Retreat!" Pendergast yelled.

They stumbled back into the storage area, Pendergast sending another gout of flame toward the creatures. In the burst of orange light, Margo saw countless more running up the access tube toward them. Instinctively, she raised the gun and squeezed off several shots. Two of the creatures pinwheeled backwards and were lost in the flickering dark. Dimly, she was aware of having lost Smithback in the confusion. There was an explosion in her ear and both barrels of Mephisto's shotgun went off. She could hear somebody shouting—perhaps it was her—and the frantic, blubbering screams of pain from the wounded creatures. There was a sharp report, then a massive explosion shook the tunnel as D'Agosta lobbed a grenade into the group.

"Quick!" Pendergast said. "Down the maintenance stairway!"

"You crazy?" D'Agosta cried. "We'll be trapped like rats!"

"We're already trapped like rats," came the reply. "There are too many of them. We don't dare fight here, we might set off the C-4. At least in the Astor Tunnels, we have a chance. *Go!*"

D'Agosta yanked open the metal banded door and the group stumbled down the stairs, Pendergast trailing, squirting tongues of fire back up the tunnel. Acrid smoke billowed down, burning Margo's eyes. Blinking back tears, she saw another cloaked figure loping after them, its hood flapping, its wrinkled face twisted in fury, a jagged flint knife raised high in one hand. Dropping into a Weaver stance, she emptied the rest of her clip into the monstrosity, noting almost with detachment how the hollow-points blossomed as they tore into the leathery flesh. The figure fell and was almost immediately replaced by a second. There was a burst from the flamethrower and the figure fell backward, dancing and convulsing in a corona of fire.

They emerged in a small, high-ceilinged room, the walls and floor covered in tiles. From beyond a Gothic archway, the red glow of the ceremony could be seen. Margo looked around quickly, scattering rounds across the floor as she desperately reloaded her clip. Smoke hung in the air, but with relief she sensed the place was deserted. It appeared to be some kind of secondary waiting area, perhaps intended for children: several low tables surrounded them, some still set for games of checkers, chess, and backgammon, the pieces thickly draped in cobwebs and mold.

"A shame for black," said Mephisto, glancing at the closest table as he broke open the shotgun and reloaded. "He was a pawn ahead."

There was sound on the stairway, and a fresh group of Wrinklers scuttled out of the darkness toward them. Pendergast crouched into position, sending the long flame licking toward them. Margo dropped into firing stance, the popping of her gun drowned out in the general roar.

There was a movement from beyond the arch, and more creatures came running toward them from the Pavilion itself. She watched as Smithback, frantically working the grenade launcher, was overcome and dragged to the ground. Pendergast had his back to the tiled wall, sending a sweeping arc of flame across the creatures around him. With a curious sense of unreality, she aimed at the heads of the running figures before her and began pulling the trigger. One creature dropped, then a second, and then she was firing on an empty clip. She moved backward as fast as she dared, grabbing in her carryall for another handful of ammunition. Then there was movement all around her—arms like steel cords wrapped around her neck and ripped the gun from her grasp—a fetid odor like the breath of a corpse filled her senses—and she closed her eyes, crying out in pain, fear, and rage, composing herself as best she could for inevitable death.

60

Snow watched as the dark figures massed, filling the mouth of the tunnel before them. They had paused in the harsh brilliance of the flare, but were now moving forward with a kind of deliberation that made Snow's skin crawl. These were not brainless creatures throwing themselves mindlessly into battle; some kind of strategy was at work.

"Listen," Donovan said quietly. "Load one of those canister rounds into the XM-148. We'll fire together on my signal. You aim at the left of the group, I'll aim at the right. Reload and fire again as fast as you can. Grenade launchers have a tendency to pull high, so keep your aim low."

Snow loaded the round into the launcher, feeling his heart thumping at the back of his throat. Beside him, he felt Donovan grow tense.

"Now!" Donovan yelled.

Snow pulled the forward trigger, and the weapon almost bucked out of his hands as the load roared toward the group. The bright plumes of the two explosions filled the narrow tunnel with orange light; Snow found he had aimed too far to the left, hitting the wall of the tunnel. Then, with a deep shudder, a section of the ceiling collapsed. Horrifying screams came from the group of hooded figures.

"Again!" Donovan cried, loading another round.

Snow reloaded and fired again, letting the barrel drift slightly to the right this time. He watched, mesmerized, as the shell erupted from the barrel and—seemingly in slow motion—pinwheeled its way over the heads of the roiling group at the tunnel's mouth. There was another shudder and a fresh burst of light.

"*Lower!*" Donovan screamed. "They're closing!"

Sobbing now, Snow ripped open the extra pouch with his teeth, loaded the round, and fired again. The bright fierce plume erupted in the midst of the figures. Muffled shrieks sounding piercingly over the roar of the explosion.

"Again!" Donovan yelled, firing his own grenade launcher at the figures. "Hit them again!"

Snow loaded, fired; the shot fell short, sending a concussive blast of heat toward them, knocking him to his knees. He righted himself, blinking against the clouds of dust and smoke that billowed through the dark space. He was out of grenades, and his finger moved from the forward trigger to the rear trigger.

Donovan held up his hand in the signal for "danger point." They waited, guns pointed into the blackness, for what seemed to Snow like several minutes. At last, Donovan relaxed his weapon.

"That was a hell of a shitstorm," he whispered. "You did all right. I want you to hang back for a moment while I recon. If you hear anything, give a holler. I doubt we'll find anything larger than a pinky waiting for us after that, but I'm not taking any chances."

He checked the magazine of his M-16, snapped on a flare, and tossed it into the drifting smoke. Then he moved forward slowly, hugging the tunnel wall. As the smoke dissipated, Snow could see the dim outlines of Donovan's head and shoulders as he moved stealthily forward, the dark bar of his shadow flickering behind him.

As Snow watched, the SEAL picked his way around the broken, smoking forms that littered the tunnel. Reaching the mouth of the tunnel, Donovan looked cautiously around, then rotated himself out into Three Points. Finally he took a step into the chamber and was swallowed up by the blackness, and Snow was left alone with only the dark for company. It suddenly occurred to him that the duffel of magnesium flares was still hanging by his side, forgotten in the fight. He fought back the urge to shrug it off and leave it behind. *Rachlin said it stays with me until the mission's over,* he thought. *So it stays.*

Rachlin... it seemed impossible that those creatures could have killed all the SEALs. They were too well armed, too battle savvy. *If the other two tunnels were like this one, maybe some of the men escaped up the ladders at the end. If so, we ought to go back and try to...*

Suddenly, Snow stopped, surprised by the coolness with which he was thinking these thoughts. Maybe he was braver than he'd thought. Or just more stupid. *If only that bastard Fernandez could see me now,* he thought.

His thoughts were interrupted as the form of Donovan once again emerged from the blackness, looked around, then motioned him forward. Snow moved quickly toward him, then slowed as a grim sight came into view. The gear was still neatly piled along the wall, a stark contrast to the dismembered, headless figures lying at crazy angles in the muck of the tunnel floor.

"Hurry up!" he heard Donovan whisper. "No time for rubbernecking."

He looked up. Donovan stood there, arms folded, surveying the equipment with an impatient scowl on his face.

Above Donovan, in the thick darkness of the vault, a black form dropped from the dangling chain with a sudden shriek and landed on his back.

Donovan staggered and managed to shrug the thing off, but two more figures dropped nearby and grappled with the SEAL, bringing him to his knees. Snow stumbled backward, aiming his gun, unable to get a clear shot. Another lunged forward, knife in hand, and Donovan screamed: an impossibly high, almost feminine sound. There was a strange sawing motion, a guttural roar of triumph, and the figure raised Donovan's head in the air. Momentarily paralyzed by the sight, Snow thought he saw Donovan's eyes rolling wildly in their sockets, dim reflections of the red glow at the rear of the tunnel.

Snow fired then, short staccato bursts as Donovan had taught him, hosing the barrel left and right toward the obscene group huddled over Donovan's body. He knew, somehow, that he was shouting, though he couldn't hear it. The magazine emptied and he slammed home the spare, screaming and firing until the clip ran dry. As his ears rang in the sudden silence, he took a step forward, waving the cordite aside, searching the gloom for the nightmare apparitions. He took another step, then another.

The blackness ahead seemed to shift—as if moving in against itself—and Snow wheeled and ran for the end of the tunnel, his feet churning through the mud and the dank water, the empty clip clattering forgotten onto the slick stones behind him.

61

Margo closed her eyes tightly, trying to empty her mind against the ultimate pain. But a moment passed, then another, and she felt herself wrenched from the ground and borne away, slung roughly from side to side, the heavy carryall chafing at her shoulder. Despite the transcendent horror, relief flooded through her: at least she was still alive.

She passed through a close, foul-smelling darkness, then into a large, dimly illuminated space. She forced her eyes open, straining to orient herself. She could see a ruined mirror, covered in what looked like countless layers of dried mud, most of its glass shattered and lost long ago. Beside it, an ancient tapestry of a unicorn in captivity, rotting from the bottom up. Then she was jostled again, and she now saw the marble walls rushing toward a high, glittering ceiling, the ruined chandelier. A tiny metal plate glinted at the ceiling's center: their viewhole, not ten minutes before. *I'm in the Crystal Pavilion,* she thought.

The foul odor was stronger here than ever, and she fought against panic and a rising despair. She was brusquely thrown to the ground, the blow knocking the breath from her lungs. Gasping, she tried to rise to one elbow. She saw she was surrounded by Wrinklers, shuffling back and forth, swathed in

439

their ragged patchwork cloaks and hoods. Despite her horror, she found herself looking at them with curiosity. *So these are the victims of glaze,* she thought, her mind clearing. She could not help feeling a stab of pity over what had happened to them. She wondered again if it was necessary for them to die, even as she knew in her heart there was no other answer. Kawakita himself had written that there was no antidote—no way to reverse what the reovirus had done to them—any more than there had been a way to reverse what had happened to Whittlesey.

But with this thought came another, and she stared around wildly. The charges had been set and would soon detonate. Even if the Wrinklers spared them—

One of the creatures bent forward, leering at her. The hood slipped back a moment, and all thoughts of pity—even thoughts of her own immediate danger—fled away in overwhelming revulsion. She had a brief, searing vision of grotesquely wrinkled skin with pendulous folds and dewlaps, surrounding two lizardlike eyes, black and dead, their pupils contracted to quivering pinpoints. She turned away.

There was a thump and Pendergast was thrown to the ground beside her. Smithback and Mephisto, struggling wildly, followed after him.

Pendergast looked at her questioningly, and she nodded that she was unhurt. There was another commotion, then Lieutenant D'Agosta was dumped nearby, his weapon tugged from him and tossed aside. He was bleeding freely from a large gash above one eye. A Wrinkler tore the pack from her shoulder and tossed it to the ground, then started toward D'Agosta.

"Keep away from me, you goddamn mutant," the policeman swore. One of the Wrinklers leaned forward and dealt him a slashing blow across the face.

"You'd better cooperate, Vincent," said Pendergast quietly. "We are slightly outnumbered."

D'Agosta rose to his knees and shook his head clear. "Why are we still alive?"

"The question of the hour," replied Pendergast. "I'm afraid it might have to do with the ceremony that's about to begin."

"Hear that, scriblerian?" Mephisto chuckled mirthlessly. "Perhaps the *Post* will buy your next story: 'How I Became a Human Sacrifice.'"

The soft chanting rose once again, and Margo felt herself pulled to her feet. A path was cleared among the shuffling throng, and she could make out the hut of skulls, perhaps twenty feet in front of them. She stared in mute horror at the macabre structure, stained and unclean, grinning a thousand grins. Several figures moved around within it, and great wafts of steam rose above the unfinished roof. It was surrounded by a paling of human longbones indifferently cleaned. Before the entrance, she could make out several ceremonial stone platforms. Inside, through the countless empty eye sockets, she could see the vague form of the sedan chair on which the shaman had been brought in. She wondered what the terrifying apparition within might look like. She was not sure she could bear to see another face such as the one that had leered at her hungrily moments before.

A hand at her back propelled her roughly forward, and she half walked, half stumbled toward the hut. Out of the corner of her eye, she could see D'Agosta struggling with the Wrinklers prodding him along. Smithback, too, was silently resisting. One of them drew a long, evil-looking stone knife from beneath the folds of his cloak and held it to the journalist's throat.

"*Cuchillos de pedernal*," Pendergast murmured. "Isn't that what the subway survivor told you?"

D'Agosta nodded.

A few feet from the paling, Margo was brought to a halt, then forced to her knees and held along with the others. Around her, the chanting and drumming had increased to a fever pitch.

Suddenly her eyes focused on the stone platforms around the hut. There were several metal objects on the nearest, lovingly arranged as if for some ritual purpose.

Then she caught her breath. "Pendergast?" she croaked.

Pendergast looked toward her inquiringly, and she gestured with her head toward the platform. "Ah," he whispered. "The larger of the souvenirs. I could only carry the smaller pieces."

"Yes," Margo replied urgently, "but I recognize one of these. It's the handbrake to a wheelchair."

A look of surprise crossed Pendergast's face.

"And that piece there is a tipping lever, broken off at the stub."

Pendergast tried to move toward the platform, but one of the figures forced him back. "This makes no sense," he said. "Why would such an arrangement be—" He stopped abruptly. "Lourdes," he said in a low whisper.

"I don't understand," Margo answered. But Pendergast said nothing more, his eyes now fixed on the figure inside the hut.

There was a rustling from within, then a small procession began to emerge. Cloaked figures stepped out in groups of two, carrying between them large cauldrons of steaming liquid. Around her, the chanting increased until it seemed to Margo one long, monotonous cacophony. The Wrinklers seated the cauldrons into depressions beaten into the floor of the Pavilion. Then the sedan chair emerged, covered in dense black material, flanked by four bearers. The bearers processed with measured step around the bone paling. Reaching the farthest, largest stone platform, they carefully placed the sedan chair upon it. The supports were drawn away, the covering removed, and the lieutenants moved slowly back into the hut.

Margo stared at the shadowed figure in the chair, his features invisible in the darkness, the only observable movement the slight flexing of thick fingers. The chanting ebbed, then swelled again, taking on an unmistakable undertone of anticipation. The figure raised his hand suddenly, and the chanting ceased in an instant. Then, as he leaned forward, the flickering firelight slanted across his face.

For Margo, it was as if time itself were suspended for a brief, terrible instant. She forgot the fear, the aching knees, the detonation timers relentlessly ticking in the dark corridors above her head. The man who sat on the litter made of lashed human bone—dressed in the familiar gabardine pants and paisley tie—was Whitney Frock.

She opened her mouth to speak, but no sound came.

"Oh, my God," Smithback said behind her.

Frock gazed across the assembled throng, his expression impassive, devoid of emotion. The huge hall was deathly silent.

Slowly, Frock's eyes swept forward to the prisoners before him. He looked at D'Agosta, then Smithback, then Pendergast. When his gaze reached Margo, he started suddenly. Something kindled in his eyes.

"My dear," he said. "How truly unfortunate. Frankly, I didn't expect to see you as science advisor for this little outing, and I am indeed sorry. No—it's true, and you needn't look· at me like that. Remember how, when it came time to get rid of that meddlesome Irishman, I spared *your* life. Against my own better judgment, I might add."

Margo, reeling in shock and disbelief, could not speak.

"However, it can't be helped." The flicker in Frock's eyes died away. "As for the rest of you, welcome. I think some introductions are in order. For example, who is this hirsute gentleman with the ragged clothes?" He turned to Mephisto. "He has the face of a wild animal caught in a trap, which I suppose is exactly what he is. One of the natives, I imagine, brought along as a guide. I will ask you again, what is your name?"

There was a silence.

He turned to one of his lieutenants. "Cut his throat if he doesn't answer. We can't tolerate rudeness, now, can we?"

"Mephisto," came the sullen reply.

"Mephisto, indeed! A little learning is a dangerous thing. Especially in a derelict. But 'Mephisto.' Really, how banal. No doubt meant to strike fear into the hearts of your scabby little followers. You don't look like much of a devil to me, just a pathetic, drug-addled bum. I should not complain, however: you and your likes have been exceedingly useful, I will admit.

Perhaps you will find an erstwhile friend amongst my children..." He swept his hand across the gathered ranks of Wrinklers. Mephisto drew himself up, saying nothing.

Margo stared at her former professor. This was like no Frock she had ever seen before. He had always been diplomatic and soft-spoken. Now there was an arrogance, a cold lack of emotion, that chilled her even beyond the fear and confusion she felt.

"And Smithback, the journalist!" Frock sneered. "Were you brought along to document this intended victory over my children? Pity you won't be able to tell the real outcome in that scandal sheet you write for."

"The jury's still out on that," Smithback said defiantly.

Frock chuckled.

"Frock, what the hell is all this?" D'Agosta said as he struggled. "You'd better explain, or—"

"Or what?" Frock turned toward the police officer. "I always thought you a crude, ill-bred fellow. But I'm surprised it's necessary to point out you are in no position to make demands of *me*. Are they disarmed?" he asked one of the hooded figures closest to him, who nodded slowly in reply.

"Check that one again," Frock said, pointing to Pendergast. "He's a tricky devil."

Pendergast was hauled roughly to his feet, searched, then shoved back to his knees. Frock slowly scanned them with his eyes, smiling coldly.

"That was your wheelchair, wasn't it?" Pendergast asked quietly, indicating the platform.

Frock nodded. "My *best* wheelchair."

Pendergast said nothing. Margo turned to Frock, finding her voice at last. "Why?" she asked simply. Frock looked at Margo for a moment, then signaled his lieutenants. The cloaked forms moved into position behind the huge cauldrons. Frock stood up, jumped down from the sedan chair, and approached the FBI agent on foot.

"*This* is why," he replied.

Then he stood proudly, lifting his arms high above his head.

"*As I am cured, so shall you be cured*!" he cried in a clear, ringing voice. "*As I am made whole, so shall you be made whole*!"

A loud answering cry came from the assembly. The cry went on and on, and Margo realized it was not an inarticulate cry, but a kind of programmed guttural response. *The creatures are speaking,* she thought. *Or trying to.*

Slowly, the cry died away and the chanting resumed. The deep, monotonous beat of the drums began again, and the lines of Wrinklers came shuffling forward toward the semicircle of cauldrons. The lieutenants brought delicate clay goblets out from within the hut. Margo stared, her mind unable to connect the beautifully formed implements with the hideous ceremony. One by one, the creatures came forward, accepting the steaming cups in horny-nailed hands, drawing them up into their hoods. She turned away, repelled by the thick slurping sounds that followed.

"*This* is why," Frock repeated, turning toward Margo. "Don't you see? Don't you see how *this* would be worth anything, anything in the world?" There seemed to be something almost imploring in his tone.

For a minute, Margo didn't understand. Then it hit her: the ceremony, the drug, the wheelchair pieces, Pendergast's reference to the Lourdes shrine with its miraculous healing powers.

"So you could walk," she said quietly. "All this, just so you could walk again."

Instantly, Frock's face hardened. "How easy for you to judge," he said. "You, who have walked all your life and *never* given it a second thought. How can you begin to know what it is like not to walk? Bad enough to be crippled from birth, but to know the gift and to have it snatched away, when the greatest achievements of your life still lie before you?" He looked at her. "Of course, to you I was always just Dr. Frock. Dear old Dr. Frock, how *unpleasant* for him to contract polio in that African bush village in the Ituri Forest. How *unfortunate* he had to give up his field work."

He brought his face closer to hers. "Field work was my *life*," he hissed.

"So you built upon Dr. Kawakita's work," Pendergast said. "You finished what he started."

Frock snorted. "Poor Gregory. He came to me in desperation. As you surely know, he'd started taking the drug prematurely." Frock waggled his finger in an uncharacteristically cynical gesture. "Tut, tut. And to think I'd always taught him to follow strict laboratory procedure. But the boy was simply too eager. He was arrogant and had visions of immortality. He took the drug before all the unpleasant side effects of the reovirus had been negated. Due to the rather, ah, *extreme* physical changes that resulted, he needed help. A surgical procedure had left him with a plate in his back. It was beginning to cause him acute pain. He was hurt, lonely, and scared. Who could he turn to but me, in my stifling, wasting retirement? And, naturally, I was able to help him. Not only in removing the plate, but in further purifying the drug. But of course, his *cruel* experimentation"— here Frock spread his hands at the multitude—"his selling of the drug—was his demise. When his subjects realized what he had done to them, they killed him."

"So you purified the drug," Pendergast said, "and took it yourself."

"We did the final work at a rather untidy little lab he'd set up along the river. Greg had lost the conviction he needed to go forward. Or perhaps he'd never had that kind of courage, that intestinal fortitude a truly visionary scientist needs to see things through to their conclusion. So I finished what he'd started. More accurately, I *perfected* what he'd started. The drug still creates morphological change, of course. However, those changes now *heal*, rather than disfigure, what nature has corrupted. It is the true destiny, the truest iteration, of the reovirus. I am living proof of its restorative power. I was the first to make the transition. In fact, it is now clear to me that no one but myself *could* have made it. My wheelchair was my cross, you see. Now it is venerated as a symbol of the new world we shall create."

"The new world," Pendergast repeated. "The Mbwun lilies growing in the Reservoir."

"Kawakita's idea," Frock said. "Aquaria are so expensive and take up so much room, you see. But that was before..." his voice trailed off.

"I think I understand," Pendergast went on, as calmly as if he was debating with an old friend at a comfortable coffeehouse table. "You'd been planning to drain the Reservoir all along."

"Naturally. Gregory had modified the plant to grow in a temperate environment. We were going to drain the Reservoir ourselves and release the lily into these tunnels. My children shun light, you see, and this makes the perfect warren. But then, friend Waxie made it all unnecessary. He is—or rather *was*—so eager to take credit for other people's ideas. If you recall, it was *I* who first suggested the notion of draining the Reservoir."

"Dr. Frock," Margo said, trying to keep her voice under control, "some of these seeds will make it out to the storm drain system, and from there to the Hudson and the open ocean. When they hit saltwater, they'll activate the virus, polluting the entire ecosystem. Do you know what that could mean for the world's food chain?"

"My dear Margo, that is the *idea*. Admittedly, it's an evolutionary step, a step into the unknown. But as a biologist, Margo, you surely realize that the human race has become degenerate. It has lost its evolutionary vigor, become grossly maladaptive. I am the instrument for the reinvigoration of the species."

"And just where were you planning to hide your fat ass during the flood?" D'Agosta asked.

Frock laughed. "No doubt you foolishly assume that, by virtue of this little excursion, you know all there is to know about this underground world. Believe me, subterranean Manhattan is far more vast, more terrible, and more wonderful, than you could imagine. I've wandered again and again, glorying in the use of my legs. Here I'm free from the dissembling I must continue aboveground. I've found natural caverns of incredible beauty. Ancient tunnels used by Dutch smugglers in the days of New Amsterdam. Snug little places where we can all retire while the water rushes past on its way to the sea. You won't find them on any maps. When twenty million cubic feet of water drains through here shortly, delivering the very ripe seeds of *Liliceae mbwunensis* into the world, my children and I will be safe in a tunnel just above the flood. And when the flood is over, we will return to our freshly scoured quarters to enjoy the fruit left behind. And, of course, to await the arrival of what I like to call the Holocene Discontinuity."

Margo stared at Frock in disbelief. He smiled in return: an arrogant, distant smile she had not seen before. He seemed supremely confident. It occurred to her that Frock might not know of the charges they'd placed.

"Yes, my dear. It's my theory of fractal evolution, taken to the logical extreme. The reovirus—'glaze,' if you will—inserted directly into the bottom of the world's food chain. How fitting, don't you think, that I myself will be its vector, its activating agent? The mass extinction at the K-T Boundary will seem minuscule by comparison. That simply made way for mammals by removing the dinosaurs. Who knows what this transformation will make room for? The prospects are tremendously exciting."

"You're a very sick man," Margo said, feeling even as she said it a chilling despair grip her heart. She'd had no idea just how much Frock must have missed the use of his legs. It was his secret obsession. He must have seen the potential for the drug's restorative effects, even from within Kawakita's misery. But he had clearly discounted the drug's potential for poisoning the mind. He could never understand—he would never believe—that in perfecting the drug's action on the body, he'd increased exponentially its ability to stimulate mania and violence, to magnify buried obsessions. And she sensed there was nothing she could now say that could bring him back.

The processions continued to shuffle up to the cauldrons. As the Wrinklers raised the cups to their lips, Margo could see shudders ripple their cloaks—through pleasure or pain, she could not tell.

"And you knew our moves all along," she heard Pendergast say. "As if you were conducting them yourself."

"In some ways, I was. I'd trained Margo here too well to hope that she could leave well enough alone. And I knew your busy mind would always be spinning. So I made sure the draining of the Reservoir couldn't be stopped. Finding one of my wounded children here, the one you shot, merely cemented my conviction. But how clever of you to send your little frogmen in as a precaution. Luckily, my children were all on their way to the Ceremony and prevented them from crashing our little party." He blinked. "For one so clever, I'm surprised you thought you could come down here and defeat us with your pathetic weapons. But no doubt you misjudged just how numerous my children have become. As you've misjudged so much else."

"I think you've left something out of the story, Doctor," Margo said suddenly, as evenly as she could.

Frock stepped closer to her, an enquiring look on his face. It was very difficult, seeing him move so nimbly on his feet; it made it hard to think straight. She took a deep breath of the noxious air. "I think it was you who killed Kawakita," she said. "You killed him, and left his body here to look like just another victim."

"Indeed," Frock replied. "Why, pray tell?"

"Two reasons," she said, speaking louder now. "I found Kawakita's journal in the wreckage of his laboratory. He was clearly having second thoughts. It mentioned thyoxin. I think he had learned about the effect salinity would have on the reovirus, and he was planning to destroy the plants before you could flush them into the Hudson. He may have been warped in mind and body, but in him, at least, some small voice of conscience must have remained."

"My dear, you don't understand. You *cannot* understand," said Frock.

"And you killed him because he knew the drug's effects were irreversible. Isn't that right? I learned that much through my own experiments. You can't cure these people, and you know it. But do *they*?"

The chanting in the ranks around them seemed to falter slightly, and Frock glanced briefly from side to side. "These are the claims of a desperate woman. This is beneath you, my dear."

They're listening, Margo thought. *Perhaps they can still be convinced.*

"Of course," the voice of Pendergast intruded on her thoughts. "Kawakita fell into this ceremony, this dispensing of the drug, because it seemed the easiest way to keep his own poor victims docile. But he didn't especially enjoy the trappings or the ritual. He didn't take them seriously. That was *your* addition. As an anthropologist, how you must have enjoyed the chance to create your own cult. Minions—or perhaps acolytes—wielding primitive knives. Your own hut of skulls. A reliquary for your wheelchair, symbol of your own transformation."

Frock stood stiffly, saying nothing.

"That's the real reason the killings have been increasing. It's not lack of the drug anymore, is it? Now you've got a reservoir full. No—there's another agenda. An obsessive one. An *architectural* one." He nodded toward the hut. "You needed a temple for your new religion. For your personal deification."

Frock looked at Pendergast, his lips twitching. "And why not? Every new age needs its new religion."

"But it's still a ceremony at its core, isn't it? And everything relies on control. If these creatures know the effects are irreversible, what hold will you have on them?"

Murmurs were rising from among the closest Wrinklers.

"Enough!" Frock cried, clapping his hands. "We don't have much time. Prepare them!" Margo felt her arms seized again, then she was dragged to her feet, a knifepoint placed against her throat. Frock looked at her, a strange mix of expressions again playing across his face. "I wish you could be here to experience the change for yourself, Margo. But many must fall in the transition. I am sorry."

Smithback lunged toward Frock, but was dragged back.

"Dr. Frock!" Pendergast cried. "Margo was your student. Remember how the three of us struggled against the Museum Beast. Even now, you're not wholly responsible for what's happened. Perhaps there is still a way for you to go back. We'll heal your mind."

"And destroy my life?" Frock leaned toward the FBI agent, lowering his voice to whisper. "Go back to what, may I ask? Being a helpless, superannuated, slightly ridiculous curator *emeritus*? One whose years are rapidly dwindling? Surely Margo's research showed you there is another side effect to the new drug: it eliminates the concentration of free radical molecules in living tissue. In short, it *extends life*! You would have me give up both my freedom of movement *and* my life?" He looked at his watch. "Twenty minutes to twelve. We're out of time."

There was a sudden puff of wind, and a series of small dust clouds arose from the skulls forming the top rank of the hut. Almost immediately, there was a sharp rattling noise, and Margo realized she was hearing the sound of automatic weapons fire.

There was a strange popping sound—then another—and suddenly the entire Pavilion exploded in a burst of brilliant light. Screams and squeals of pain sounded from all sides. There was another burst, and the knifepoint vanished from her neck. Margo shook her head, stunned, temporarily blinded by the fierce glare. The chanting died away into confusion, and Margo heard angry howls arise from the group. While her eyes were closed, there was yet another burst of light, accompanied by more screams of pain. Margo felt one of the Wrinklers drop his hold. With the instinctive speed of desperation, she twisted out of the grasp of her other captor and lunged toward the ground, rolling away, scrambling onto her hands and knees, blinking desperately in an effort to restore her sight. As the spots of black and white began to clear, she could see several plumes of smoke rising from the floor, burning impossibly bright. Wrinklers everywhere had fallen to the ground, pawing at their faces, hiding their heads beneath their cloaks, convulsing with pain. Nearby, Pendergast and D'Agosta had also broken free and were rushing to the aid of Smithback.

Suddenly there was a loud explosion, and one side of the hut collapsed in a gout of flame. A shrapnel cloud of shattered bone flew across the closest ranks.

"Some of the SEALs must still be alive," Pendergast shouted, pulling Smithback toward them. "That shooting is coming from the platform outside the Pavilion. Let's head for it while we still can. Where's Mephisto?"

"Stop them!" Frock boomed, shading his own eyes. But the blinded Wrinklers milled about in confusion.

Just then another shell landed in the clearing before the hut, bursting the paling into countless pieces and shattering two of the cauldrons. A great gush of steaming liquid began pouring across the floor, gleaming in the torchlight. Cries of dismay rose from the Wrinklers, and several of those on the ground nearby began to lap up the precious fluid. Frock was shouting, gesturing in the direction from which the shells had come.

D'Agosta and the others ran toward the free ground at the rear of the hut. Margo hesitated, looking around desperately for her carryall. The intense light was dropping, and a few of the creatures were beginning to shamble toward them now, hands up against the glare, stone knives glinting evilly.

"Dr. Green, *now*!" Pendergast cried.

Suddenly, she saw it, lying torn and open on the dusty ground. She grabbed for it, then sprinted after Smithback. The group had halted near the tunnel leading toward the platform, their exit blocked by a ragged line of Wrinklers.

"Shit," D'Agosta muttered fervently.

"Hey!" Margo heard the unmistakable voice of Mephisto shouting above the noise and confusion. "Fat Napoleon!"

She turned to see Mephisto scrambling onto one of the empty platforms, turquoise necklace swinging wildly around his neck. There was another blast, farther away this time; a gout of flame arose from the midst of one of the scattered processions.

Frock turned in his direction, squinting.

"Drug-addled bum, am I? Take a look!" Mephisto dug deep into the crotch of his filthy pants and drew out what looked to Margo like a kidney-shaped disk of green plastic. "You know what this is? Antipersonnel mine. Chock-full of metal splinters coated in Teflon, propelled by a charge equal to twenty grenades. Very ugly."

Mephisto shook it in Frock's direction. "It's armed. So tell your leathery minions to back off."

The Wrinklers paused.

"A bluff," Frock said calmly. "You may be filth, but you're not a suicide."

"Are you so sure?" Mephisto grinned. "Tell you what. I'd rather be blown to pieces than end up decorating that little A-frame of yours." He nodded toward Pendergast. "Yo, Grant's Tomb! You'll forgive me, I hope, for appropriating this tidbit from your armory. Promises are all very nice, but I planned to make sure *nobody* ever rousted Route 666 again. Now you'd best hie yourself over here if we're going to get topside."

Pendergast shook his head and tapped his wrist, signifying they'd run out of time. Frock gestured frantically to the hooded figures surrounding the platforms. "Cut his throat!" he cried. The Wrinklers swarmed toward Mephisto, who pulled himself up to the center of the platform.

"Good-bye, Mayor Whitey!" he called. "Remember your promise!" Margo turned away in horror as he tossed the disk into the masses surging around his feet. There was a sudden orange flash—the dank, filthy space filled with the heat of the sun—then the overwave of pressure hit, a massive blast that threw her to the ground. Rising to her knees, she looked back to see a great sheet of flame roar up behind the ruined hut, red against the brilliant white of the flares. For a moment, she could see the silhouette of Frock—standing as if triumphant, his arms outstretched, his white hair tinted orange by a thousand tongues of fire—before all was engulfed in roiling smoke and flames.

In the confusion, the ragged group of Wrinklers before them was parting.

"Move!" Pendergast cried over the roar of the firestorm. Hoisting her pack, Margo followed them under the archway at the far end of the Crystal Pavilion. On the railway platform beyond, she could see D'Agosta and Smithback come to a halt beside a slightly built man in a black wetsuit, his face slick with sweat and camouflage paint.

There were wet wheezing sounds behind her. The Wrinklers had closed ranks and were bearing down on them. At the narrow mouth of the archway, Margo stopped and turned.

"Margo!" Pendergast shouted from the platform. "What are you doing?"

"We've got to stop them here!" Margo cried, digging into her pack. "We'll never outrun them!"

"Don't be a fool!" Pendergast said.

Ignoring him, Margo grabbed two of the liter bottles, one in each hand. Gripping them tightly, she hosed a stream of liquid across the archway entrance. "Stop!" she cried. "I've got two billion units of vitamin D_3 in these bottles!"

The Wrinklers came on, their eyes blood red and streaming, their skin mottled and burned from the intense light.

She shook the squeeze bottles. "Hear me? Activated 7-dehydrocholesterol! Enough to kill all of you ten times over!" As the first Wrinkler reached her, knife raised, she hosed it in the face, and then hit a second Wrinkler just behind it. They fell backward, writhing horribly, small wisps of acrid smoke rising from their skin.

The other Wrinklers paused, a gibbering sound rising from their ranks.

"Vitamin D!" Margo repeated. "Bottled sunlight!"

She raised her arms and sent two delicate streams of liquid arcing over the milling crowd. A wail rose up, some falling and tearing at their cloaks, splattering droplets on their companions. Margo stepped forward and hosed the rest of the front rank. They fell backward in sheer panic, the sounds of gibbering and wailing filling the air. She advanced again, spraying a thick line of solution from left to right, and then the mass of Wrinklers broke and turned, scrambling over one another to get away, leaving a dozen convulsing, smoking bodies on the floor, ripping desperately at their cloaks.

Margo stepped back, and hosed the rest of the solution across the floor of the archway, then up along its sides and ceiling, leaving the exit tunnel wet and dripping. She tossed the empty containers into the Pavilion. "Let's go!"

She ran after the others, catching up to them by an open grating at the far end of the platform.

"We've got to get back to the rally point," the black-suited figure said. "Those charges are set to go off in ten minutes."

"You first, Margo," D'Agosta said.

As she dropped to the level of the tracks and began to descend into the drain below, a series of shattering explosions sounded behind and above her.

"Our charges!" D'Agosta cried. "The fires must have set them off prematurely!"

Pendergast turned to answer, but his voice was drowned in a rumble which, like an earthquake, was felt first in the feet, then in the gut, growing in violence and volume. A strange wind kicked up in the passageway—a gathering roar of air, forced along by the collapse of the Crystal Pavilion—pushing dust, smoke, scraps of paper, and the ripe smell of blood before it.

62

Margo dropped through the drain into a long, low tunnel, lit only by the sputtering glow of a dying flare. Several piles of rubble were strewn here and there, poking up from the standing water on the tunnel floor. Above her, the passages still rumbled and shook from the aftereffects of the concussion. Dust and debris drifted down through the drain, settling onto her shoulders.

Smithback fell into the water beside her, followed by Pendergast, D'Agosta, and the diver.

"Who the hell are you?" D'Agosta asked. "And what happened to the rest of the SEALs?"

"I'm not a SEAL, sir," the man said. "I'm a police diver. Officer Snow, sir."

"Well, well," said D'Agosta. "The guy who started it all. Got a light, Snow?"

The diver snapped a new flare to life, and suddenly the tunnel was illuminated by a harsh crimson glare.

"Oh, God!" Margo heard Smithback murmur beside her. Then she realized that what she had thought to be piles of rubble were actually rubber-suited divers, battered and headless, their bodies splayed in mute agony. The surrounding walls were pocked and scarred by countless bullet holes and the charred tracings of shells.

"SEAL Team Gamma," Snow muttered. "After my partner bought it, I ran back here to make a stand. Those creatures chased me up the drain, but then abandoned the chase on those tracks up there."

"Guess they were late for the debutante's ball," D'Agosta said, looking around at the massacre site, his face hard.

"You didn't see any of the other SEALs in there, sir?" Snow asked. "I followed the prints. I hoped some of them might have survived..." his voice trailed off when he saw the look on D'Agosta's face. There was a moment of awkward silence.

"Come on," Snow urged, once again animated. "There's still forty pounds of C-4 around here, waiting to go off."

Margo stumbled forward in a dark daze. She felt the floor of the tunnel solid beneath her feet, and she tried to draw that solidity up through her feet, her legs, and her arms. She knew she could not allow herself to think about what she had seen, what she had learned, inside the Crystal Pavilion: if she stopped to do that, she would be unable to go on.

The tunnel took a long, shallow bend. Ahead, Margo could see Snow and D'Agosta already moving into a large vaulted space at the end of the tunnel.

Beside her, she could hear Smithback's breathing turn choppy. Her eyes drifted toward the tunnel floor. Around her lay the torn and bloodied bodies of perhaps a dozen Wrinklers. She caught a glimpse of a dirty hood, burned away to expose skin seamed and veined to an extraordinary thickness.

"Striking," Pendergast murmured at her side. "The reptilian traits are unmistakable, yet the human attributes remain dominant. An early way station, so to speak, on the way to the full-blown Mbwun-hood. Odd, though, how the metamorphosis is so much greater in certain specimens than in others. No doubt due to Kawakita's continual refinements and experimentations. Shame there's no time for further study."

The echoes of their footfalls grew broader as they moved into the large space at the end of the tunnel. There were several more still forms lying scattered in the shallow water.

"This was our rally point," Snow said as he sorted quickly through the rows of equipment lining one side of the vaulted space. Margo could hear the sharp edge of nervousness in his voice. "There's more than enough scuba equipment here to get us out, but no suits. Look, we've got to move quickly. If we're still here when those charges blow, this whole place is going to come down on top of us."

Pendergast handed her a set of tanks. "Dr. Green, we have you to thank for our escape," he said. "You were right about the vitamin D. And you were able to contain the creatures within the Pavilion until the explosions blocked their escape. I promise you'll be welcome on any further excursions we may make."

Margo nodded as she snugged her feet into a pair of flippers. "Thanks, but once was enough."

The FBI agent turned toward Snow. "What's the exit strategy?"

"We came in through the Sewage Treatment Plant on the Hudson," Snow replied, shouldering his air tank and strapping on a headlamp. "But there's no way to return through the plant. We were to leave via the north branch of the West Side Lateral, to the One Hundred Twenty-fifth Street Canal."

"Can you get us there?" Pendergast asked, quickly passing air tanks to Smithback and helping to fit them.

"I think so," Snow panted, pulling masks out of the equipment pile. "I had a good long look at the Commander's maps. We retrace our route as far as the first flow riser. If we ascend the riser instead of descend, we should reach the access spillway leading out into the Lateral. But it's a long swim, and we'll have to be extremely careful. There are sluice gates and evacuation shunts. Get lost down those, and..." His voice petered off.

"Understood," Pendergast said, shrugging into a set of air tanks. "Mr. Smithback, Dr. Green, ever used scuba gear before?"

"Took a few lessons in college," Smithback said, accepting the proffered mask.

"Skin-dived in the Bahamas," Margo said.

"The principle's the same," Pendergast said to her. "We'll adjust your regulator. Just breathe normally, stay calm, and you'll do fine."

"Hurry!" Snow said, real urgency in his voice now. He began to jog toward the far end of the vaulted space, Smithback and Pendergast close behind him. Margo forced herself to follow, tightening her tank belt as she ran.

Suddenly, she was brought up short by Pendergast, who had stopped and was looking over his shoulder.

"Vincent?" he asked.

Margo turned. D'Agosta was standing behind them in the center of the vault, the air tanks and mask still in a pile by his feet.

"You go on ahead," he said.

Pendergast looked inquiringly at him.

"Can't swim," D'Agosta explained simply.

Margo heard Snow curse fervently under his breath. For a moment, nobody moved. Then Smithback stepped back toward the Lieutenant.

"I'll help you out," he said. "You can follow me."

"I *told* you, I grew up in Queens, I don't know how to swim," D'Agosta snapped. "I'll sink like a damn stone."

"Not with all that blubber, you won't," Smithback said, snatching a tank off the ground and placing it on D'Agosta's back. "Just hold on to me. I'll swim for both of us, if need be. You kept your head above water back in the subbasement, remember? Just do what I do and you'll be okay." He thrust a mask into D'Agosta's hands, then pushed him ahead toward the group.

At the far end of the chamber, an underground river ran off into darkness. Margo watched as first Snow, then Pendergast, adjusted their masks and eased themselves into the dark liquid.

Pulling her mask down over her eyes and placing the regulator in her mouth, she slid in after them. The air of the tanks was a welcome relief after the foul atmosphere of the tunnel. Behind her, she could hear a loud splashing as D'Agosta half swam, half floundered through the viscous, lukewarm liquid, Smithback urging him on.

Margo swam as quickly as she could through the tunnel, following the flickering light of Snow's headlamp, expecting at any moment to feel the massive concussion of the SEAL charges bring the ancient stone ceiling down behind them. Ahead, Pendergast and Snow had stopped, and she pulled up beside them.

"We go down here," Snow said, popping the regulator from his mouth and pointing downward. "Be careful not to scratch yourself, and for God's sake don't swallow anything. There's an old iron pipe at the base of the tunnel here that leads—"

At that moment they felt, rather than heard, a vibration begin over their heads: a low, rhythmic rumbling that grew to a terrible intensity.

"What's that?" Smithback gasped, coming up with D'Agosta. "The charges?"

"No," Pendergast whispered. "Listen: it's one continuous stream of sound. It must be the dumping of the Reservoir. Prematurely."

They hung there in the foul liquid, mesmerized despite the danger by the long rolling sound of millions of gallons of water roaring down the ancient network of pipes that crossed and recrossed above their heads, heading directly for them.

"Thirty seconds until the rest of the charges go," Pendergast said quietly, checking his watch.

Margo waited, trying to steady her breathing. She knew that if the charges failed, they'd be dead within minutes.

The tunnel began to vibrate violently, the surface of the water jiggling and dancing. Small pieces of masonry and cement began to rain down into the water around them. Snow tightened his mask and took a last look around, then sank beneath the surface. Smithback followed, pushing the protesting D'Agosta before him. Pendergast motioned Margo to go next. She sank into the darkness, trying to follow the faint light of Snow's headlamp as it descended into a narrow, rust-coated pipe. She could see the ungainly thrashing of D'Agosta subside into more regular movements as he became used to breathing tank air.

The tunnel leveled out, then snaked around two bends. Margo took a quick look behind to reassure herself that Pendergast was following. In the dim light of the swirling orange effluent, she could see the FBI agent motion her forward.

Now, she could see the group pausing at a junction ahead of her. The ancient iron pipe ended and a gleaming steel tube continued onward. Beneath her feet, at the point where the two tunnels met, Margo could see a narrow tube leading downward. Snow gestured ahead, then pointed upward with his finger, indicating that the vent riser to the West Side Lateral was directly ahead.

Suddenly, there was a roar from behind them: an ominous, deep rolling sound, horribly magnified in the tight water-filled space. Then a sharp concussion sounded, and another, following one upon the other in rapid succession. Beneath the wildly flickering beam of his headlamp, Margo could see Snow's eyes widen. The final set of charges had gone off barely in time, crushing the spillways from the Devil's Attic, sealing it forever.

As Snow frantically signaled them toward the riser, Margo felt a sudden tug at her legs, as if a tidal undertow were pulling her back toward the rally point. The feeling stopped as quickly as it had begun, and the water around her seemed to grow strangely dense. For a split second she had the strange sensation of hanging motionless, suspended in the eye of a hurricane.

Then an enormous blast of overpressure boiled up from the iron pipe behind them, a roiling cyclone of muddy water that caused the tunnel itself to jerk and dance spasmodically. Margo felt herself battered against its iron flanks. Her mouthpiece came loose and she reached for it frantically, hands grabbing through the storm of bubbles and thrashing sediment that surrounded her. There was another burst of pressure and she felt herself forced downward, sucked into the pipe beneath her feet. She righted herself desperately and fought to swim back up to the junction, but a horrible suction only pulled her deeper into unguessable depths. The roaring sound continued like the rushing of blood in her ears. She felt herself being knocked from side to side against the walls of the pipe, a piece of flotsam in the flood. Far above her head now she could see, through the dim illumination of Snow's headlamp, Pendergast staring at her, his hand reaching down, tiny as a doll's, from what seemed countless miles away. Then there was another blast, the narrow tunnel collapsed above her head with a shriek of protesting metal, and as the endless rumbling continued, she felt herself falling ever farther into a watery darkness.

63

Hayward jogged up the Mall toward the Bandshell and Cherry Hill, Officer Carlin by her side. For all his bulk, he ran easily, with the grace of a natural athlete. Didn't even break a sweat. The encounter with the moles, the tear gas—even the chaos they'd found when they regained the street—hadn't fazed him.

Here, in the darkness of the Park, the noise that had seemed so distant before was now much louder: a strange, ululating cry, continuously rising and falling, possessing a life of its own. Odd flickers and gouts of flame arose, blushing the underside of the ragged clouds overhead with patches of bright crimson.

"Jesus," Carlin said as he jogged. "It sounds like a million people, all trying to murder each other."

"Maybe that's what it is," Hayward replied as she watched a troop of National Guardsmen double-timing northward ahead of them.

They trotted over Bow Bridge and skirted the Ramble, approaching the rear line of the police defenses. A long, unbroken string of news vehicles was parked along the Transverse, engines idling. Overhead, a fat-bellied helicopter glided, its huge prop smacking the air as it moved at treetop level. A row of policemen had formed a ring around the Castle terrace, and a lieutenant waved her through. With Carlin in tow, she crossed the terrace, then moved up the steps toward the Castle ramparts. There—amidst a milling throng of police brass, city officials, National Guardsmen, and nervous-looking men speaking into portable telephones—was Chief Horlocker, looking about ten years older than when Hayward had seen him barely four hours before. He was speaking with a slight, well-dressed woman in her late fifties. Or, rather, he was listening as the woman spoke in clipped, decisive sentences. Hayward moved closer and recognized the woman as the leader of Take Back Our City, the mother of Pamela Wisher.

"... atrocity unlike anything ever seen in this city before!" Mrs. Wisher was saying. "A dozen of my personal friends are lying in hospital beds as we speak. And who knows how many hundreds more from among our ranks have been wounded? I promise you, and I promise the mayor, that lawsuits are going to fall like rain on this city. Like *rain,* Chief Horlocker!"

Horlocker made a valiant attempt. "Mrs. Wisher, our reports indicate that it was the younger element among your own marchers that incited this rioting—"

But Mrs. Wisher was not listening. "And when this is all over," she continued, "and the Park and the streets are scrubbed free of the filth and ruin that litter them now, our organization will be stronger than ever. If the mayor feared us before tonight, he will fear us ten times more tomorrow! The death of my daughter was the spark that set our cause on fire, but this outrageous assault on our liberties and our persons has set it ablaze! And don't think that..."

Hayward backed off, deciding this was perhaps not the best time to approach the Chief. She felt a tugging at her sleeve, and turned to find Carlin looking at her. Wordlessly, he pointed over the Esplanade toward the Great Lawn. Hayward glanced over, then froze, stupefied.

In the close summer darkness, the Great Lawn had become a plain of fire. Several dozen groups of people were clashing, withdrawing, attacking, retreating, in a scene of pandemonium. The flickering light of numerous small fires in the trash cans that dotted the outskirts showed that the lawn, once a beautiful carpet of grass, had become a sea of dirt. The combination of darkness and dirt made it impossible to determine which of the rioters were homeless and which were not. To the west and east, double lines of police vehicles had positioned themselves, headlights pointed in toward the scene. In one corner, a large group of well-dressed marchers—Take Back Our City's last remaining elite remnants—were retreating behind the police barricades, apparently realizing that the midnight vigil could not possibly take place. Squads of police and National Guardsmen were moving forward slowly from the periphery, breaking up fistfights, wielding batons, making arrests.

"Shit," Hayward breathed with fervent conviction. "What a balls-up."

Carlin turned toward her in surprise, then coughed disapprovingly into his hand.

There was a sudden flurry of movement behind them, and Hayward turned to see Mrs. Wisher moving gracefully away, head held high, leading a small knot of retainers and bodyguards. In her wake, Horlocker looked like a fighter who'd finished a bad twelve rounds. He leaned against the sand-colored stone of the Castle wall as if seeking its support.

"Have they finished dosing the Reservoir with—well, with whatever it's called?" he asked at last, fetching a ragged breath.

"Thyoxin," said a well-dressed man standing by a battery-powered radio. "Yes, they finished fifteen minutes ago."

Horlocker looked around with sunken eyes. "Why the hell haven't we heard anything?" His eyes landed on Hayward. "You, there!" he barked. "What's your name, Harris?"

Hayward stepped forward. "It's Hayward, sir."

"Whatever." Horlocker pushed himself away from the wall. "Heard anything from D'Agosta?"

"No, sir."

"Captain Waxie?"

"No, sir."

Abruptly, Horlocker sank back again. "Jesus Christ," he muttered. Then he looked at his watch. "Ten minutes to midnight."

He turned to an officer at his right. "Why the hell are they still at it?" he said, pointing out toward the Great Lawn.

"When we try to round them up, they just break and reform somewhere else. And more seem to be joining, leaking through the perimeter at the south end of the Park. It's hard without tear gas."

"Well, why the hell don't you use it, then?" Horlocker demanded.

"Your orders, sir."

"*My* order? Wisher's people are gone now, you idiot. Gas them. Now."

"Yes, sir."

There was a deep booming sound, strangely muffled, seemingly from the center of the earth itself. Suddenly, life returned once again to Horlocker's limbs. He sprang forward. "Hear that?" he demanded. "Those were the charges! The goddamn charges!"

A scattering of applause rang out from the cops manning the various communications devices. Carlin turned toward Hayward, a puzzled look on his face. "Charges?" he asked.

Hayward shrugged. "Beats me. What are they so happy about, with all hell breaking loose down there?"

As if on an unspoken signal, they both turned back toward the Great Lawn. The spectacle below was perversely fascinating. Cries and shouts rushed up toward them, a sonic wave almost physical in its force. Every few moments, a single sound would separate itself from the roar: a curse, a scream, the smack of fist on flesh.

Suddenly, from beyond the Great Lawn, Hayward heard a strange sighing sound, as if the very foundation of Manhattan had decided to give way. At first she was unable to pinpoint its location. Then she noticed that the surface of the Central Park Reservoir, normally as calm as a mill pond, was suddenly in motion. Little wavelets broke the surface like whitecaps, and a series of bubbles began to roil its center.

A silence fell in the Command Center as all eyes turned to the Reservoir.

"Breakers," Carlin whispered. "In the Central Park Reservoir. I'll be goddamned."

There was a deep-throated belching sound, followed by the awesome rumbling of millions of cubic feet of water pouring with incredible force into underground Manhattan. On the plain of the Great Lawn, out of sight of the Reservoir, the rioting continued. But beneath the sounds of conflict, Hayward heard, or rather felt, a great hollow rushing, as of vast underground galleries and long-forgotten tunnels filling with the onslaught of water.

"It's too early!" Horlocker cried.

As Hayward watched, the surface of the Reservoir began visibly dropping, first slowly, then more rapidly. In the reflected glow of the spotlights and the innumerable fires, she could see the exposed crescent of Reservoir wall, its banks boiling and frothing from the force of a great central whirlpool.

"Stop," Horlocker whispered.

The level continued to drop inexorably.

"Please stop," Horlocker whispered, staring fixedly northward.

The Reservoir was draining faster now, and Hayward could see the surface of the water surging downward by the moment, exposing more and more of the cracked far wall abutting the East Meadow and the Ball Field. Suddenly, the rumbling sound seemed to falter, and the turbulence lessened. The water grew calmer, slowing in its rapid descent. The silence in the Command Center was absolute.

Hayward stared as a narrow band of bubbles flowed into the Reservoir from its northward end; first a fine jet, then more and more until it had expanded into a heavy roar.

"Son of a bitch," Horlocker whispered. "They did it."

With the exits below sealed off, the Reservoir ceased draining. However, water continued to pour into the Reservoir from the upstate aquifers. With great sizzles and pops, the level of the water began to rise again. The churning at the northward end of the Reservoir grew until the entire mass of water seemed to tremble from some kind of subterranean pressure. With a steady surge of thunder, the water rose, and rose, until at last it trembled on the edge of the embankment. Then, suddenly, it crested.

"Jesus," Carlin said. "I guess they're going swimming."

A massive flood of water spilled over the top of the Reservoir and hurried away into the lambent darkness of the Park, drowning the sound of fighting with its splashing, hissing, tumbling roar. Frozen in place, staring at the awe-inspiring sight, Hayward was reminded of a vast bathtub that had been allowed to overflow. She watched as the onrush of water leveled mounds of earth and worried away the ground among small trees and copses. It was like a huge river, she thought: gentle, shallow, but irresistible. And there was no mistake about where it was headed—the low ground of the Great Lawn.

There was a moment of unbearable suspense as the onrushing water was hidden from the rioting plain that stretched beneath the Castle ramparts. Then it appeared between the trees at the northern end of the Lawn, a glistening swath of black, churning sticks and weeds and garbage before it. As it struck the edges of the crowd, Hayward could hear the noise of the fighting shift in tone and volume. A sudden uncertainty rippled through the rioters. Hayward watched as knots of people dispersed, reformed, dispersed again. Then the water was rushing over the length of the Great Lawn, and the shrieking mob was breaking for the high ground of the trees, supping and stumbling over each other as they struggled toward the Park exits and safety.

And still the water advanced, licking around the baseball diamonds, swallowing up countless fires, knocking over trash cans. It swept into the Delacorte Theater with an immense gurgling sound, surrounded and then swallowed up Turtle Pond, and swirled around the base of Belvedere Castle itself, breaking against the stones in dark rivulets of foam. Then at last the sound of rushing water began to die away. As the newly made lake grew still, bright points of reflected light appeared on its surface, more and still more as the water grew quieter, looking at last like a vast mirror of stars.

For another long moment, the entire Command Center remained still, awed by the spectacle. Then a spontaneous cheering burst out, filling the chambers and turrets of the Castle and swirling upward into the crisp summer night air.

"I wish my old daddy could've seen that," Hayward said over the noise, turning to Carlin with a grin. "He would have said it was just like water on a dogfight. I'll bet money he would."

64

The early morning sun snuck in low over the Atlantic, kissing the sandy fork of Long Island, gliding over coves and harbors, villages and resorts, bringing a cool summer sweat to asphalt and pavement. Farther west, the brilliant arc illuminated the nearest reaches of New York City, briefly turning the gray welter of buildings a pale shade of rose. Following the ecliptic, the rays hit the East River, then burnished the windows of ten thousand buildings to a temporary sparkle, as if washing the city new in heat and light.

Beneath the thick tangles of railroad track and overhead wire that crossed the narrow canal known as the Humboldt Kill, no light penetrated. The tenements that reared up, vacant and gray as vast dead teeth, were too numerous and too tall. At their feet, the water lay still and thick, its only currents formed by the rumble of the subway trains passing infrequently on the rail bridge above.

As the sun followed its inexorable course west, a single beam of light slanted down through the labyrinth of wood and steel, blood red against the rusted iron, as sudden and sharp as a knife wound. It winked out again, as quickly as it had arrived, but not before illuminating a strange sight: a figure, muddy and battered, curled motionless upon a thin revetment of brick that jutted mere inches above the dark water.

Darkness and silence returned, and the foul canal was left to itself once again. Then its sleep was disturbed a second time: a low rumble sounded in the distance, approached in the dim gray dawn, passed overhead, receded, then returned. And beneath this rumble followed another: deeper, more immediate. The surface of the canal began to shake and quiver, as if jostled reluctantly to life.

In the bow of the Coast Guard cutter, D'Agosta stood, stiff and vigilant as a sentry.

"There she is!" he cried, pointing to a dark figure lying on the embankment. He turned to the pilot. "Get those choppers the hell away! They're stirring the stink up off the water. Besides, we might need to get a medevac in here."

The pilot glanced up at the craggy, burnt-out facades and the steel bridges overhead, a look of doubt crossing his face, but he said nothing.

Smithback crowded to the rail, straining to see in the lightening gloom. "What is this place?" he asked, tugging his shirt up over his nose.

"Humboldt Kill," D'Agosta replied curtly. He turned to the pilot. "Bring us in closer; let the doctor get a look at her."

Smithback straightened up and glanced over at D'Agosta. He knew the Lieutenant was wearing a brown suit—he always wore brown suits—but the color was now completely undetectable beneath a damp mantle of mud, dust, blood, and oil. The gash above his eye was a ragged red line. Smithback watched the Lieutenant give his face a savage wipe with his sleeve. "God, let her be okay," D'Agosta muttered to himself.

The boat eased up to the revetment, the pilot backing the throttle into neutral. In a flash D'Agosta and the doctor were over the side and onto the revetment, bending low over the prone figure. Pendergast stood in the shadows aft, silent, an intense look on his pale face.

Margo suddenly jerked awake and blinked around at her surroundings. She tried to sit up, then clapped a hand to her head with a groan.

"Margo!" D'Agosta said. "It's Lieutenant D'Agosta."

"Don't move," the doctor said, gently feeling her neck.

Ignoring him, Margo pushed herself into a sitting position. "What the hell took you guys?" she asked, then broke into a series of racking coughs.

"Anything broken?" the doctor asked.

"Everything," she replied, wincing. "Actually, my left leg, I think."

The doctor moved his attentions to her leg, slicing off her muddy jeans with an expert hand. He quickly examined the rest of her body, then said something to D'Agosta.

"She's okay!" D'Agosta called up. "Have the medevac meet us at the dock."

"So?" Margo prompted. "Where were you?"

"We got sidetracked," Pendergast said, now at the side. "One of your flippers was found in a settling tank at the Treatment Plant, badly chewed up. We were afraid that..." He paused. "Well, it was awhile before we decided to check all the secondary exit points of the West Side Lateral."

"Is anything broken?" Smithback called down.

"Might be a small green-splint fracture," the doctor said. "Let's get the stretcher lowered."

Margo sat forward. "I think I can manage the—"

"You listen to the doc," D'Agosta said, frowning paternally.

As the cutter rode the water next to the dank brickwork, Smithback and the pilot lowered the stretcher over the side, then Smithback jumped down to help Margo onto the narrow canvas. It took the three of them to lift her back over the side. D'Agosta followed Smithback and the doctor back on board, then nodded to the pilot. "Get us the hell out of here."

There was a rumble of the diesel engine and the boat backed off the revetment and surged into the canal. Margo leaned back carefully, resting her head on a flotation pillow as Smithback dabbed her face and hands clean with a damp towel.

"Feels good," she whispered.

"Ten minutes, and we'll have you on dry land," Pendergast said, taking a seat next to her. "Ten more, and we'll have you in a hospital bed."

Margo opened her mouth to protest, but Pendergast's look silenced her. "Our friend Officer Snow told us about some of the things that grow in the Humboldt Kill," he said. "Believe me, it'll be for the best."

"What happened?" Margo said, closing her eyes and feeling the reassuring vibration of the boat's engines.

"That depends," Pendergast answered. "What do you remember?"

"I remember being separated," Margo said. "The explosion—"

"The explosion knocked you into a drainage tunnel," Pendergast said. "With Snow's help, we made it up the riser and eventually into the Hudson. You must have been sucked into the Lateral sluice that drains into the Humboldt Kill."

"Seems you followed the same path those two corpses took when the storm washed them out," D'Agosta said.

Margo seemed to doze for a moment. Then her lips moved again. "Frock—"

Pendergast immediately touched his fingertips to her lips. "Later," he said. "There will be plenty of time for that, later."

Margo shook her head. "How could he have done it," she murmured. "How could he have taken that drug, built that terrible hut?" She stopped.

"It's unsettling to learn just how little you really know about even your closest friends," Pendergast replied. "Who can say what secret desires fuel the inner flames that keep them alive? We could never have known just how much Frock missed the use of his legs. That he was arrogant was always obvious. All great scientists are arrogant, to a point. He must have seen how Kawakita had already perfected the drug through many stages.

After all, the drug that Kawakita took himself was obviously a later strain than that which created the Wrinklers. Frock must have been supremely self-confident in his ability to correct that which Kawakita had overlooked. He saw the drug's potential to correct physical flaws, and he pushed that potential to its limit. But the final iteration of the drug warped the mind far more than it mended the body. And his deepest desires—his most secret lusts—were thus brought to the fore, magnified, perverted, and allowed to govern his actions. The hut itself is the ultimate example of this corruption. He wanted to be God—*his* God, the God of evolution."

Margo winced, then took a deep breath, dropping her hands to her sides and allowing the rocking of the boat to carry her thoughts far away. They moved out of the Cloaca, through the Spuyten Dyvil, and into the fresh air of the Hudson. Already the pale light of dawn was giving way to a warm late-summer day. D'Agosta stared off silently into the creamy wake of the cutter.

Idly, Margo realized that her right hand was lying over a bulge in her pocket. She reached in and pulled out the waterlogged envelope that Mephisto had given her in the black tunnel not so many hours before. Curiously, she opened it. A brief note lay inside, but whatever message it had contained was now washed into faint swirls and stains of ink. Enclosed by the note was a damp black-and-white photograph, faded and heavily creased. It showed a young boy in a dusty front yard, wearing coveralls and a pint-sized version of a train engineer's cap, riding a wooden horse with wheels. The chubby face was smiling at the camera. In the background was an old house trailer, framed by cacti. Behind the trailer was a mountain range, low and distant. Margo stared for a moment, seeing in the happy little face the ghost of the man he would become. She carefully replaced the photograph and envelope in her pocket.

"What about the Reservoir?" she asked Pendergast in a quiet voice.

"The level hasn't fluctuated in the last six hours," Pendergast replied. "Apparently, the water has been contained."

"So we did it," she said.

Pendergast did not reply.

"Didn't we?" she asked, her eyes suddenly sharp.

Pendergast looked away. "It would seem so," he said at last.

"Then what is it?" she prodded. "You're not sure, are you?"

He turned back to her, his pale eyes staring at her face. "With luck, the collapsed tunnels held and there was no leakage. In another twenty hours or so, the thyoxin will have destroyed the plants remaining in the Reservoir and in the tunnels below. But none of us can be sure—not yet."

"Then how will we ever know?" Margo asked.

D'Agosta grinned. "Tell you what. One year from today, I'm gonna head down to Mercer's on South Street and have one of those two-pound swordfish steaks, nice and rare. And if I don't catch a good buzz, then maybe we can all breathe easier."

Just then, the sun broke over Washington Heights, turning the dark water to the color of beaten electrum. Smithback, looking up from patting Margo's face dry, gazed at the scene: the tall buildings of Midtown flashing purple and gold in the morning light, the George Washington Bridge swept with silver light.

"As for myself," Pendergast said slowly, "I think I, too, will avoid *frutti del mare* for the foreseeable future." Margo looked at him quickly, trying to read the joke in his expression. But his gaze remained steady. And, eventually, she simply nodded her understanding.

Author's Note

While the events and characters portrayed in this novel are fictitious, much of the underground setting and its population are not. It has been estimated that as many as five thousand or more homeless people have lived in the vast warren of underground tracks, subway tunnels, ancient aqueducts, coal tunnels, old sewers, abandoned stations and waiting rooms, disused gas mains, old machine rooms, and other spaces that riddle underground Manhattan. Grand Central Station alone sits above seven stories of tunnels, and in some places the underground works extend more than thirty stories beneath the city. The Astor Tunnels, with their elegant stations crumbling into dust, actually exist, on a smaller scale and under a different name. No comprehensive maps exist of underground Manhattan. It is a truly unexplored and dangerous territory.

Much of what is described in *Reliquary* about the underground homeless—or Mole people—is true. (Some prefer to call themselves "houseless," for they consider their underground spaces home.) In many underground areas the homeless have organized themselves into communities. Some of the Mole people who live in these communities have not been aboveground for weeks or months—or even longer—and their eyes have adjusted to the extremely low levels of light. They live on food brought down by "runners," sometimes supplemented with "track rabbit" as described in the novel. They cook on campfires or steam pipes, and purloin electricity and water from the many conduits and pipes that run underground. At least one of these communities has a part-time schoolteacher—for there are also children living underground, often brought down by their mothers to avoid having them taken away by the state and put in foster care. Mole people do communicate in the dark over long distances by tapping on pipes. And finally, there are homeless who claim to have seen a fabulous, decaying nineteenth-century waiting room deep underground, with mirrored and tiled walls, a fountain, a grand piano, and a huge crystal chandelier, similar to the Crystal Pavilion described in *Reliquary*.

It should also be noted that in certain important instances the authors have altered, moved, or embellished what exists under Manhattan for purposes of the story.

The authors feel that it is not asking too much of our wealthy country that the underground homeless be given the medical care, psychiatric help, shelter, and respect that should be the basic rights of all human beings in a civilized society.

The authors are indebted to the book *The Mole People*, by Jennifer Toth (Chicago Review Press, 1993). Readers interested in the factual account of the *subterra incognita* of Manhattan are urged to read this excellent, thought-provoking, and at times frightening study.

Acknowledgments

The authors wish to thank the following people for helping, in myriad ways, this book see the light of day: Bob Gleason, Matthew Snyder, Denis Kelly, Stephen de las Heras, Jim Cush, Linda Quinten, Tom Espensheid, Dan Rabinowitz, Caleb Rabinowitz, Karen Lovell, Mark Gallagher, Bob Wincott, Lee Suckno, and Georgette Piligian.

Special thanks to Tom Doherty and Harvey Klinger, without whose guidance and diligent effort *Reliquary* would not have been possible.

Thanks also to everyone on the Tor/Forge sales force for all their hard work and dedication.

We would also like to acknowledge all those readers who have supported us, whether it be by calling during radio or television interviews, speaking with us at book signings, sending mail both conventional and electronic, or simply by reading and enjoying our books. Your enthusiasm for *Relic* was the motivating force behind this sequel.

To all of you—and to those of you who should have been mentioned, but were not—our deepest thanks.

A letter from the publisher

We hope you enjoyed this book. We are an independent publisher dedicated to discovering brilliant books, new authors and great storytelling. If you want to hear more, why not join our community of book-lovers at:

www.headofzeus.com

We'll keep you up-to-date with our latest books, author blogs, tempting offers, chances to win signed editions, events across the UK and much more.

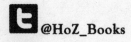 @HoZ_Books

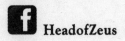 HeadofZeus

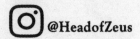 @HeadofZeus

HEAD *of* ZEUS